Disney

COMICS

AND STORIES

FRIENDS FORE[V]

Facebook: **facebook.com/idwpublishing**
Twitter: **@idwpublishing**
YouTube: **youtube.com/idwpublishing**
Tumblr: **tumblr.idwpublishing.com**
Instagram: **instagram.com/idwpublishing**

COVER ARTIST
ALESSANDRO PERINA

COVER COLORIST
VALERIA TURATI

SERIES ASSISTANT EDITORS
ELIZABETH BREI
& ANNI PERHEENTUPA

SERIES EDITOR
CHRIS CERASI

COLLECTION EDITORS
JUSTIN EISINGER
& ALONZO SIMON

COLLECTION DESIGNER
CLYDE GRAPA

ISBN: 978-1-68405-504-3   22 21 20 19   1 2 3 4

Originally published as DISNEY COMICS AND STORIES issues #1–4 (Legacy issues #744–747).

Chris Ryall, President, Publisher, & Chief Creative Officer
John Barber, Editor-In-Chief
Cara Morrison, Chief Financial Officer
Matt Ruzicka, Chief Accounting Officer
David Hedgecock, Associate Publisher
Jerry Bennington, VP of New Product Development
Lorelei Bunjes, VP of Digital Services
Justin Eisinger, Editorial Director, Graphic Novels & Collections
Eric Moss, Senior Director, Licensing and Business Development

Ted Adams and Robbie Robbins, IDW Founders

Special thanks to Stefano Ambrosio, Stefano Attardi, Julie Dorris, Marco Ghiglione, Jodi Hammerwold, Behnoosh Khalili, Manny Mederos, Eugene Paraszczuk, Carlotta Quattrocolo, Roberto Santillo, Christopher Troise, and Camilla Vedove.

My Friend Mickey
FROM ITALIAN TOPOLINO #3052, 2014
WRITER: VITO STABILE
ARTIST: MARCO MAZZARELLO
COLORIST: DISNEY ITALIA
LETTERER: TOM B. LONG
TRANSLATION AND DIALOGUE: ERIN BRADY

Mickey and the Ghostchasers
FROM ITALIAN TOPOLINO #2838, 2010
WRITER: STEFANO AMBROSIO
ARTIST: CLAUDIO SCIARRONE
COLORIST: DISNEY ITALIA
LETTERER: TOM B. LONG
TRANSLATION AND DIALOGUE: ERIN BRADY

The Night in Sleepyhead Valley
FROM ITALIAN TOPOLINO #2842, 2010
WRITER AND ARTIST: ENRICO FACCINI
COLORIST: DISNEY ITALIA
LETTERER: TOM B. LONG
TRANSLATION AND DIALOGUE: ERIN BRADY

The Art of the Perfect Traveler
FROM ITALIAN TOPOLINO #3185, 2016
WRITER: GIULIO D'ANTONA
ARTIST: MASSIMO ASARO
COLORIST: DISNEY ITALIA
LETTERER: TOM B. LONG
TRANSLATION AND DIALOGUE: ERIN BRADY

Run, Fethry, Run!
FROM ITALIAN TOPOLINO #3268, 2018
WRITER AND ARTIST: ENRICO FACCINI
COLORIST: DISNEY ITALIA
LETTERER: TOM B. LONG
TRANSLATION AND DIALOGUE: ERIN BRADY

Oh, Grow Up!
FROM DANISH ANDERS AND & CO #21/2004
WRITER: BYRON ERICKSON
ARTIST: FRANCISCO RODRIGUEZ PEINADO
COLORIST: EGMONT
LETTERER: TOM B. LONG

Donald Duck: Sports Photographer
FROM DANISH ANDERS AND & CO #30/1984
WRITERS: PER WIKING AND TOM ANDERSON
ARTIST: VICAR
COLORIST: EGMONT
LETTERER: TOM B. LONG
TRANSLATION AND DIALOGUE: ERIN BRADY

Mickey Mouse and the Unreachable Island
FROM ITALIAN TOPOLINO #2879, 2011
WRITER: FAUSTO VITALIANO
ARTIST: SILVIA ZICHE
COLORIST: DISNEY ITALIA
LETTERER: TOM B. LONG
TRANSLATION AND DIALOGUE: ERIN BRADY

3 x 2
FROM ITALIAN TOPOLINO #2297, 1999
WRITER: TITO FARACI
ARTIST: SILVIA ZICHE
COLORIST: DISNEY ITALIA
LETTERER: TOM B. LONG
TRANSLATION AND DIALOGUE: ERIN BRADY

Fethry at Work
FROM ITALIAN TOPOLINO #2803, 2009
WRITER AND ARTIST: ENRICO FACCINI
COLORIST: DISNEY ITALIA
LETTERER: TOM B. LONG
TRANSLATION AND DIALOGUE: ERIN BRADY

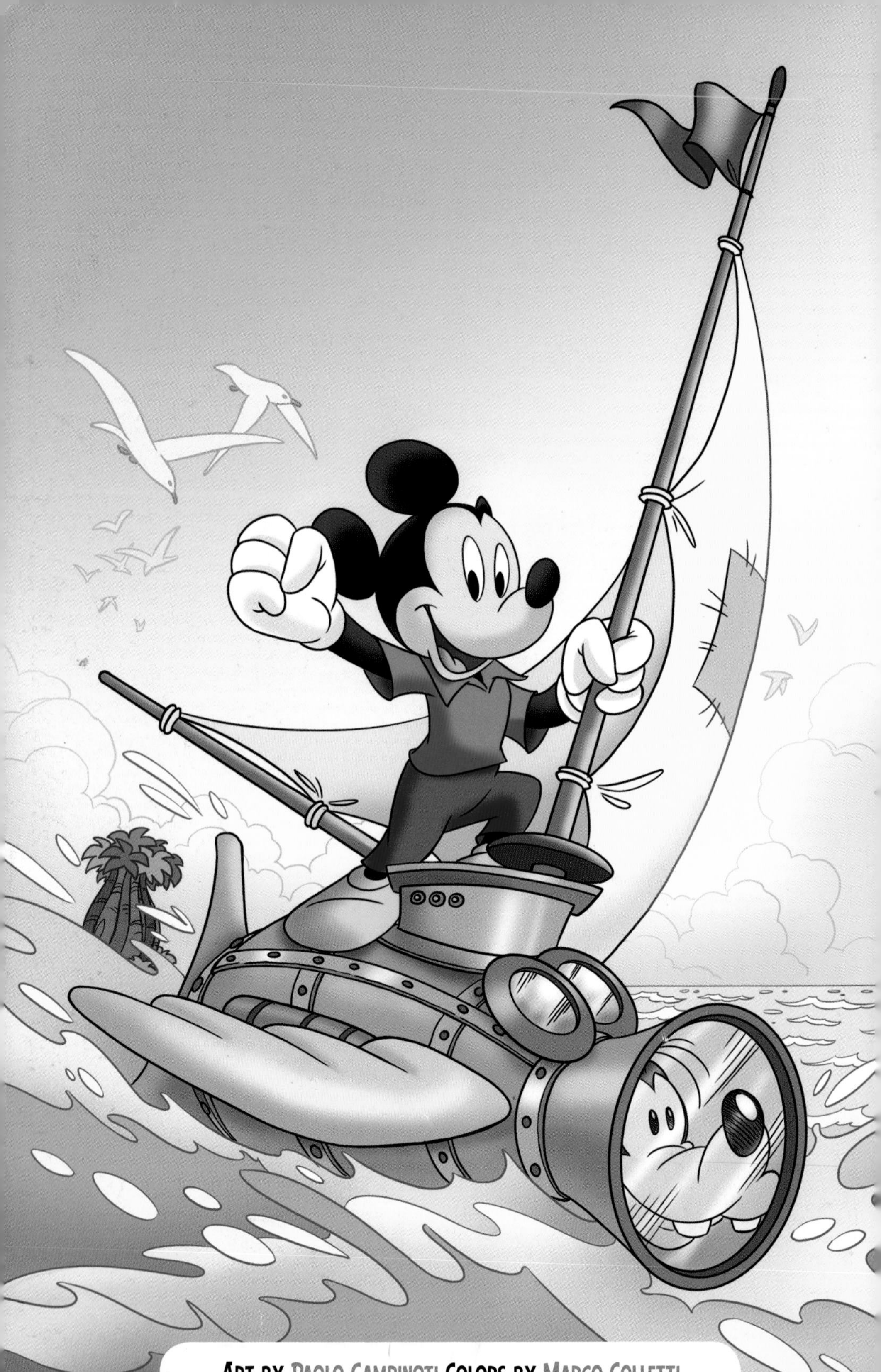

Art by Paolo Campinoti Colors by Marco Colletti

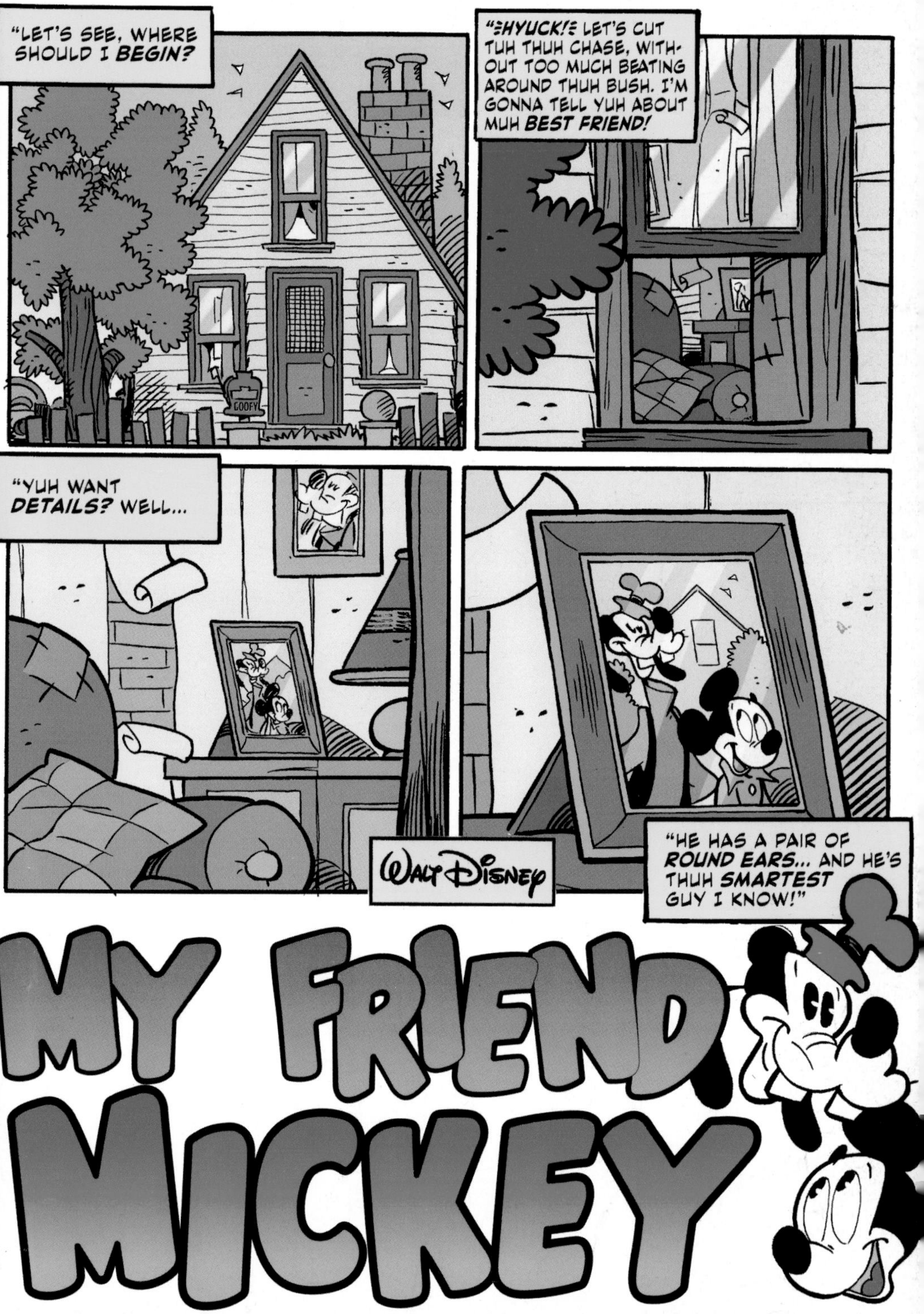
"LET'S SEE, WHERE SHOULD I *BEGIN?*
GOOFY
"*HYUCK!* LET'S CUT TUH THUH CHASE, WITH-OUT TOO MUCH BEATING AROUND THUH BUSH. I'M GONNA TELL YUH ABOUT MUH *BEST FRIEND!*
"YUH WANT *DETAILS?* WELL...
WALT DISNEY
"HE HAS A PAIR OF *ROUND EARS...* AND HE'S THUH *SMARTEST* GUY I KNOW!"
MY FRIEND MICKEY

ORIGINALLY PUBLISHED IN **TOPOLINO #3052** (ITALY, 2014) • **FIRST USA PUBLICATION**

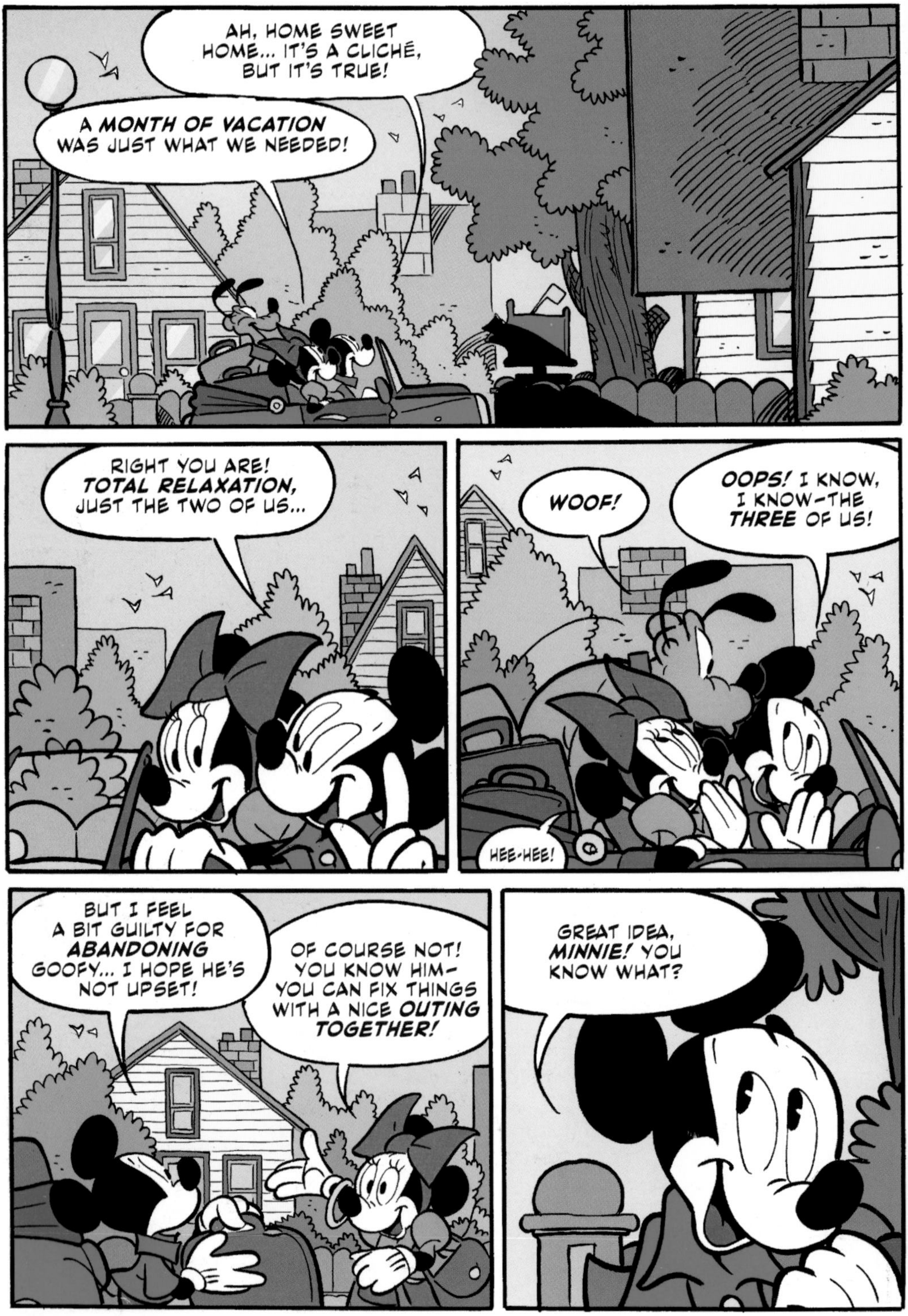
AH, HOME SWEET HOME... IT'S A CLICHÉ, BUT IT'S TRUE!
A MONTH OF VACATION WAS JUST WHAT WE NEEDED!
RIGHT YOU ARE! TOTAL RELAXATION, JUST THE TWO OF US...
WOOF!
OOPS! I KNOW, I KNOW—THE THREE OF US!
HEE-HEE!
BUT I FEEL A BIT GUILTY FOR ABANDONING GOOFY... I HOPE HE'S NOT UPSET!
OF COURSE NOT! YOU KNOW HIM— YOU CAN FIX THINGS WITH A NICE OUTING TOGETHER!
GREAT IDEA, MINNIE! YOU KNOW WHAT?

WELCOME BACK, MICKEY! A *PICNIC,* YUH SAY? OF COURSE I'LL COME!

GREAT! YOU CAN MAKE THE *CHEESE SANDWICHES...*

I'D RATHER *EAT* 'EM! ≋HYUCK!≋

GOOD OLD GOOFY! I REALLY MISSED HI–*HUH?*

DING DONG

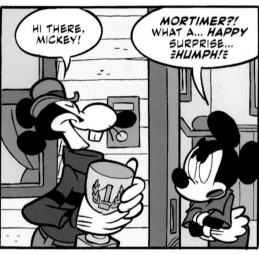

HI THERE, MICKEY!

MORTIMER?! WHAT A... *HAPPY* SURPRISE... ≋HUMPH!≋

I JUST *HAPPENED* TO PASS BY, AND I THOUGHT I'D SHOW YOU MY IMPORTANT *TROPHY!*

HAH! DID YOU WIN A *BRAGGING* CONTEST?

FUNNY! I WROTE THE *BEST POEM* IN A CONTEST! WANNA HEAR IT?

IF I HAVE TO...

7

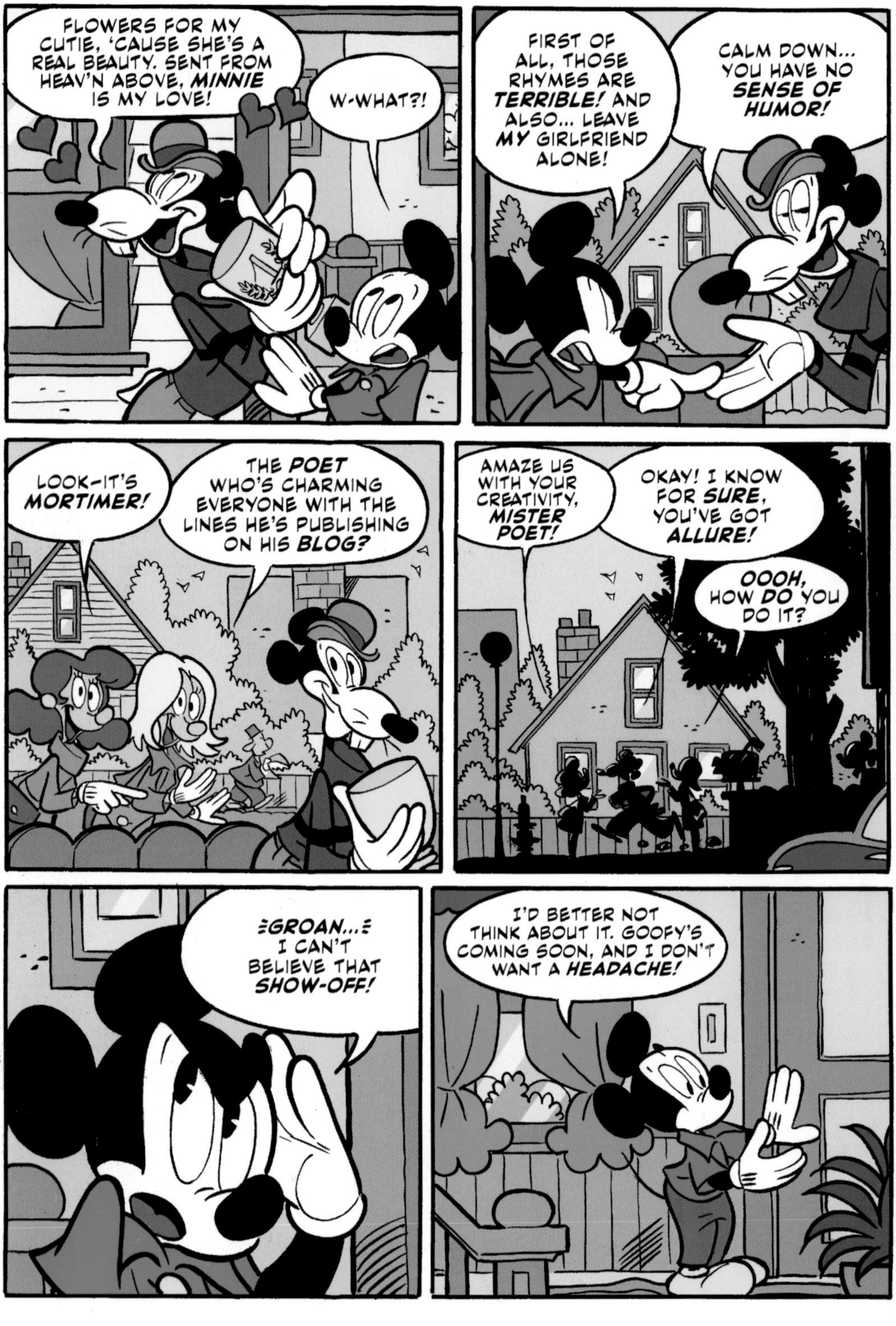
FLOWERS FOR MY CUTIE, 'CAUSE SHE'S A REAL BEAUTY. SENT FROM HEAV'N ABOVE, MINNIE IS MY LOVE!
W-WHAT?!
FIRST OF ALL, THOSE RHYMES ARE TERRIBLE! AND ALSO... LEAVE MY GIRLFRIEND ALONE!
CALM DOWN... YOU HAVE NO SENSE OF HUMOR!
LOOK--IT'S MORTIMER!
THE POET WHO'S CHARMING EVERYONE WITH THE LINES HE'S PUBLISHING ON HIS BLOG?
AMAZE US WITH YOUR CREATIVITY, MISTER POET!
OKAY! I KNOW FOR SURE, YOU'VE GOT ALLURE!
OOOH, HOW DO YOU DO IT?
GROAN... I CAN'T BELIEVE THAT SHOW-OFF!
I'D BETTER NOT THINK ABOUT IT. GOOFY'S COMING SOON, AND I DON'T WANT A HEADACHE!

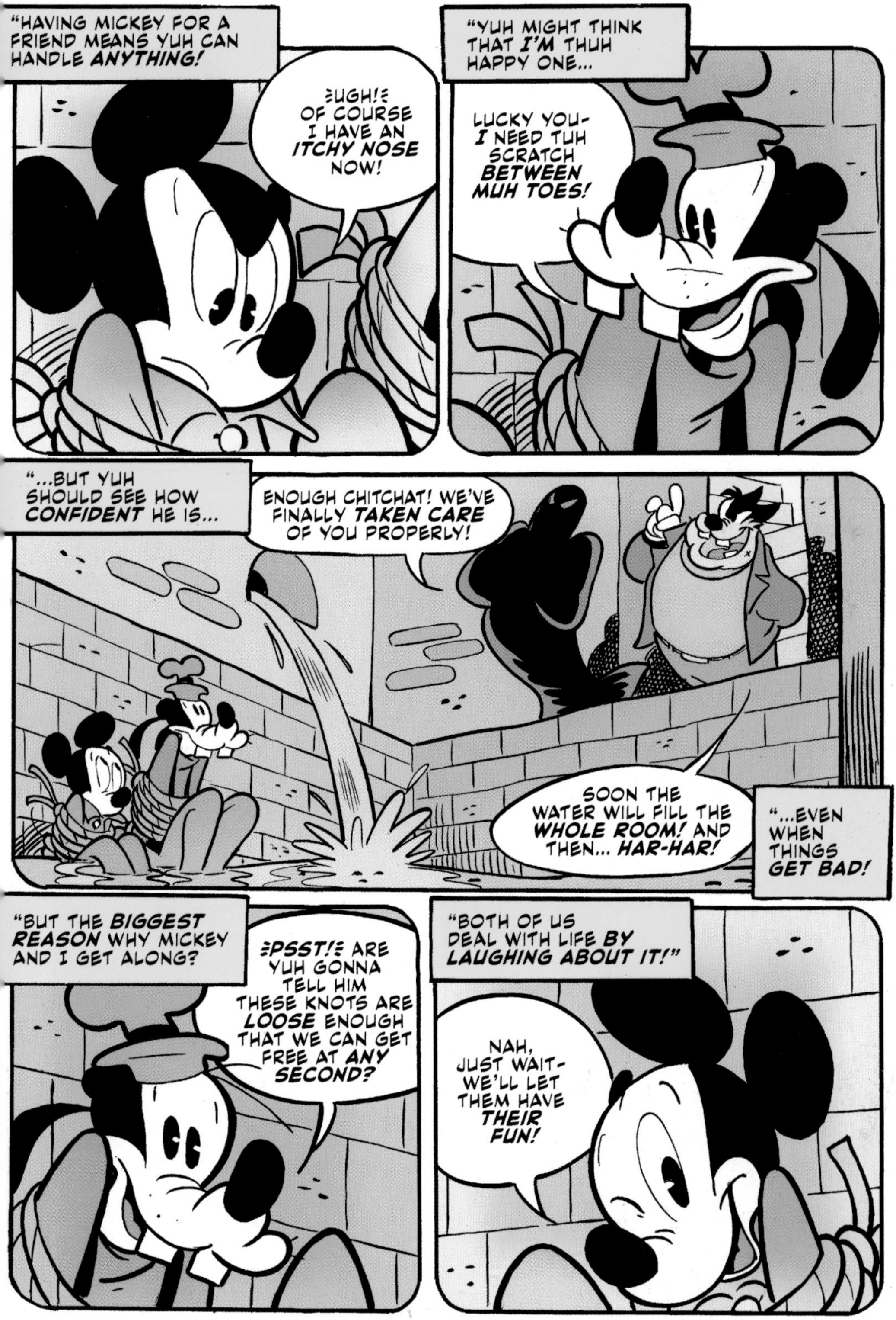

"HAVING MICKEY FOR A FRIEND MEANS YUH CAN HANDLE ANYTHING!
UGH! OF COURSE I HAVE AN ITCHY NOSE NOW!
"YUH MIGHT THINK THAT I'M THUH HAPPY ONE...
LUCKY YOU- I NEED TUH SCRATCH BETWEEN MUH TOES!
"...BUT YUH SHOULD SEE HOW CONFIDENT HE IS...
ENOUGH CHITCHAT! WE'VE FINALLY TAKEN CARE OF YOU PROPERLY!
SOON THE WATER WILL FILL THE WHOLE ROOM! AND THEN... HAR-HAR!
"...EVEN WHEN THINGS GET BAD!
"BUT THE BIGGEST REASON WHY MICKEY AND I GET ALONG?
PSST! ARE YUH GONNA TELL HIM THESE KNOTS ARE LOOSE ENOUGH THAT WE CAN GET FREE AT ANY SECOND?
"BOTH OF US DEAL WITH LIFE BY LAUGHING ABOUT IT!"
NAH, JUST WAIT- WE'LL LET THEM HAVE THEIR FUN!

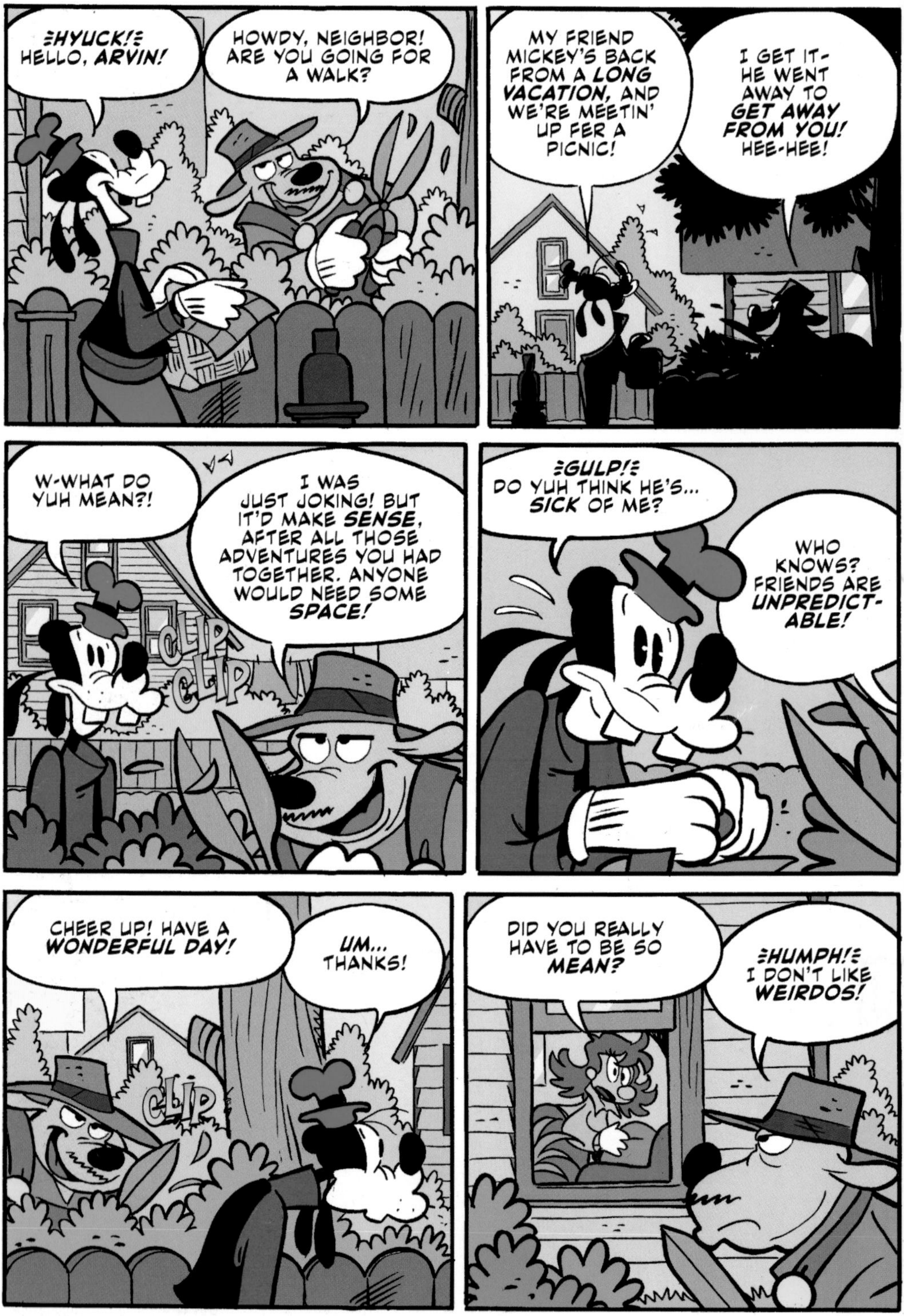

HYUCK! HELLO, ARVIN!
HOWDY, NEIGHBOR! ARE YOU GOING FOR A WALK?
MY FRIEND MICKEY'S BACK FROM A LONG VACATION, AND WE'RE MEETIN' UP FER A PICNIC!
I GET IT- HE WENT AWAY TO GET AWAY FROM YOU! HEE-HEE!
W-WHAT DO YUH MEAN?!
I WAS JUST JOKING! BUT IT'D MAKE SENSE, AFTER ALL THOSE ADVENTURES YOU HAD TOGETHER. ANYONE WOULD NEED SOME SPACE!
CLIP
CLIP
GULP! DO YUH THINK HE'S... SICK OF ME?
WHO KNOWS? FRIENDS ARE UNPREDICT-ABLE!
CHEER UP! HAVE A WONDERFUL DAY!
UM... THANKS!
CLIP
DID YOU REALLY HAVE TO BE SO MEAN?
HUMPH! I DON'T LIKE WEIRDOS!

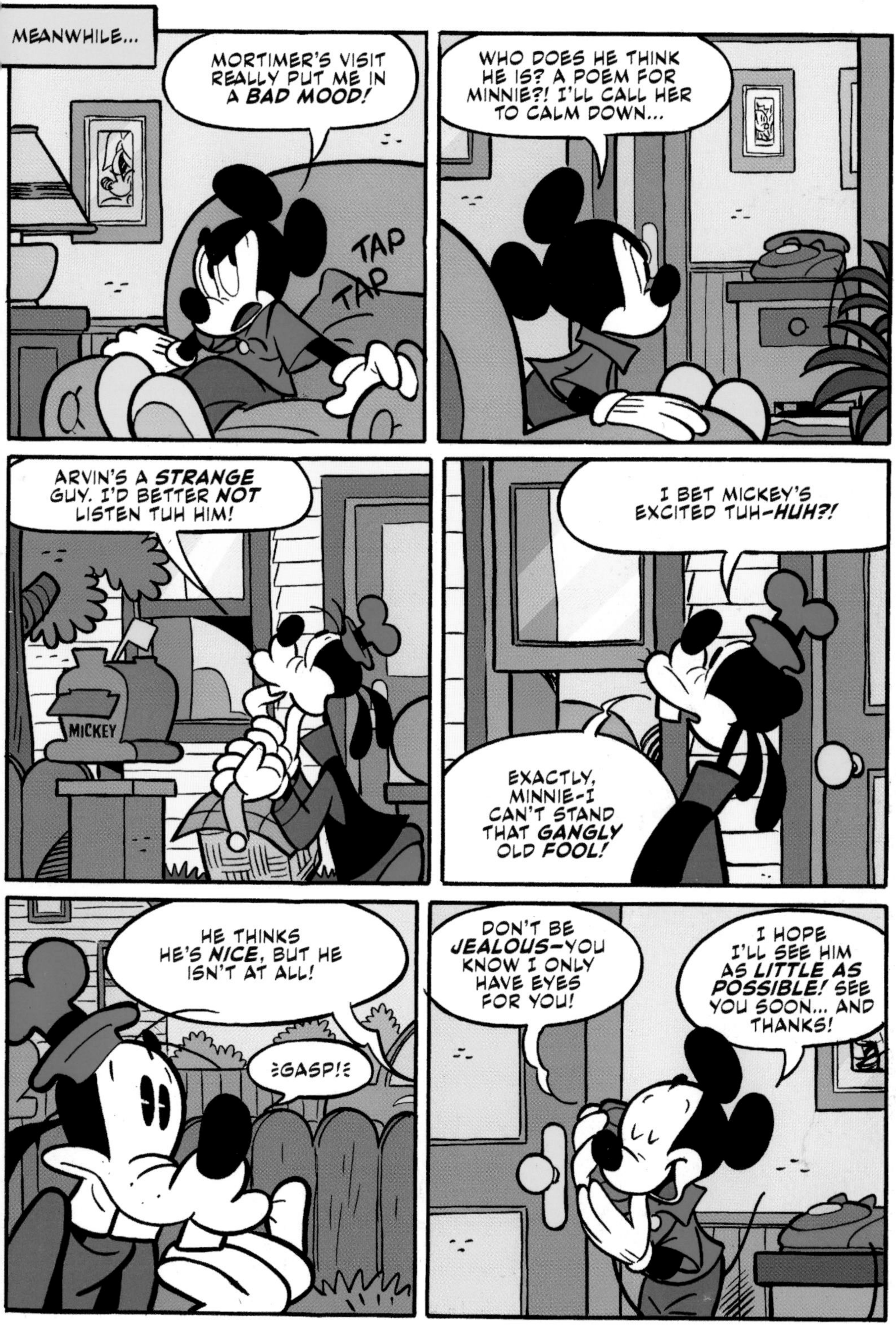
MEANWHILE...
MORTIMER'S VISIT REALLY PUT ME IN A BAD MOOD!
TAP TAP
WHO DOES HE THINK HE IS? A POEM FOR MINNIE?! I'LL CALL HER TO CALM DOWN...
ARVIN'S A STRANGE GUY. I'D BETTER NOT LISTEN TUH HIM!
MICKEY
I BET MICKEY'S EXCITED TUH–HUH?!
EXACTLY, MINNIE–I CAN'T STAND THAT GANGLY OLD FOOL!
HE THINKS HE'S NICE, BUT HE ISN'T AT ALL!
GASP!
DON'T BE JEALOUS–YOU KNOW I ONLY HAVE EYES FOR YOU!
I HOPE I'LL SEE HIM AS LITTLE AS POSSIBLE! SEE YOU SOON... AND THANKS!

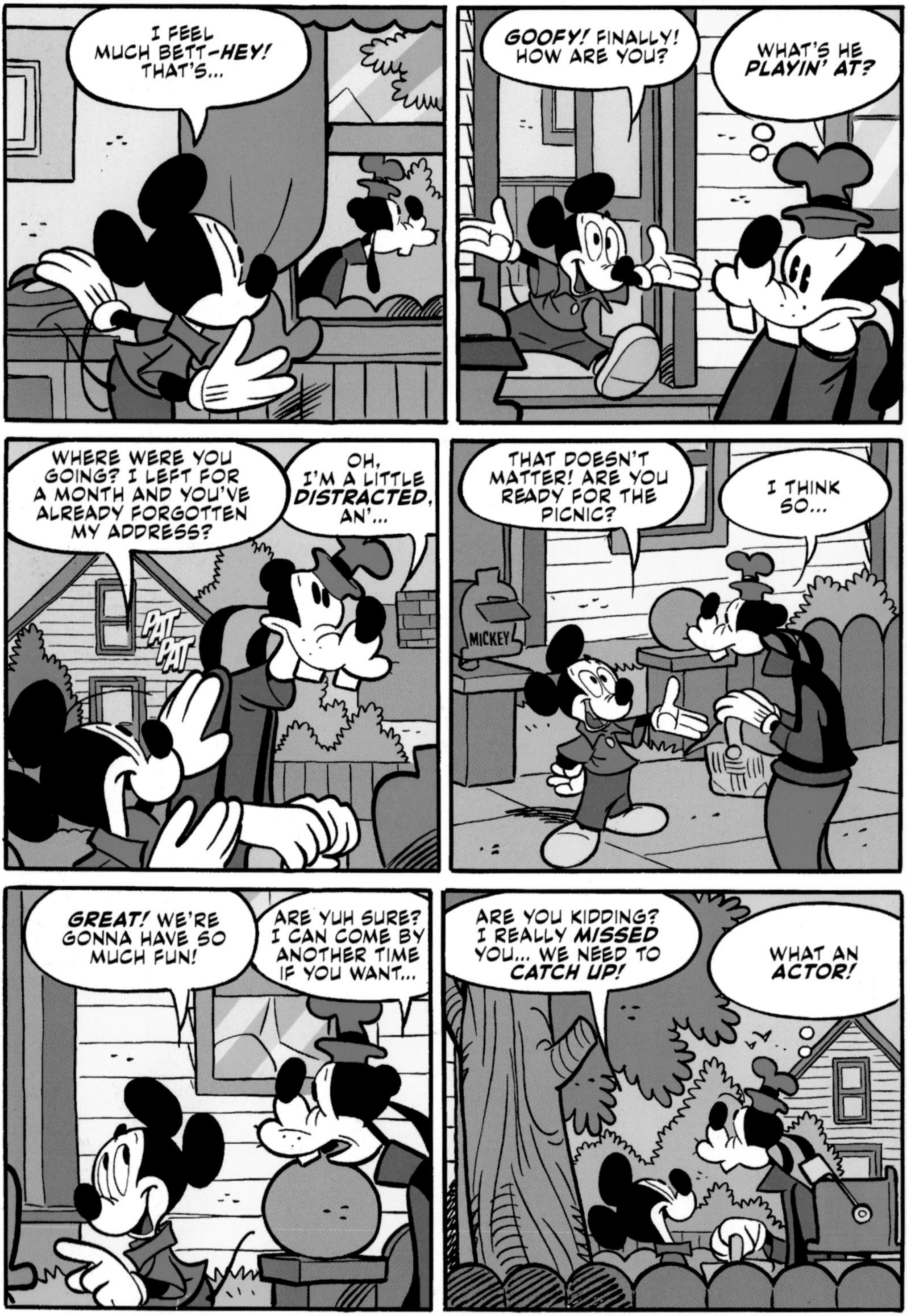
I FEEL MUCH BETT-HEY! THAT'S...
GOOFY! FINALLY! HOW ARE YOU?
WHAT'S HE PLAYIN' AT?
WHERE WERE YOU GOING? I LEFT FOR A MONTH AND YOU'VE ALREADY FORGOTTEN MY ADDRESS?
PAT PAT
OH, I'M A LITTLE DISTRACTED, AN'...
THAT DOESN'T MATTER! ARE YOU READY FOR THE PICNIC?
MICKEY
I THINK SO...
GREAT! WE'RE GONNA HAVE SO MUCH FUN!
ARE YUH SURE? I CAN COME BY ANOTHER TIME IF YOU WANT...
ARE YOU KIDDING? I REALLY MISSED YOU... WE NEED TO CATCH UP!
WHAT AN ACTOR!

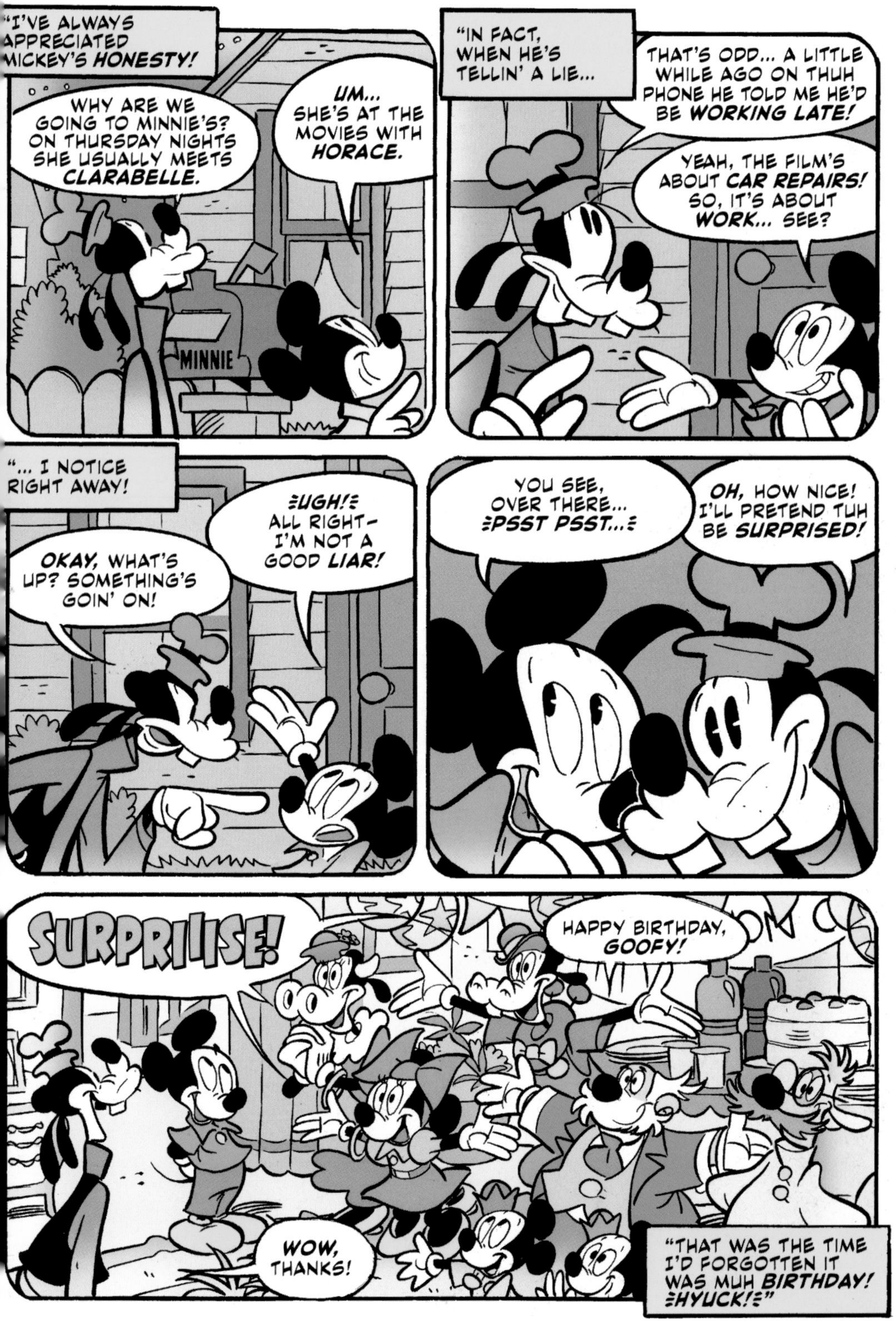
"I'VE ALWAYS APPRECIATED MICKEY'S HONESTY!
WHY ARE WE GOING TO MINNIE'S? ON THURSDAY NIGHTS SHE USUALLY MEETS CLARABELLE.
UM... SHE'S AT THE MOVIES WITH HORACE.
MINNIE
"IN FACT, WHEN HE'S TELLIN' A LIE...
THAT'S ODD... A LITTLE WHILE AGO ON THUH PHONE HE TOLD ME HE'D BE WORKING LATE!
YEAH, THE FILM'S ABOUT CAR REPAIRS! SO, IT'S ABOUT WORK... SEE?
"... I NOTICE RIGHT AWAY!
OKAY, WHAT'S UP? SOMETHING'S GOIN' ON!
UGH! ALL RIGHT— I'M NOT A GOOD LIAR!
YOU SEE, OVER THERE... PSST PSST...
OH, HOW NICE! I'LL PRETEND TUH BE SURPRISED!
SURPRIIISE!
HAPPY BIRTHDAY, GOOFY!
WOW, THANKS!
"THAT WAS THE TIME I'D FORGOTTEN IT WAS MUH BIRTHDAY! HYUCK!"

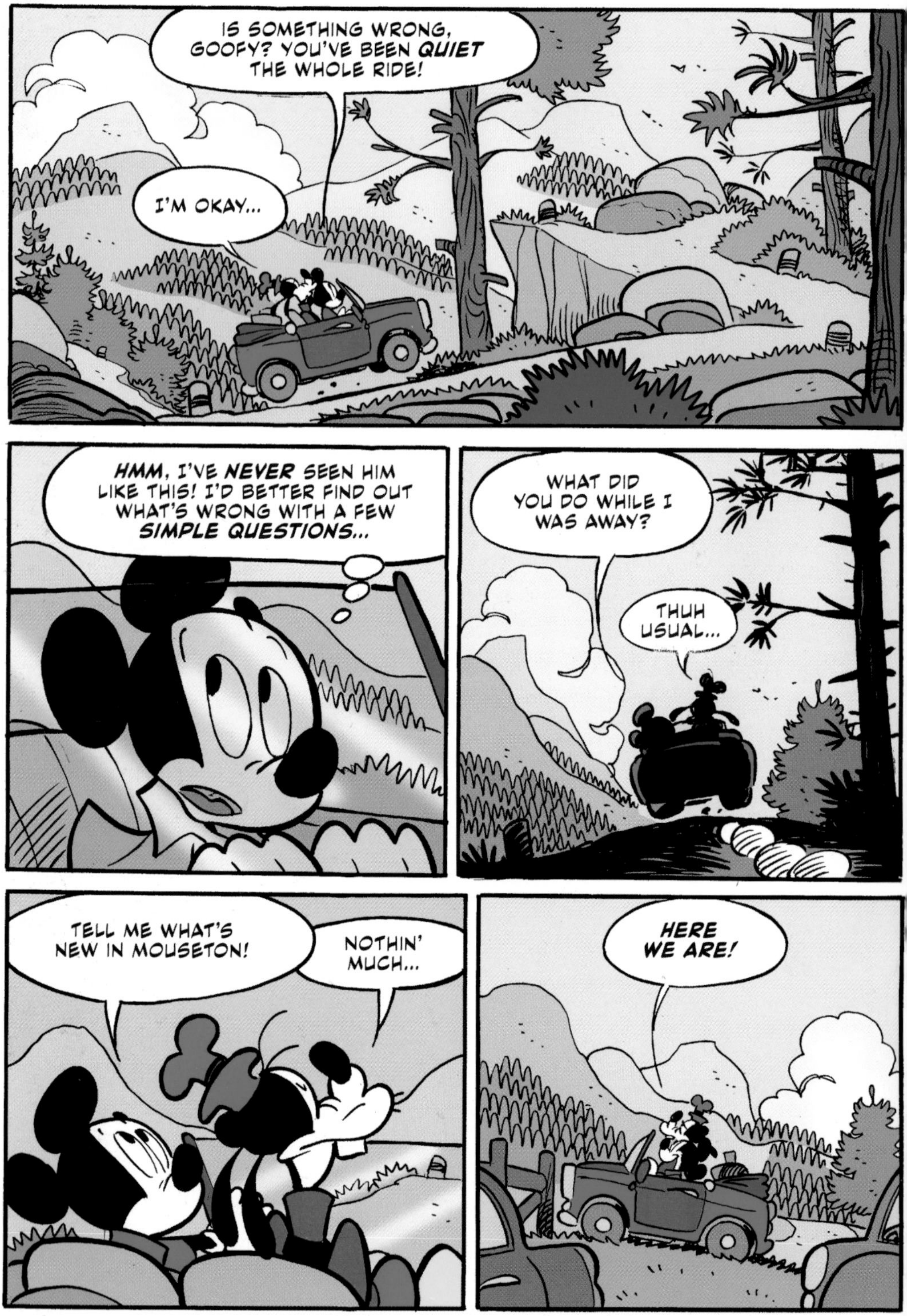
IS SOMETHING WRONG, GOOFY? YOU'VE BEEN QUIET THE WHOLE RIDE!
I'M OKAY...
HMM, I'VE NEVER SEEN HIM LIKE THIS! I'D BETTER FIND OUT WHAT'S WRONG WITH A FEW SIMPLE QUESTIONS...
WHAT DID YOU DO WHILE I WAS AWAY?
THUH USUAL...
TELL ME WHAT'S NEW IN MOUSETON!
NOTHIN' MUCH...
HERE WE ARE!

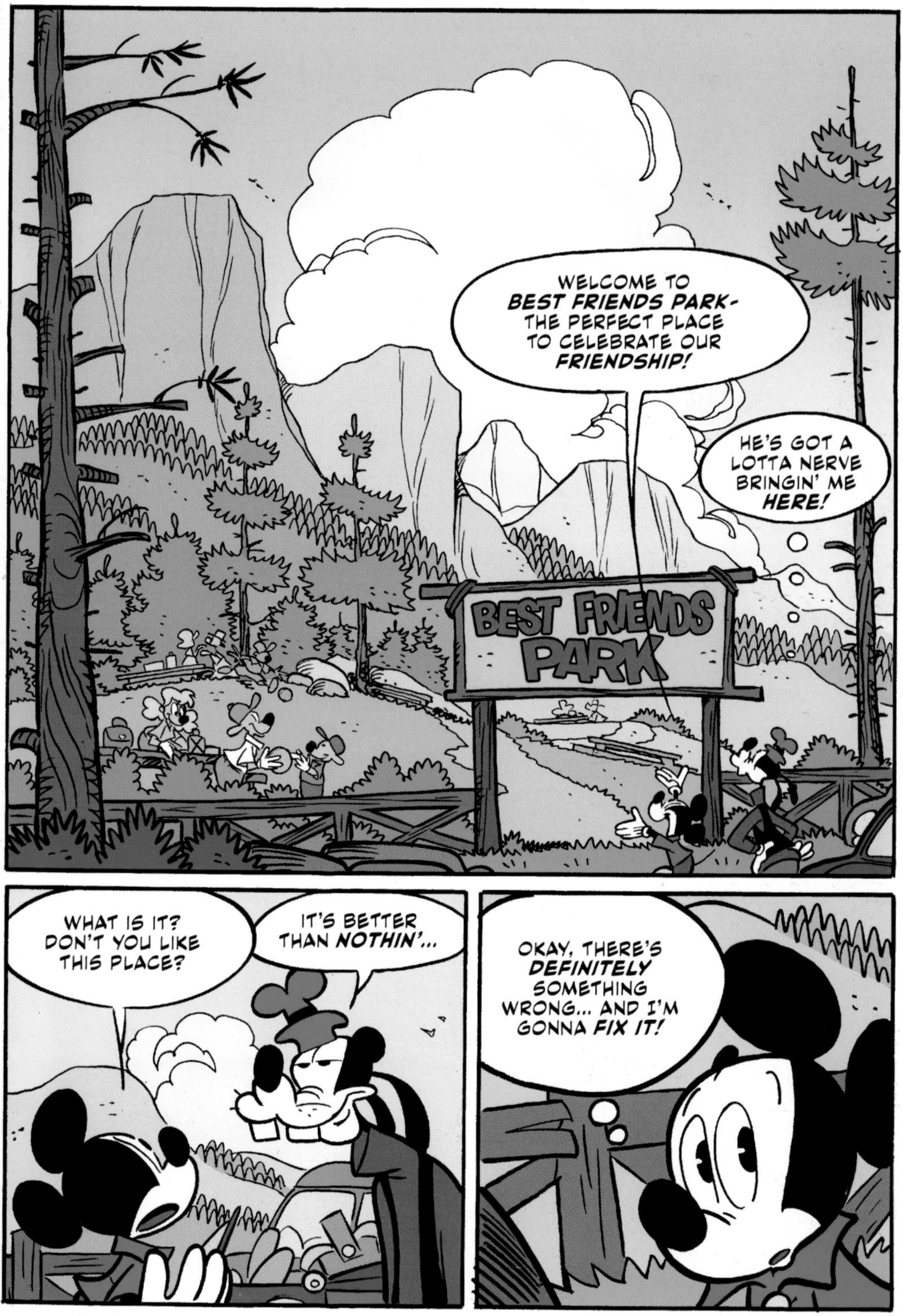
WELCOME TO BEST FRIENDS PARK- THE PERFECT PLACE TO CELEBRATE OUR FRIENDSHIP!
HE'S GOT A LOTTA NERVE BRINGIN' ME HERE!
BEST FRIENDS PARK
WHAT IS IT? DON'T YOU LIKE THIS PLACE?
IT'S BETTER THAN NOTHIN'...
OKAY, THERE'S DEFINITELY SOMETHING WRONG... AND I'M GONNA FIX IT!

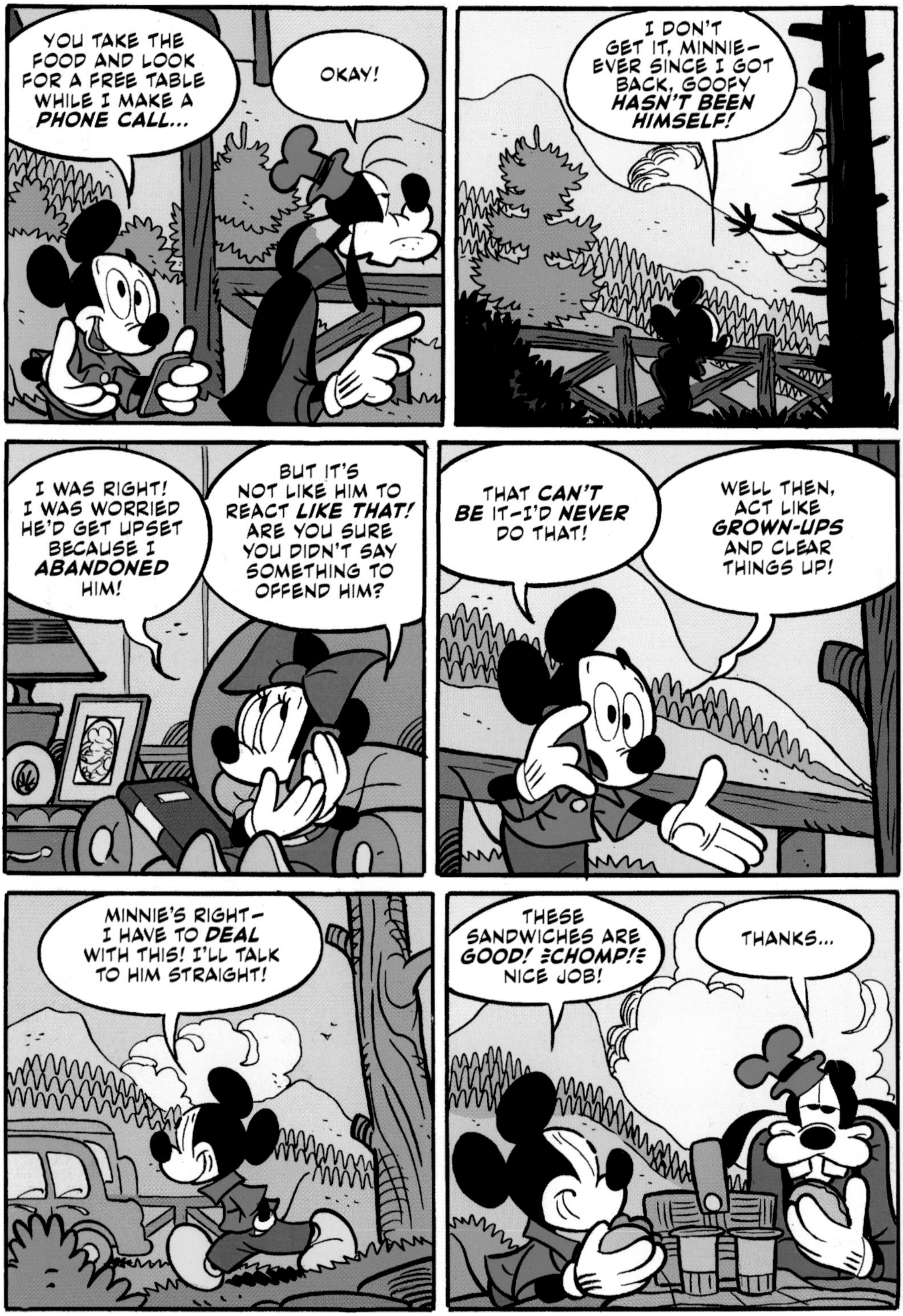
YOU TAKE THE FOOD AND LOOK FOR A FREE TABLE WHILE I MAKE A PHONE CALL...
OKAY!
I DON'T GET IT, MINNIE— EVER SINCE I GOT BACK, GOOFY HASN'T BEEN HIMSELF!
I WAS RIGHT! I WAS WORRIED HE'D GET UPSET BECAUSE I ABANDONED HIM!
BUT IT'S NOT LIKE HIM TO REACT LIKE THAT! ARE YOU SURE YOU DIDN'T SAY SOMETHING TO OFFEND HIM?
THAT CAN'T BE IT—I'D NEVER DO THAT!
WELL THEN, ACT LIKE GROWN-UPS AND CLEAR THINGS UP!
MINNIE'S RIGHT— I HAVE TO DEAL WITH THIS! I'LL TALK TO HIM STRAIGHT!
THESE SANDWICHES ARE GOOD! CHOMP! NICE JOB!
THANKS...

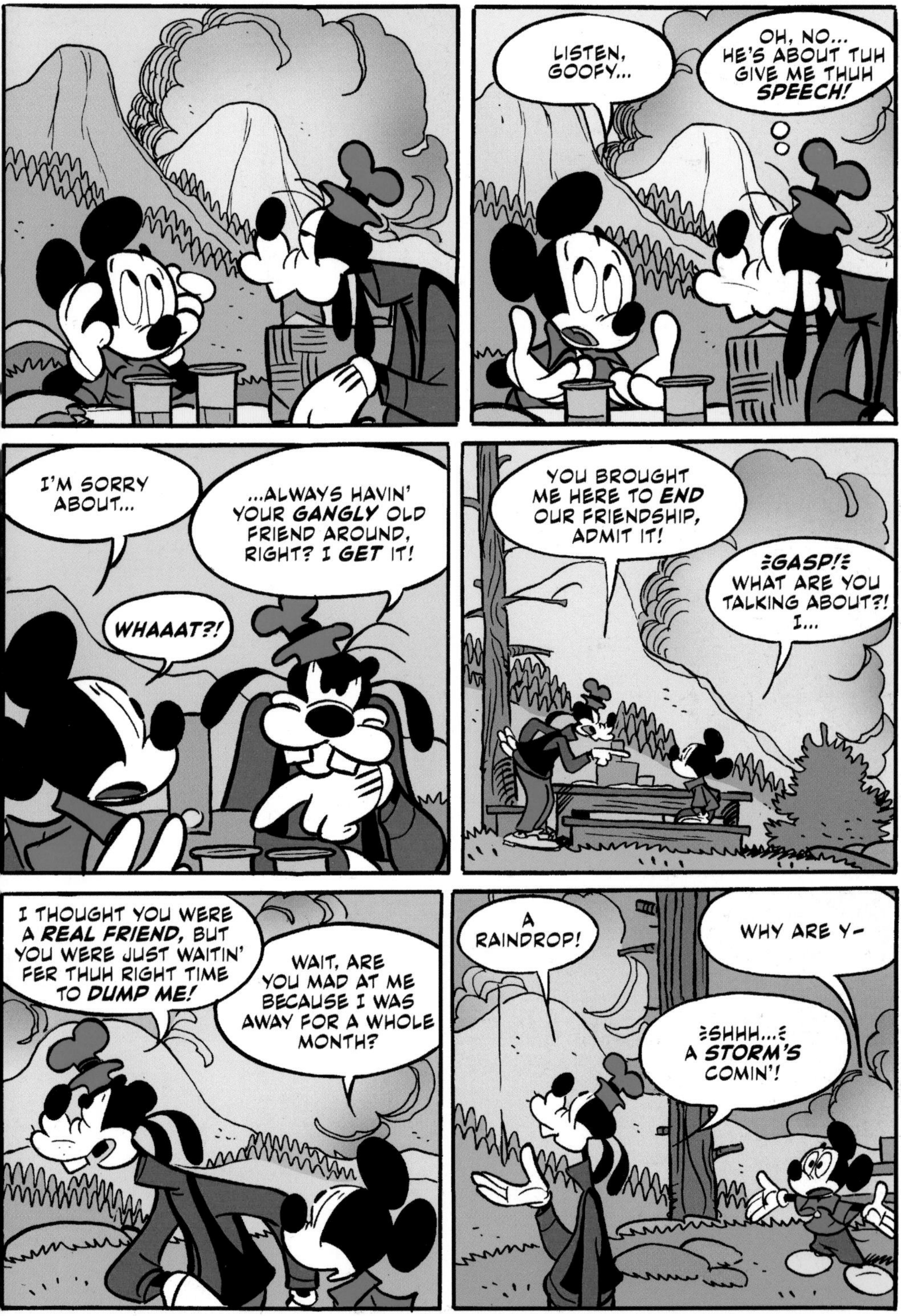
LISTEN, GOOFY...
OH, NO... HE'S ABOUT TUH GIVE ME THUH SPEECH!
I'M SORRY ABOUT...
...ALWAYS HAVIN' YOUR GANGLY OLD FRIEND AROUND, RIGHT? I GET IT!
WHAAAT?!
YOU BROUGHT ME HERE TO END OUR FRIENDSHIP, ADMIT IT!
GASP! WHAT ARE YOU TALKING ABOUT?! I...
I THOUGHT YOU WERE A REAL FRIEND, BUT YOU WERE JUST WAITIN' FER THUH RIGHT TIME TO DUMP ME!
WAIT, ARE YOU MAD AT ME BECAUSE I WAS AWAY FOR A WHOLE MONTH?
A RAINDROP!
WHY ARE Y-
SHHH... A STORM'S COMIN'!

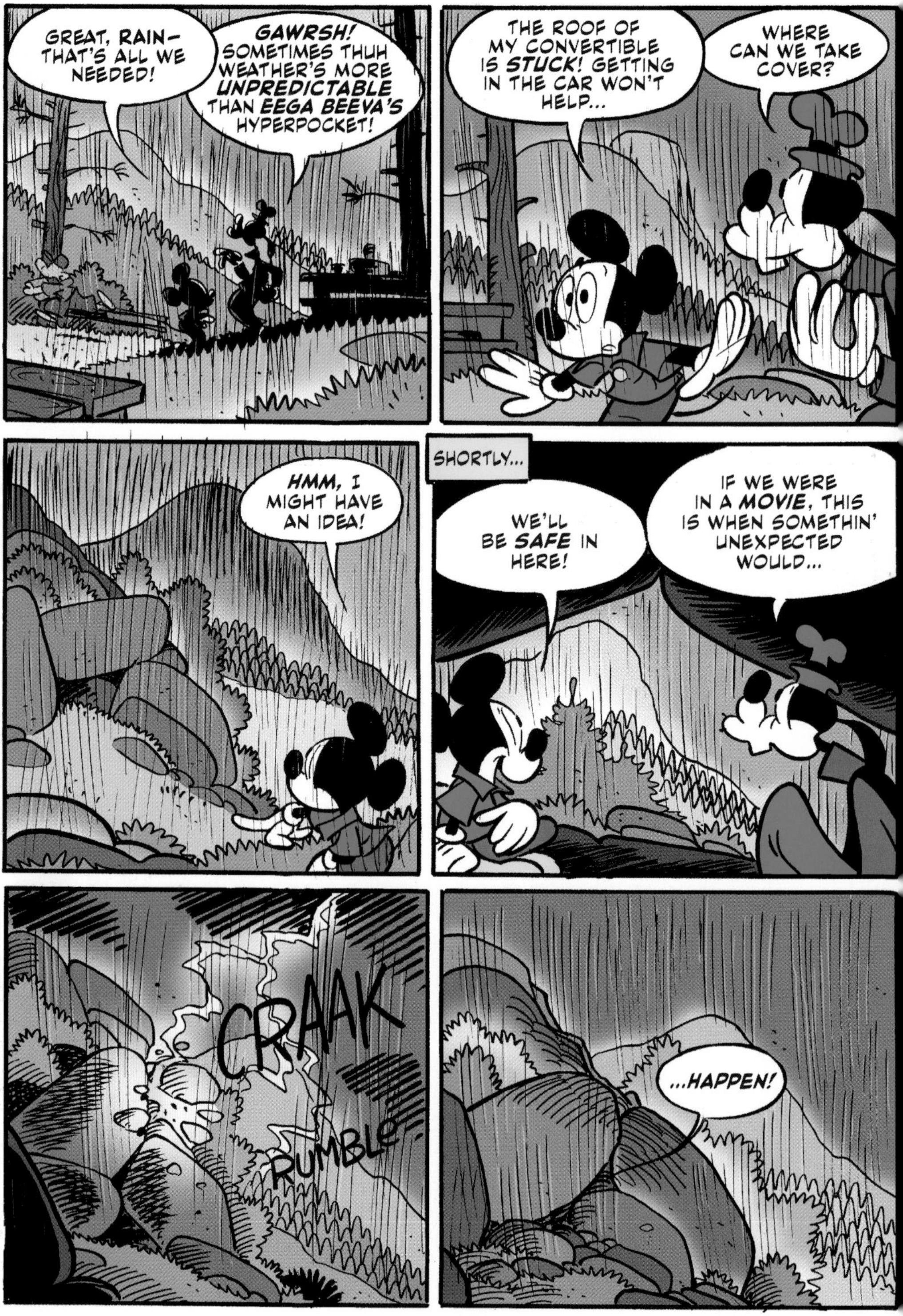
GREAT, **RAIN**— THAT'S ALL WE NEEDED!
GAWRSH! SOMETIMES THUH WEATHER'S MORE ***UNPREDICTABLE*** THAN ***EEGA BEEVA'S*** HYPERPOCKET!
THE ROOF OF MY CONVERTIBLE IS ***STUCK!*** GETTING IN THE CAR WON'T HELP...
WHERE CAN WE TAKE COVER?
HMM, I MIGHT HAVE AN IDEA!
SHORTLY...
WE'LL BE ***SAFE*** IN HERE!
IF WE WERE IN A ***MOVIE***, THIS IS WHEN SOMETHIN' UNEXPECTED WOULD...
CRAAK
RUMBLE
...HAPPEN!

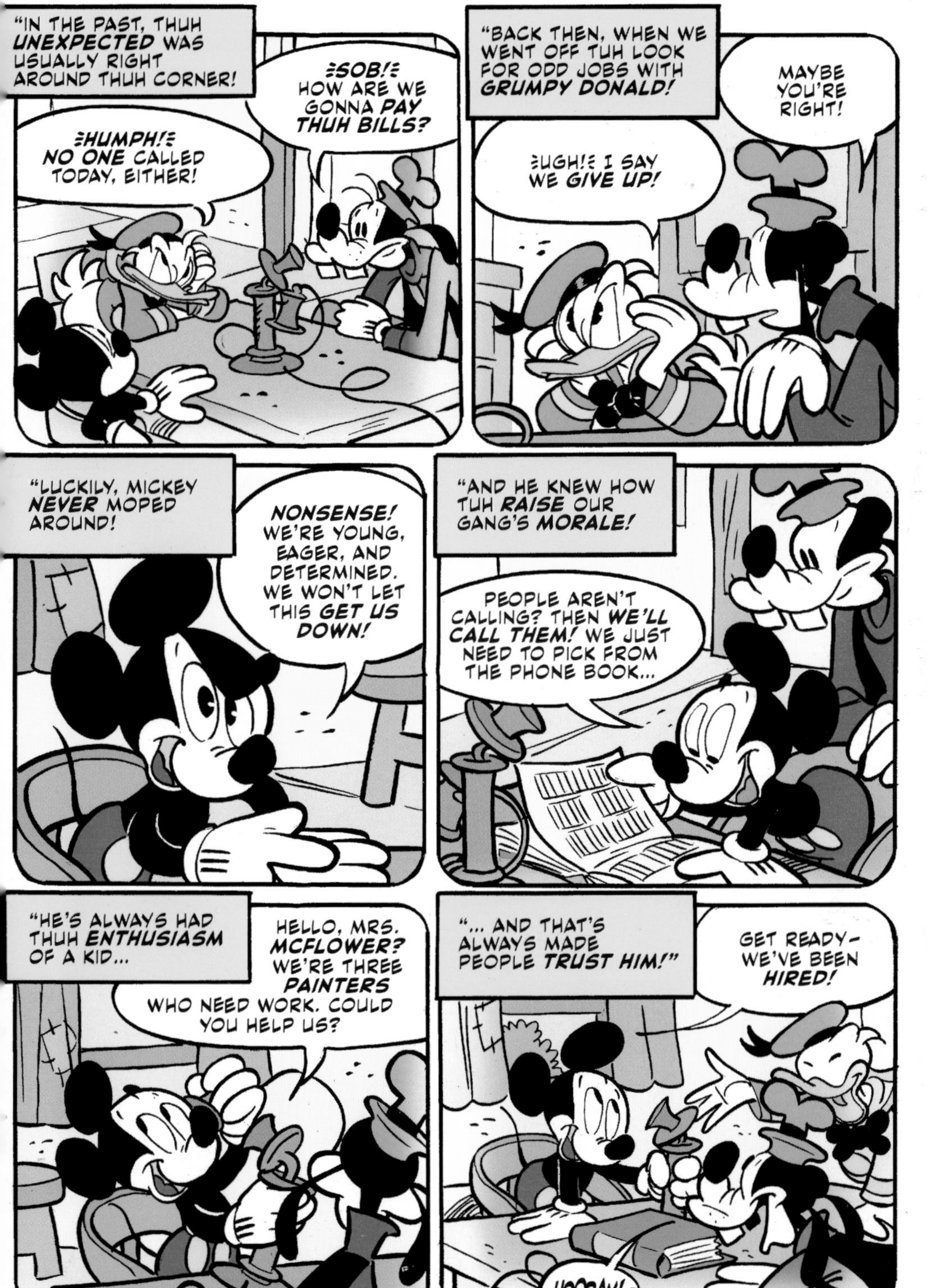
"IN THE PAST, THUH UNEXPECTED WAS USUALLY RIGHT AROUND THUH CORNER!
SOB! HOW ARE WE GONNA PAY THUH BILLS?
HUMPH! NO ONE CALLED TODAY, EITHER!
"BACK THEN, WHEN WE WENT OFF TUH LOOK FOR ODD JOBS WITH GRUMPY DONALD!
MAYBE YOU'RE RIGHT!
UGH! I SAY WE GIVE UP!
"LUCKILY, MICKEY NEVER MOPED AROUND!
NONSENSE! WE'RE YOUNG, EAGER, AND DETERMINED. WE WON'T LET THIS GET US DOWN!
"AND HE KNEW HOW TUH RAISE OUR GANG'S MORALE!
PEOPLE AREN'T CALLING? THEN WE'LL CALL THEM! WE JUST NEED TO PICK FROM THE PHONE BOOK...
"HE'S ALWAYS HAD THUH ENTHUSIASM OF A KID...
HELLO, MRS. MCFLOWER? WE'RE THREE PAINTERS WHO NEED WORK. COULD YOU HELP US?
"... AND THAT'S ALWAYS MADE PEOPLE TRUST HIM!"
GET READY- WE'VE BEEN HIRED!
HOORAY!

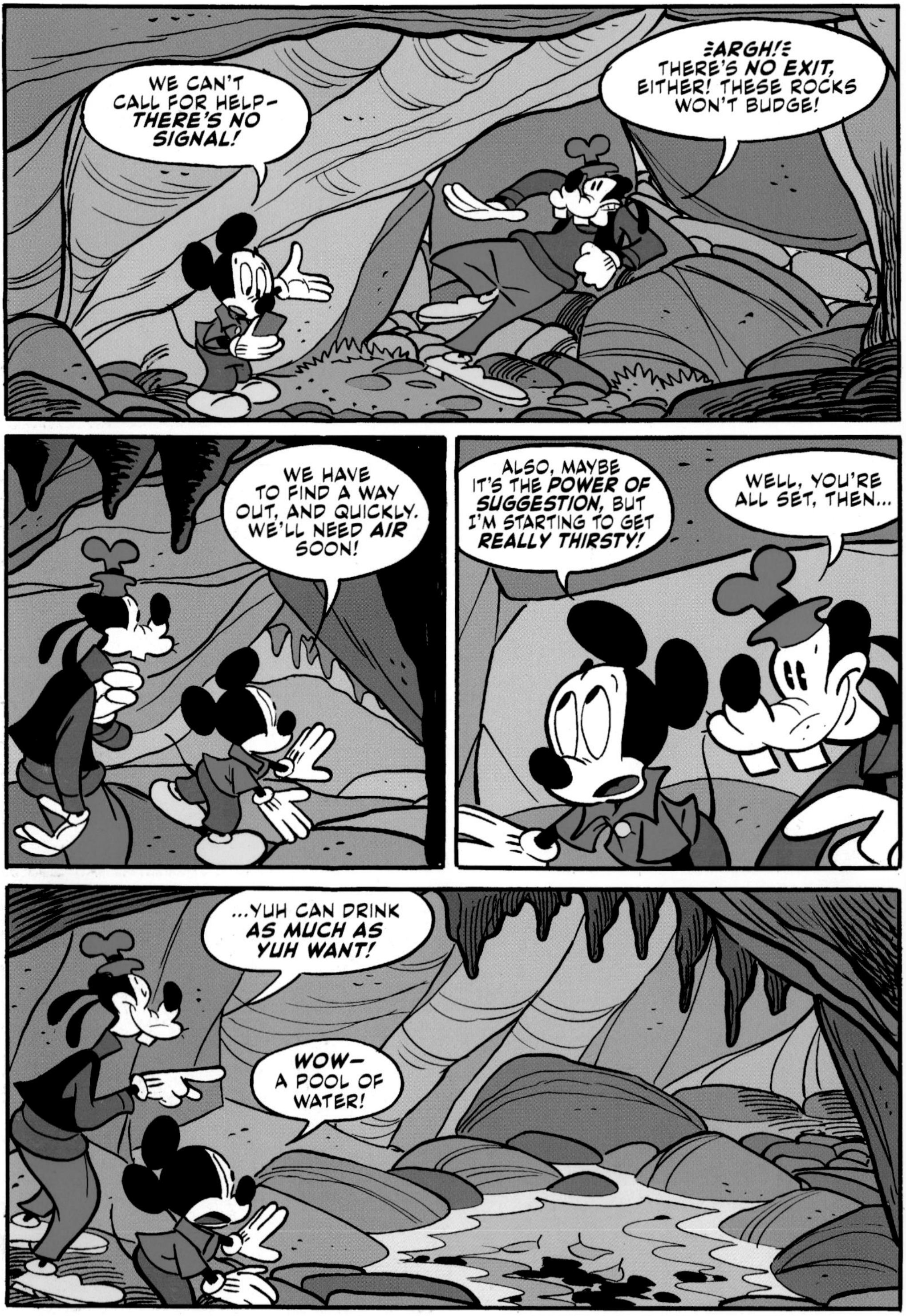
WE CAN'T CALL FOR HELP- THERE'S NO SIGNAL!
ARGH! THERE'S NO EXIT, EITHER! THESE ROCKS WON'T BUDGE!
WE HAVE TO FIND A WAY OUT, AND QUICKLY. WE'LL NEED AIR SOON!
ALSO, MAYBE IT'S THE POWER OF SUGGESTION, BUT I'M STARTING TO GET REALLY THIRSTY!
WELL, YOU'RE ALL SET, THEN...
...YUH CAN DRINK AS MUCH AS YUH WANT!
WOW- A POOL OF WATER!

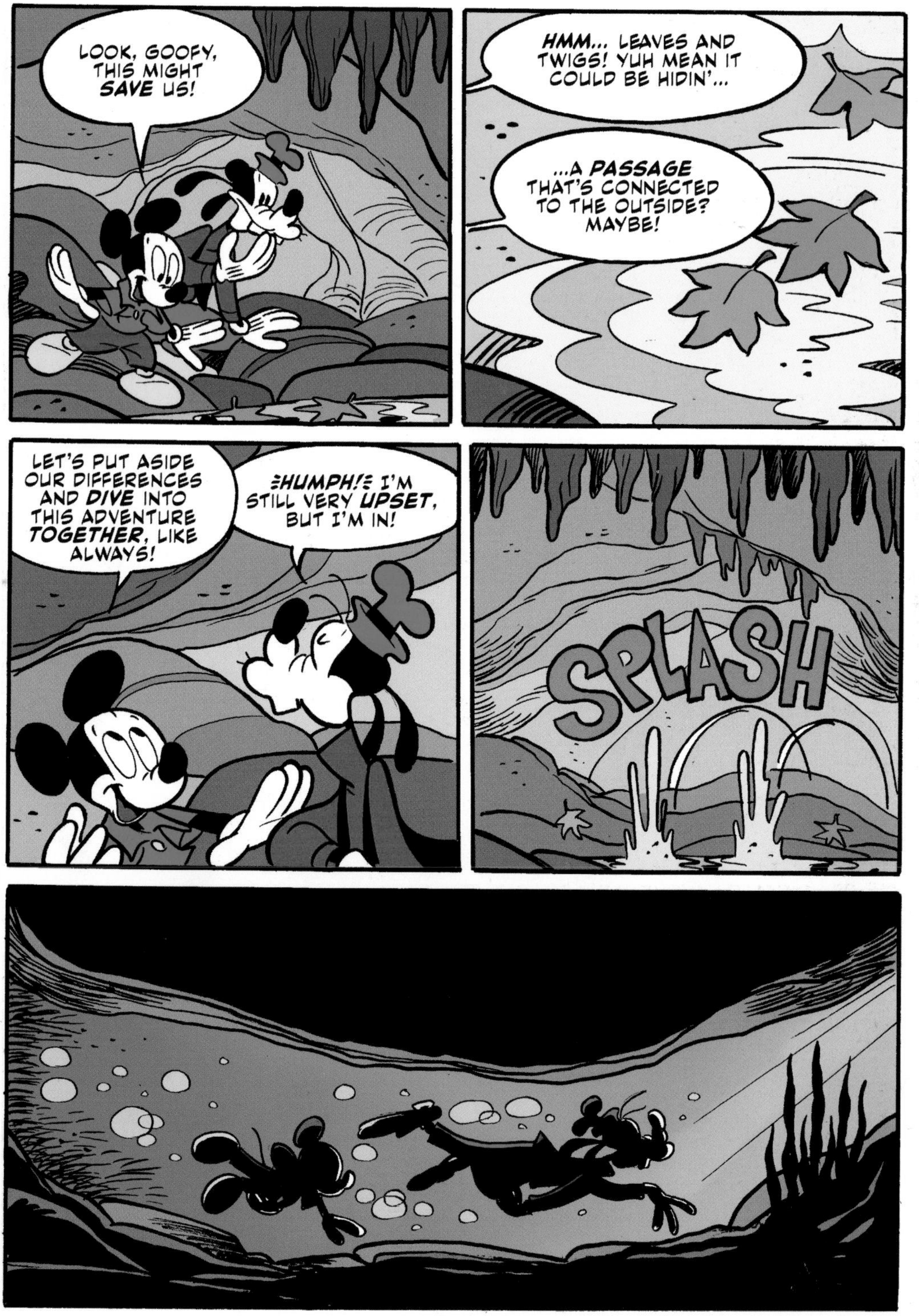

LOOK, GOOFY, THIS MIGHT SAVE US!
HMM... LEAVES AND TWIGS! YUH MEAN IT COULD BE HIDIN'...
...A PASSAGE THAT'S CONNECTED TO THE OUTSIDE? MAYBE!
LET'S PUT ASIDE OUR DIFFERENCES AND DIVE INTO THIS ADVENTURE TOGETHER, LIKE ALWAYS!
HUMPH! I'M STILL VERY UPSET, BUT I'M IN!
SPLASH

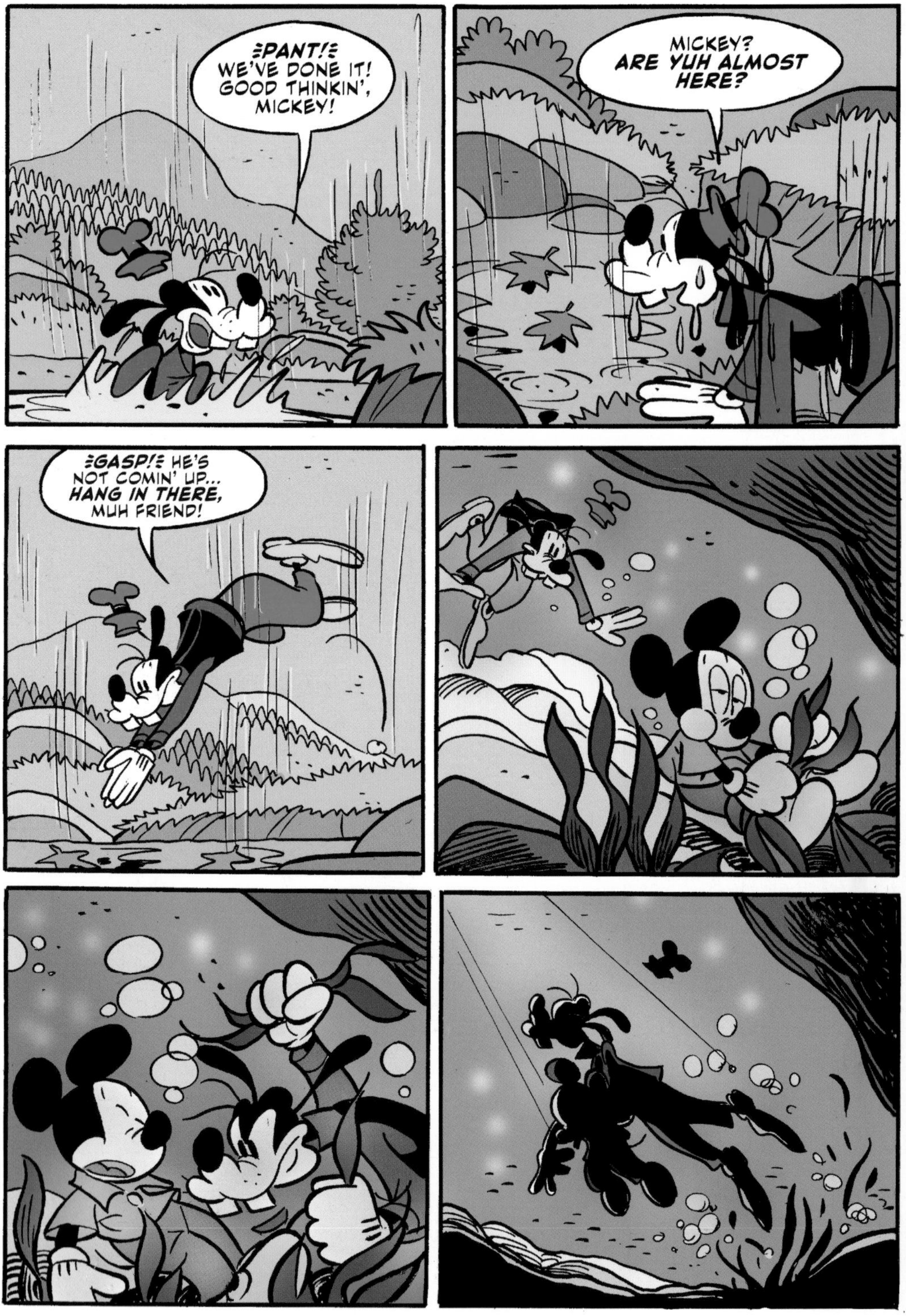
PANT! WE'VE DONE IT! GOOD THINKIN', MICKEY!
MICKEY? ARE YUH ALMOST HERE?
GASP! HE'S NOT COMIN' UP... HANG IN THERE, MUH FRIEND!

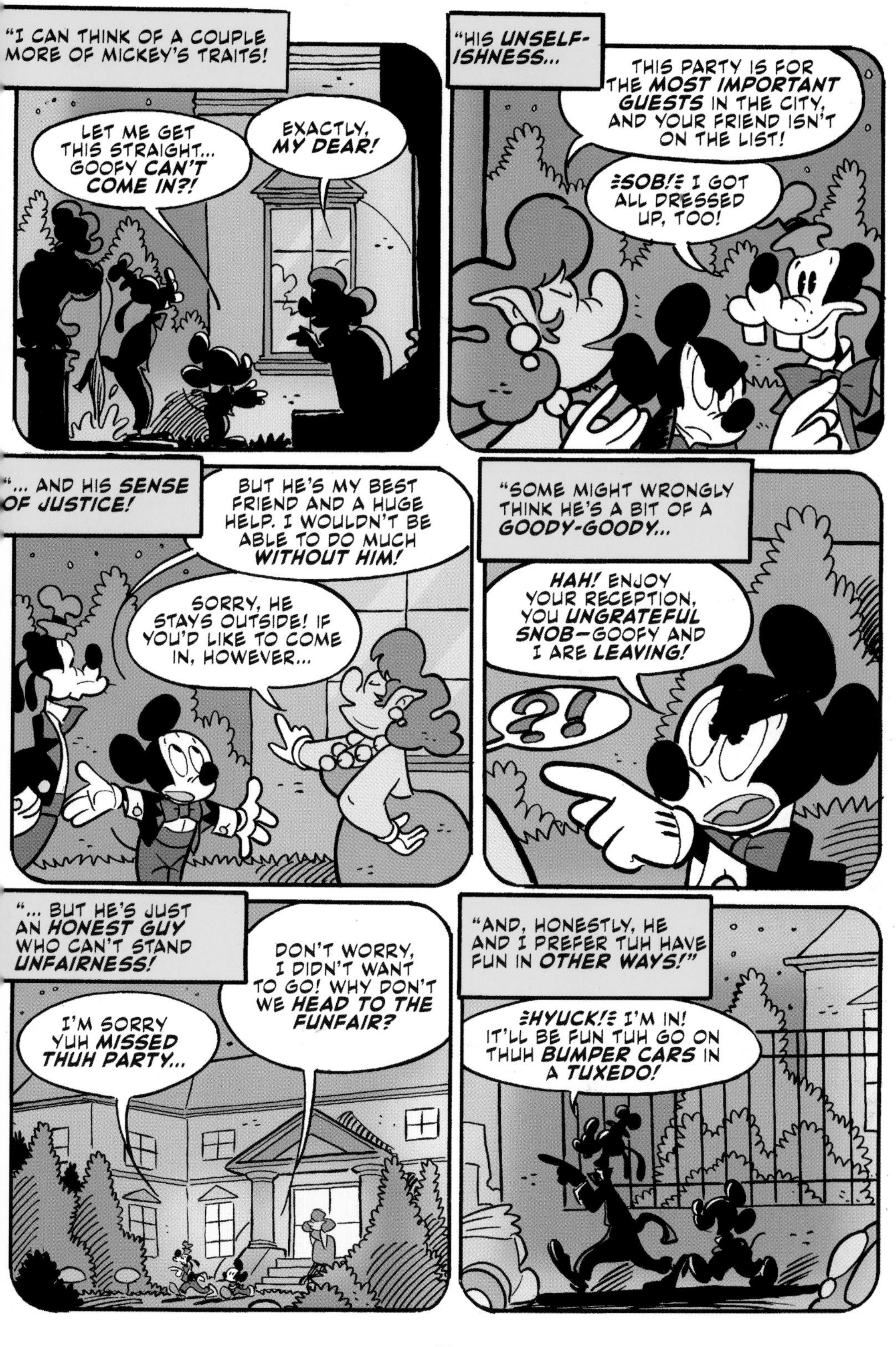
"I CAN THINK OF A COUPLE MORE OF MICKEY'S TRAITS!
LET ME GET THIS STRAIGHT... GOOFY CAN'T COME IN?!
EXACTLY, MY DEAR!
"HIS UNSELF-ISHNESS...
THIS PARTY IS FOR THE MOST IMPORTANT GUESTS IN THE CITY, AND YOUR FRIEND ISN'T ON THE LIST!
SOB! I GOT ALL DRESSED UP, TOO!
"... AND HIS SENSE OF JUSTICE!
BUT HE'S MY BEST FRIEND AND A HUGE HELP. I WOULDN'T BE ABLE TO DO MUCH WITHOUT HIM!
SORRY, HE STAYS OUTSIDE! IF YOU'D LIKE TO COME IN, HOWEVER...
"SOME MIGHT WRONGLY THINK HE'S A BIT OF A GOODY-GOODY...
HAH! ENJOY YOUR RECEPTION, YOU UNGRATEFUL SNOB—GOOFY AND I ARE LEAVING!
?!
"... BUT HE'S JUST AN HONEST GUY WHO CAN'T STAND UNFAIRNESS!
I'M SORRY YUH MISSED THUH PARTY...
DON'T WORRY, I DIDN'T WANT TO GO! WHY DON'T WE HEAD TO THE FUNFAIR?
"AND, HONESTLY, HE AND I PREFER TUH HAVE FUN IN OTHER WAYS!"
HYUCK! I'M IN! IT'LL BE FUN TUH GO ON THUH BUMPER CARS IN A TUXEDO!

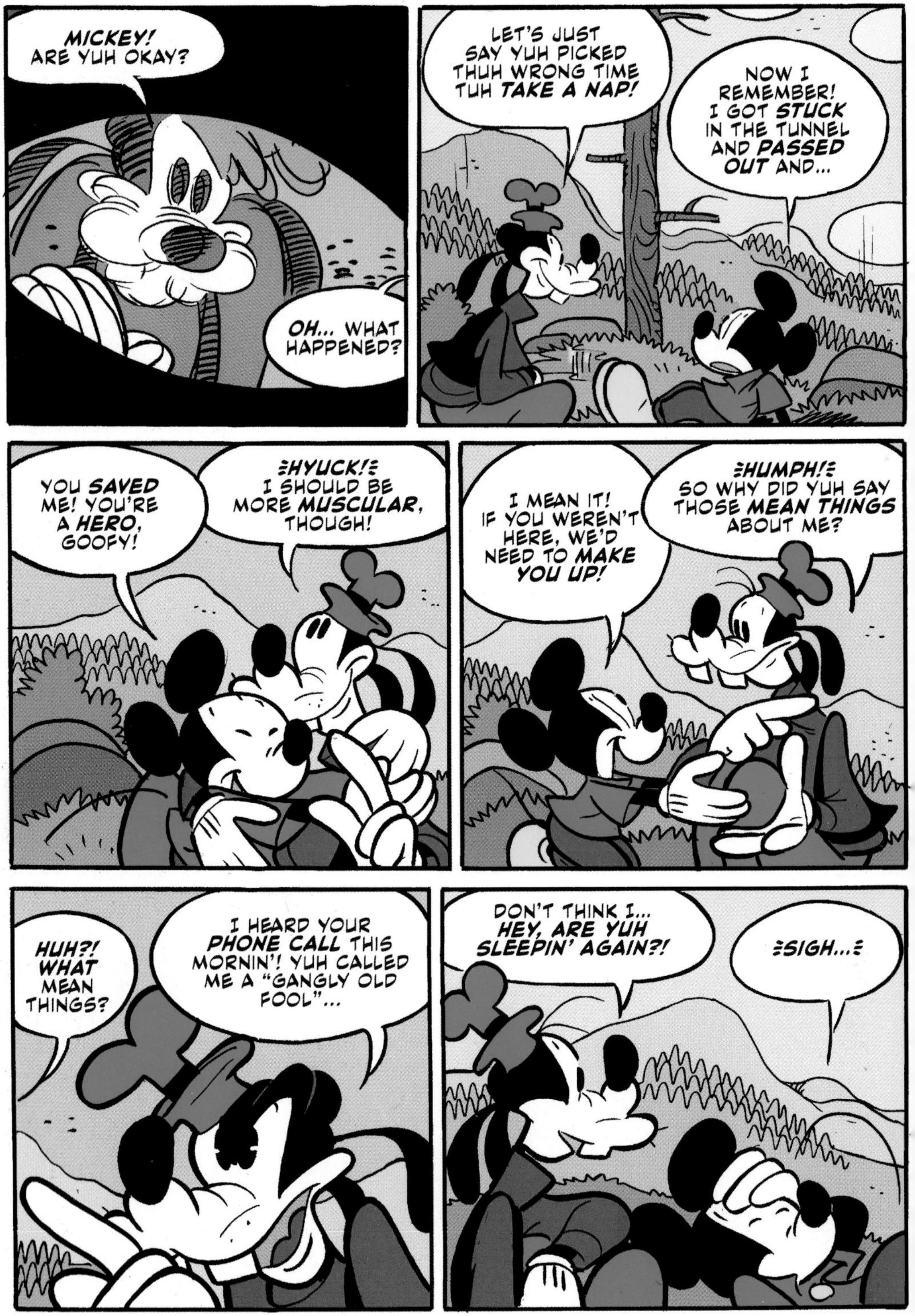
MICKEY! ARE YUH OKAY?
OH... WHAT HAPPENED?
LET'S JUST SAY YUH PICKED THUH WRONG TIME TUH TAKE A NAP!
NOW I REMEMBER! I GOT STUCK IN THE TUNNEL AND PASSED OUT AND...
YOU SAVED ME! YOU'RE A HERO, GOOFY!
≡HYUCK!≡ I SHOULD BE MORE MUSCULAR, THOUGH!
I MEAN IT! IF YOU WEREN'T HERE, WE'D NEED TO MAKE YOU UP!
≡HUMPH!≡ SO WHY DID YUH SAY THOSE MEAN THINGS ABOUT ME?
HUH?! WHAT MEAN THINGS?
I HEARD YOUR PHONE CALL THIS MORNIN'! YUH CALLED ME A "GANGLY OLD FOOL"...
DON'T THINK I... HEY, ARE YUH SLEEPIN' AGAIN?!
≡SIGH...≡

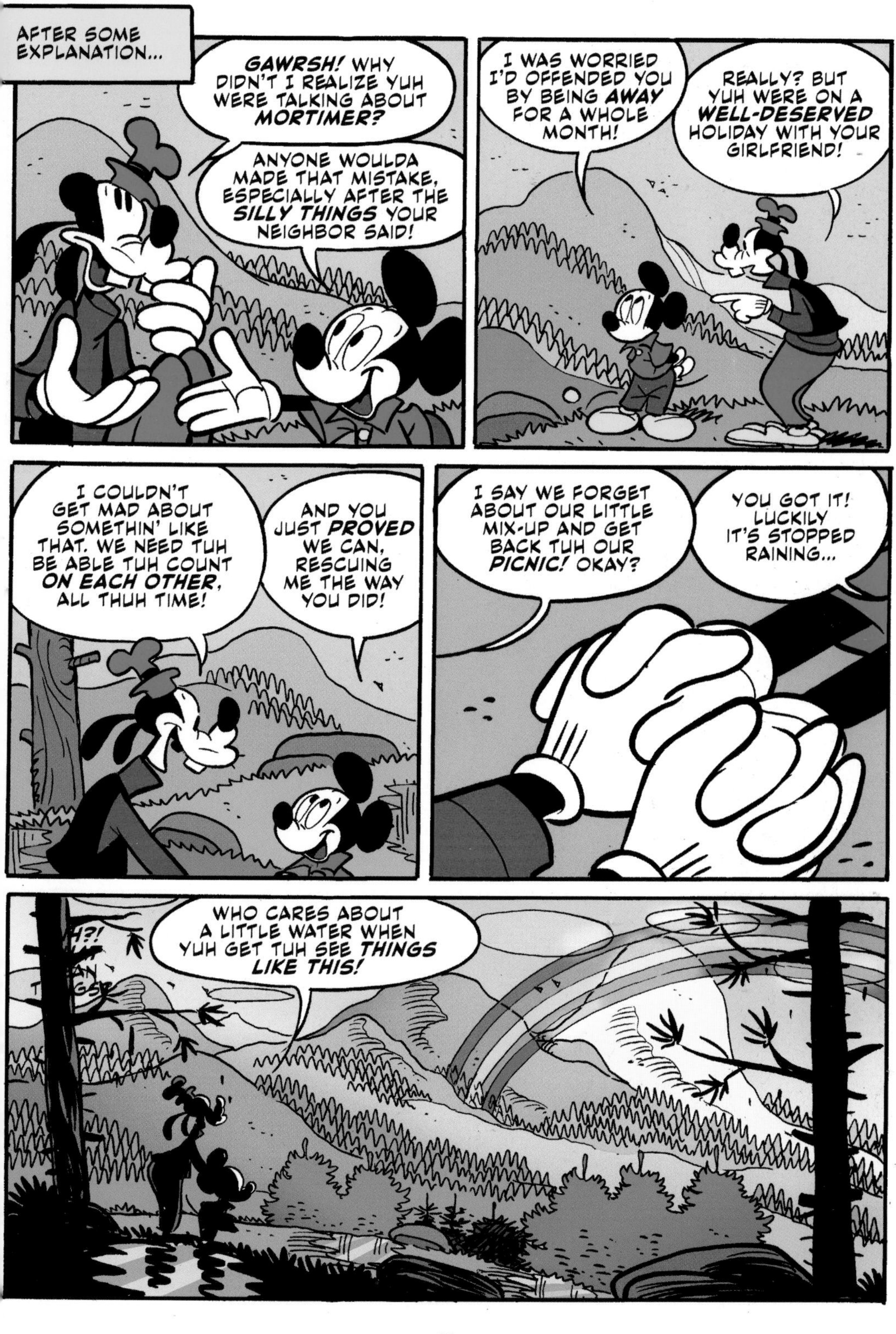
AFTER SOME EXPLANATION...
GAWRSH! WHY DIDN'T I REALIZE YUH WERE TALKING ABOUT MORTIMER?
ANYONE WOULDA MADE THAT MISTAKE, ESPECIALLY AFTER THE SILLY THINGS YOUR NEIGHBOR SAID!
I WAS WORRIED I'D OFFENDED YOU BY BEING AWAY FOR A WHOLE MONTH!
REALLY? BUT YUH WERE ON A WELL-DESERVED HOLIDAY WITH YOUR GIRLFRIEND!
I COULDN'T GET MAD ABOUT SOMETHIN' LIKE THAT. WE NEED TUH BE ABLE TUH COUNT ON EACH OTHER, ALL THUH TIME!
AND YOU JUST PROVED WE CAN, RESCUING ME THE WAY YOU DID!
I SAY WE FORGET ABOUT OUR LITTLE MIX-UP AND GET BACK TUH OUR PICNIC! OKAY?
YOU GOT IT! LUCKILY IT'S STOPPED RAINING...
WHO CARES ABOUT A LITTLE WATER WHEN YUH GET TUH SEE THINGS LIKE THIS!

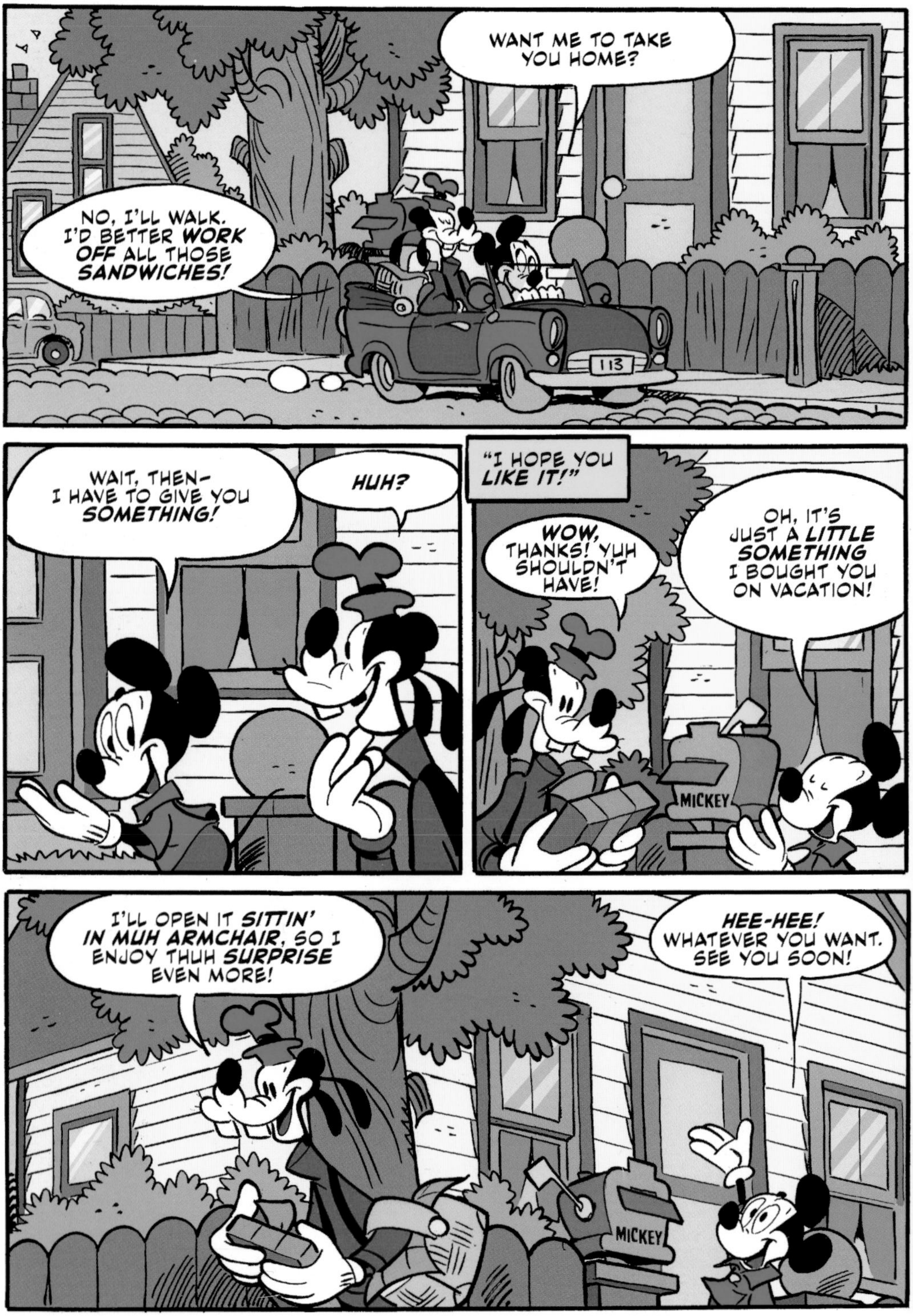

WANT ME TO TAKE YOU HOME?
NO, I'LL WALK. I'D BETTER **WORK OFF** ALL THOSE **SANDWICHES!**
113
WAIT, THEN– I HAVE TO GIVE YOU **SOMETHING!**
HUH?
"I HOPE YOU **LIKE IT!**"
WOW, THANKS! YUH SHOULDN'T HAVE!
OH, IT'S JUST A **LITTLE SOMETHING** I BOUGHT YOU ON VACATION!
MICKEY
I'LL OPEN IT **SITTIN' IN MUH ARMCHAIR**, SO I ENJOY THUH **SURPRISE** EVEN MORE!
HEE-HEE! WHATEVER YOU WANT. SEE YOU SOON!
MICKEY

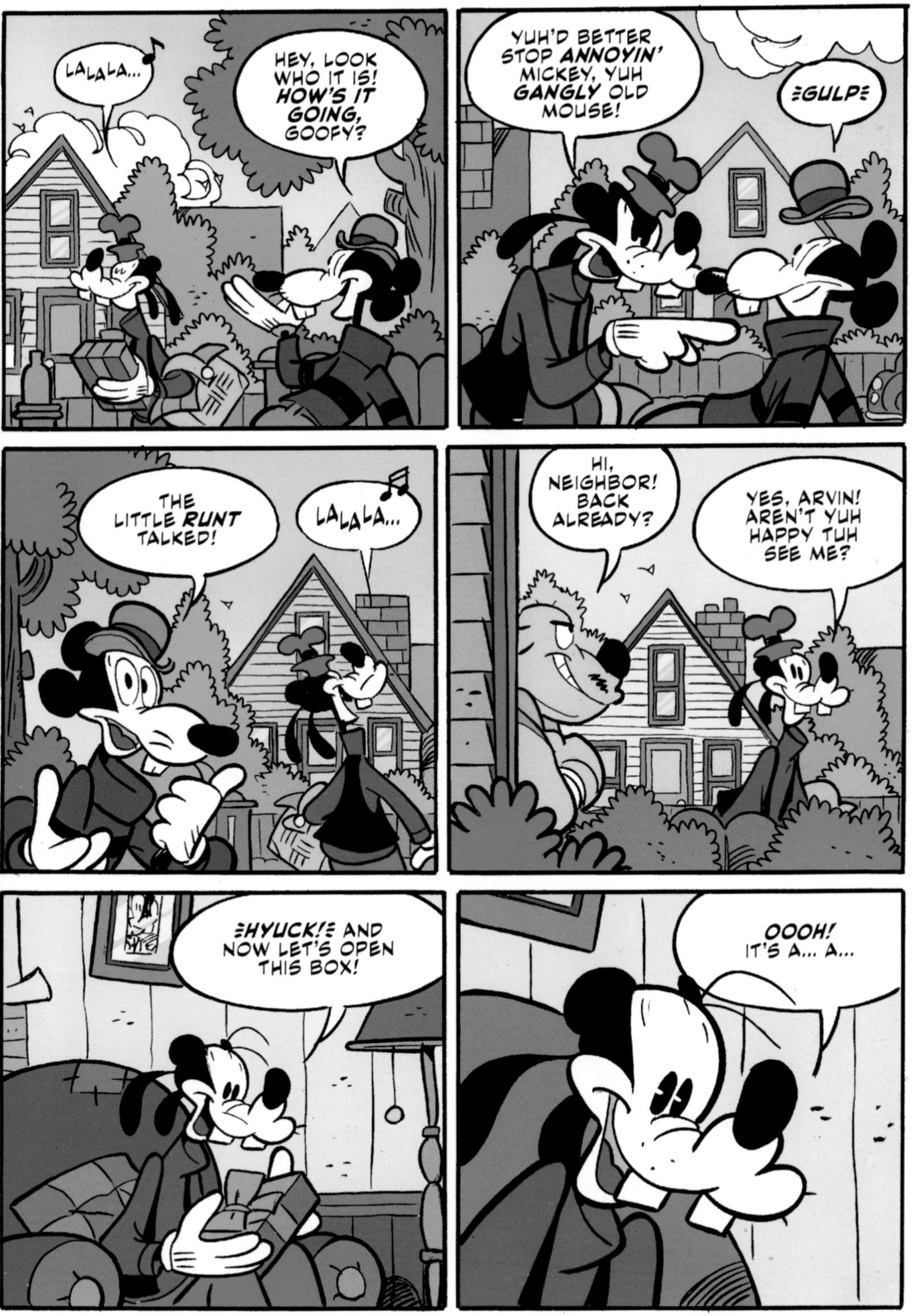
LALALA...
HEY, LOOK WHO IT IS! HOW'S IT GOING, GOOFY?
YUH'D BETTER STOP ANNOYIN' MICKEY, YUH GANGLY OLD MOUSE!
GULP
THE LITTLE RUNT TALKED!
LALALA...
HI, NEIGHBOR! BACK ALREADY?
YES, ARVIN! AREN'T YUH HAPPY TUH SEE ME?
HYUCK! AND NOW LET'S OPEN THIS BOX!
OOOH! IT'S A... A...

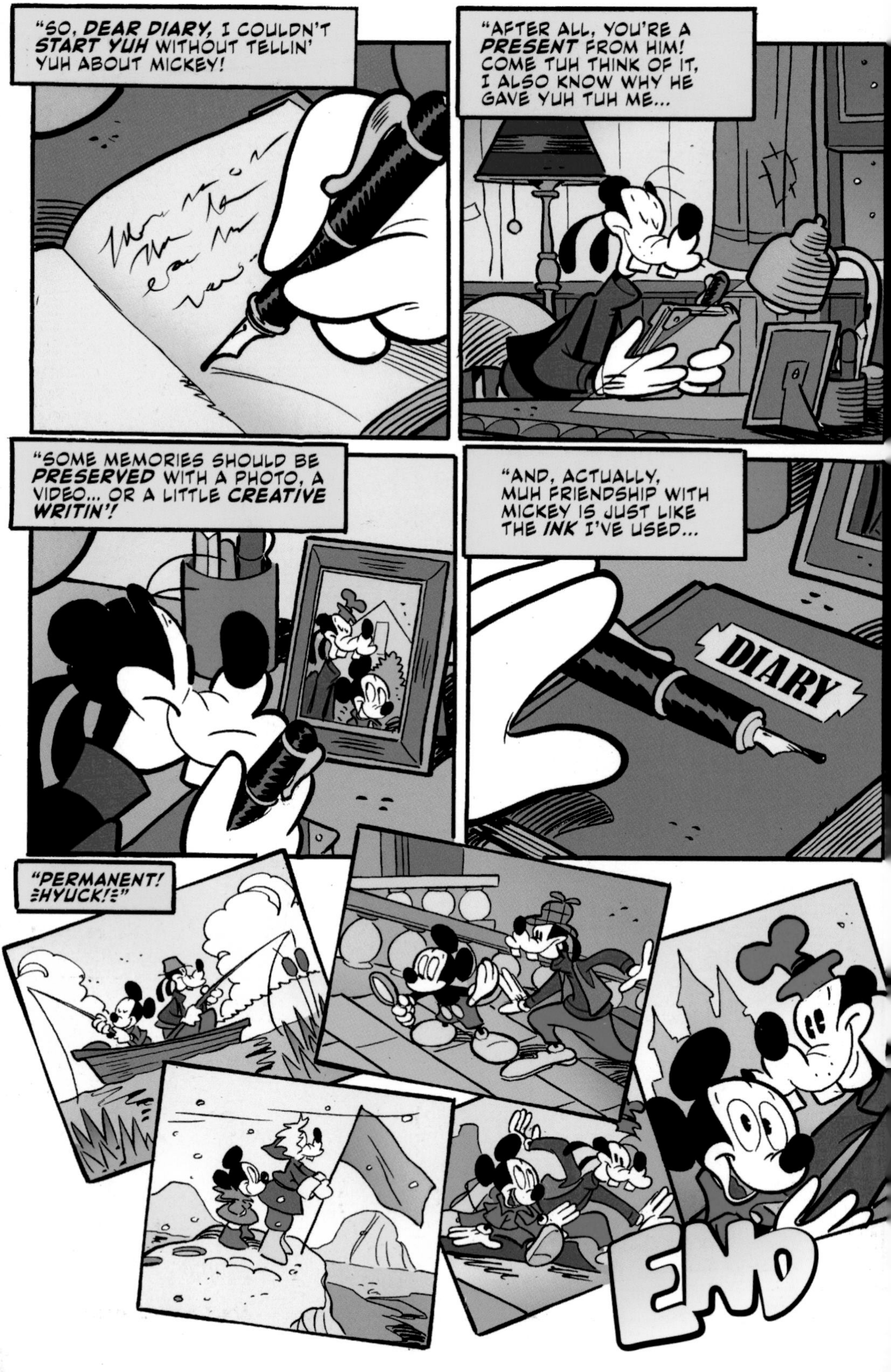
"SO, DEAR DIARY, I COULDN'T START YUH WITHOUT TELLIN' YUH ABOUT MICKEY!
"AFTER ALL, YOU'RE A PRESENT FROM HIM! COME TUH THINK OF IT, I ALSO KNOW WHY HE GAVE YUH TUH ME...
"SOME MEMORIES SHOULD BE PRESERVED WITH A PHOTO, A VIDEO... OR A LITTLE CREATIVE WRITIN'!
"AND, ACTUALLY, MUH FRIENDSHIP WITH MICKEY IS JUST LIKE THE INK I'VE USED...
DIARY
"PERMANENT! HYUCK!"
END

Walt Disney's Donald Duck in OH, GROW UP!

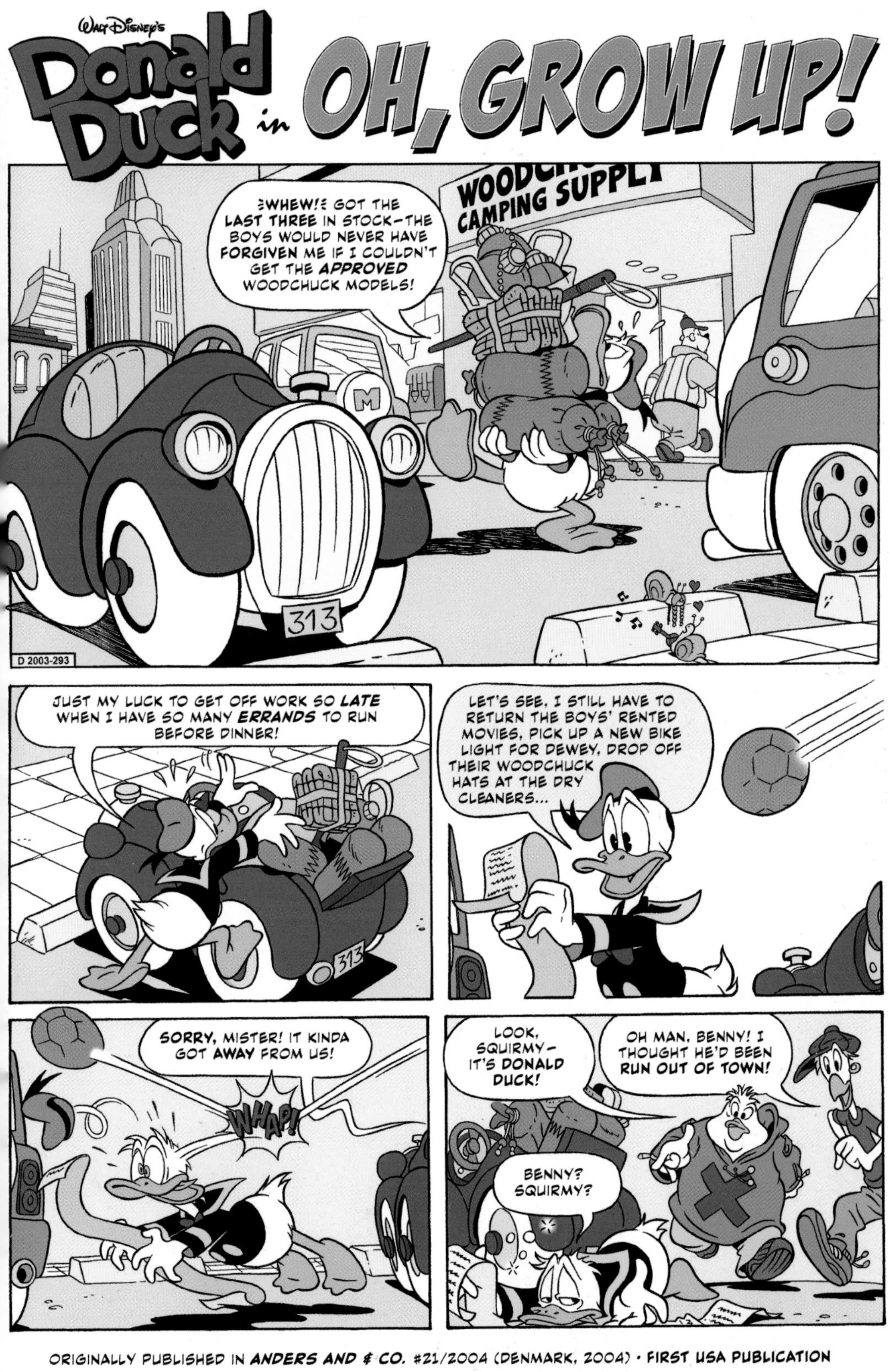
WOODCHUCK CAMPING SUPPLY
WHEW! GOT THE LAST THREE IN STOCK—THE BOYS WOULD NEVER HAVE FORGIVEN ME IF I COULDN'T GET THE APPROVED WOODCHUCK MODELS!
313
D 2003-293
JUST MY LUCK TO GET OFF WORK SO LATE WHEN I HAVE SO MANY ERRANDS TO RUN BEFORE DINNER!
313
LET'S SEE. I STILL HAVE TO RETURN THE BOYS' RENTED MOVIES, PICK UP A NEW BIKE LIGHT FOR DEWEY, DROP OFF THEIR WOODCHUCK HATS AT THE DRY CLEANERS...
SORRY, MISTER! IT KINDA GOT AWAY FROM US!
WHAP!
LOOK, SQUIRMY— IT'S DONALD DUCK!
OH MAN, BENNY! I THOUGHT HE'D BEEN RUN OUT OF TOWN!
BENNY? SQUIRMY?

ORIGINALLY PUBLISHED IN *ANDERS AND & CO.* #21/2004 (DENMARK, 2004) • FIRST USA PUBLICATION

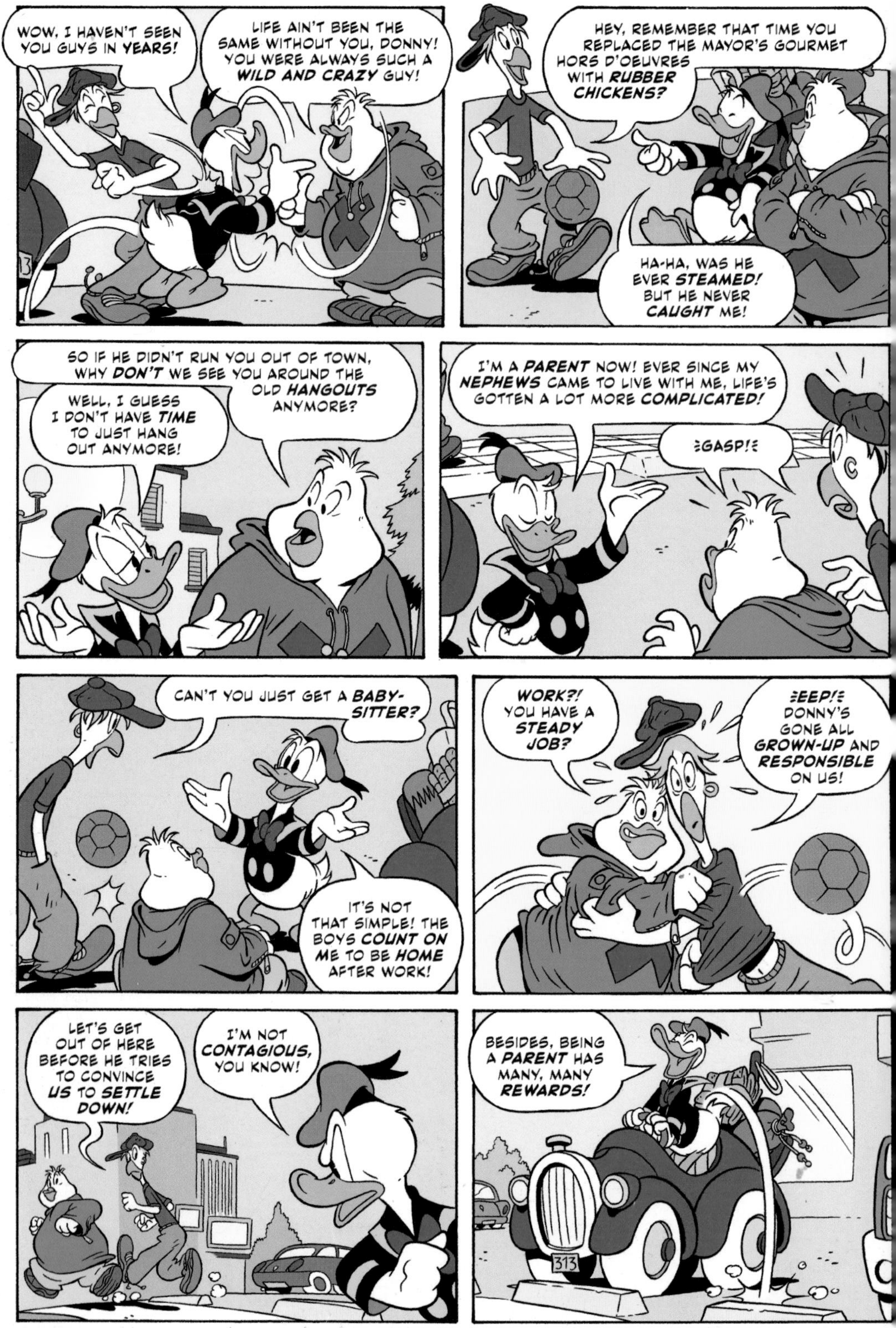

WOW, I HAVEN'T SEEN YOU GUYS IN YEARS!
LIFE AIN'T BEEN THE SAME WITHOUT YOU, DONNY! YOU WERE ALWAYS SUCH A WILD AND CRAZY GUY!
HEY, REMEMBER THAT TIME YOU REPLACED THE MAYOR'S GOURMET HORS D'OEUVRES WITH RUBBER CHICKENS?
HA-HA, WAS HE EVER STEAMED! BUT HE NEVER CAUGHT ME!
SO IF HE DIDN'T RUN YOU OUT OF TOWN, WHY DON'T WE SEE YOU AROUND THE OLD HANGOUTS ANYMORE?
WELL, I GUESS I DON'T HAVE TIME TO JUST HANG OUT ANYMORE!
I'M A PARENT NOW! EVER SINCE MY NEPHEWS CAME TO LIVE WITH ME, LIFE'S GOTTEN A LOT MORE COMPLICATED!
GASP!
CAN'T YOU JUST GET A BABY-SITTER?
IT'S NOT THAT SIMPLE! THE BOYS COUNT ON ME TO BE HOME AFTER WORK!
WORK?! YOU HAVE A STEADY JOB?
EEP! DONNY'S GONE ALL GROWN-UP AND RESPONSIBLE ON US!
LET'S GET OUT OF HERE BEFORE HE TRIES TO CONVINCE US TO SETTLE DOWN!
I'M NOT CONTAGIOUS, YOU KNOW!
BESIDES, BEING A PARENT HAS MANY, MANY REWARDS!
313

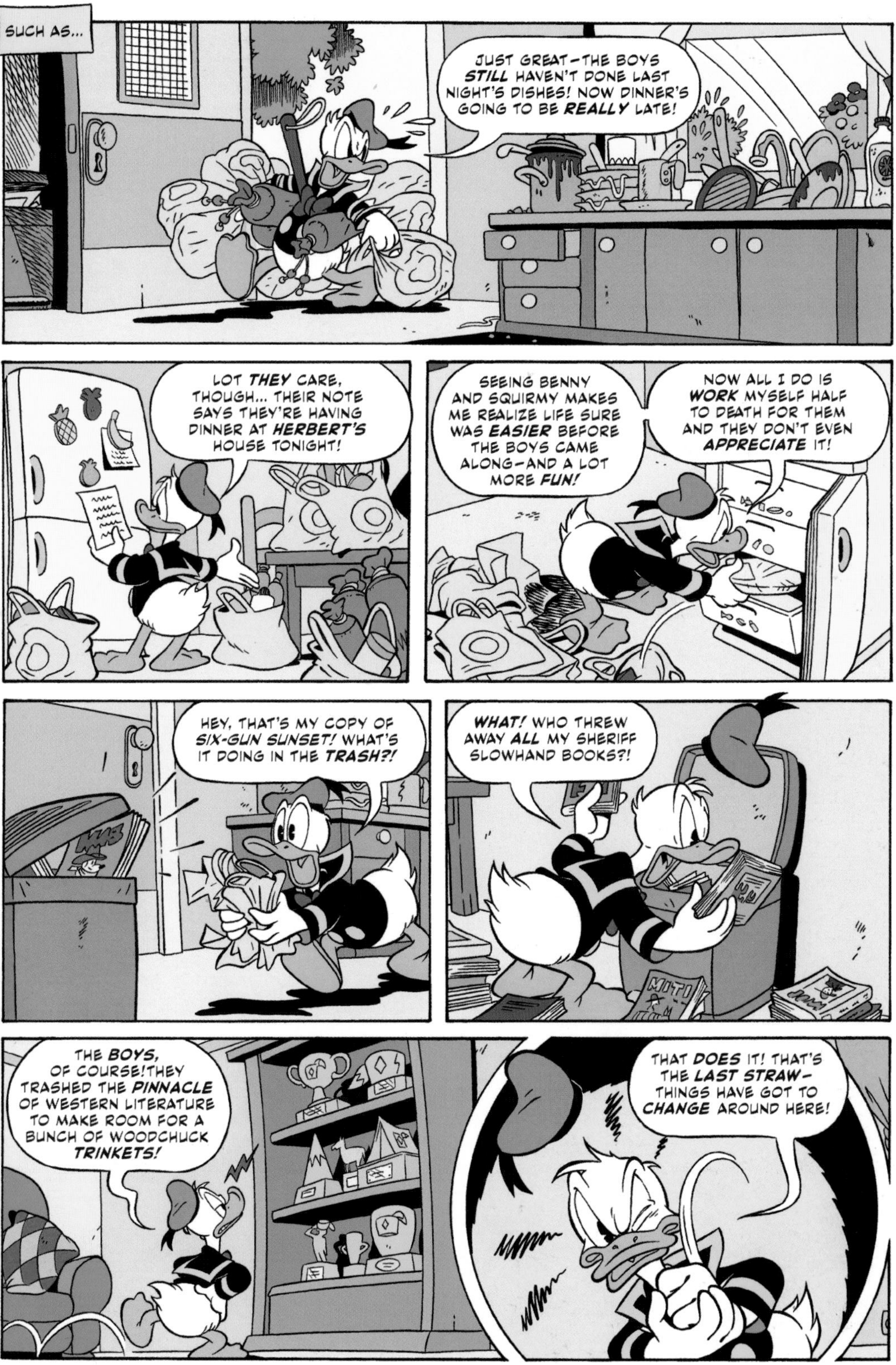
SUCH AS...
JUST GREAT—THE BOYS STILL HAVEN'T DONE LAST NIGHT'S DISHES! NOW DINNER'S GOING TO BE REALLY LATE!
LOT THEY CARE, THOUGH... THEIR NOTE SAYS THEY'RE HAVING DINNER AT HERBERT'S HOUSE TONIGHT!
SEEING BENNY AND SQUIRMY MAKES ME REALIZE LIFE SURE WAS EASIER BEFORE THE BOYS CAME ALONG—AND A LOT MORE FUN!
NOW ALL I DO IS WORK MYSELF HALF TO DEATH FOR THEM AND THEY DON'T EVEN APPRECIATE IT!
HEY, THAT'S MY COPY OF SIX-GUN SUNSET! WHAT'S IT DOING IN THE TRASH?!
WHAT! WHO THREW AWAY ALL MY SHERIFF SLOWHAND BOOKS?!
THE BOYS, OF COURSE! THEY TRASHED THE PINNACLE OF WESTERN LITERATURE TO MAKE ROOM FOR A BUNCH OF WOODCHUCK TRINKETS!
THAT DOES IT! THAT'S THE LAST STRAW—THINGS HAVE GOT TO CHANGE AROUND HERE!

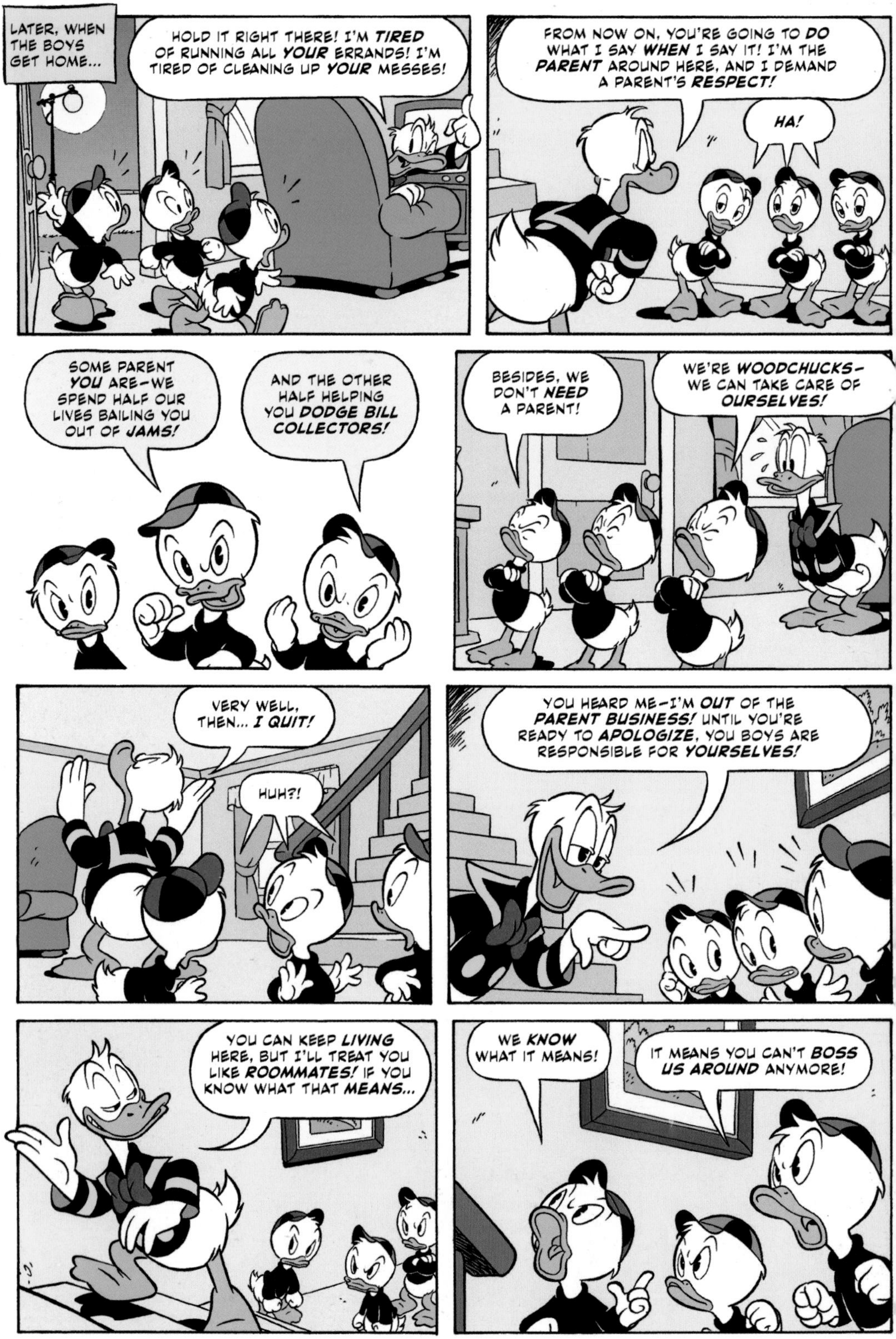
LATER, WHEN THE BOYS GET HOME...
HOLD IT RIGHT THERE! I'M TIRED OF RUNNING ALL YOUR ERRANDS! I'M TIRED OF CLEANING UP YOUR MESSES!
FROM NOW ON, YOU'RE GOING TO DO WHAT I SAY WHEN I SAY IT! I'M THE PARENT AROUND HERE, AND I DEMAND A PARENT'S RESPECT!
HA!
SOME PARENT YOU ARE—WE SPEND HALF OUR LIVES BAILING YOU OUT OF JAMS!
AND THE OTHER HALF HELPING YOU DODGE BILL COLLECTORS!
BESIDES, WE DON'T NEED A PARENT!
WE'RE WOODCHUCKS—WE CAN TAKE CARE OF OURSELVES!
VERY WELL, THEN... I QUIT!
HUH?!
YOU HEARD ME—I'M OUT OF THE PARENT BUSINESS! UNTIL YOU'RE READY TO APOLOGIZE, YOU BOYS ARE RESPONSIBLE FOR YOURSELVES!
YOU CAN KEEP LIVING HERE, BUT I'LL TREAT YOU LIKE ROOMMATES! IF YOU KNOW WHAT THAT MEANS...
WE KNOW WHAT IT MEANS!
IT MEANS YOU CAN'T BOSS US AROUND ANYMORE!

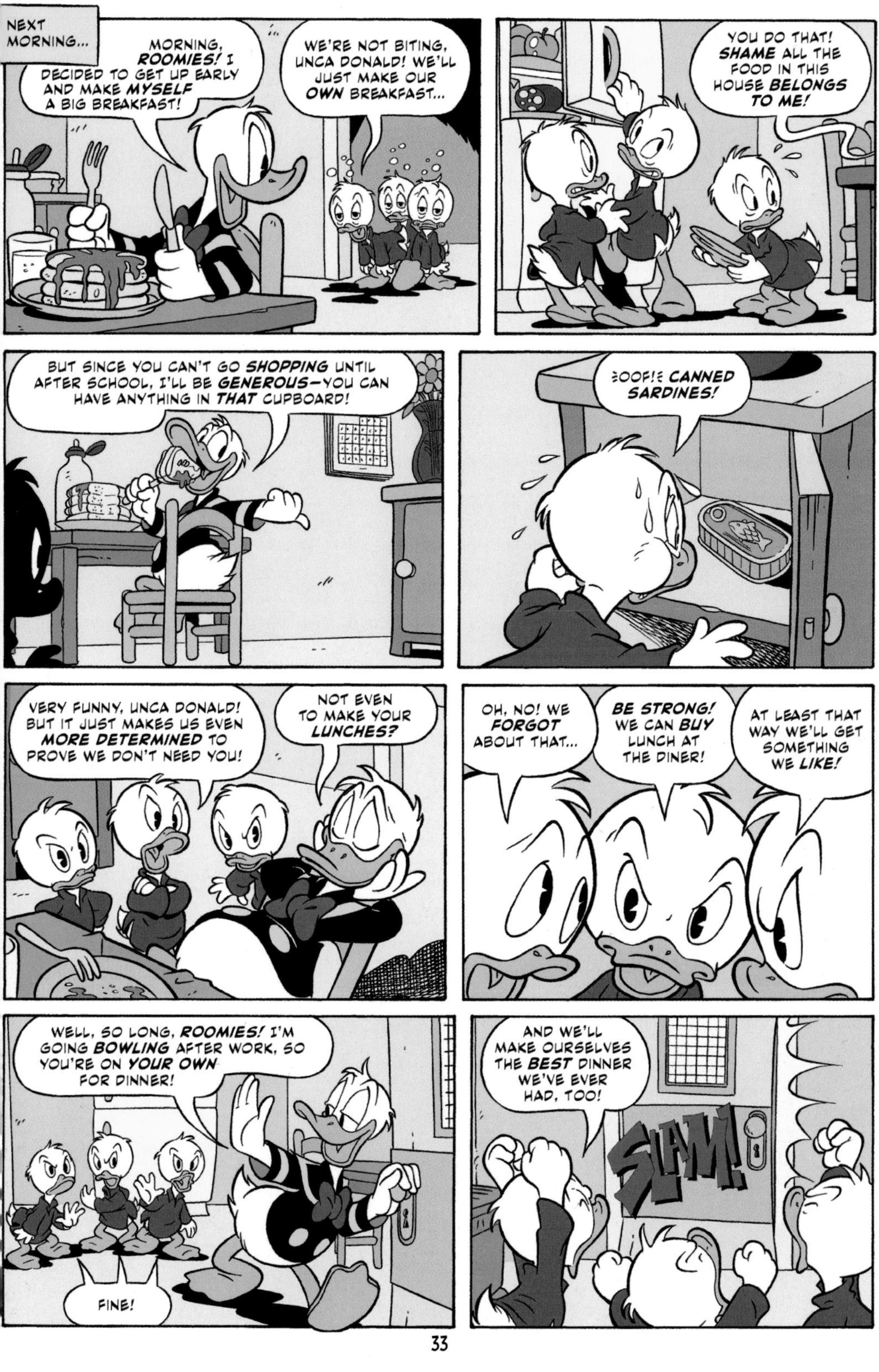
NEXT MORNING...
MORNING, ROOMIES! I DECIDED TO GET UP EARLY AND MAKE MYSELF A BIG BREAKFAST!
WE'RE NOT BITING, UNCA DONALD! WE'LL JUST MAKE OUR OWN BREAKFAST...
YOU DO THAT! SHAME ALL THE FOOD IN THIS HOUSE BELONGS TO ME!
BUT SINCE YOU CAN'T GO SHOPPING UNTIL AFTER SCHOOL, I'LL BE GENEROUS—YOU CAN HAVE ANYTHING IN THAT CUPBOARD!
OOF! CANNED SARDINES!
VERY FUNNY, UNCA DONALD! BUT IT JUST MAKES US EVEN MORE DETERMINED TO PROVE WE DON'T NEED YOU!
NOT EVEN TO MAKE YOUR LUNCHES?
OH, NO! WE FORGOT ABOUT THAT...
BE STRONG! WE CAN BUY LUNCH AT THE DINER!
AT LEAST THAT WAY WE'LL GET SOMETHING WE LIKE!
WELL, SO LONG, ROOMIES! I'M GOING BOWLING AFTER WORK, SO YOU'RE ON YOUR OWN FOR DINNER!
FINE!
AND WE'LL MAKE OURSELVES THE BEST DINNER WE'VE EVER HAD, TOO!
SLAM!

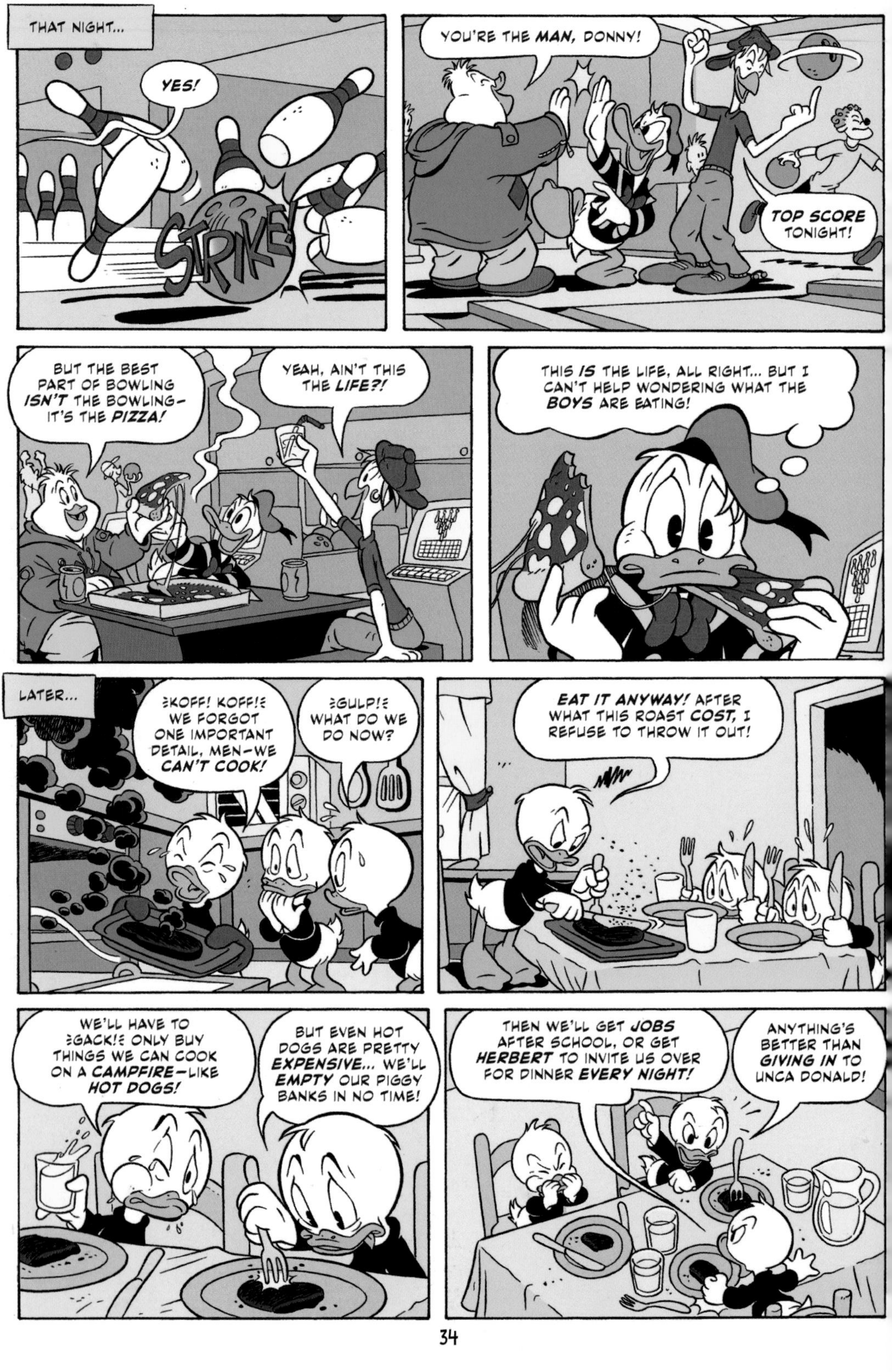
THAT NIGHT...
YES!
STRIKE!
YOU'RE THE MAN, DONNY!
TOP SCORE TONIGHT!
BUT THE BEST PART OF BOWLING ISN'T THE BOWLING– IT'S THE PIZZA!
YEAH, AIN'T THIS THE LIFE?!
THIS IS THE LIFE, ALL RIGHT... BUT I CAN'T HELP WONDERING WHAT THE BOYS ARE EATING!
LATER...
KOFF! KOFF! WE FORGOT ONE IMPORTANT DETAIL, MEN–WE CAN'T COOK!
GULP! WHAT DO WE DO NOW?
EAT IT ANYWAY! AFTER WHAT THIS ROAST COST, I REFUSE TO THROW IT OUT!
WE'LL HAVE TO GACK! ONLY BUY THINGS WE CAN COOK ON A CAMPFIRE–LIKE HOT DOGS!
BUT EVEN HOT DOGS ARE PRETTY EXPENSIVE... WE'LL EMPTY OUR PIGGY BANKS IN NO TIME!
THEN WE'LL GET JOBS AFTER SCHOOL, OR GET HERBERT TO INVITE US OVER FOR DINNER EVERY NIGHT!
ANYTHING'S BETTER THAN GIVING IN TO UNCA DONALD!

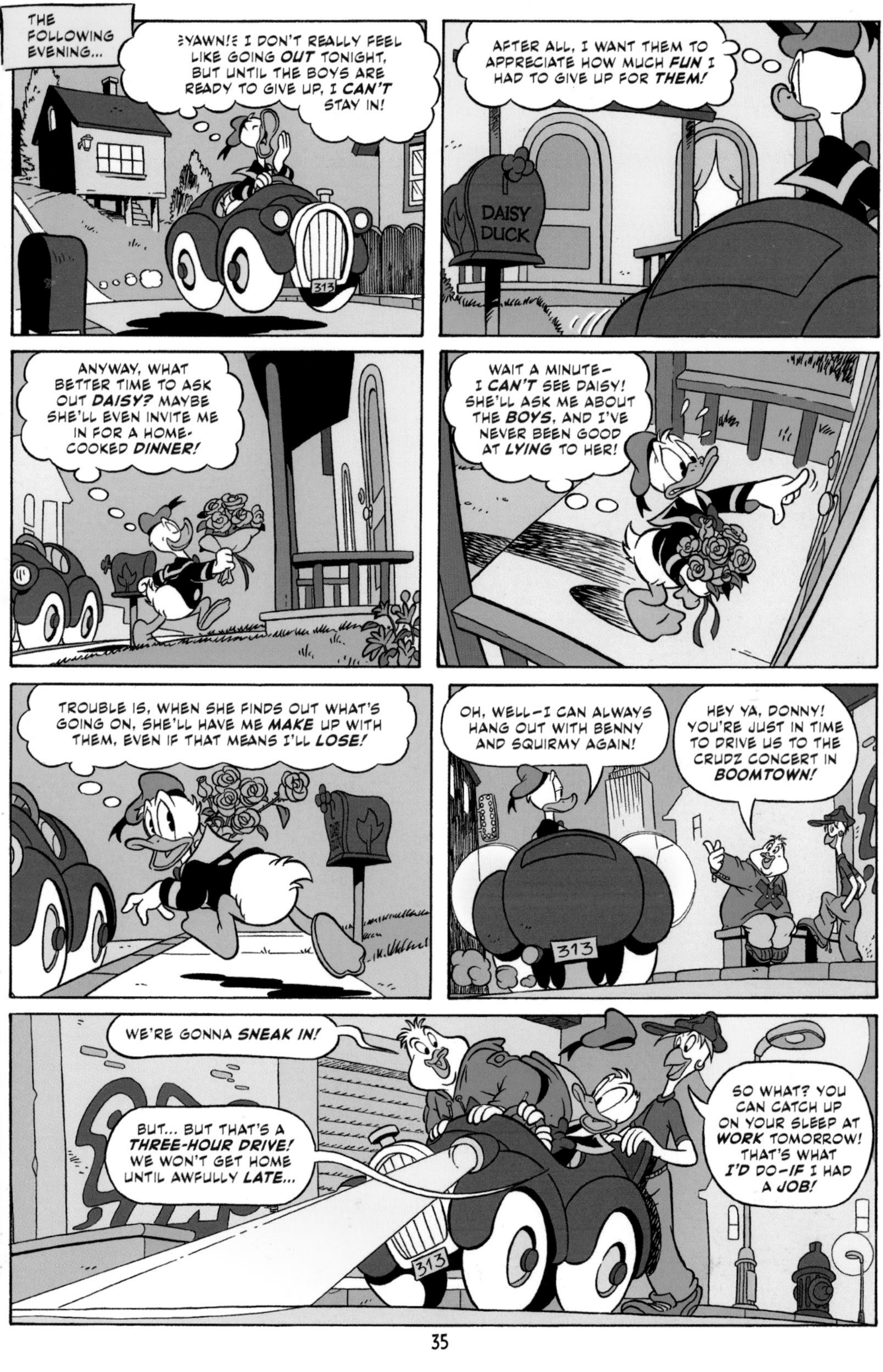
THE FOLLOWING EVENING...
ƸYAWN!Ƹ I DON'T REALLY FEEL LIKE GOING OUT TONIGHT, BUT UNTIL THE BOYS ARE READY TO GIVE UP, I CAN'T STAY IN!
313
AFTER ALL, I WANT THEM TO APPRECIATE HOW MUCH FUN I HAD TO GIVE UP FOR THEM!
DAISY DUCK
ANYWAY, WHAT BETTER TIME TO ASK OUT DAISY? MAYBE SHE'LL EVEN INVITE ME IN FOR A HOME-COOKED DINNER!
WAIT A MINUTE— I CAN'T SEE DAISY! SHE'LL ASK ME ABOUT THE BOYS, AND I'VE NEVER BEEN GOOD AT LYING TO HER!
TROUBLE IS, WHEN SHE FINDS OUT WHAT'S GOING ON, SHE'LL HAVE ME MAKE UP WITH THEM, EVEN IF THAT MEANS I'LL LOSE!
OH, WELL—I CAN ALWAYS HANG OUT WITH BENNY AND SQUIRMY AGAIN!
HEY YA, DONNY! YOU'RE JUST IN TIME TO DRIVE US TO THE CRUDZ CONCERT IN BOOMTOWN!
313
WE'RE GONNA SNEAK IN!
BUT... BUT THAT'S A THREE-HOUR DRIVE! WE WON'T GET HOME UNTIL AWFULLY LATE...
SO WHAT? YOU CAN CATCH UP ON YOUR SLEEP AT WORK TOMORROW! THAT'S WHAT I'D DO—IF I HAD A JOB!
313

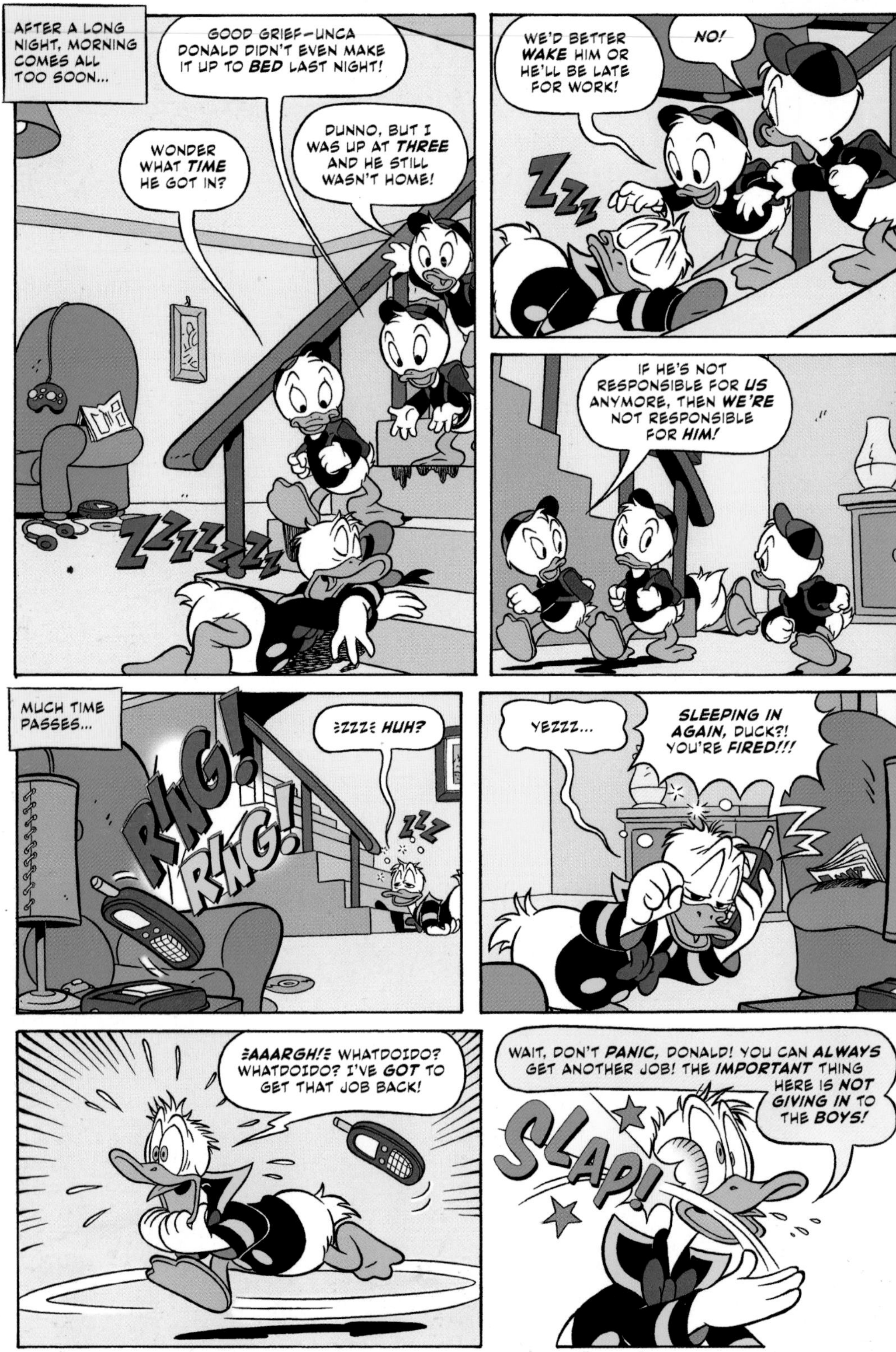
AFTER A LONG NIGHT, MORNING COMES ALL TOO SOON...
GOOD GRIEF—UNCA DONALD DIDN'T EVEN MAKE IT UP TO BED LAST NIGHT!
WONDER WHAT TIME HE GOT IN?
DUNNO, BUT I WAS UP AT THREE AND HE STILL WASN'T HOME!
ZZZZZZZZ
WE'D BETTER WAKE HIM OR HE'LL BE LATE FOR WORK!
NO!
ZZZ
IF HE'S NOT RESPONSIBLE FOR US ANYMORE, THEN WE'RE NOT RESPONSIBLE FOR HIM!
MUCH TIME PASSES...
RING! RING!
ZZZZ HUH?
ZZZ
YEZZZ...
SLEEPING IN AGAIN, DUCK?! YOU'RE FIRED!!!
AAARGH! WHATDOIDO? WHATDOIDO? I'VE GOT TO GET THAT JOB BACK!
WAIT, DON'T PANIC, DONALD! YOU CAN ALWAYS GET ANOTHER JOB! THE IMPORTANT THING HERE IS NOT GIVING IN TO THE BOYS!
SLAP!

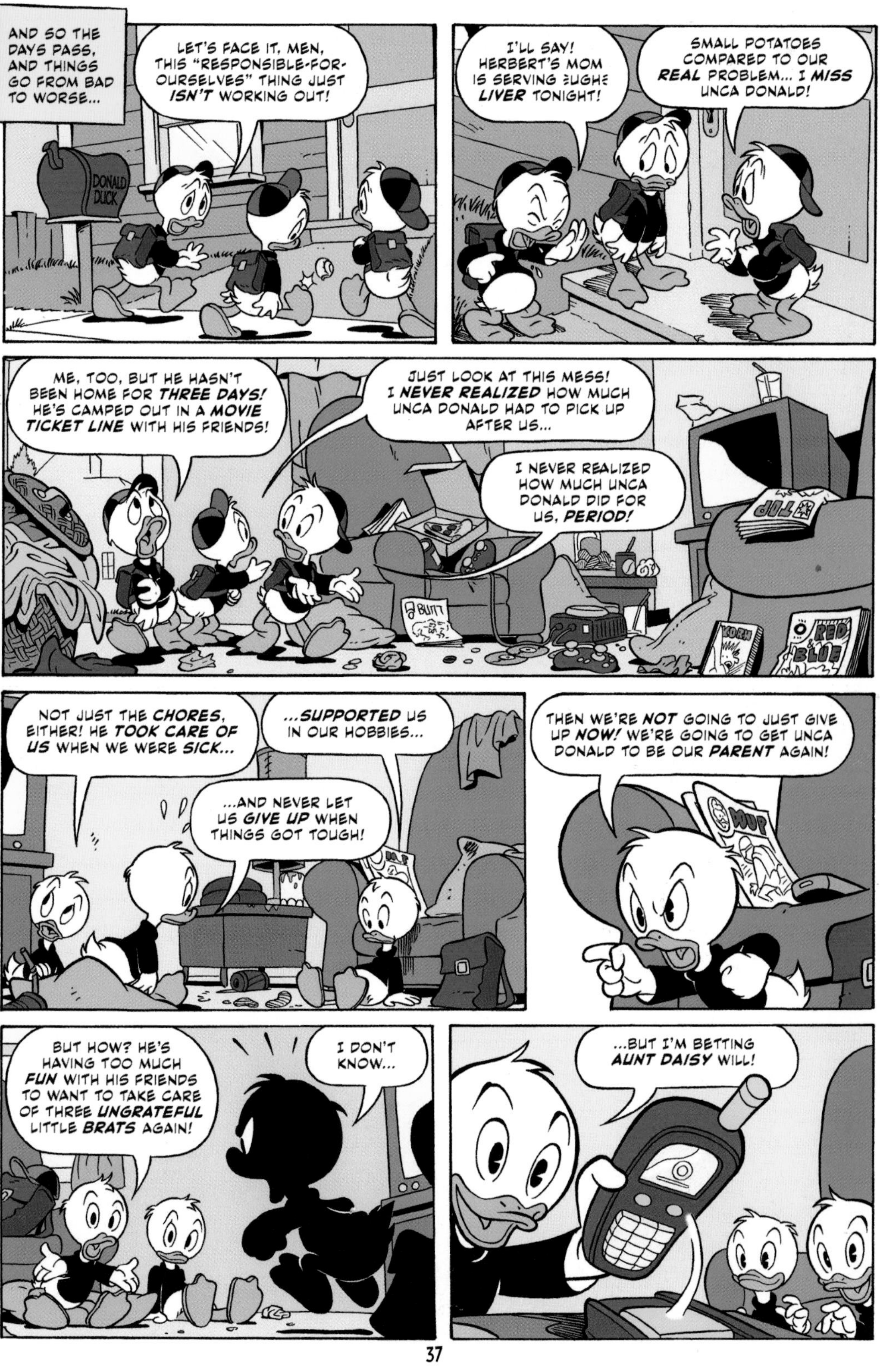

AND SO THE DAYS PASS, AND THINGS GO FROM BAD TO WORSE...
LET'S FACE IT, MEN, THIS "RESPONSIBLE-FOR-OURSELVES" THING JUST ISN'T WORKING OUT!
DONALD DUCK
I'LL SAY! HERBERT'S MOM IS SERVING UGH LIVER TONIGHT!
SMALL POTATOES COMPARED TO OUR REAL PROBLEM... I MISS UNCA DONALD!
ME, TOO, BUT HE HASN'T BEEN HOME FOR THREE DAYS! HE'S CAMPED OUT IN A MOVIE TICKET LINE WITH HIS FRIENDS!
JUST LOOK AT THIS MESS! I NEVER REALIZED HOW MUCH UNCA DONALD HAD TO PICK UP AFTER US...
I NEVER REALIZED HOW MUCH UNCA DONALD DID FOR US, PERIOD!
TOP
RED & BLUE
NOT JUST THE CHORES, EITHER! HE TOOK CARE OF US WHEN WE WERE SICK...
...SUPPORTED US IN OUR HOBBIES...
...AND NEVER LET US GIVE UP WHEN THINGS GOT TOUGH!
THEN WE'RE NOT GOING TO JUST GIVE UP NOW! WE'RE GOING TO GET UNCA DONALD TO BE OUR PARENT AGAIN!
BUT HOW? HE'S HAVING TOO MUCH FUN WITH HIS FRIENDS TO WANT TO TAKE CARE OF THREE UNGRATEFUL LITTLE BRATS AGAIN!
I DON'T KNOW...
...BUT I'M BETTING AUNT DAISY WILL!

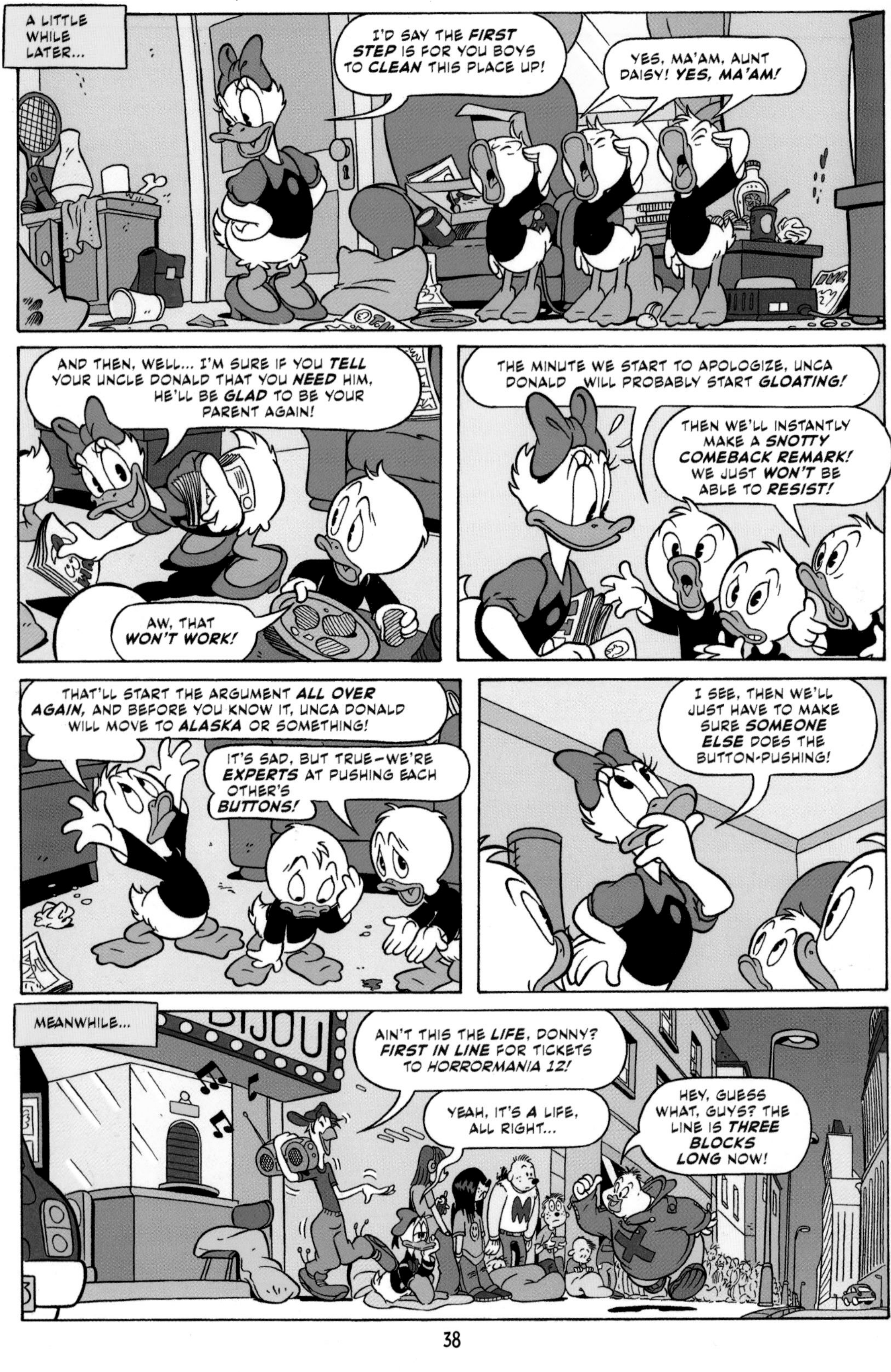
A LITTLE WHILE LATER...
I'D SAY THE FIRST STEP IS FOR YOU BOYS TO CLEAN THIS PLACE UP!
YES, MA'AM, AUNT DAISY! YES, MA'AM!
AND THEN, WELL... I'M SURE IF YOU TELL YOUR UNCLE DONALD THAT YOU NEED HIM, HE'LL BE GLAD TO BE YOUR PARENT AGAIN!
AW, THAT WON'T WORK!
THE MINUTE WE START TO APOLOGIZE, UNCA DONALD WILL PROBABLY START GLOATING!
THEN WE'LL INSTANTLY MAKE A SNOTTY COMEBACK REMARK! WE JUST WON'T BE ABLE TO RESIST!
THAT'LL START THE ARGUMENT ALL OVER AGAIN, AND BEFORE YOU KNOW IT, UNCA DONALD WILL MOVE TO ALASKA OR SOMETHING!
IT'S SAD, BUT TRUE—WE'RE EXPERTS AT PUSHING EACH OTHER'S BUTTONS!
I SEE. THEN WE'LL JUST HAVE TO MAKE SURE SOMEONE ELSE DOES THE BUTTON-PUSHING!
MEANWHILE...
BIJOU
AIN'T THIS THE LIFE, DONNY? FIRST IN LINE FOR TICKETS TO HORRORMANIA 12!
YEAH, IT'S A LIFE, ALL RIGHT...
HEY, GUESS WHAT, GUYS? THE LINE IS THREE BLOCKS LONG NOW!

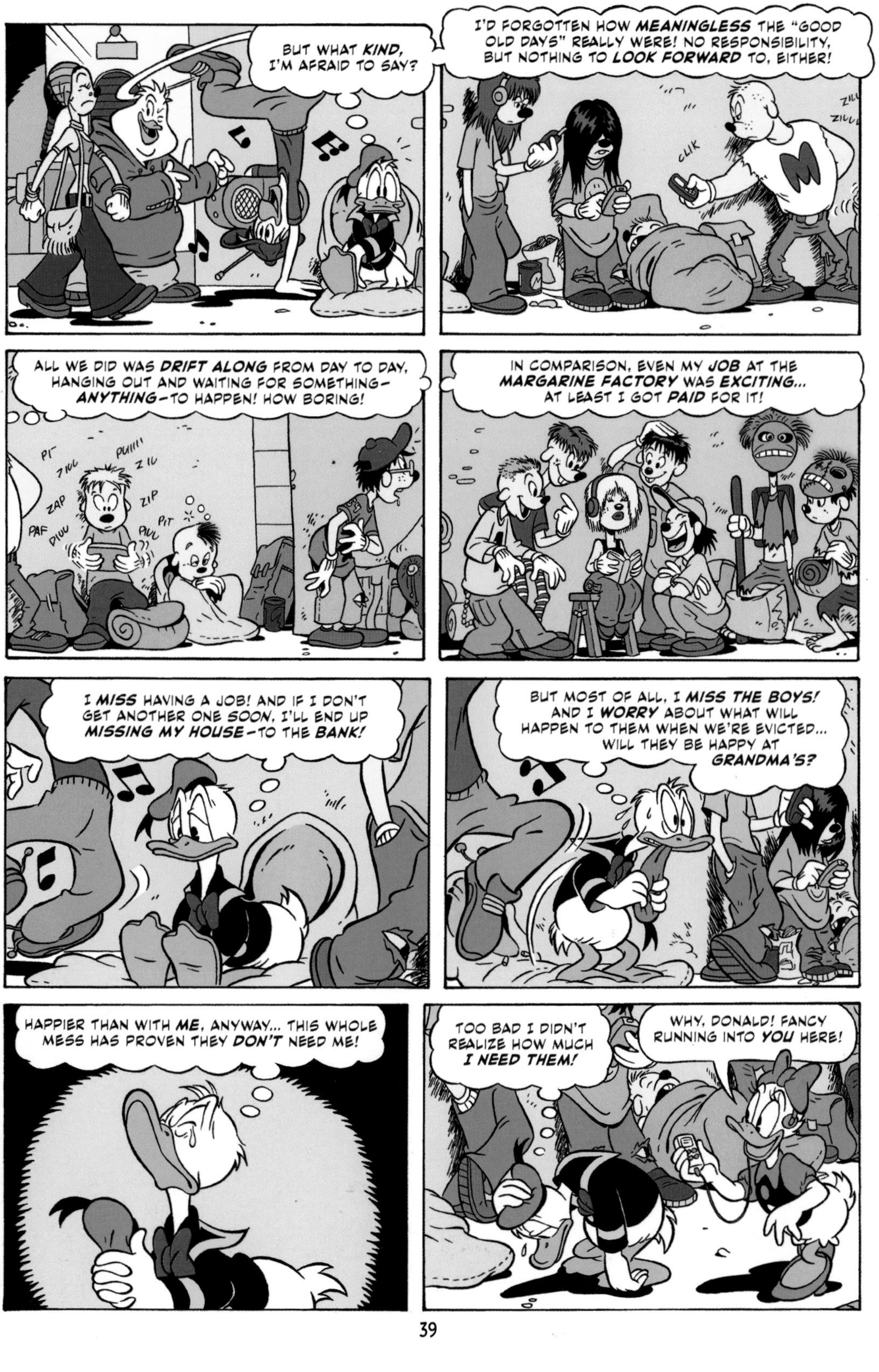
BUT WHAT KIND, I'M AFRAID TO SAY?
I'D FORGOTTEN HOW MEANINGLESS THE "GOOD OLD DAYS" REALLY WERE! NO RESPONSIBILITY, BUT NOTHING TO LOOK FORWARD TO, EITHER!
CLIK
ALL WE DID WAS DRIFT ALONG FROM DAY TO DAY, HANGING OUT AND WAITING FOR SOMETHING—ANYTHING—TO HAPPEN! HOW BORING!
ZAP
ZIP
PAF
IN COMPARISON, EVEN MY JOB AT THE MARGARINE FACTORY WAS EXCITING... AT LEAST I GOT PAID FOR IT!
I MISS HAVING A JOB! AND IF I DON'T GET ANOTHER ONE SOON, I'LL END UP MISSING MY HOUSE—TO THE BANK!
BUT MOST OF ALL, I MISS THE BOYS! AND I WORRY ABOUT WHAT WILL HAPPEN TO THEM WHEN WE'RE EVICTED... WILL THEY BE HAPPY AT GRANDMA'S?
HAPPIER THAN WITH ME, ANYWAY... THIS WHOLE MESS HAS PROVEN THEY DON'T NEED ME!
TOO BAD I DIDN'T REALIZE HOW MUCH I NEED THEM!
WHY, DONALD! FANCY RUNNING INTO YOU HERE!

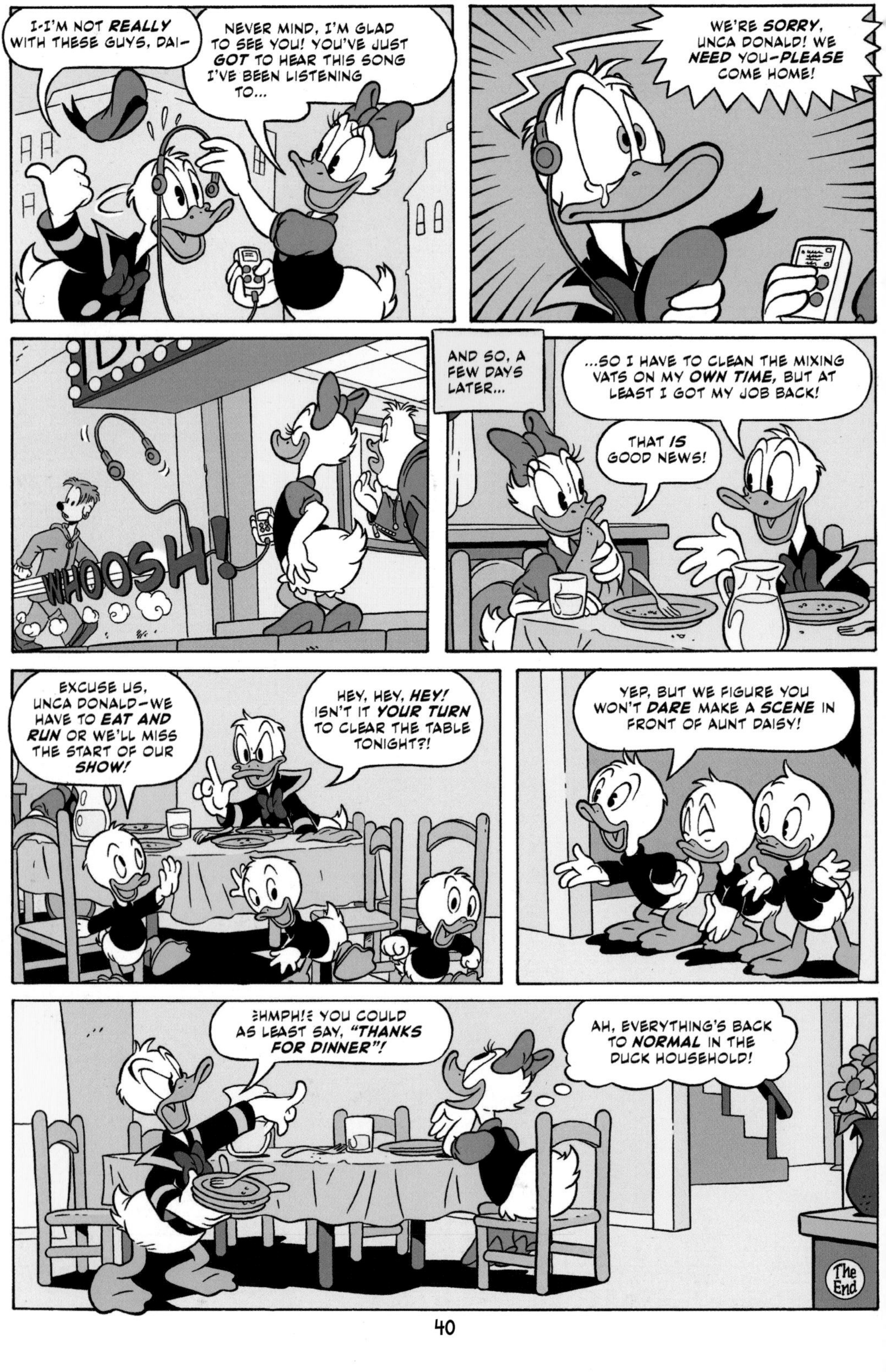
I-I'M NOT REALLY WITH THESE GUYS, DAI–
NEVER MIND, I'M GLAD TO SEE YOU! YOU'VE JUST GOT TO HEAR THIS SONG I'VE BEEN LISTENING TO...
WE'RE SORRY, UNCA DONALD! WE NEED YOU–PLEASE COME HOME!
WHOOSH!
AND SO, A FEW DAYS LATER...
...SO I HAVE TO CLEAN THE MIXING VATS ON MY OWN TIME, BUT AT LEAST I GOT MY JOB BACK!
THAT IS GOOD NEWS!
EXCUSE US, UNCA DONALD–WE HAVE TO EAT AND RUN OR WE'LL MISS THE START OF OUR SHOW!
HEY, HEY, HEY! ISN'T IT YOUR TURN TO CLEAR THE TABLE TONIGHT?!
YEP, BUT WE FIGURE YOU WON'T DARE MAKE A SCENE IN FRONT OF AUNT DAISY!
ƎHMPH!Ǝ YOU COULD AS LEAST SAY, "THANKS FOR DINNER"!
AH, EVERYTHING'S BACK TO NORMAL IN THE DUCK HOUSEHOLD!
The End

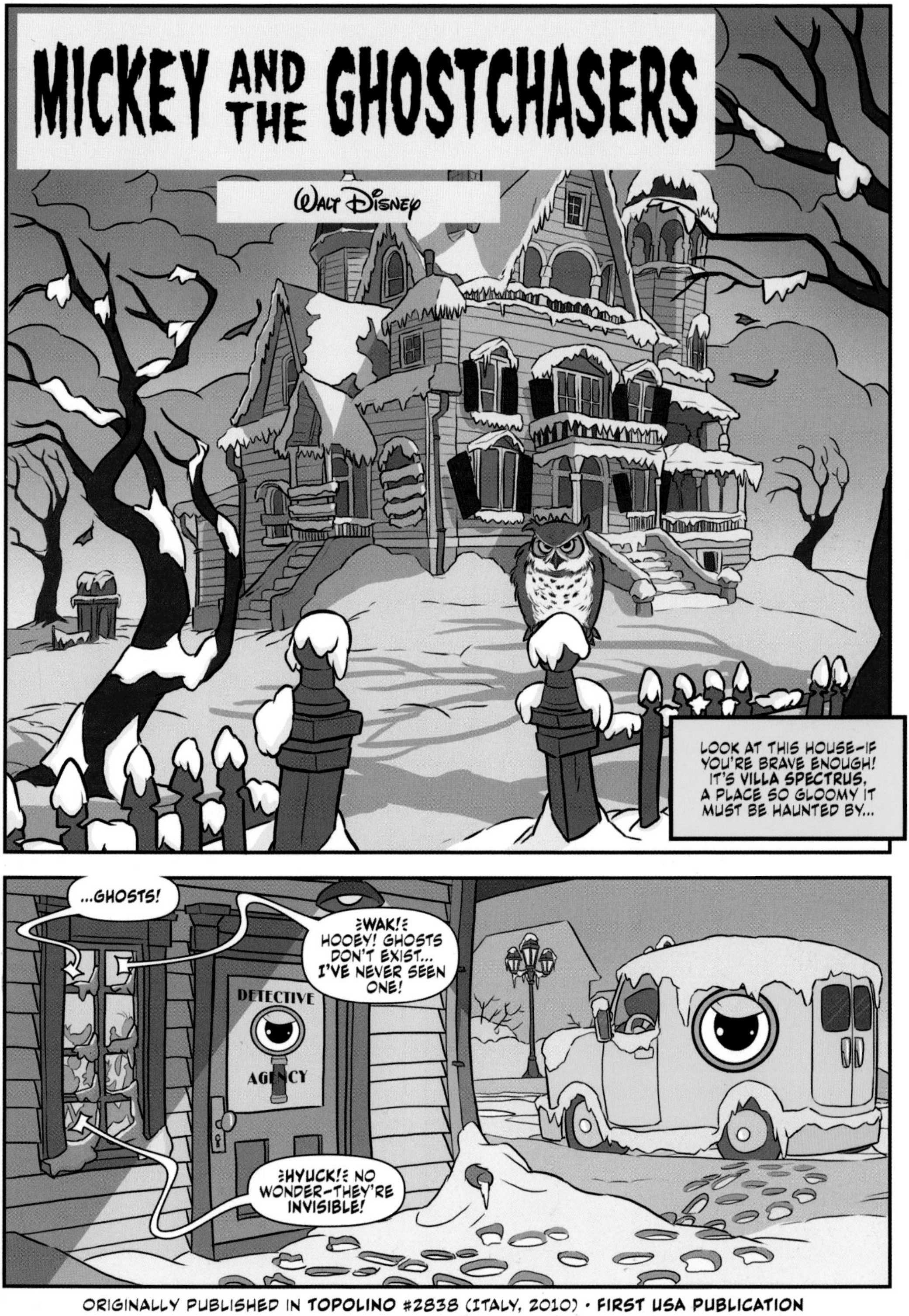
MICKEY AND THE GHOSTCHASERS
WALT DISNEY
LOOK AT THIS HOUSE—IF YOU'RE BRAVE ENOUGH! IT'S VILLA SPECTRUS, A PLACE SO GLOOMY IT MUST BE HAUNTED BY...
...GHOSTS!
WAK! HOOEY! GHOSTS DON'T EXIST... I'VE NEVER SEEN ONE!
DETECTIVE AGENCY
HYUCK! NO WONDER—THEY'RE INVISIBLE!

ORIGINALLY PUBLISHED IN **TOPOLINO #2838** (ITALY, 2010) • **FIRST USA PUBLICATION**

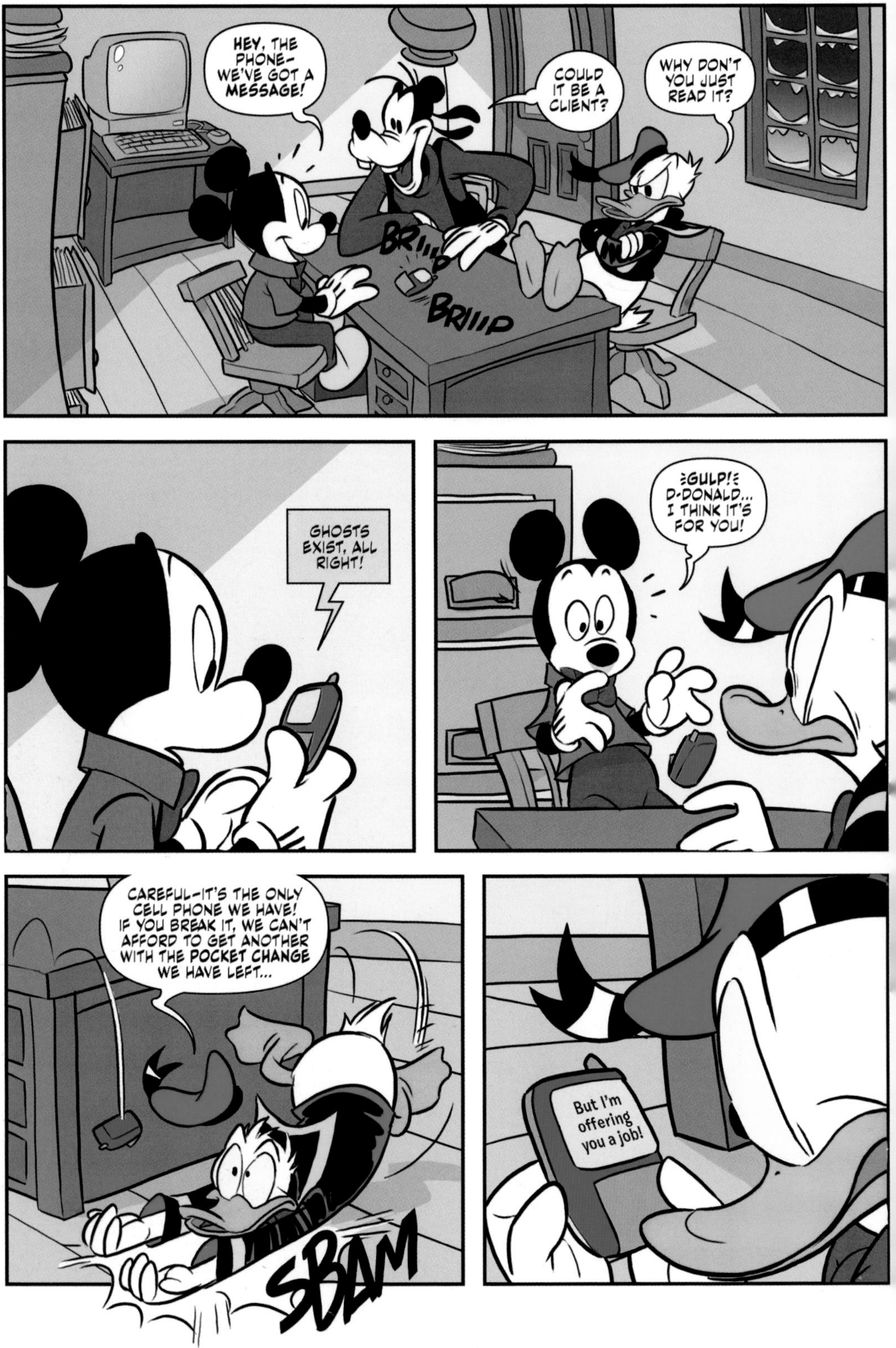
HEY, THE PHONE-WE'VE GOT A MESSAGE!
COULD IT BE A CLIENT?
WHY DON'T YOU JUST READ IT?
BRIIIP
BRIIIP
GHOSTS EXIST, ALL RIGHT!
GULP! D-DONALD... I THINK IT'S FOR YOU!
CAREFUL-IT'S THE ONLY CELL PHONE WE HAVE! IF YOU BREAK IT, WE CAN'T AFFORD TO GET ANOTHER WITH THE POCKET CHANGE WE HAVE LEFT...
SBAM
But I'm offering you a job!

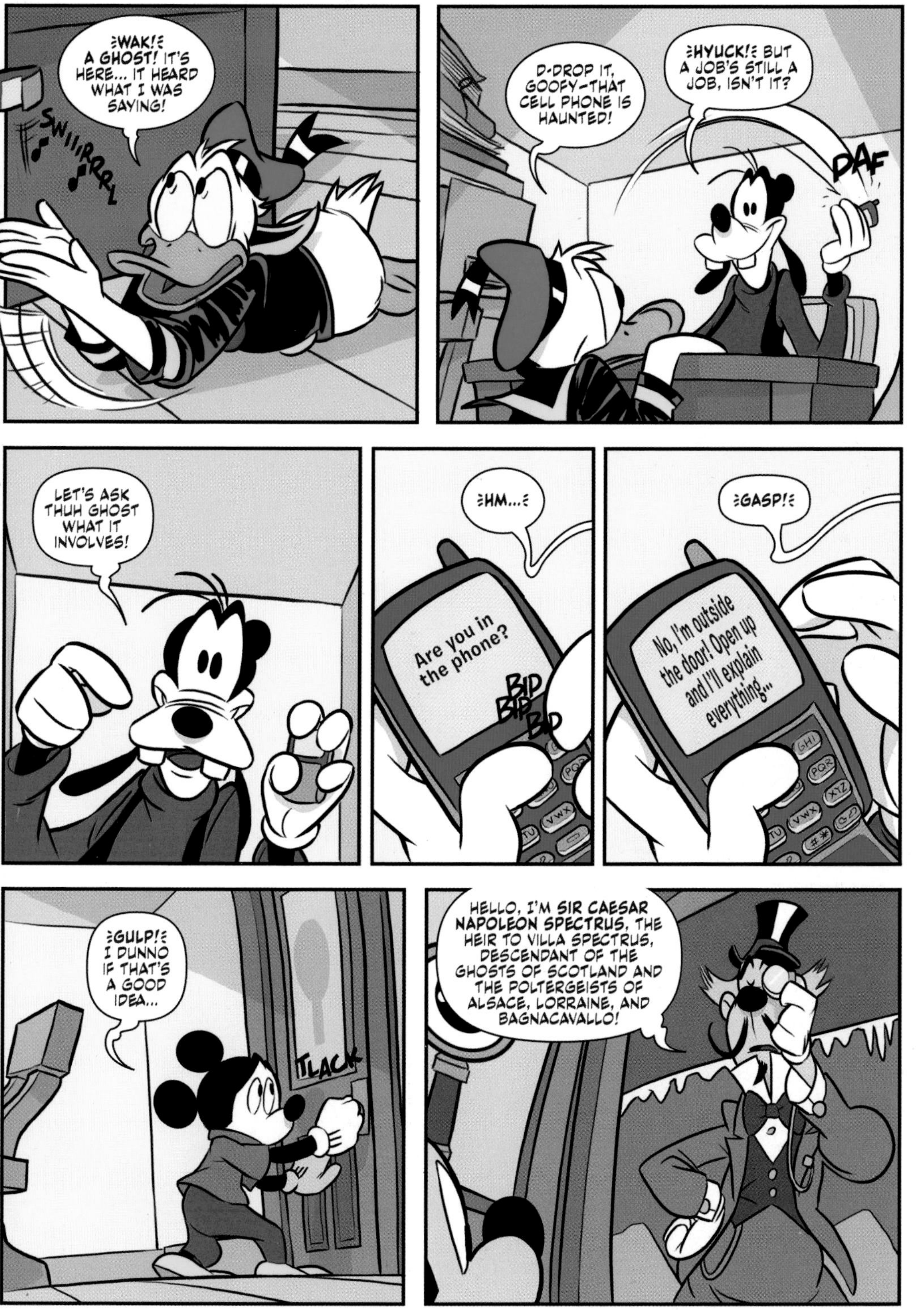
WAK! A GHOST! IT'S HERE... IT HEARD WHAT I WAS SAYING!
SWIIIRRRL
D-DROP IT, GOOFY—THAT CELL PHONE IS HAUNTED!
HYUCK! BUT A JOB'S STILL A JOB, ISN'T IT?
DAF
LET'S ASK THUH GHOST WHAT IT INVOLVES!
HM...
Are you in the phone?
BIP BIP BIP
GASP!
No, I'm outside the door! Open up and I'll explain everything...
GULP! I DUNNO IF THAT'S A GOOD IDEA...
TLACK
HELLO, I'M SIR CAESAR NAPOLEON SPECTRUS, THE HEIR TO VILLA SPECTRUS, DESCENDANT OF THE GHOSTS OF SCOTLAND AND THE POLTERGEISTS OF ALSACE, LORRAINE, AND BAGNACAVALLO!

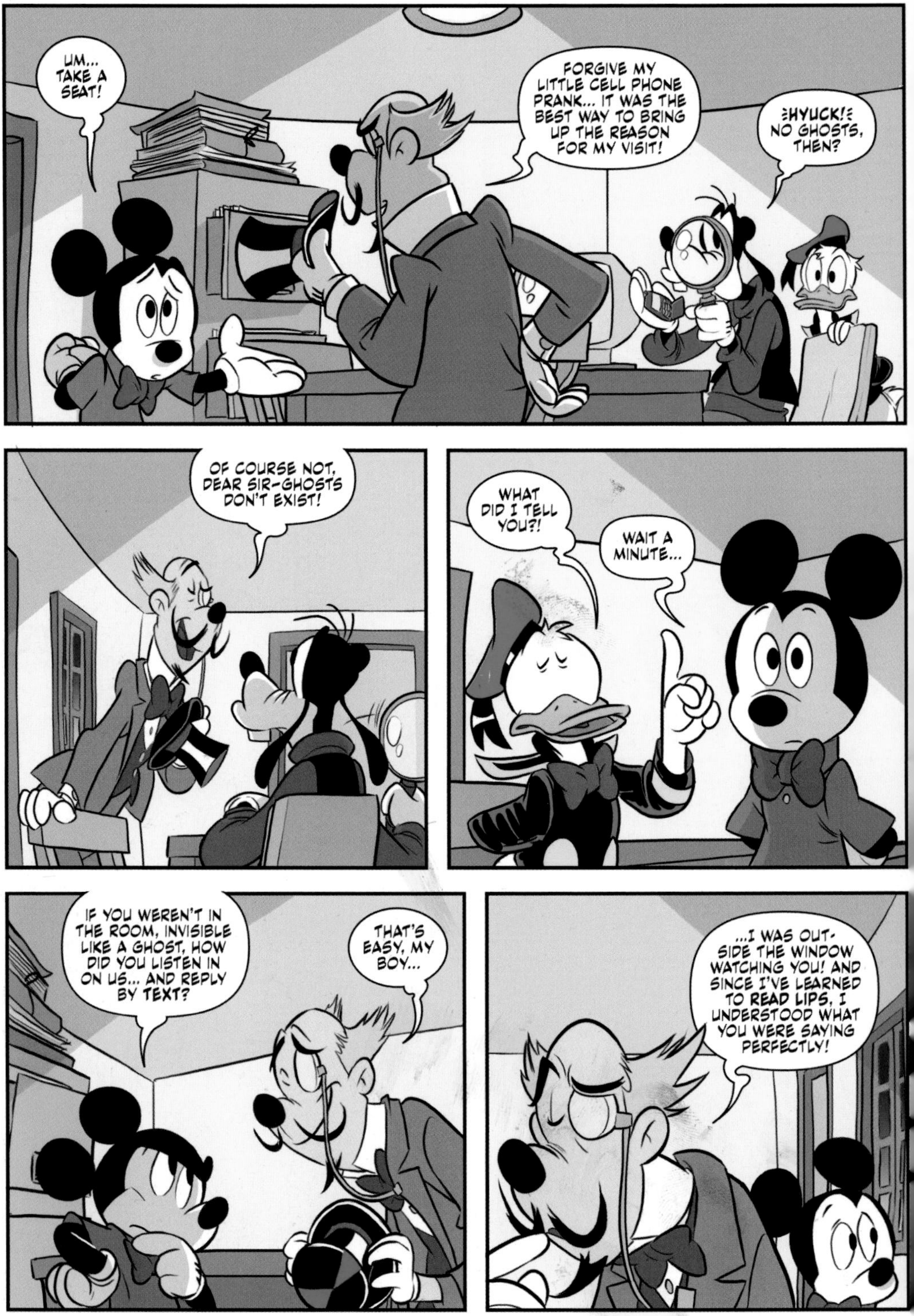
UM... TAKE A SEAT!
FORGIVE MY LITTLE CELL PHONE PRANK... IT WAS THE BEST WAY TO BRING UP THE REASON FOR MY VISIT!
HYUCK! NO GHOSTS, THEN?
OF COURSE NOT, DEAR SIR-GHOSTS DON'T EXIST!
WHAT DID I TELL YOU?!
WAIT A MINUTE...
IF YOU WEREN'T IN THE ROOM, INVISIBLE LIKE A GHOST, HOW DID YOU LISTEN IN ON US... AND REPLY BY TEXT?
THAT'S EASY, MY BOY...
...I WAS OUT-SIDE THE WINDOW WATCHING YOU! AND SINCE I'VE LEARNED TO READ LIPS, I UNDERSTOOD WHAT YOU WERE SAYING PERFECTLY!

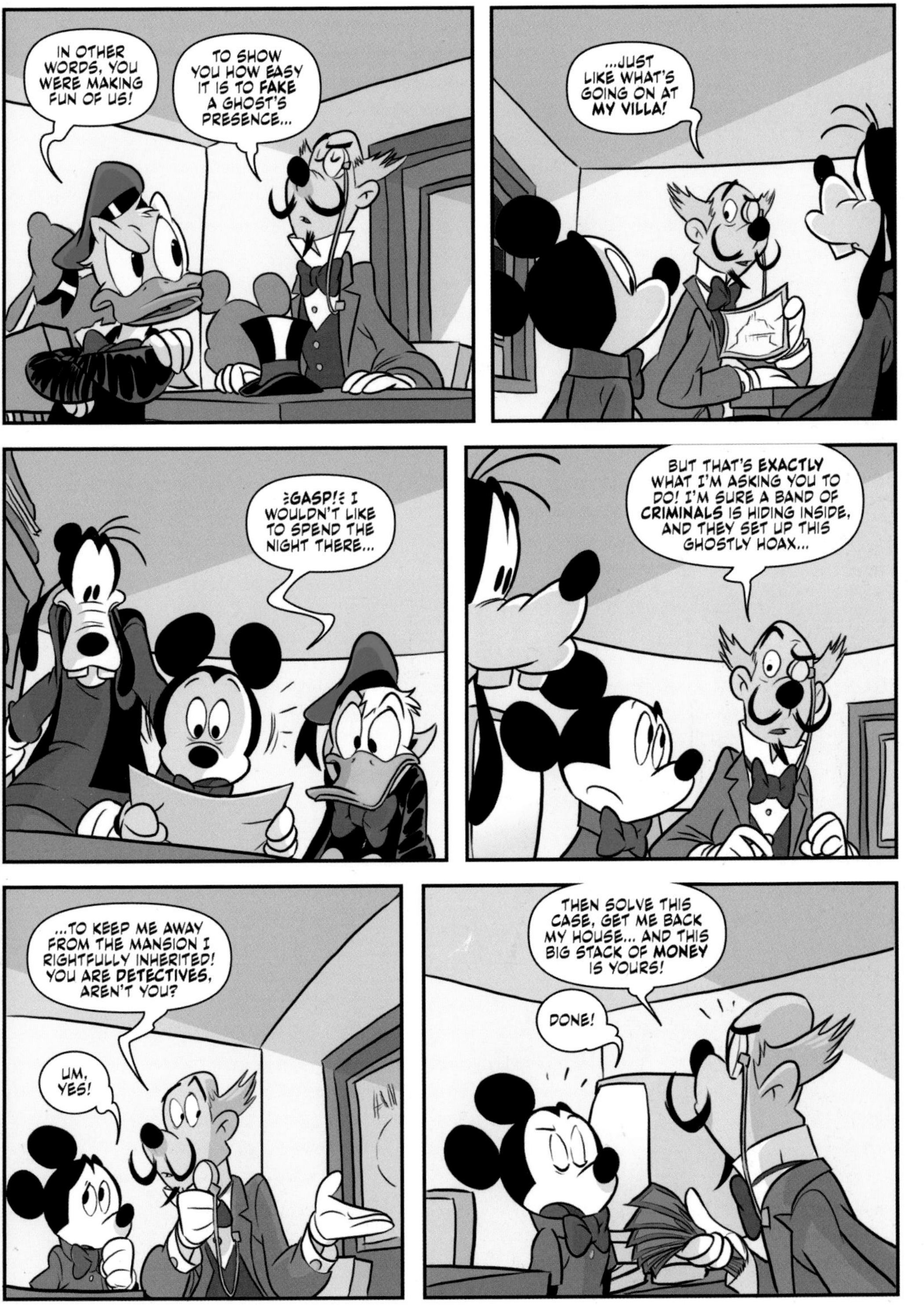
IN OTHER WORDS, YOU WERE MAKING FUN OF US!
TO SHOW YOU HOW EASY IT IS TO FAKE A GHOST'S PRESENCE...
...JUST LIKE WHAT'S GOING ON AT MY VILLA!
GASP! I WOULDN'T LIKE TO SPEND THE NIGHT THERE...
BUT THAT'S EXACTLY WHAT I'M ASKING YOU TO DO! I'M SURE A BAND OF CRIMINALS IS HIDING INSIDE, AND THEY SET UP THIS GHOSTLY HOAX...
...TO KEEP ME AWAY FROM THE MANSION I RIGHTFULLY INHERITED! YOU ARE DETECTIVES, AREN'T YOU?
UM, YES!
THEN SOLVE THIS CASE, GET ME BACK MY HOUSE... AND THIS BIG STACK OF MONEY IS YOURS!
DONE!

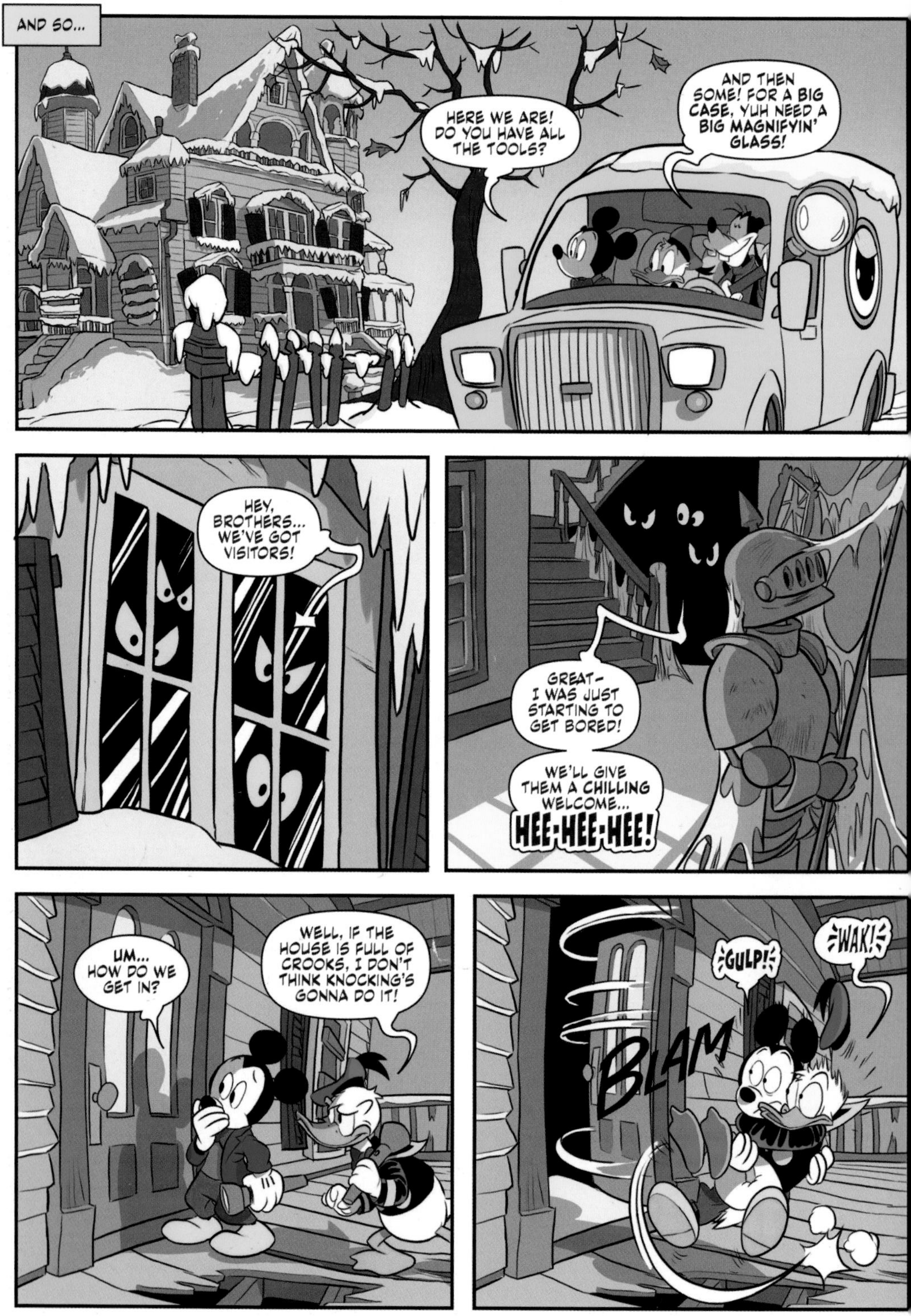
AND SO...
HERE WE ARE! DO YOU HAVE ALL THE TOOLS?
AND THEN SOME! FOR A BIG CASE, YUH NEED A BIG MAGNIFYIN' GLASS!
HEY, BROTHERS... WE'VE GOT VISITORS!
GREAT- I WAS JUST STARTING TO GET BORED!
WE'LL GIVE THEM A CHILLING WELCOME... HEE-HEE-HEE!
UM... HOW DO WE GET IN?
WELL, IF THE HOUSE IS FULL OF CROOKS, I DON'T THINK KNOCKING'S GONNA DO IT!
BLAM
GULP!
WAK!

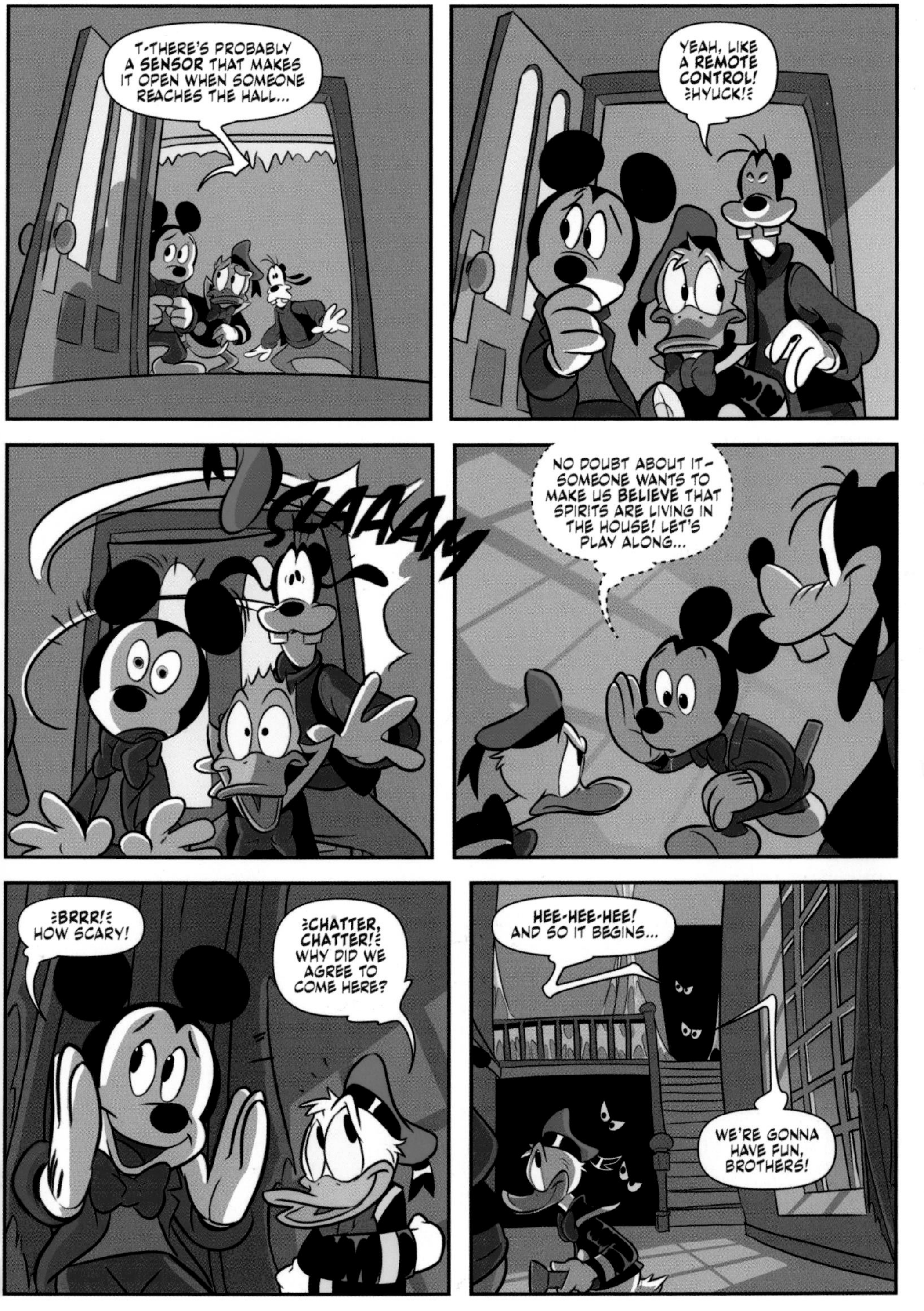
T-THERE'S PROBABLY A SENSOR THAT MAKES IT OPEN WHEN SOMEONE REACHES THE HALL...
YEAH, LIKE A REMOTE CONTROL! HYUCK!
SLAAAM
NO DOUBT ABOUT IT- SOMEONE WANTS TO MAKE US BELIEVE THAT SPIRITS ARE LIVING IN THE HOUSE! LET'S PLAY ALONG...
BRRR! HOW SCARY!
CHATTER, CHATTER! WHY DID WE AGREE TO COME HERE?
HEE-HEE-HEE! AND SO IT BEGINS...
WE'RE GONNA HAVE FUN, BROTHERS!

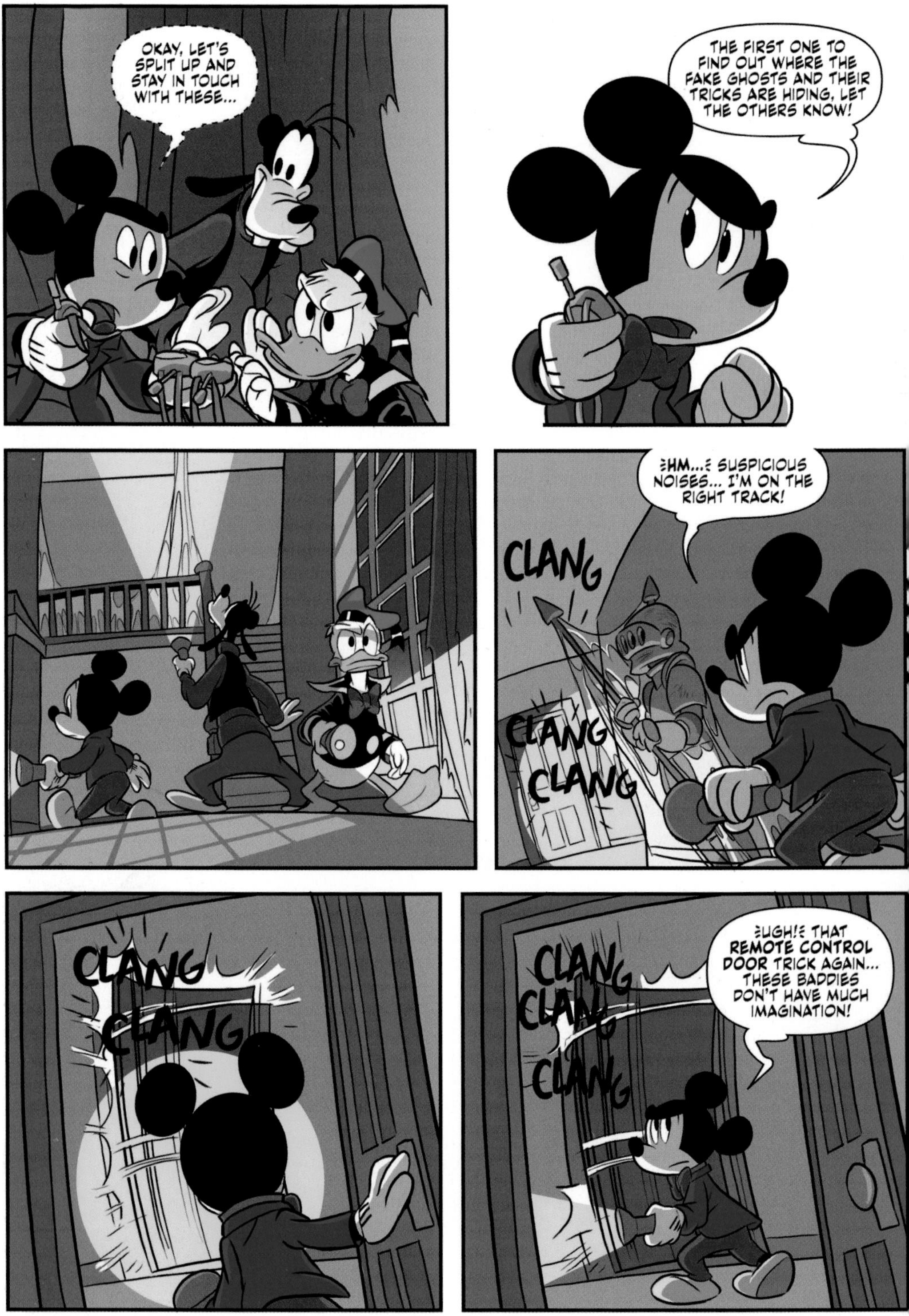
OKAY, LET'S SPLIT UP AND STAY IN TOUCH WITH THESE...
THE FIRST ONE TO FIND OUT WHERE THE FAKE GHOSTS AND THEIR TRICKS ARE HIDING, LET THE OTHERS KNOW!
HM... SUSPICIOUS NOISES... I'M ON THE RIGHT TRACK!
CLANG
CLANG
CLANG
CLANG
CLANG
CLANG
CLANG
CLANG
UGH! THAT REMOTE CONTROL DOOR TRICK AGAIN... THESE BADDIES DON'T HAVE MUCH IMAGINATION!

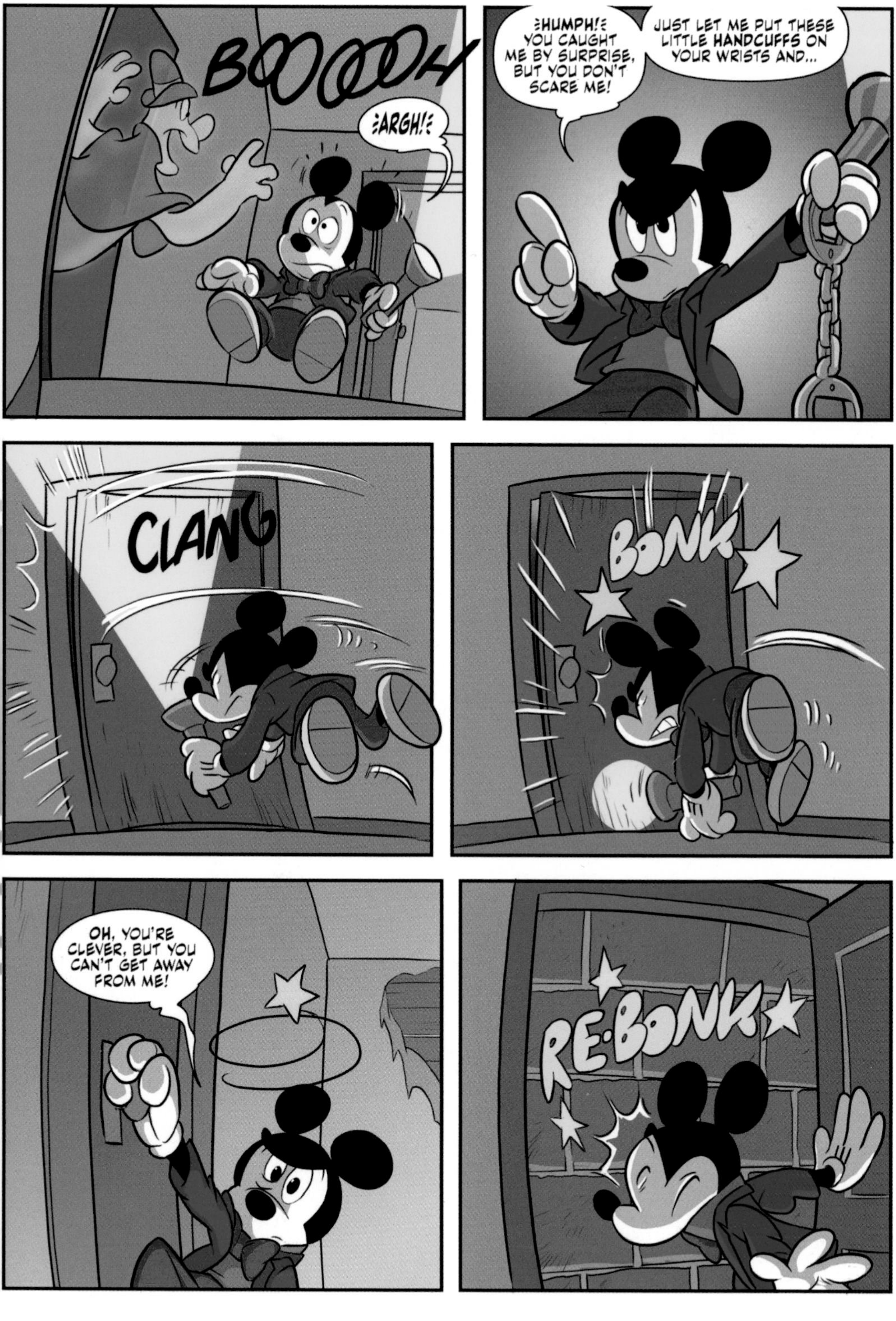
BOOOOOH
ARGH!
HUMPH! YOU CAUGHT ME BY SURPRISE, BUT YOU DON'T SCARE ME!
JUST LET ME PUT THESE LITTLE HANDCUFFS ON YOUR WRISTS AND...
CLANG
BONK
OH, YOU'RE CLEVER, BUT YOU CAN'T GET AWAY FROM ME!
RE-BONK

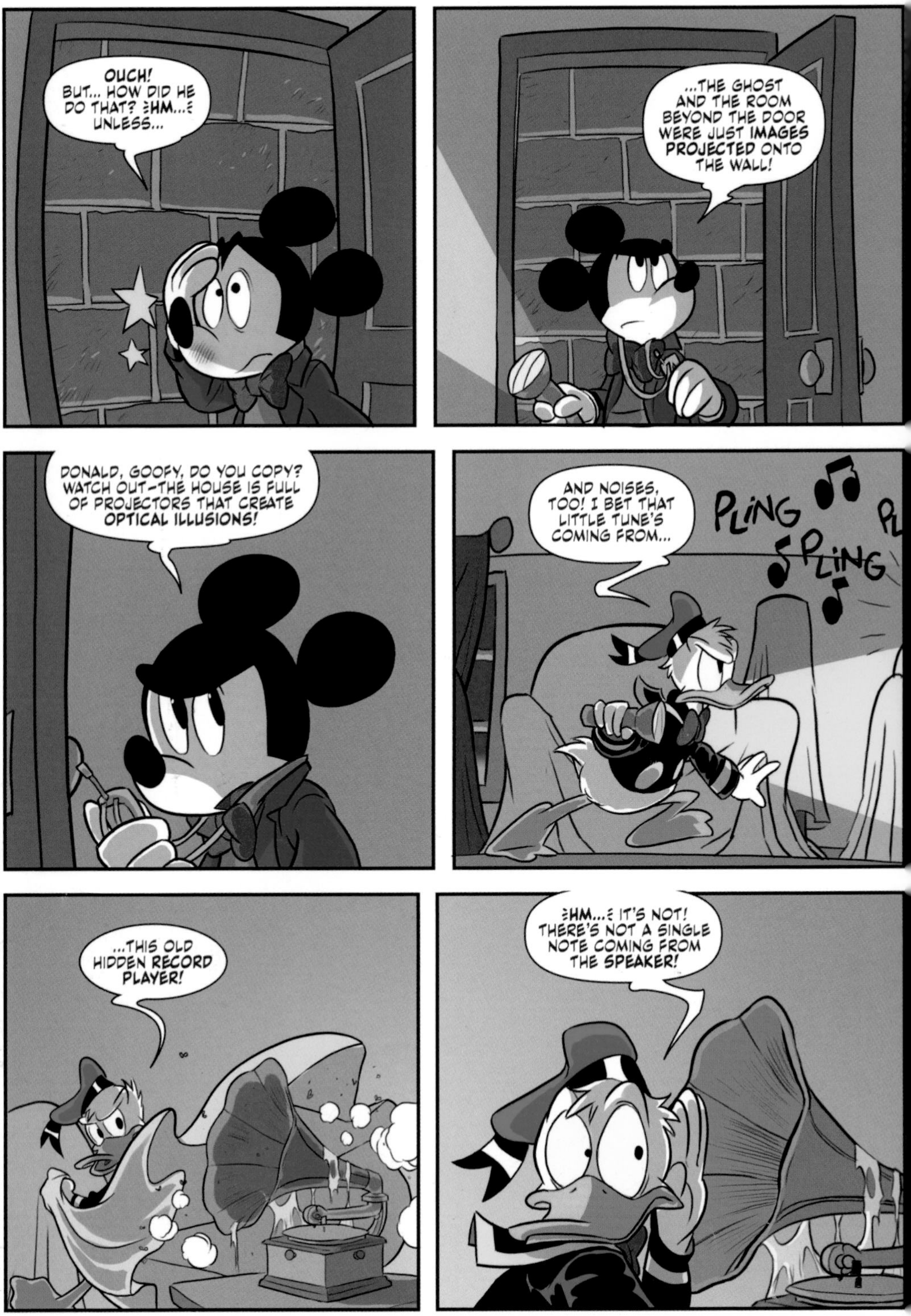
OUCH! BUT... HOW DID HE DO THAT? HM... UNLESS...
...THE GHOST AND THE ROOM BEYOND THE DOOR WERE JUST IMAGES PROJECTED ONTO THE WALL!
DONALD, GOOFY, DO YOU COPY? WATCH OUT–THE HOUSE IS FULL OF PROJECTORS THAT CREATE OPTICAL ILLUSIONS!
AND NOISES, TOO! I BET THAT LITTLE TUNE'S COMING FROM...
PLING
PLING
...THIS OLD HIDDEN RECORD PLAYER!
HM... IT'S NOT! THERE'S NOT A SINGLE NOTE COMING FROM THE SPEAKER!

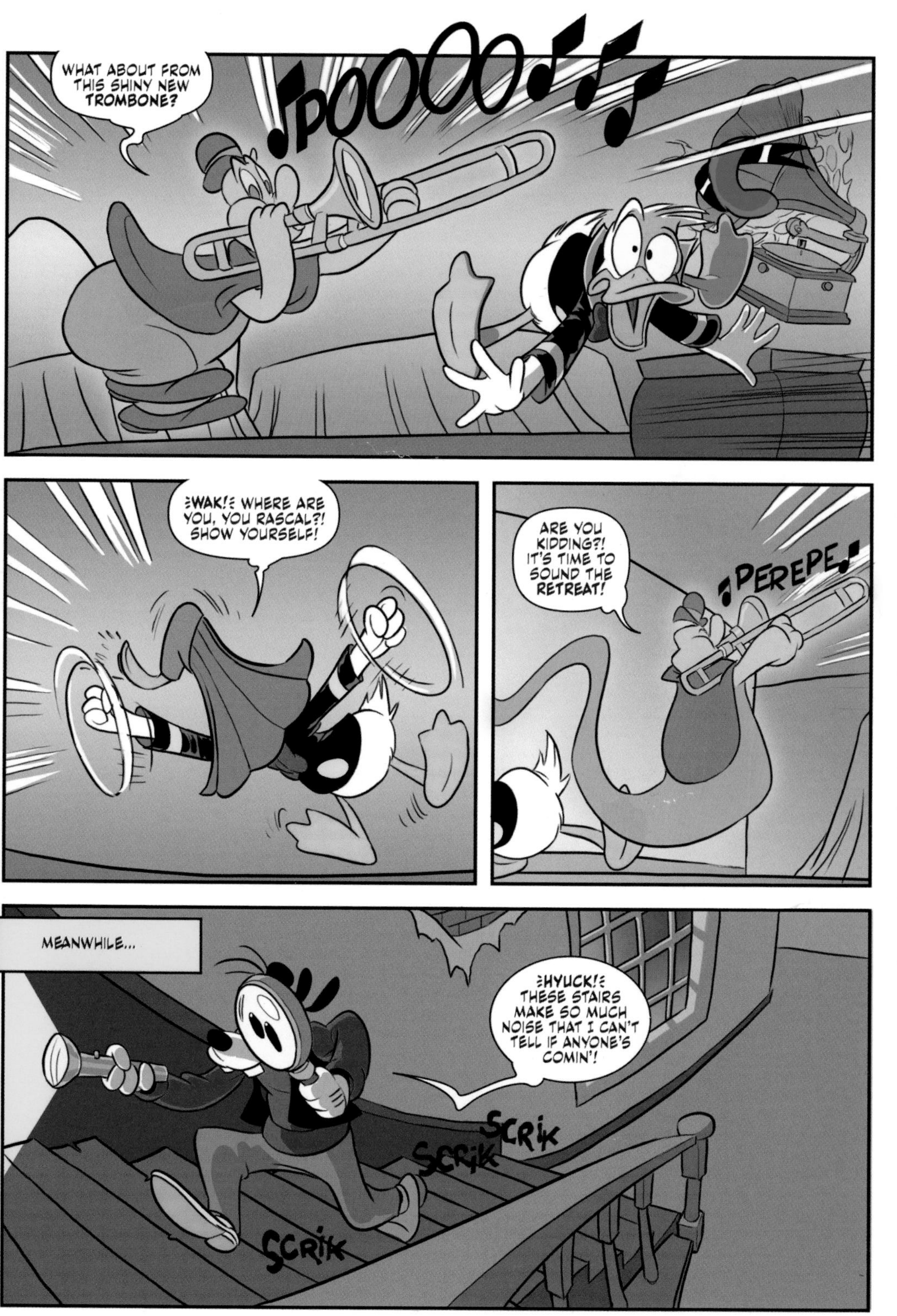
WHAT ABOUT FROM THIS SHINY NEW TROMBONE?
POOOOO
WAK! WHERE ARE YOU, YOU RASCAL?! SHOW YOURSELF!
ARE YOU KIDDING?! IT'S TIME TO SOUND THE RETREAT!
PEREPE
MEANWHILE...
HYUCK! THESE STAIRS MAKE SO MUCH NOISE THAT I CAN'T TELL IF ANYONE'S COMIN'!
SCRIK
SCRIK
SCRIK

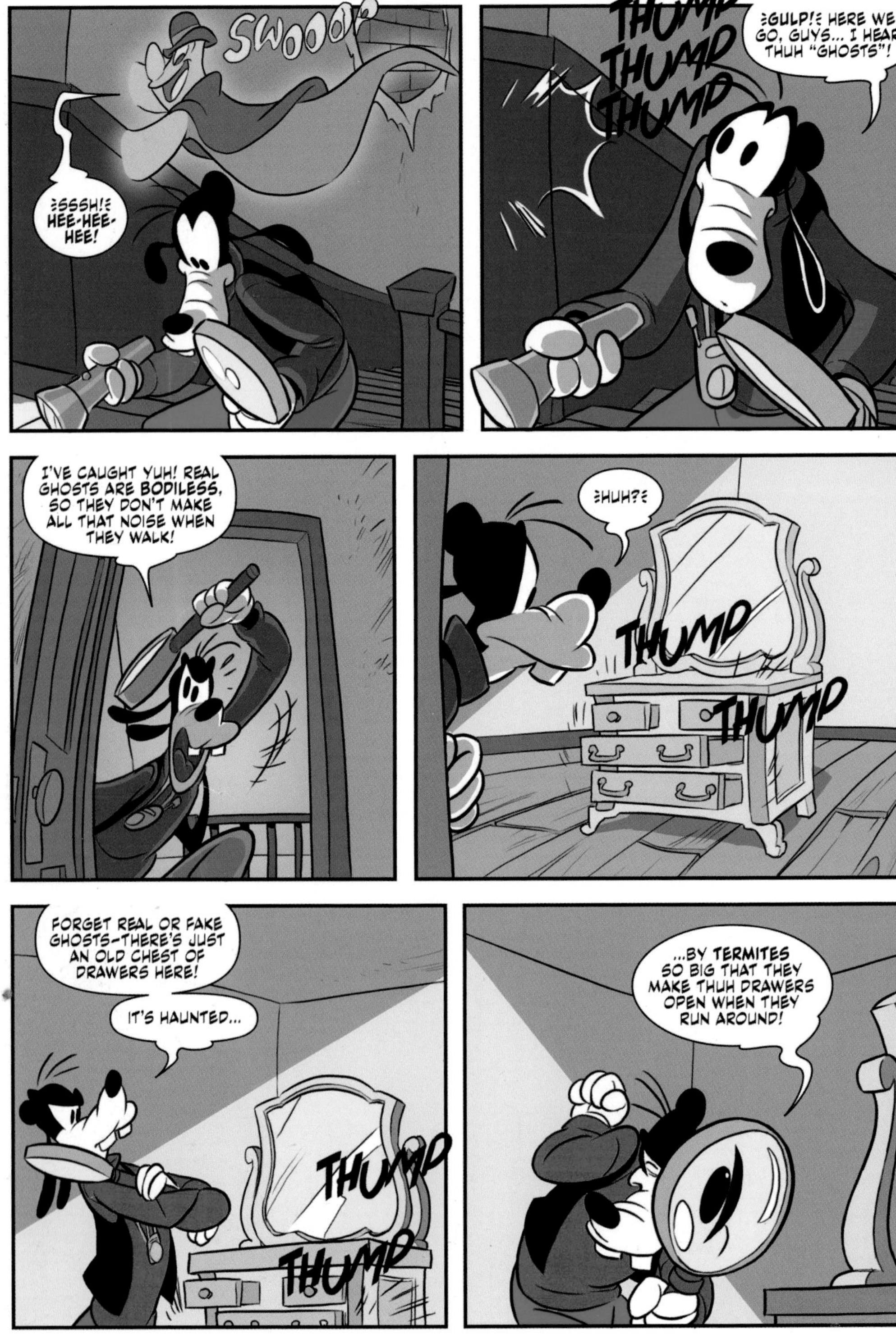
SWOOOP
≷SSSH!≶ HEE-HEE-HEE!
THUMP THUMP THUMP
≷GULP!≶ HERE WE GO, GUYS... I HEAR THUH "GHOSTS"!
I'VE CAUGHT YUH! REAL GHOSTS ARE BODILESS, SO THEY DON'T MAKE ALL THAT NOISE WHEN THEY WALK!
≷HUH?≶
THUMP
THUMP
FORGET REAL OR FAKE GHOSTS—THERE'S JUST AN OLD CHEST OF DRAWERS HERE!
IT'S HAUNTED...
THUMP
THUMP
...BY TERMITES SO BIG THAT THEY MAKE THUH DRAWERS OPEN WHEN THEY RUN AROUND!

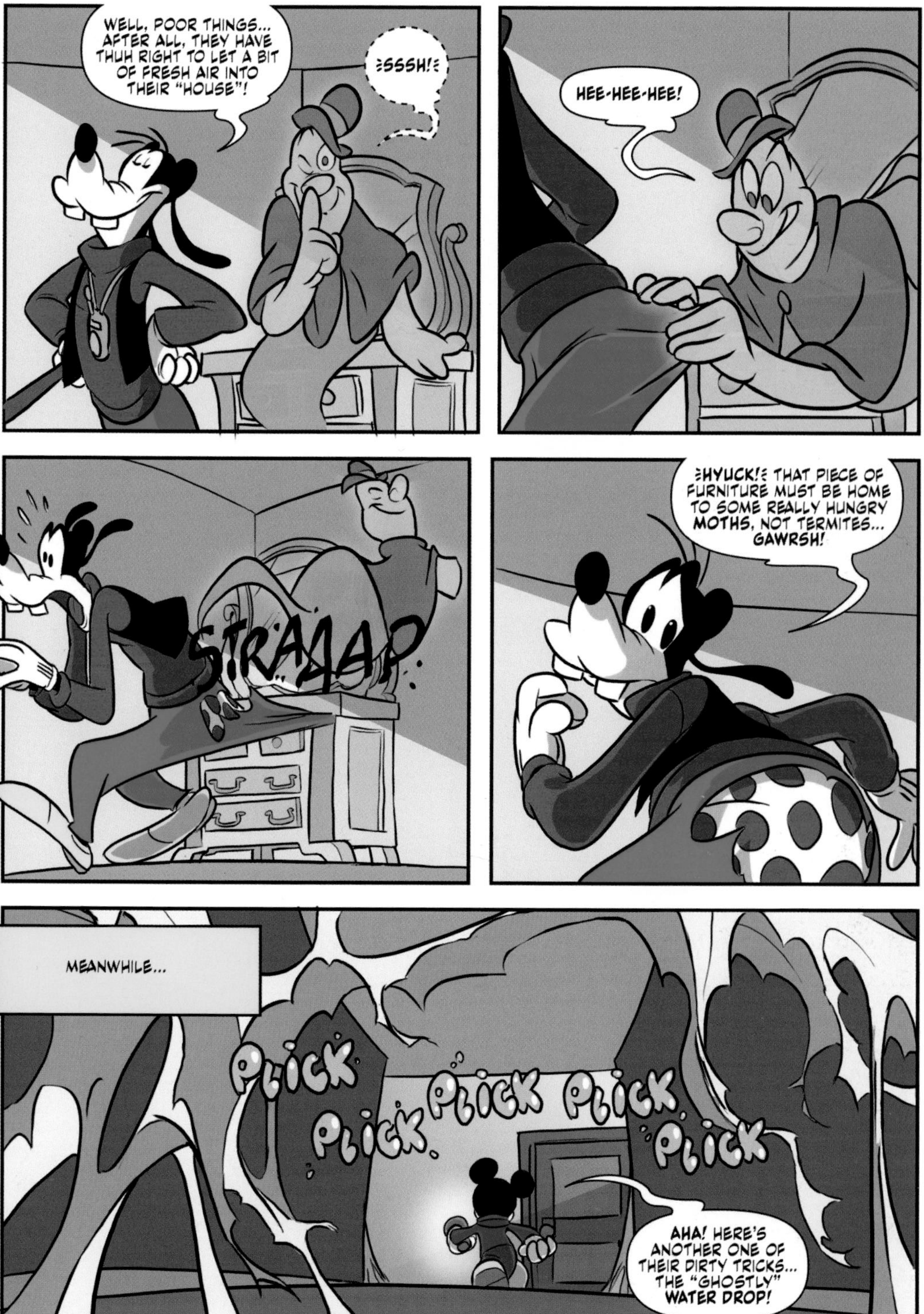
WELL, POOR THINGS... AFTER ALL, THEY HAVE THUH RIGHT TO LET A BIT OF FRESH AIR INTO THEIR "HOUSE"!
SSSH!
HEE-HEE-HEE!
STRAAAP
HYUCK! THAT PIECE OF FURNITURE MUST BE HOME TO SOME REALLY HUNGRY MOTHS, NOT TERMITES... GAWRSH!
MEANWHILE...
PLICK
PLICK
PLICK
PLICK
PLICK
AHA! HERE'S ANOTHER ONE OF THEIR DIRTY TRICKS... THE "GHOSTLY" WATER DROP!

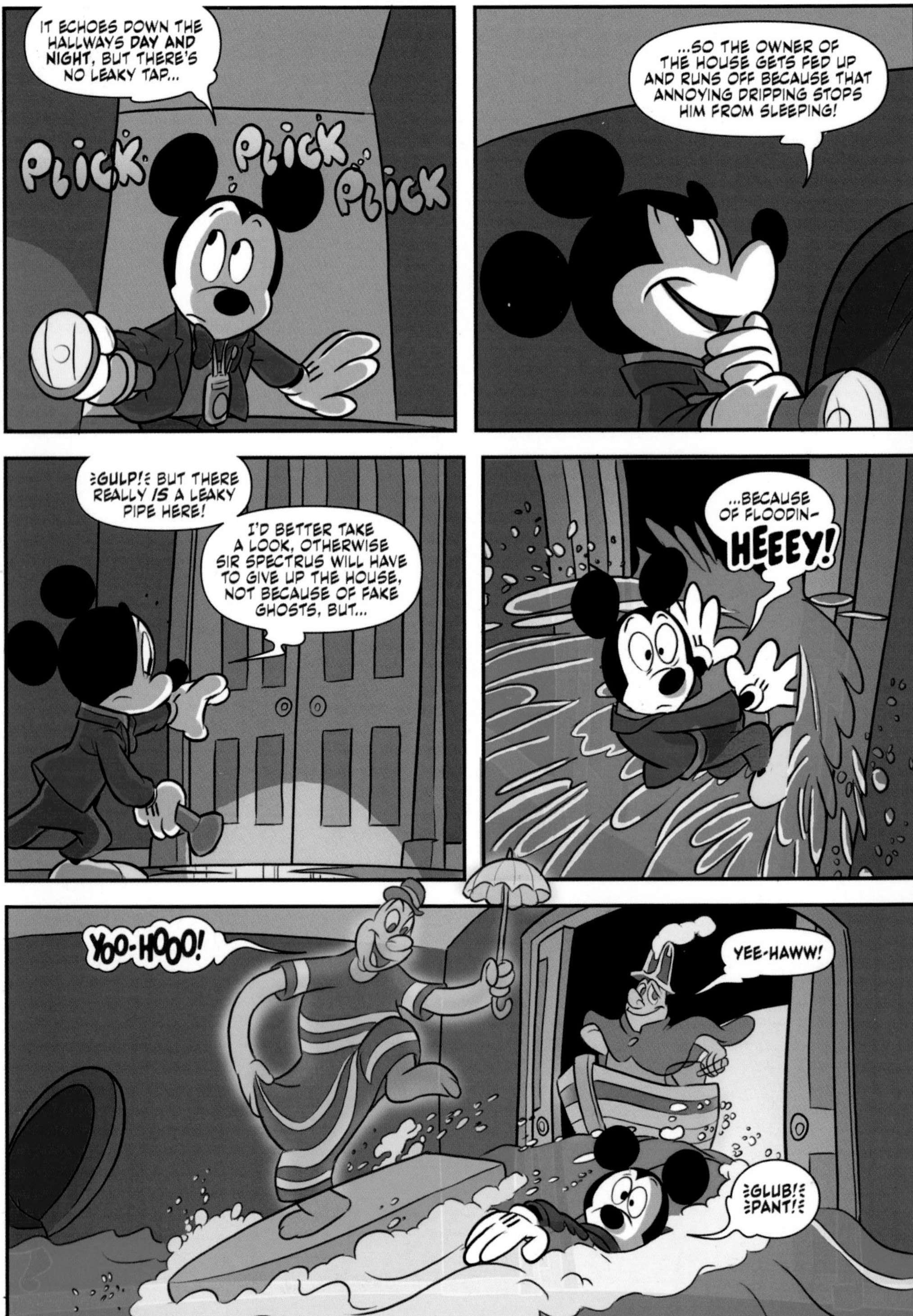
IT ECHOES DOWN THE HALLWAYS DAY AND NIGHT, BUT THERE'S NO LEAKY TAP...
PLICK PLICK PLICK
...SO THE OWNER OF THE HOUSE GETS FED UP AND RUNS OFF BECAUSE THAT ANNOYING DRIPPING STOPS HIM FROM SLEEPING!
GULP! BUT THERE REALLY IS A LEAKY PIPE HERE!
I'D BETTER TAKE A LOOK, OTHERWISE SIR SPECTRUS WILL HAVE TO GIVE UP THE HOUSE, NOT BECAUSE OF FAKE GHOSTS, BUT...
...BECAUSE OF FLOODIN-
HEEEY!
YOO-HOOO!
YEE-HAWW!
GLUB! PANT!

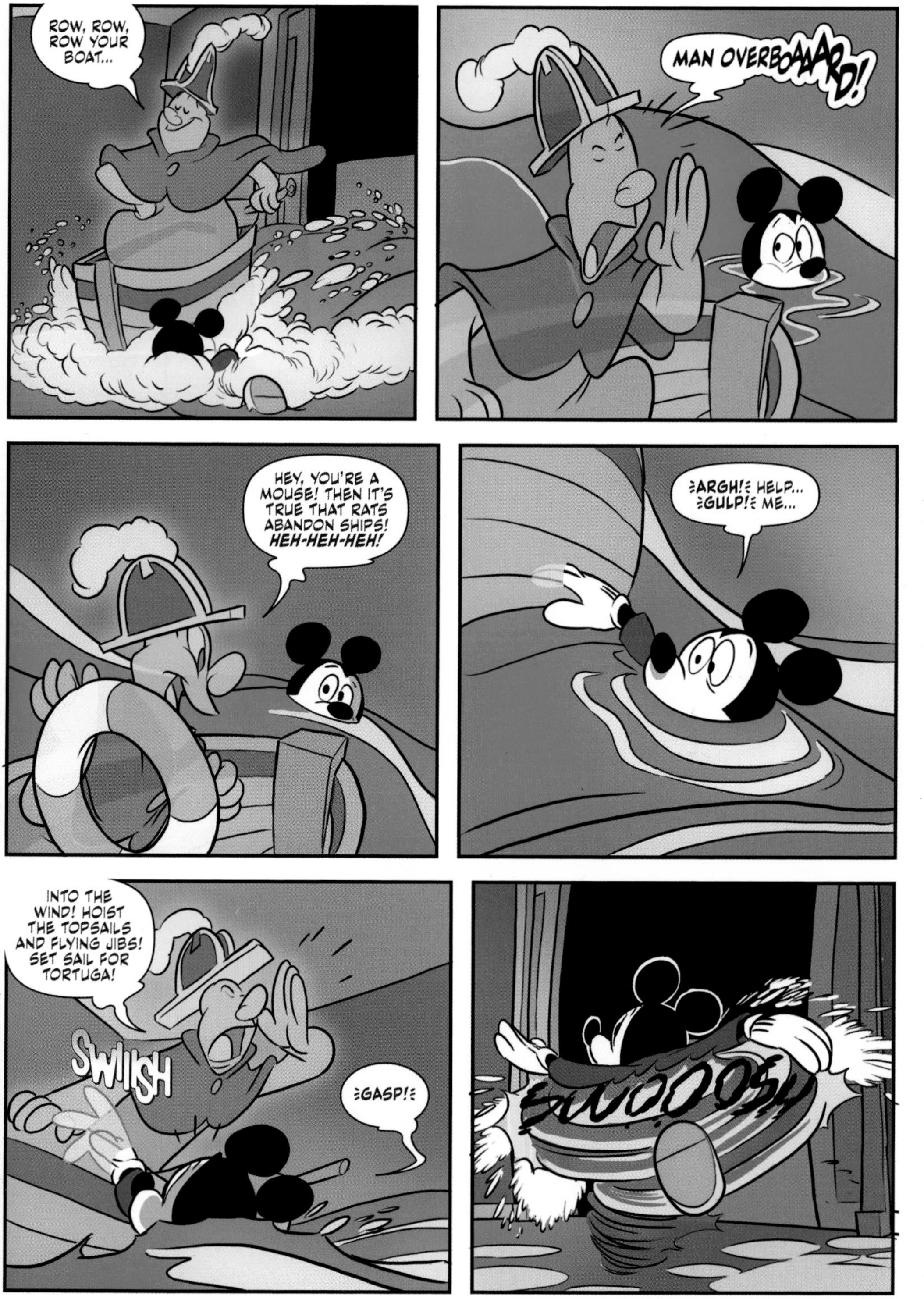
ROW, ROW, ROW YOUR BOAT...
MAN OVERBOAAARD!
HEY, YOU'RE A MOUSE! THEN IT'S TRUE THAT RATS ABANDON SHIPS! HEH-HEH-HEH!
ARGH! HELP... GULP! ME...
INTO THE WIND! HOIST THE TOPSAILS AND FLYING JIBS! SET SAIL FOR TORTUGA!
SWIIISH
GASP!
SWOOOSH

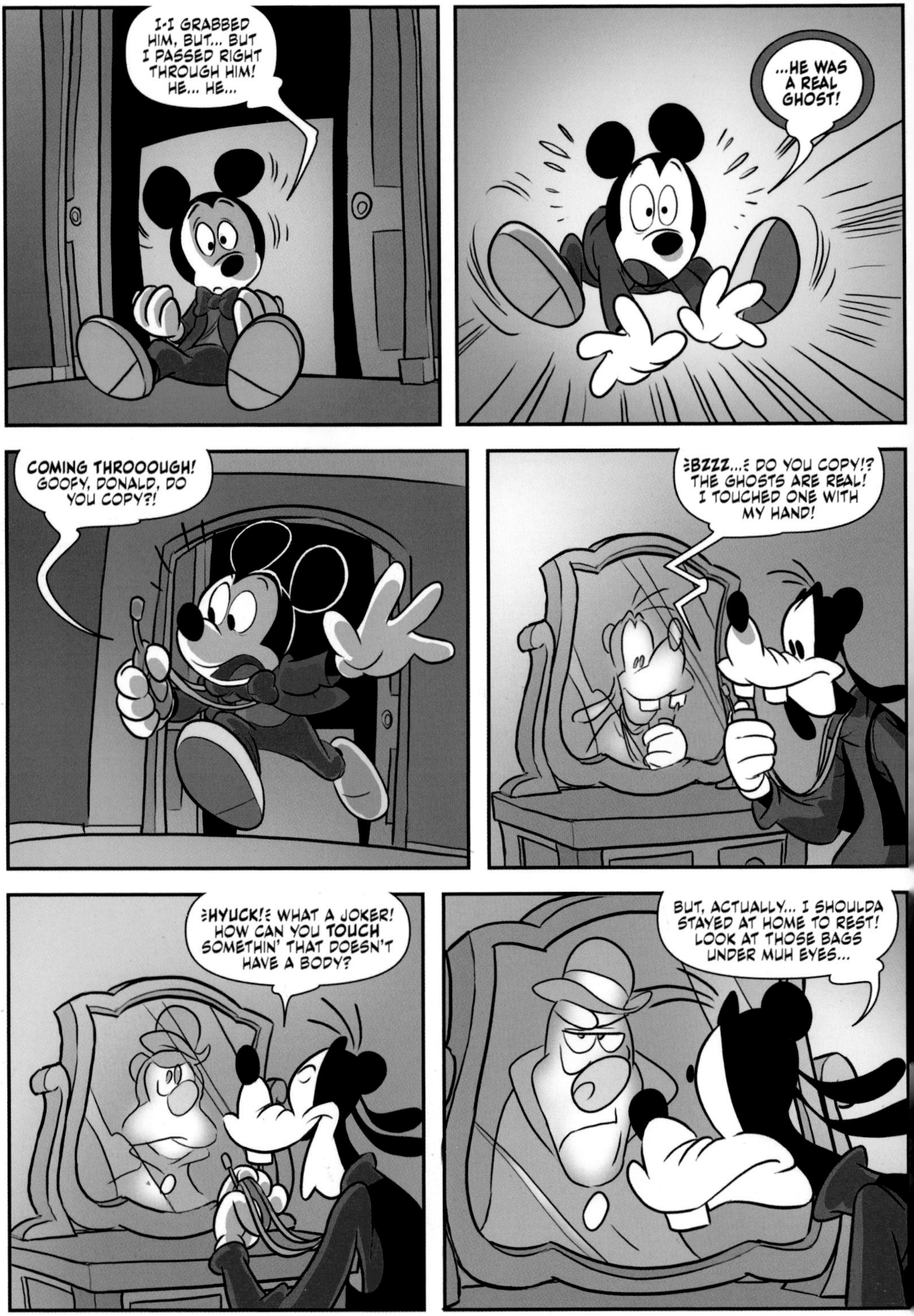
I-I GRABBED HIM, BUT... BUT I PASSED RIGHT THROUGH HIM! HE... HE...
...HE WAS A REAL GHOST!
COMING THROOOUGH! GOOFY, DONALD, DO YOU COPY?!
BZZZ... DO YOU COPY!? THE GHOSTS ARE REAL! I TOUCHED ONE WITH MY HAND!
HYUCK! WHAT A JOKER! HOW CAN YOU TOUCH SOMETHIN' THAT DOESN'T HAVE A BODY?
BUT, ACTUALLY... I SHOULDA STAYED AT HOME TO REST! LOOK AT THOSE BAGS UNDER MUH EYES...

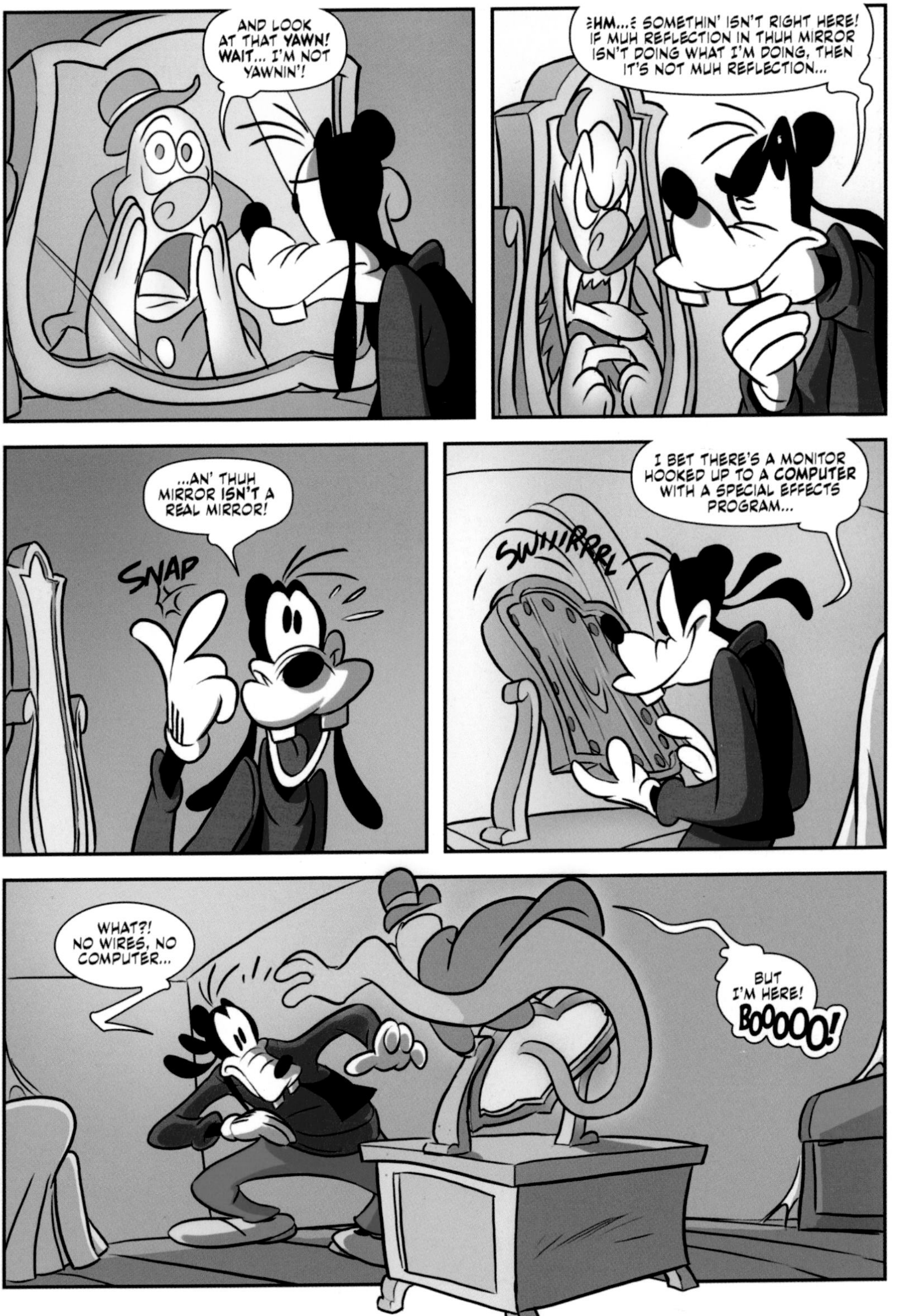
AND LOOK AT THAT YAWN! WAIT... I'M NOT YAWNIN'!
HM... SOMETHIN' ISN'T RIGHT HERE! IF MUH REFLECTION IN THUH MIRROR ISN'T DOING WHAT I'M DOING, THEN IT'S NOT MUH REFLECTION...
SNAP
...AN' THUH MIRROR ISN'T A REAL MIRROR!
I BET THERE'S A MONITOR HOOKED UP TO A COMPUTER WITH A SPECIAL EFFECTS PROGRAM...
SWHIRRRL
WHAT?! NO WIRES, NO COMPUTER...
BUT I'M HERE! BOOOOO!

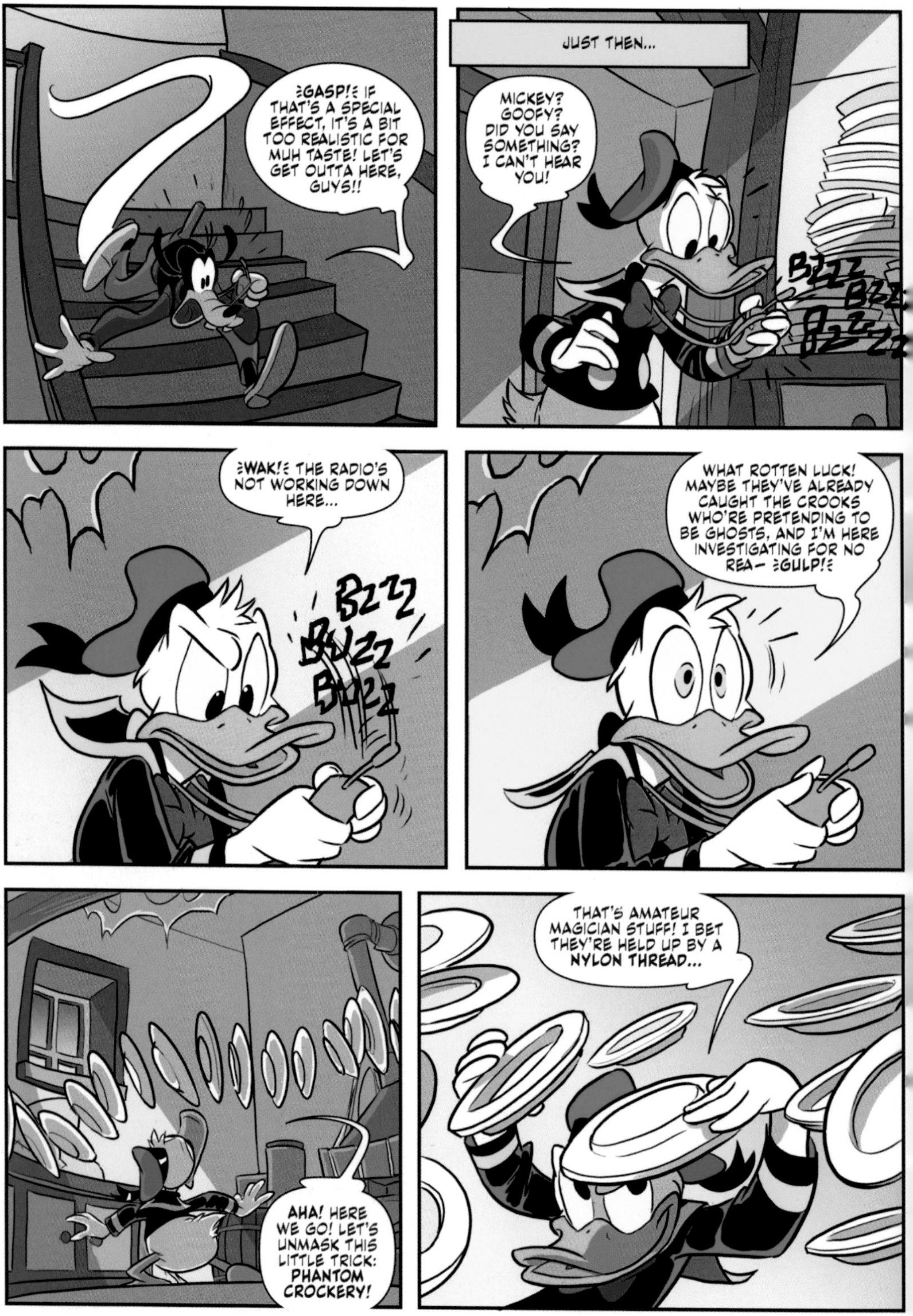

≷GASP!≶ IF THAT'S A SPECIAL EFFECT, IT'S A BIT TOO REALISTIC FOR MUH TASTE! LET'S GET OUTTA HERE, GUYS!!
JUST THEN...
MICKEY? GOOFY? DID YOU SAY SOMETHING? I CAN'T HEAR YOU!
BZZZ BZZZ BZZZ
≷WAK!≶ THE RADIO'S NOT WORKING DOWN HERE...
BZZZ BUZZ BUZZ
WHAT ROTTEN LUCK! MAYBE THEY'VE ALREADY CAUGHT THE CROOKS WHO'RE PRETENDING TO BE GHOSTS, AND I'M HERE INVESTIGATING FOR NO REA— ≷GULP!≶
AHA! HERE WE GO! LET'S UNMASK THIS LITTLE TRICK: PHANTOM CROCKERY!
THAT'S AMATEUR MAGICIAN STUFF! I BET THEY'RE HELD UP BY A NYLON THREAD...

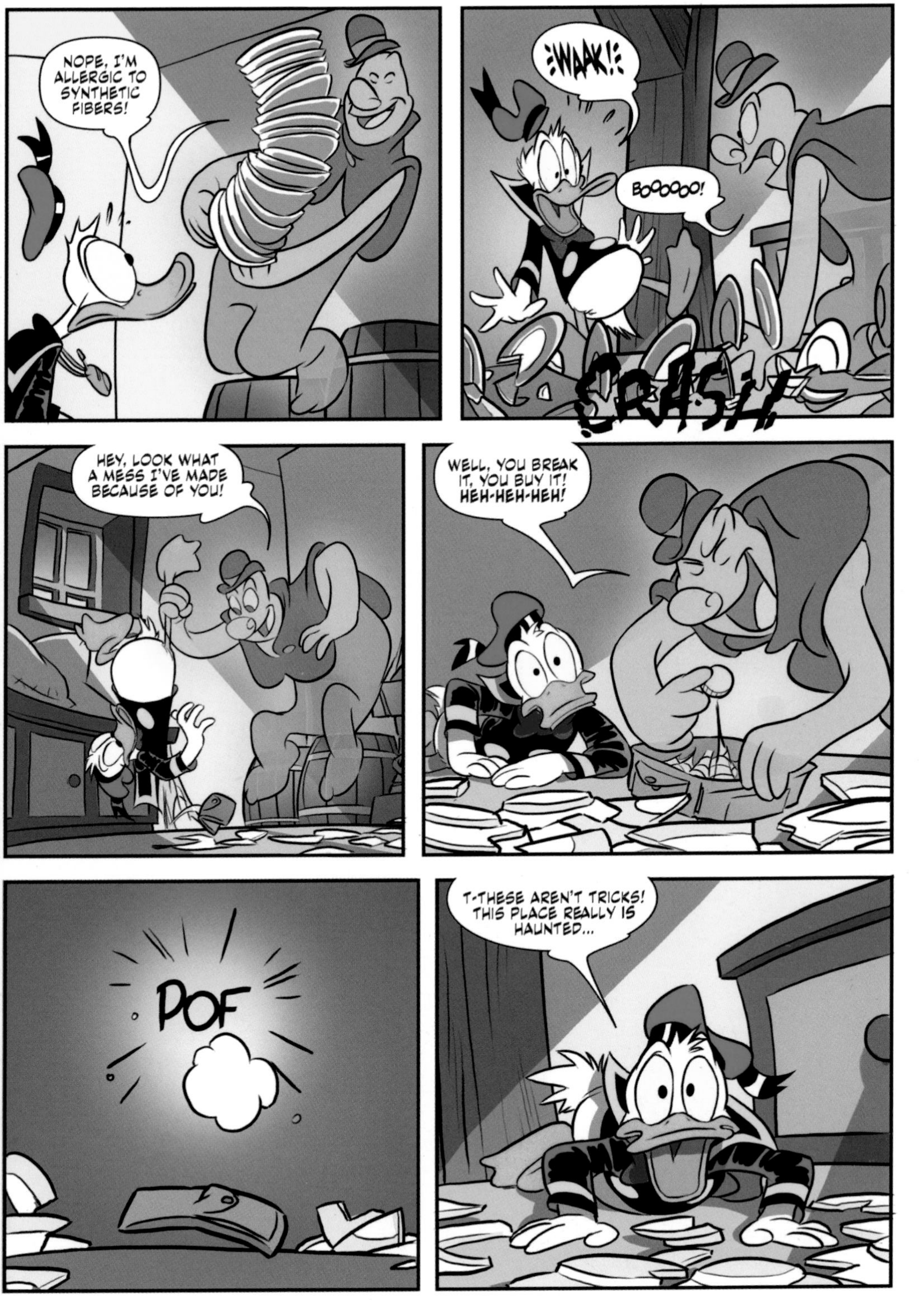
NOPE, I'M ALLERGIC TO SYNTHETIC FIBERS!
WAAK!
BOOOOOO!
CRASH!
HEY, LOOK WHAT A MESS I'VE MADE BECAUSE OF YOU!
WELL, YOU BREAK IT, YOU BUY IT! HEH-HEH-HEH!
POF
T-THESE AREN'T TRICKS! THIS PLACE REALLY IS HAUNTED...

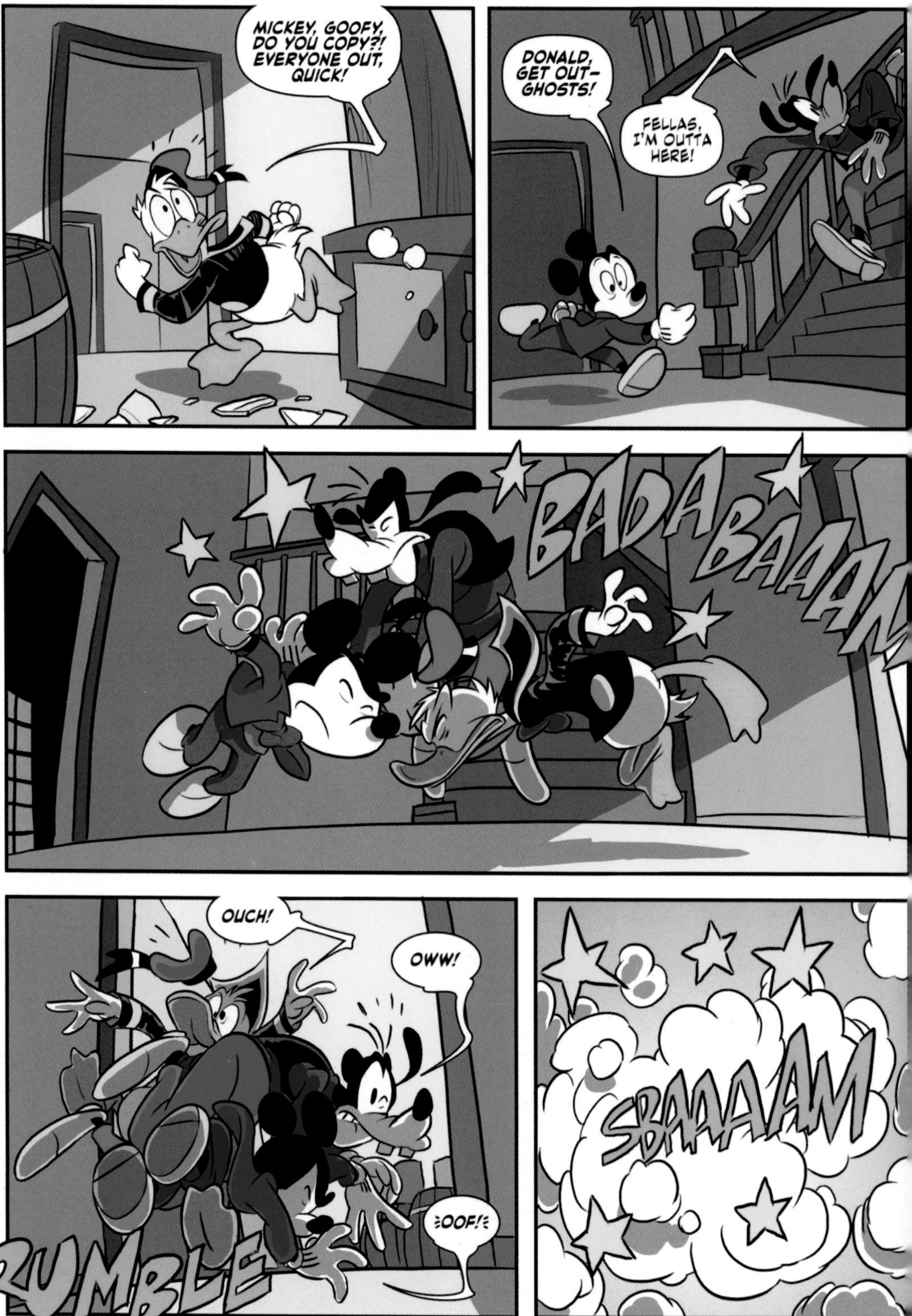
MICKEY, GOOFY, DO YOU COPY?! EVERYONE OUT, QUICK!
DONALD, GET OUT— GHOSTS!
FELLAS, I'M OUTTA HERE!
BADA BAAAAM
OUCH!
OWW!
OOF!
RUMBLE
SBAAAAM

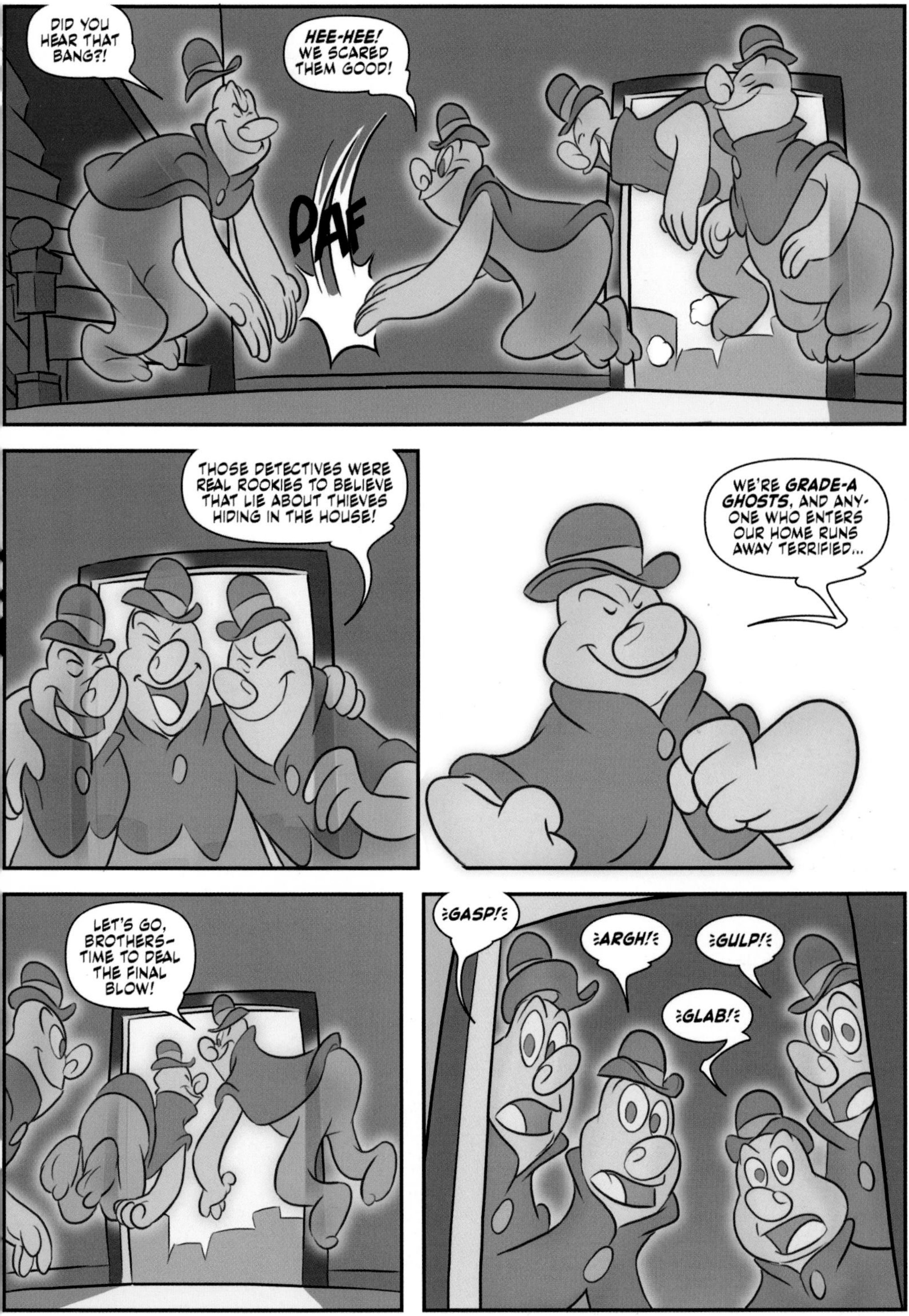
DID YOU HEAR THAT BANG?!
HEE-HEE! WE SCARED THEM GOOD!
PAF
THOSE DETECTIVES WERE REAL ROOKIES TO BELIEVE THAT LIE ABOUT THIEVES HIDING IN THE HOUSE!
WE'RE GRADE-A GHOSTS, AND ANYONE WHO ENTERS OUR HOME RUNS AWAY TERRIFIED...
LET'S GO, BROTHERS— TIME TO DEAL THE FINAL BLOW!
GASP!
ARGH!
GULP!
GLAB!

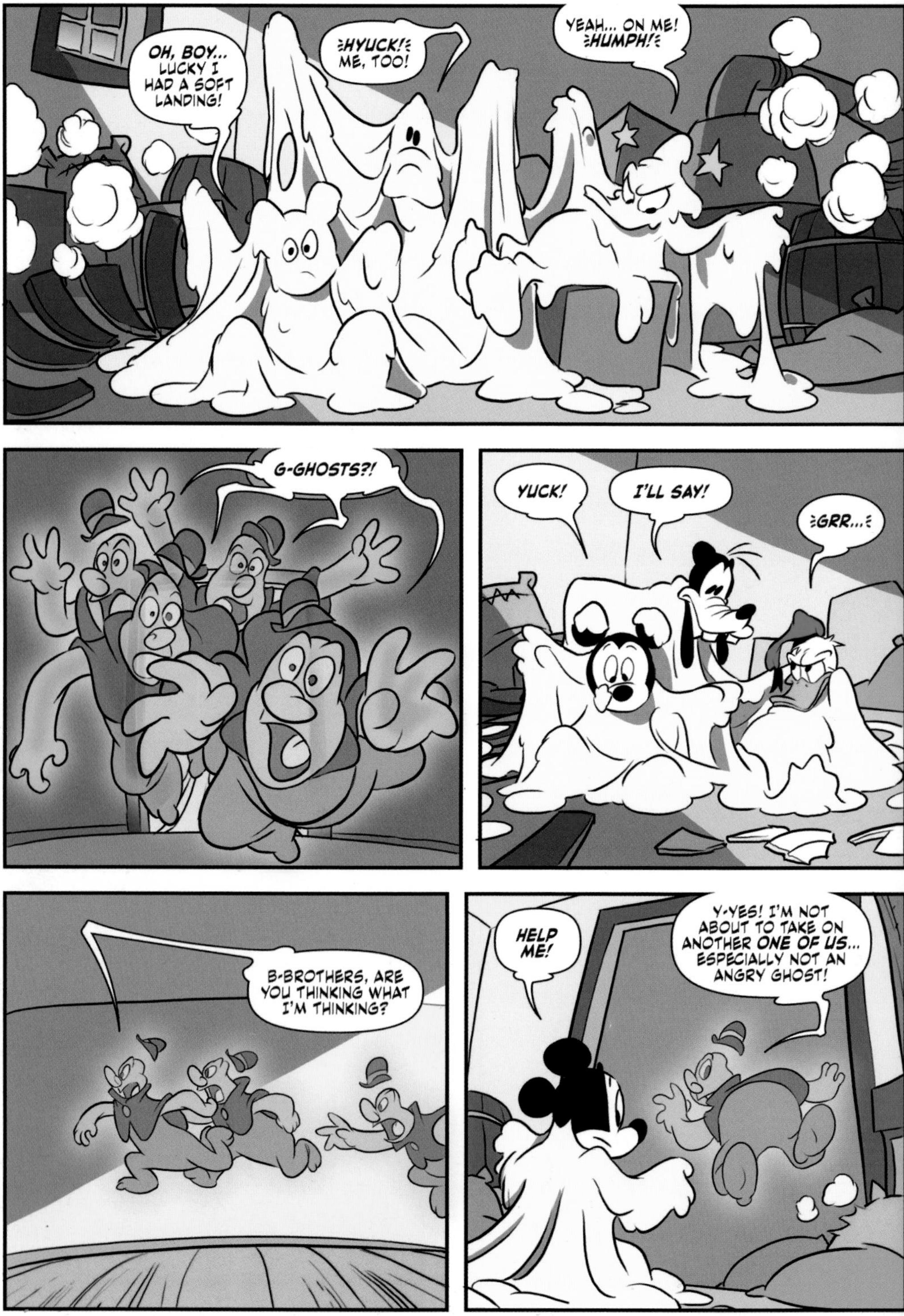
OH, BOY... LUCKY I HAD A SOFT LANDING!
HYUCK! ME, TOO!
YEAH... ON ME! HUMPH!
G-GHOSTS?!
YUCK!
I'LL SAY!
GRR...
B-BROTHERS, ARE YOU THINKING WHAT I'M THINKING?
HELP ME!
Y-YES! I'M NOT ABOUT TO TAKE ON ANOTHER ONE OF US... ESPECIALLY NOT AN ANGRY GHOST!

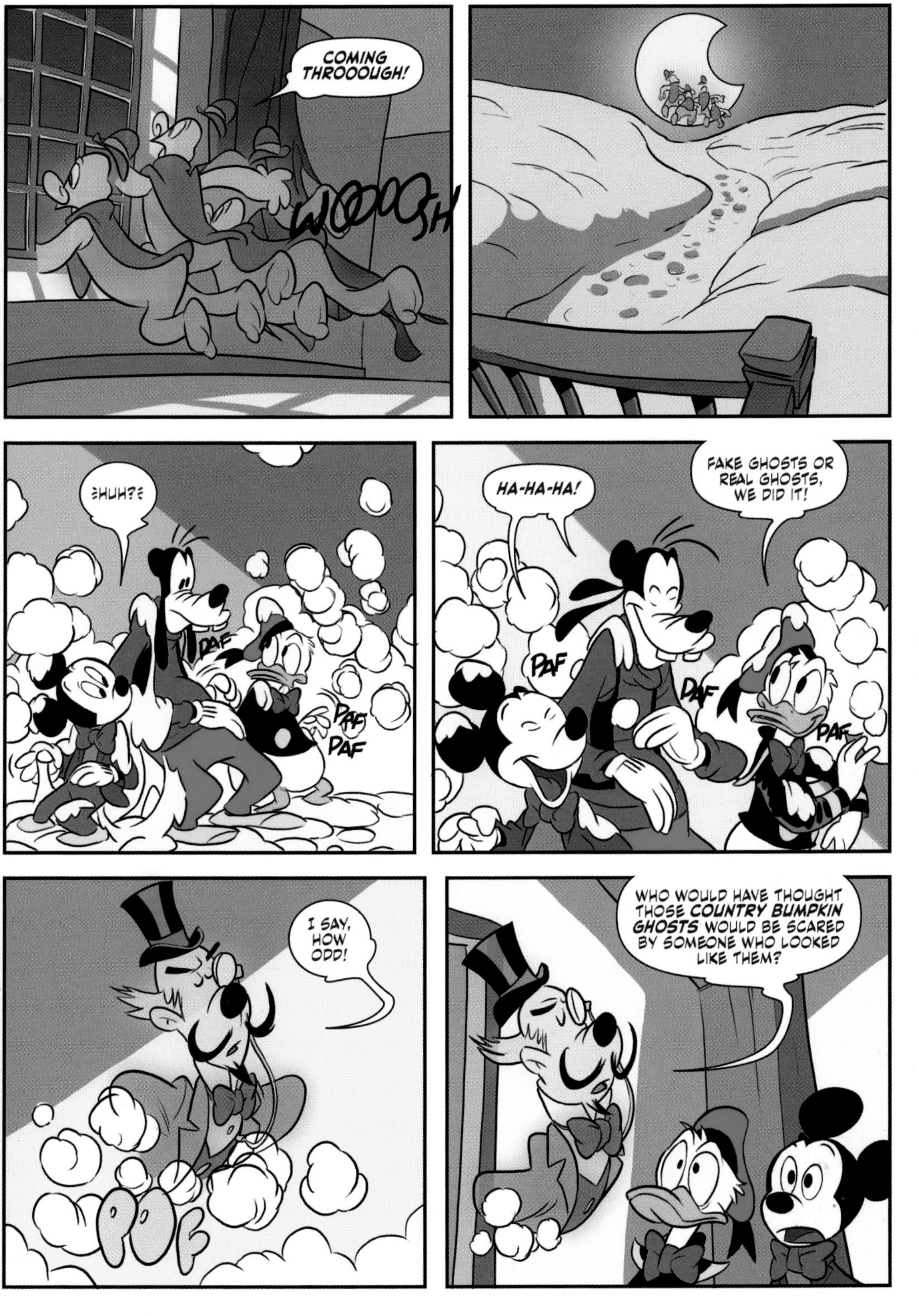
COMING THROOOUGH!
WOOOOSH
HUH?
PAF
PAF
PAF
HA-HA-HA!
FAKE GHOSTS OR REAL GHOSTS, WE DID IT!
PAF
PAF
PAF
I SAY, HOW ODD!
POOF
WHO WOULD HAVE THOUGHT THOSE COUNTRY BUMPKIN GHOSTS WOULD BE SCARED BY SOMEONE WHO LOOKED LIKE THEM?

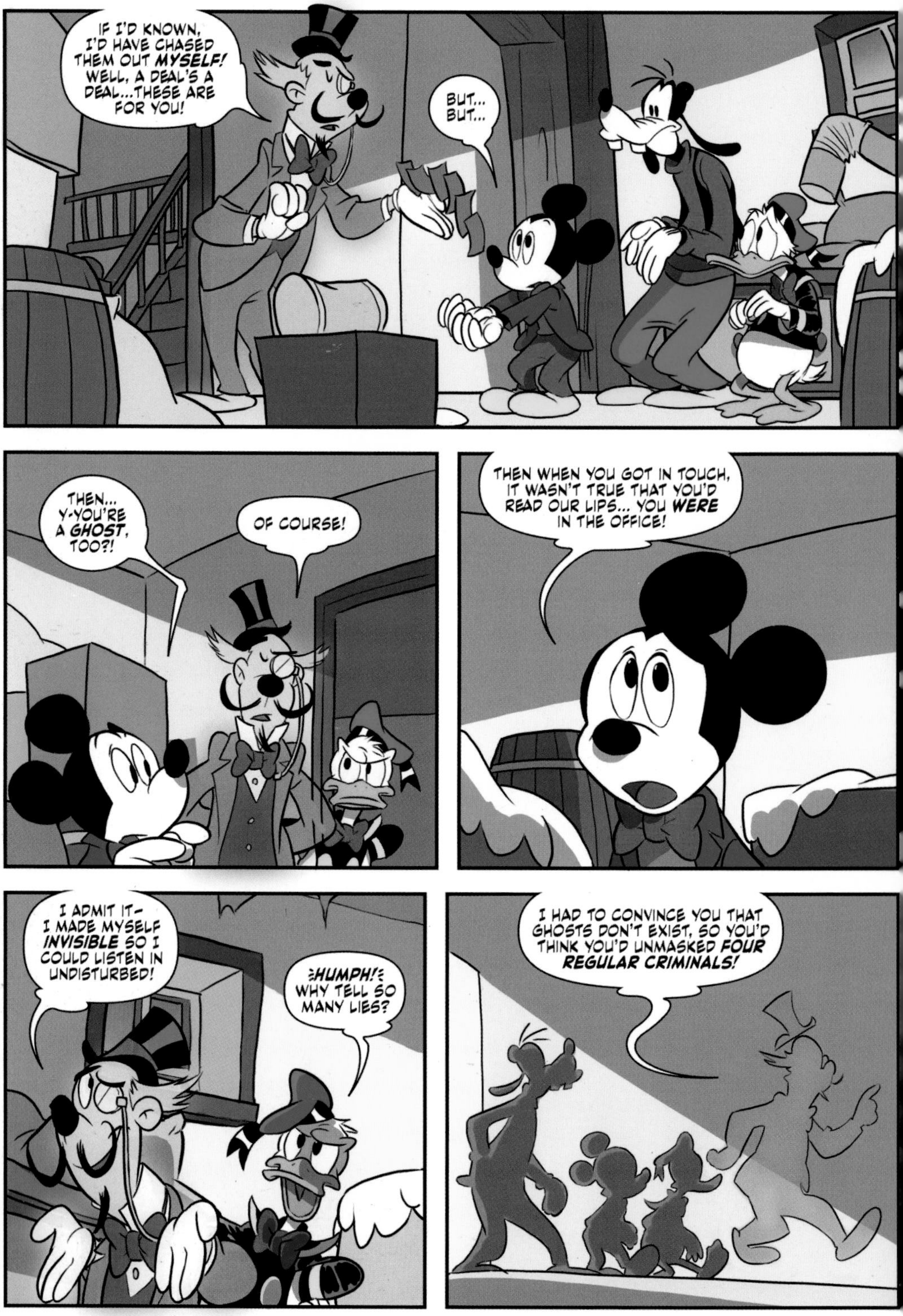
IF I'D KNOWN, I'D HAVE CHASED THEM OUT MYSELF! WELL, A DEAL'S A DEAL...THESE ARE FOR YOU!
BUT... BUT...
THEN... Y-YOU'RE A GHOST, TOO?!
OF COURSE!
THEN WHEN YOU GOT IN TOUCH, IT WASN'T TRUE THAT YOU'D READ OUR LIPS... YOU WERE IN THE OFFICE!
I ADMIT IT— I MADE MYSELF INVISIBLE SO I COULD LISTEN IN UNDISTURBED!
HUMPH! WHY TELL SO MANY LIES?
I HAD TO CONVINCE YOU THAT GHOSTS DON'T EXIST, SO YOU'D THINK YOU'D UNMASKED FOUR REGULAR CRIMINALS!

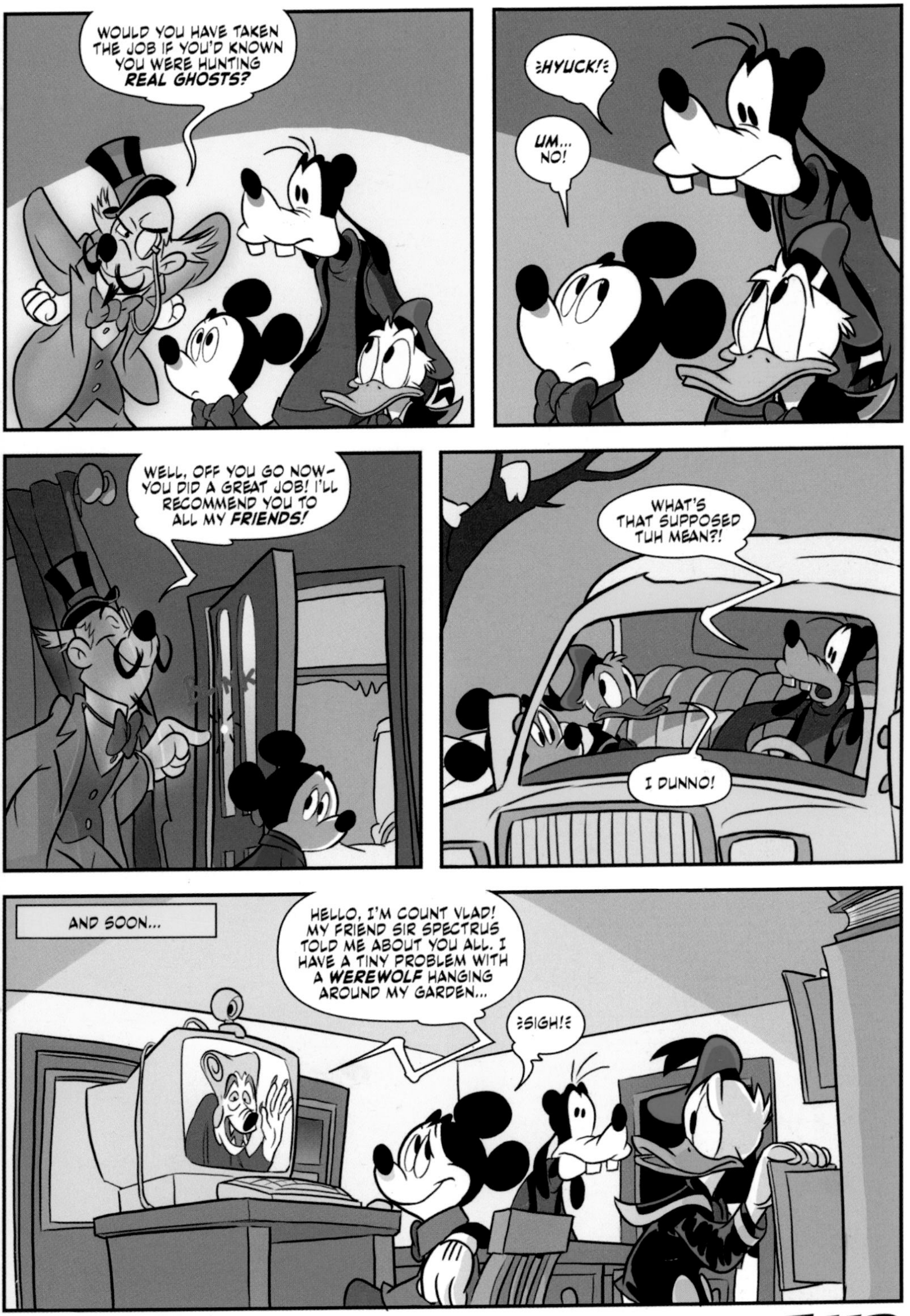
WOULD YOU HAVE TAKEN THE JOB IF YOU'D KNOWN YOU WERE HUNTING REAL GHOSTS?
HYUCK!
UM... NO!
WELL, OFF YOU GO NOW--YOU DID A GREAT JOB! I'LL RECOMMEND YOU TO ALL MY FRIENDS!
WHAT'S THAT SUPPOSED TUH MEAN?!
I DUNNO!
AND SOON...
HELLO, I'M COUNT VLAD! MY FRIEND SIR SPECTRUS TOLD ME ABOUT YOU ALL. I HAVE A TINY PROBLEM WITH A WEREWOLF HANGING AROUND MY GARDEN...
SIGH!
END

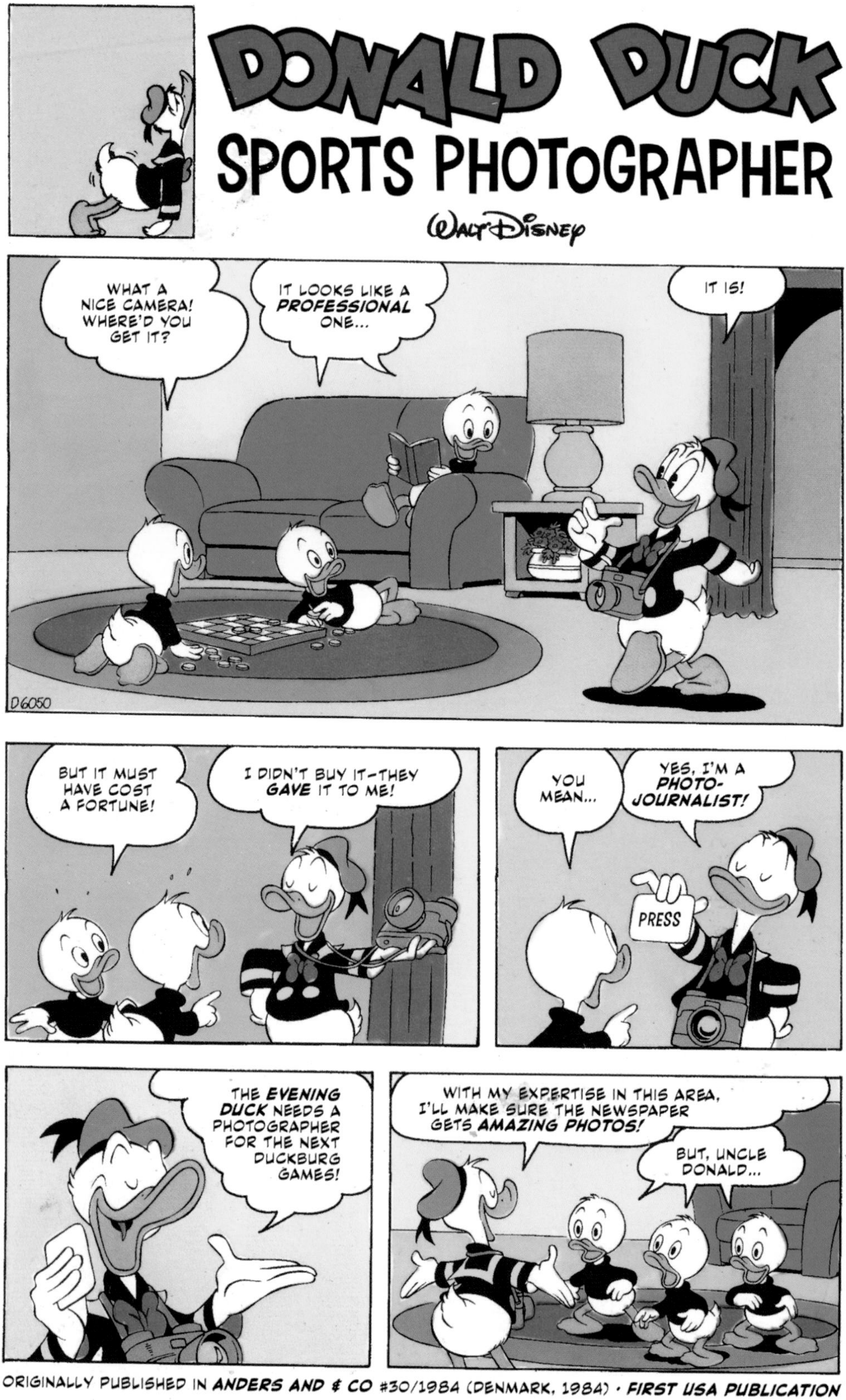
DONALD DUCK
SPORTS PHOTOGRAPHER
WALT DISNEY
WHAT A NICE CAMERA! WHERE'D YOU GET IT?
IT LOOKS LIKE A PROFESSIONAL ONE...
IT IS!
D6050
BUT IT MUST HAVE COST A FORTUNE!
I DIDN'T BUY IT—THEY GAVE IT TO ME!
YOU MEAN...
YES, I'M A PHOTO-JOURNALIST!
PRESS
THE EVENING DUCK NEEDS A PHOTOGRAPHER FOR THE NEXT DUCKBURG GAMES!
WITH MY EXPERTISE IN THIS AREA, I'LL MAKE SURE THE NEWSPAPER GETS AMAZING PHOTOS!
BUT, UNCLE DONALD...

ORIGINALLY PUBLISHED IN ***ANDERS AND & CO*** #30/1984 (DENMARK, 1984) · ***FIRST USA PUBLICATION***

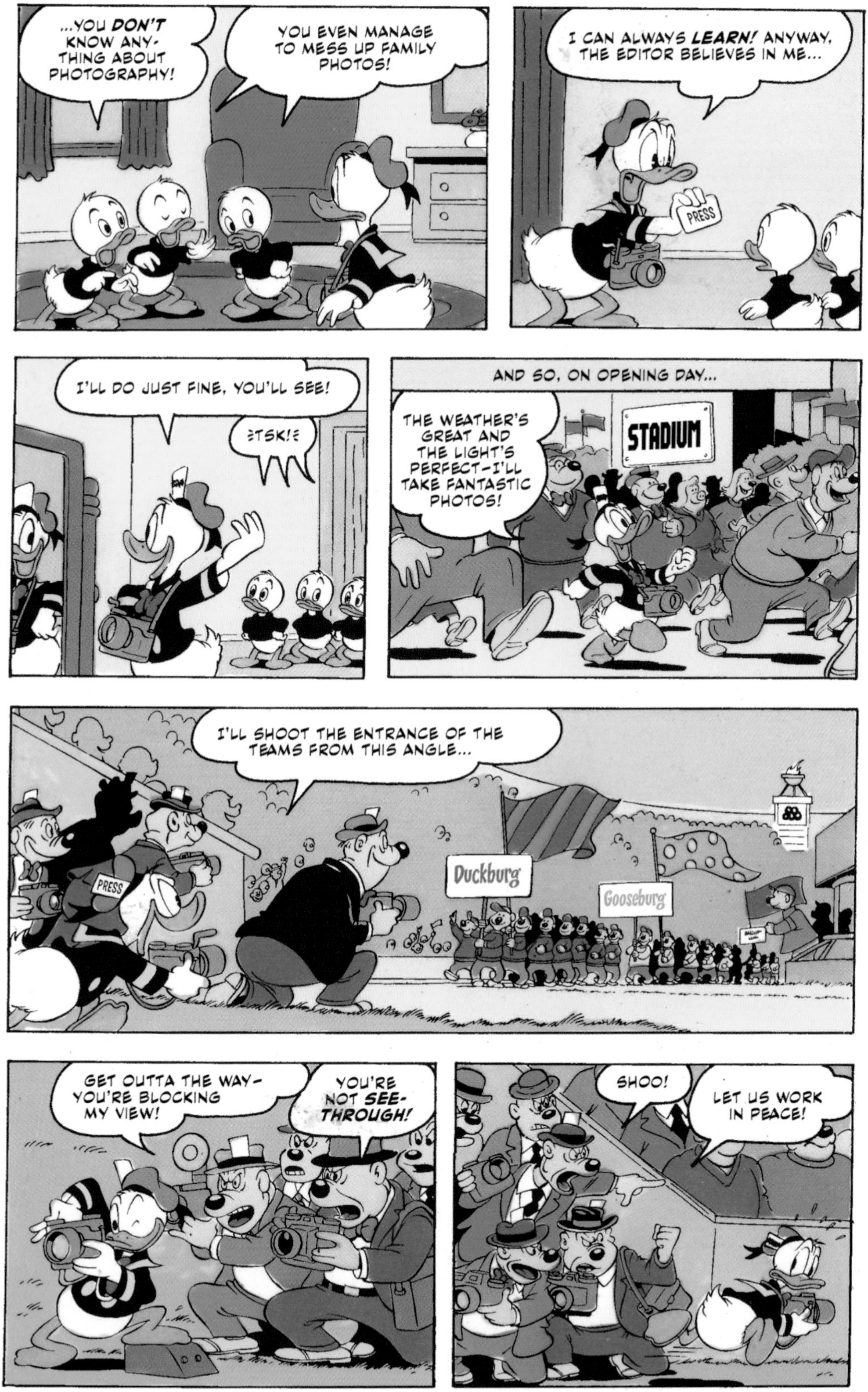
...YOU DON'T KNOW ANYTHING ABOUT PHOTOGRAPHY!
YOU EVEN MANAGE TO MESS UP FAMILY PHOTOS!
I CAN ALWAYS LEARN! ANYWAY, THE EDITOR BELIEVES IN ME...
PRESS
I'LL DO JUST FINE, YOU'LL SEE!
TSK!
AND SO, ON OPENING DAY...
THE WEATHER'S GREAT AND THE LIGHT'S PERFECT—I'LL TAKE FANTASTIC PHOTOS!
STADIUM
I'LL SHOOT THE ENTRANCE OF THE TEAMS FROM THIS ANGLE...
PRESS
Duckburg
Gooseburg
GET OUTTA THE WAY—YOU'RE BLOCKING MY VIEW!
YOU'RE NOT SEE-THROUGH!
SHOO!
LET US WORK IN PEACE!

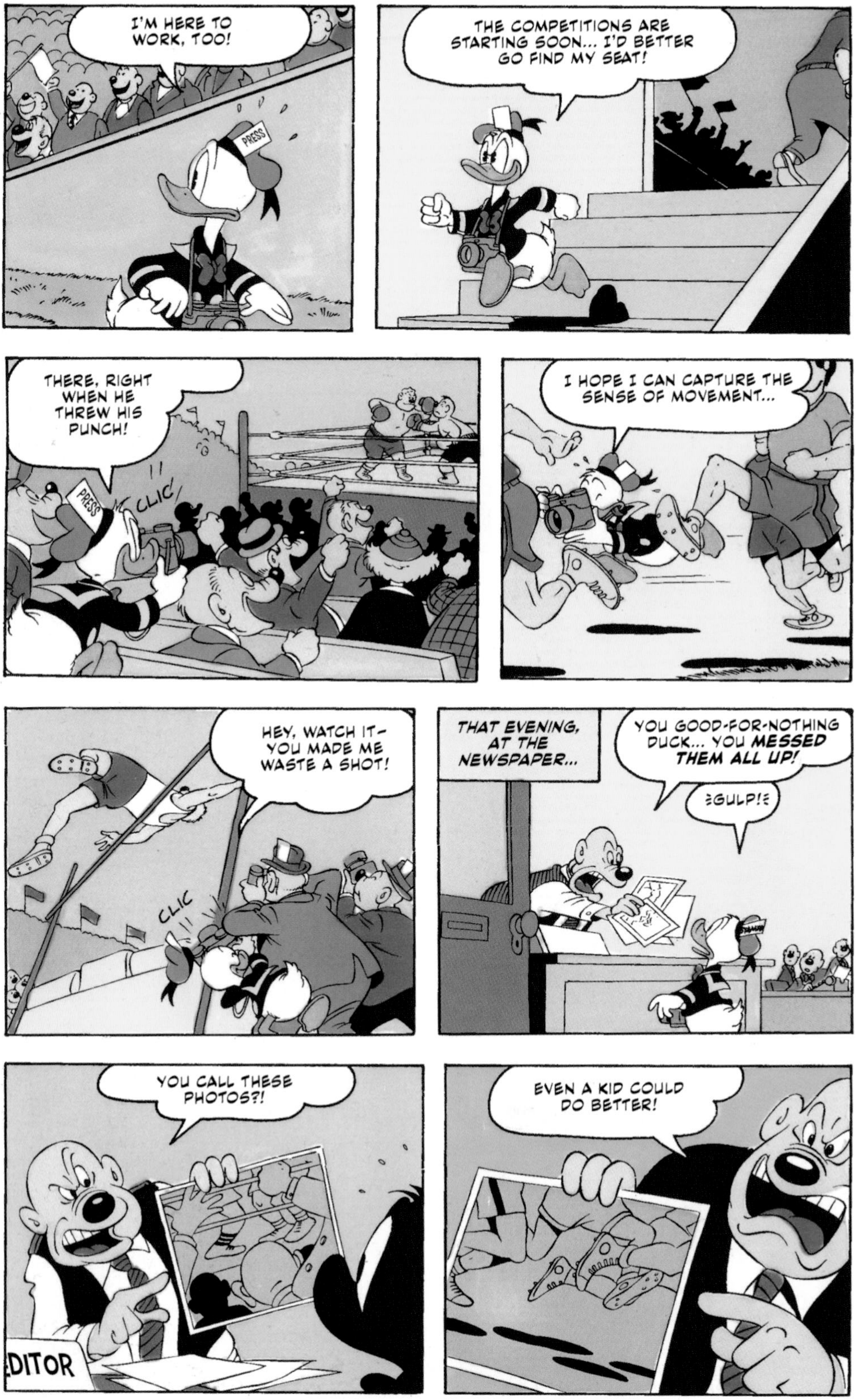
I'M HERE TO WORK, TOO!
PRESS
THE COMPETITIONS ARE STARTING SOON... I'D BETTER GO FIND MY SEAT!
THERE, RIGHT WHEN HE THREW HIS PUNCH!
PRESS
CLIC
I HOPE I CAN CAPTURE THE SENSE OF MOVEMENT...
HEY, WATCH IT-- YOU MADE ME WASTE A SHOT!
CLIC
THAT EVENING, AT THE NEWSPAPER...
YOU GOOD-FOR-NOTHING DUCK... YOU **MESSED THEM ALL UP!**
GULP!
YOU CALL THESE PHOTOS?!
EDITOR
EVEN A KID COULD DO BETTER!

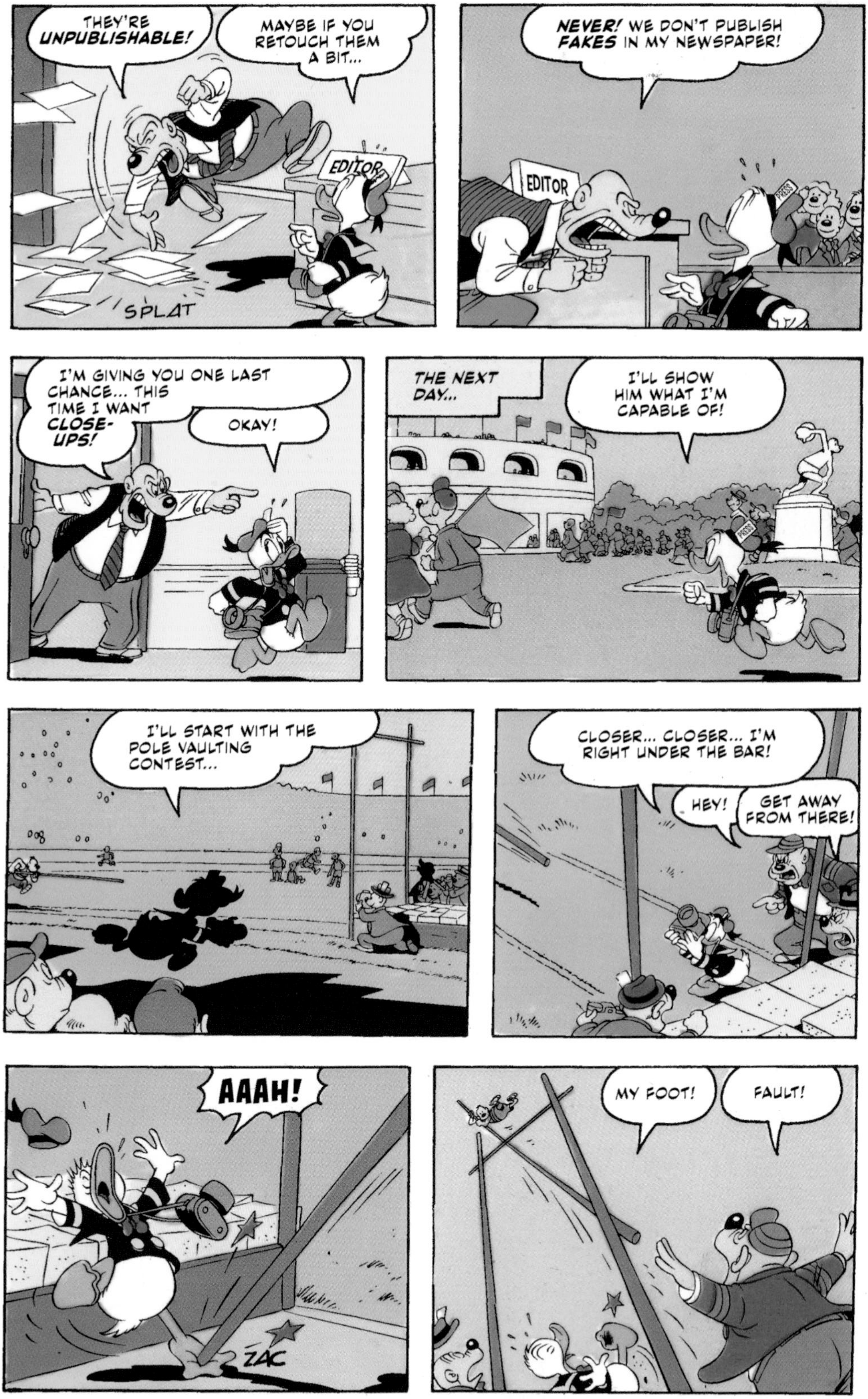
THEY'RE UNPUBLISHABLE!
MAYBE IF YOU RETOUCH THEM A BIT...
EDITOR
SPLAT
NEVER! WE DON'T PUBLISH FAKES IN MY NEWSPAPER!
EDITOR
PRESS
I'M GIVING YOU ONE LAST CHANCE... THIS TIME I WANT CLOSE-UPS!
OKAY!
THE NEXT DAY...
I'LL SHOW HIM WHAT I'M CAPABLE OF!
PRESS
I'LL START WITH THE POLE VAULTING CONTEST...
CLOSER... CLOSER... I'M RIGHT UNDER THE BAR!
HEY!
GET AWAY FROM THERE!
AAAH!
ZAC
MY FOOT!
FAULT!

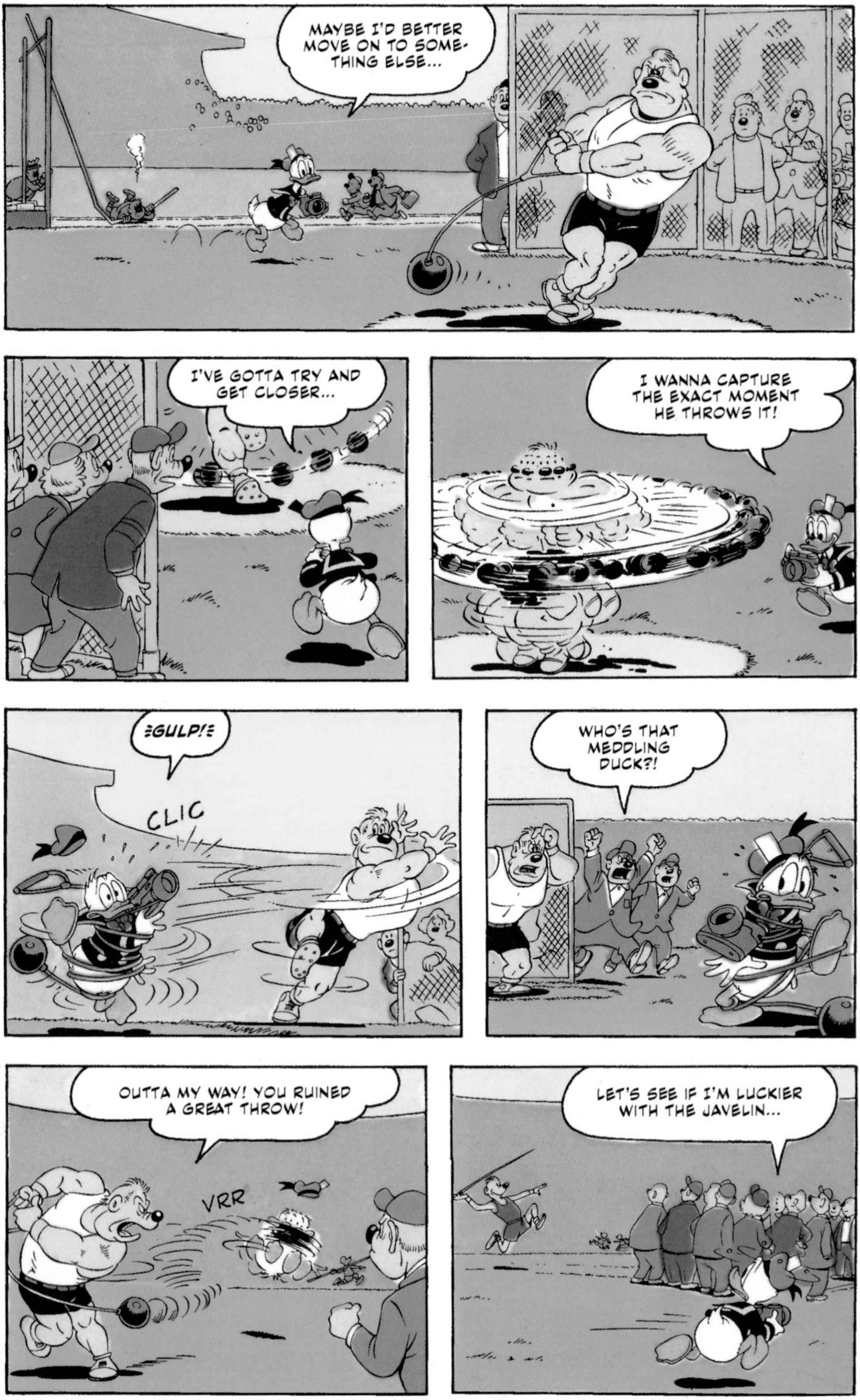
MAYBE I'D BETTER MOVE ON TO SOMETHING ELSE...
I'VE GOTTA TRY AND GET CLOSER...
I WANNA CAPTURE THE EXACT MOMENT HE THROWS IT!
GULP!
CLIC
WHO'S THAT MEDDLING DUCK?!
OUTTA MY WAY! YOU RUINED A GREAT THROW!
VRR
LET'S SEE IF I'M LUCKIER WITH THE JAVELIN...

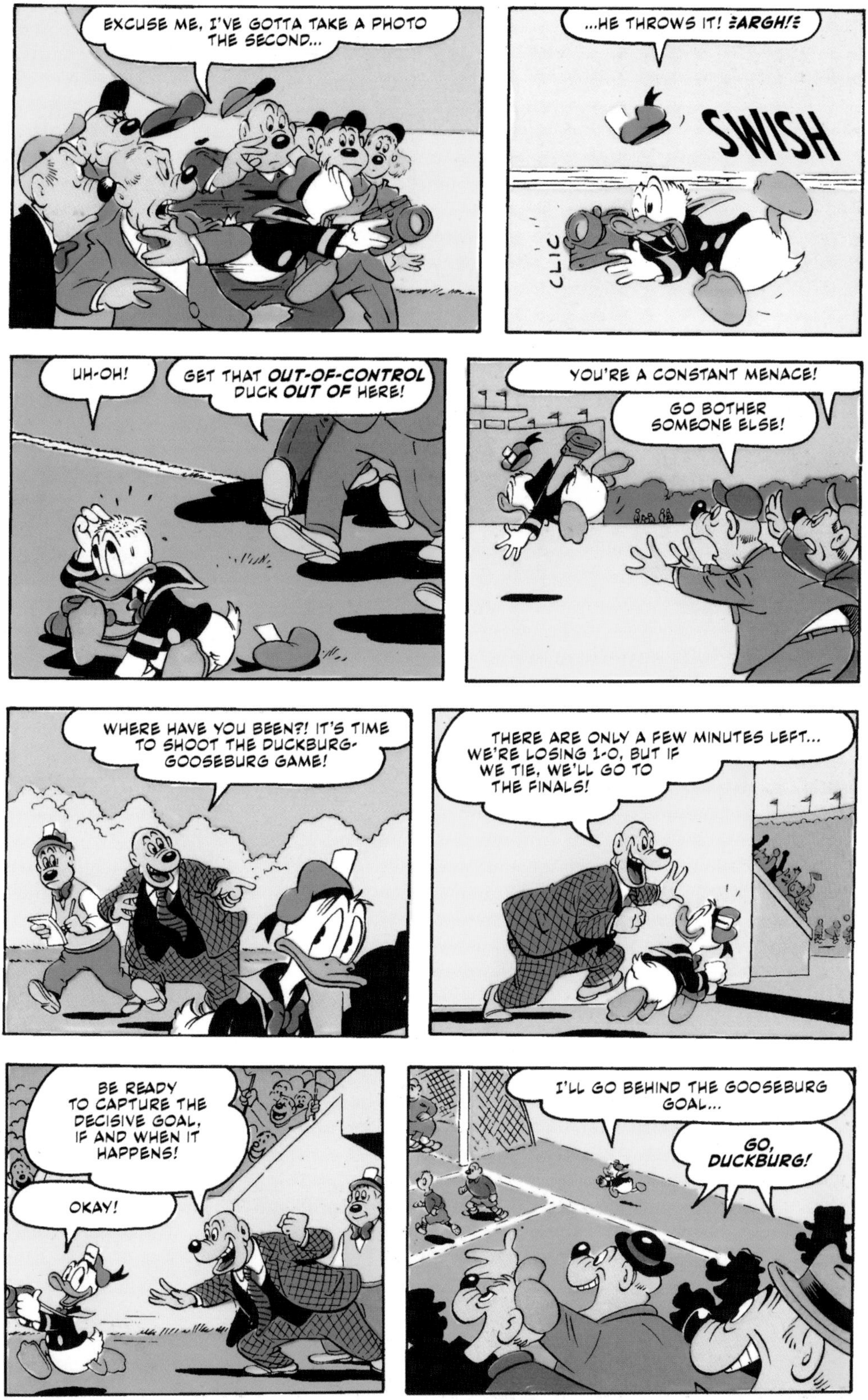
EXCUSE ME, I'VE GOTTA TAKE A PHOTO THE SECOND...
...HE THROWS IT! ARGH!
SWISH
CLIC
UH-OH!
GET THAT OUT-OF-CONTROL DUCK OUT OF HERE!
YOU'RE A CONSTANT MENACE!
GO BOTHER SOMEONE ELSE!
WHERE HAVE YOU BEEN?! IT'S TIME TO SHOOT THE DUCKBURG-GOOSEBURG GAME!
THERE ARE ONLY A FEW MINUTES LEFT... WE'RE LOSING 1-0, BUT IF WE TIE, WE'LL GO TO THE FINALS!
BE READY TO CAPTURE THE DECISIVE GOAL, IF AND WHEN IT HAPPENS!
OKAY!
I'LL GO BEHIND THE GOOSEBURG GOAL...
GO, DUCKBURG!

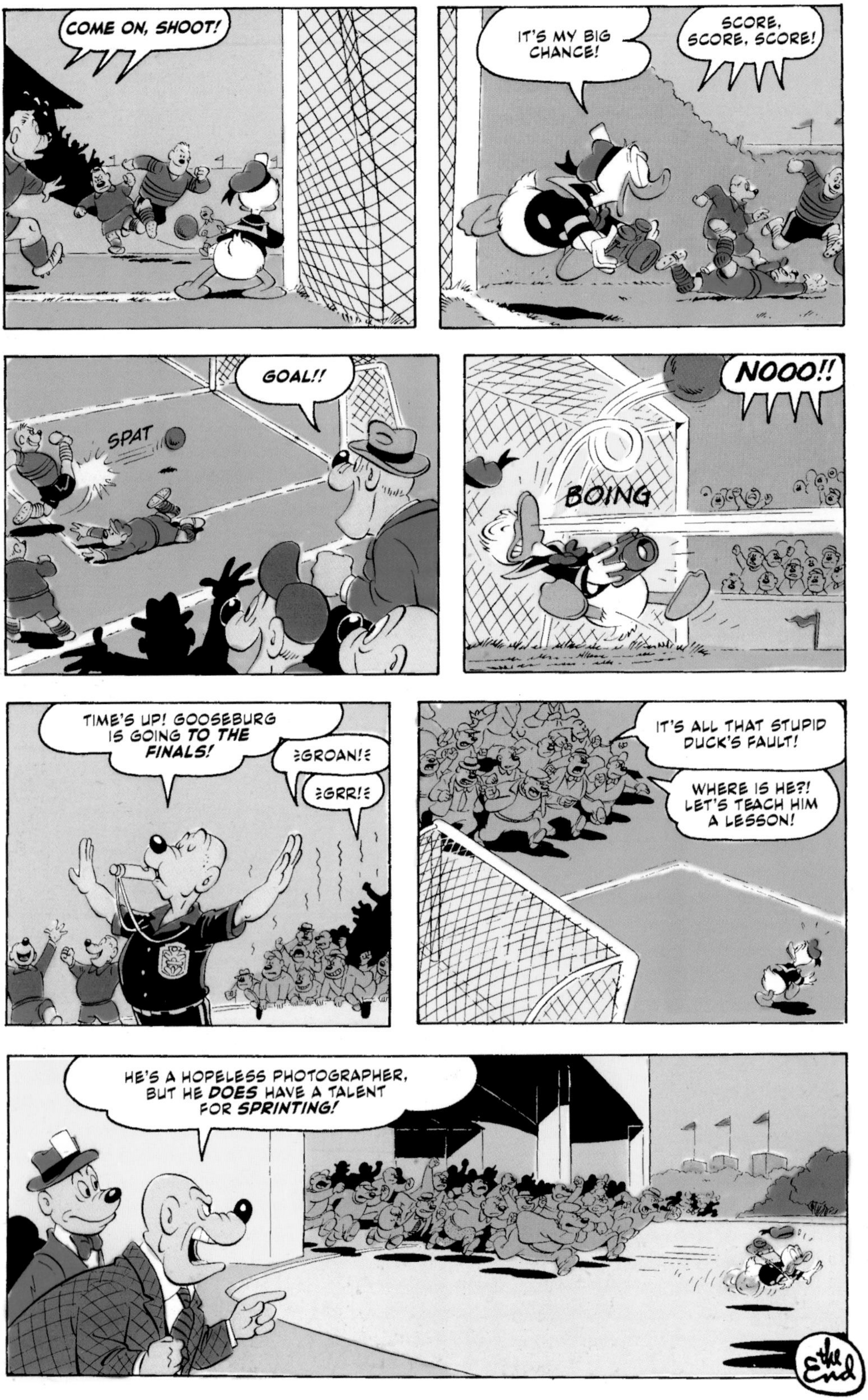
COME ON, SHOOT!
IT'S MY BIG CHANCE!
SCORE, SCORE, SCORE!
GOAL!!
SPAT
NOOO!!
BOING
TIME'S UP! GOOSEBURG IS GOING TO THE FINALS!
GROAN!
GRR!
IT'S ALL THAT STUPID DUCK'S FAULT!
WHERE IS HE?! LET'S TEACH HIM A LESSON!
HE'S A HOPELESS PHOTOGRAPHER, BUT HE DOES HAVE A TALENT FOR SPRINTING!
the End

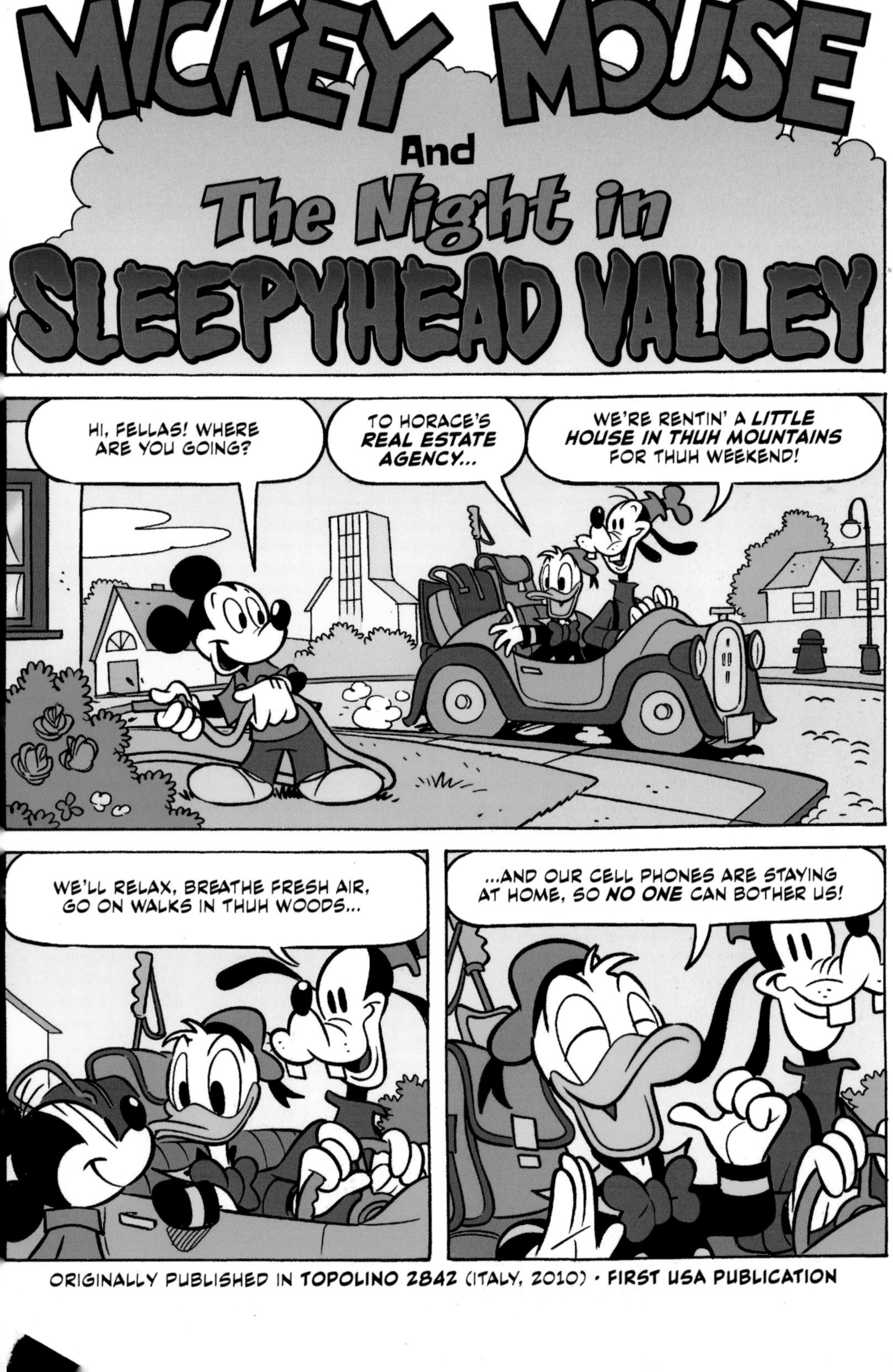
MICKEY MOUSE
And
The Night in
SLEEPYHEAD VALLEY
HI, FELLAS! WHERE ARE YOU GOING?
TO HORACE'S REAL ESTATE AGENCY...
WE'RE RENTIN' A LITTLE HOUSE IN THUH MOUNTAINS FOR THUH WEEKEND!
WE'LL RELAX, BREATHE FRESH AIR, GO ON WALKS IN THUH WOODS...
...AND OUR CELL PHONES ARE STAYING AT HOME, SO NO ONE CAN BOTHER US!

ORIGINALLY PUBLISHED IN **TOPOLINO 2842** (ITALY, 2010) • **FIRST USA PUBLICATION**

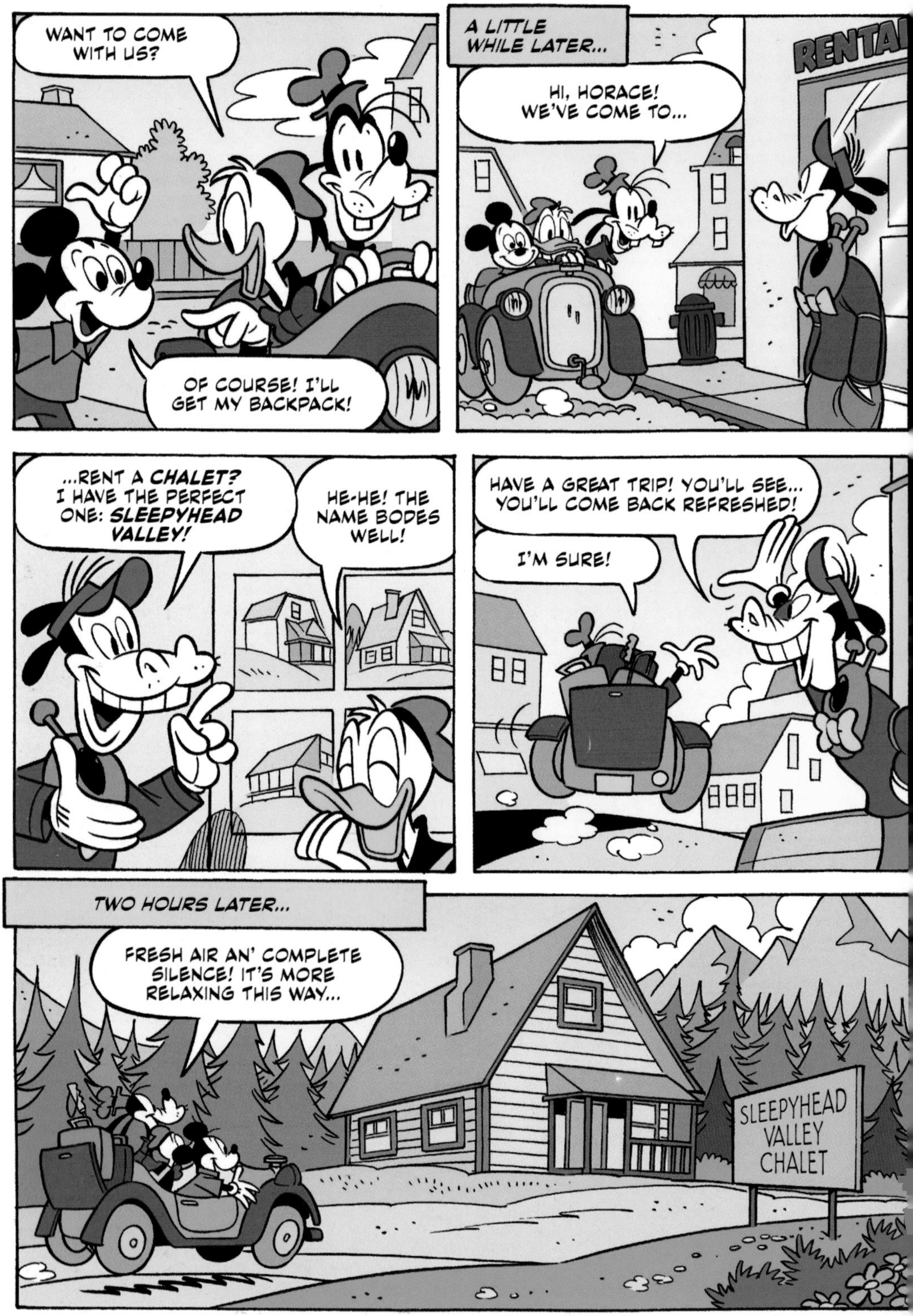
WANT TO COME WITH US?
OF COURSE! I'LL GET MY BACKPACK!
A LITTLE WHILE LATER...
HI, HORACE! WE'VE COME TO...
RENTAL
...RENT A CHALET? I HAVE THE PERFECT ONE: SLEEPYHEAD VALLEY!
HE-HE! THE NAME BODES WELL!
HAVE A GREAT TRIP! YOU'LL SEE... YOU'LL COME BACK REFRESHED!
I'M SURE!
TWO HOURS LATER...
FRESH AIR AN' COMPLETE SILENCE! IT'S MORE RELAXING THIS WAY...
SLEEPYHEAD VALLEY CHALET

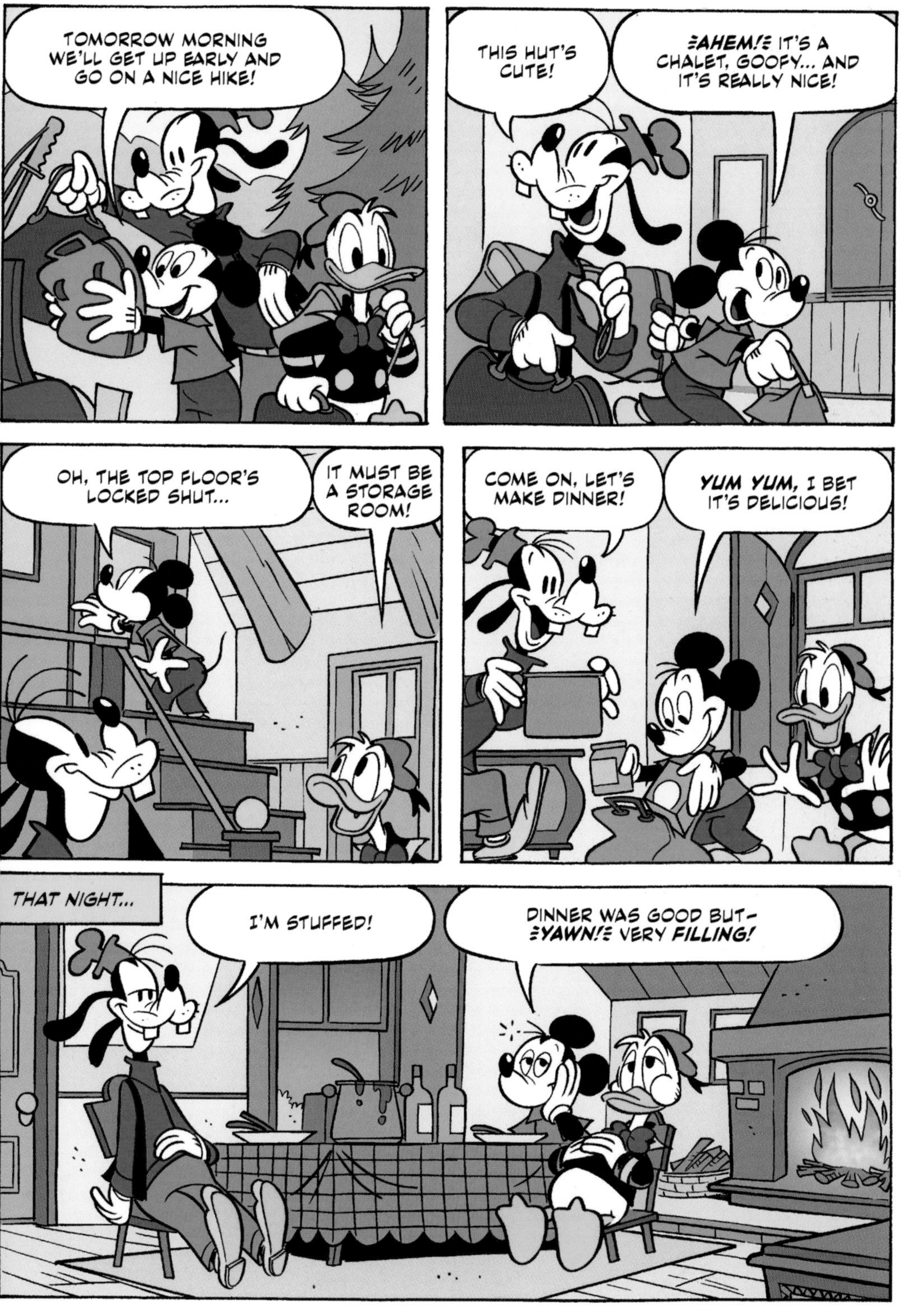

TOMORROW MORNING WE'LL GET UP EARLY AND GO ON A NICE HIKE!
THIS HUT'S CUTE!
AHEM! IT'S A CHALET, GOOFY... AND IT'S REALLY NICE!
OH, THE TOP FLOOR'S LOCKED SHUT...
IT MUST BE A STORAGE ROOM!
COME ON, LET'S MAKE DINNER!
YUM YUM, I BET IT'S DELICIOUS!
THAT NIGHT...
I'M STUFFED!
DINNER WAS GOOD BUT– YAWN! VERY FILLING!

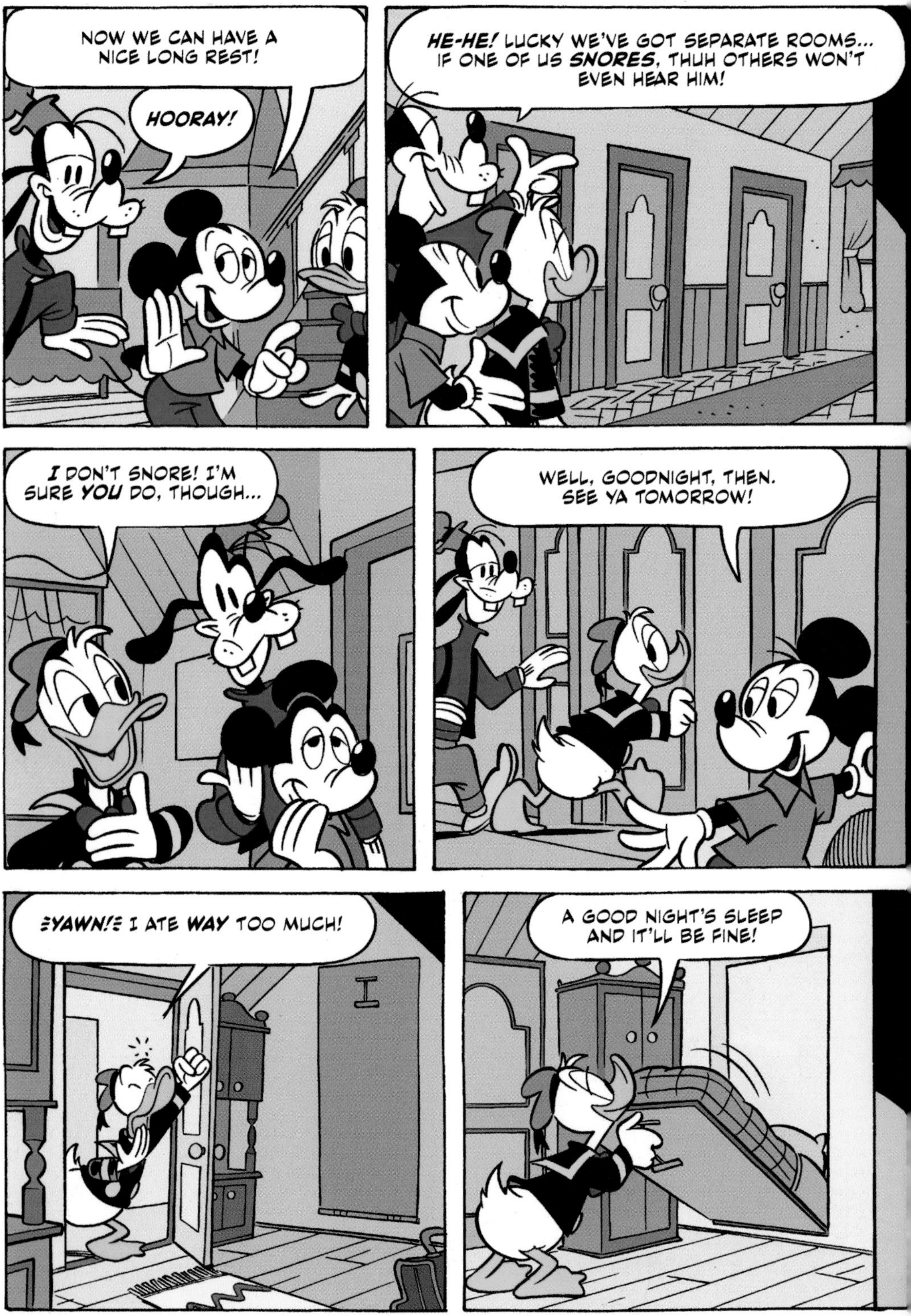
NOW WE CAN HAVE A NICE LONG REST!
HOORAY!
HE-HE! LUCKY WE'VE GOT SEPARATE ROOMS... IF ONE OF US SNORES, THUH OTHERS WON'T EVEN HEAR HIM!
I DON'T SNORE! I'M SURE YOU DO, THOUGH...
WELL, GOODNIGHT, THEN. SEE YA TOMORROW!
YAWN! I ATE WAY TOO MUCH!
A GOOD NIGHT'S SLEEP AND IT'LL BE FINE!

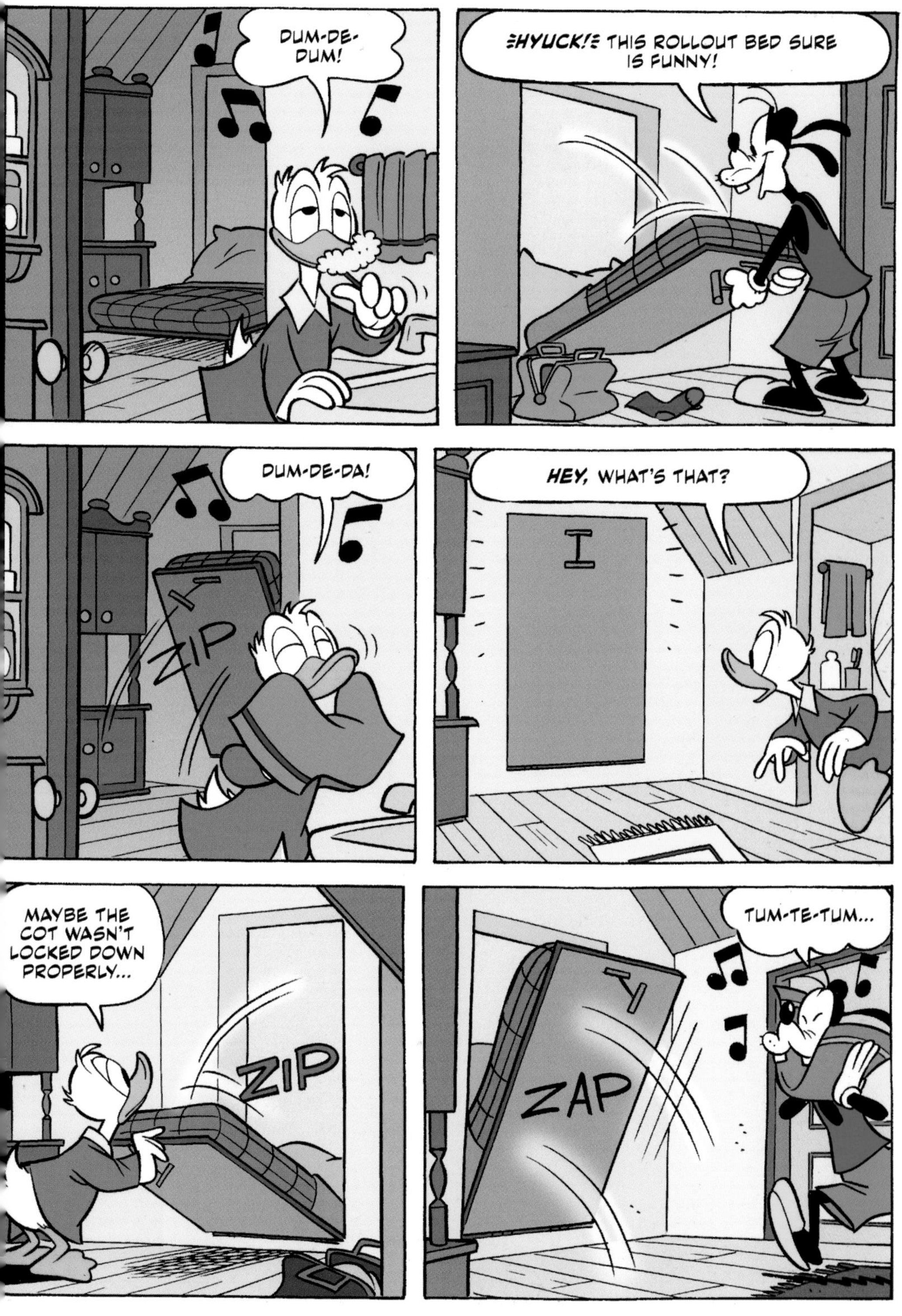
DUM-DE-DUM!
=HYUCK!= THIS ROLLOUT BED SURE IS FUNNY!
DUM-DE-DA!
ZIP
HEY, WHAT'S THAT?
MAYBE THE COT WASN'T LOCKED DOWN PROPERLY...
ZIP
TUM-TE-TUM...
ZAP

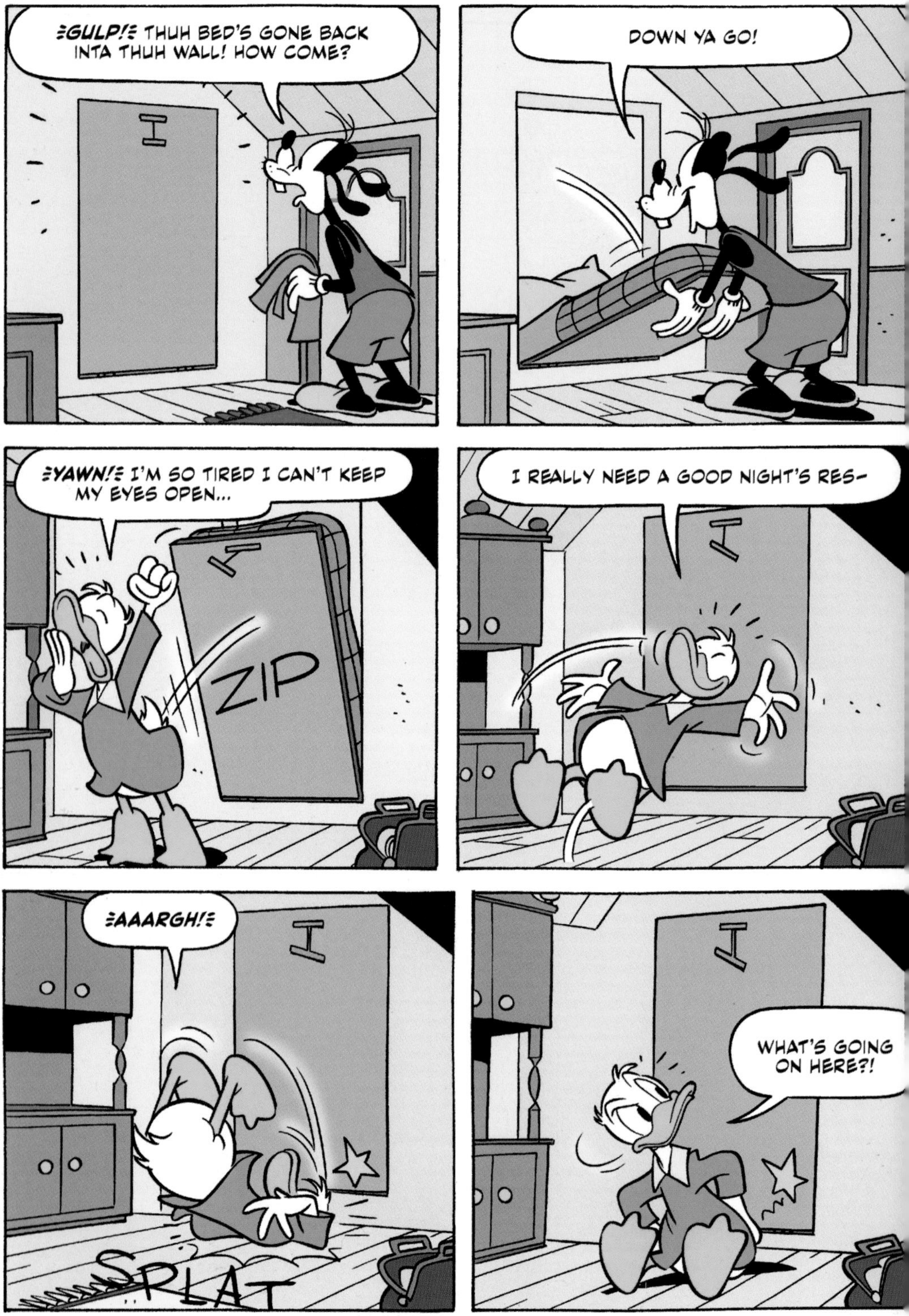

=GULP!= THUH BED'S GONE BACK INTA THUH WALL! HOW COME?
DOWN YA GO!
=YAWN!= I'M SO TIRED I CAN'T KEEP MY EYES OPEN...
ZIP
I REALLY NEED A GOOD NIGHT'S RES-
=AAARGH!=
SPLAT
WHAT'S GOING ON HERE?!

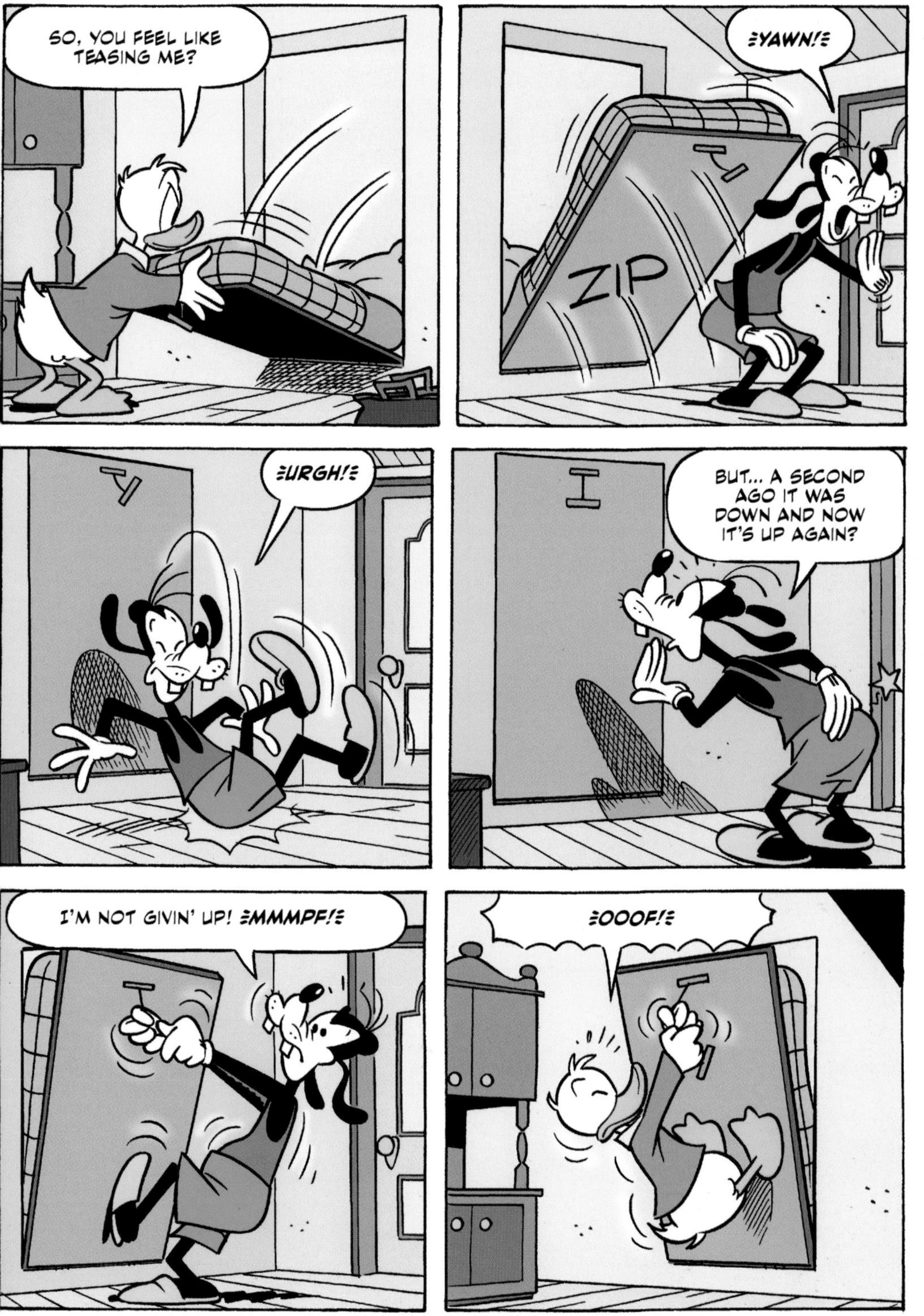
SO, YOU FEEL LIKE TEASING ME?
ZIP
=YAWN!=
=URGH!=
BUT... A SECOND AGO IT WAS DOWN AND NOW IT'S UP AGAIN?
I'M NOT GIVIN' UP! =MMMPF!=
=OOOF!=

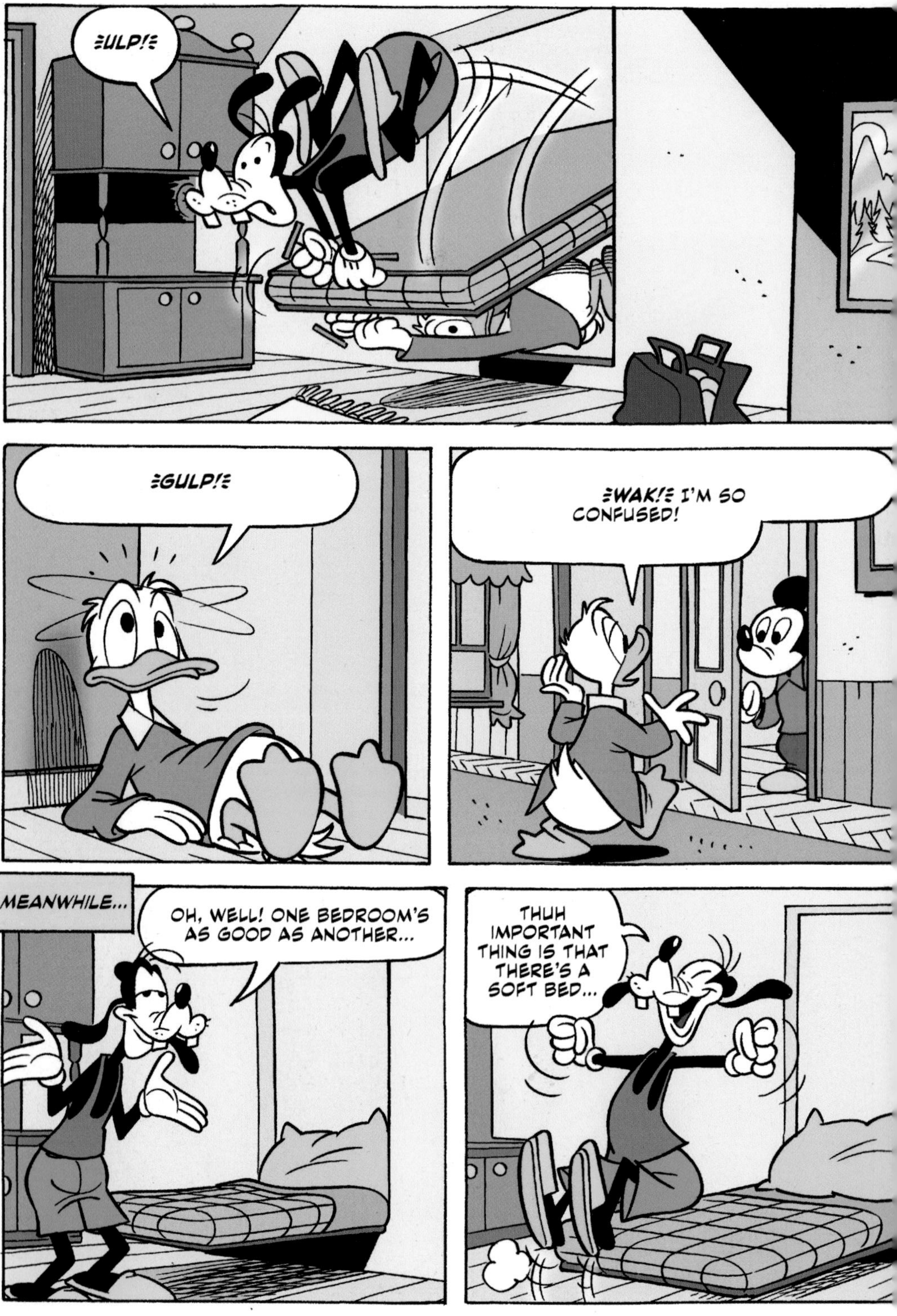

≋ULP!≋
≋GULP!≋
≋WAK!≋ I'M SO CONFUSED!
MEANWHILE...
OH, WELL! ONE BEDROOM'S AS GOOD AS ANOTHER...
THUH IMPORTANT THING IS THAT THERE'S A SOFT BED...

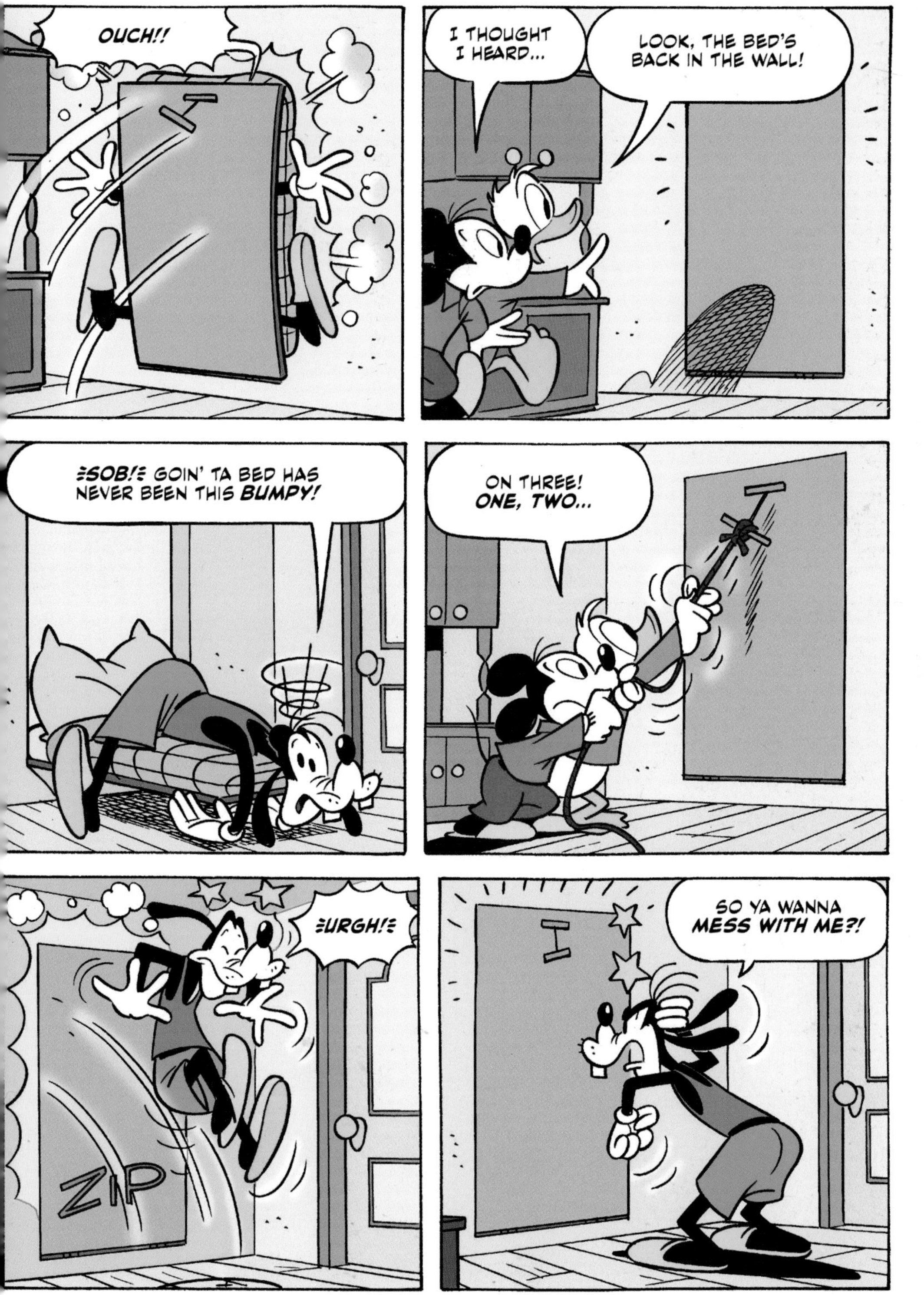
OUCH!!
I THOUGHT I HEARD...
LOOK, THE BED'S BACK IN THE WALL!
≡SOB!≡ GOIN' TA BED HAS NEVER BEEN THIS BUMPY!
ON THREE! ONE, TWO...
≡URGH!≡
ZIP
SO YA WANNA MESS WITH ME?!

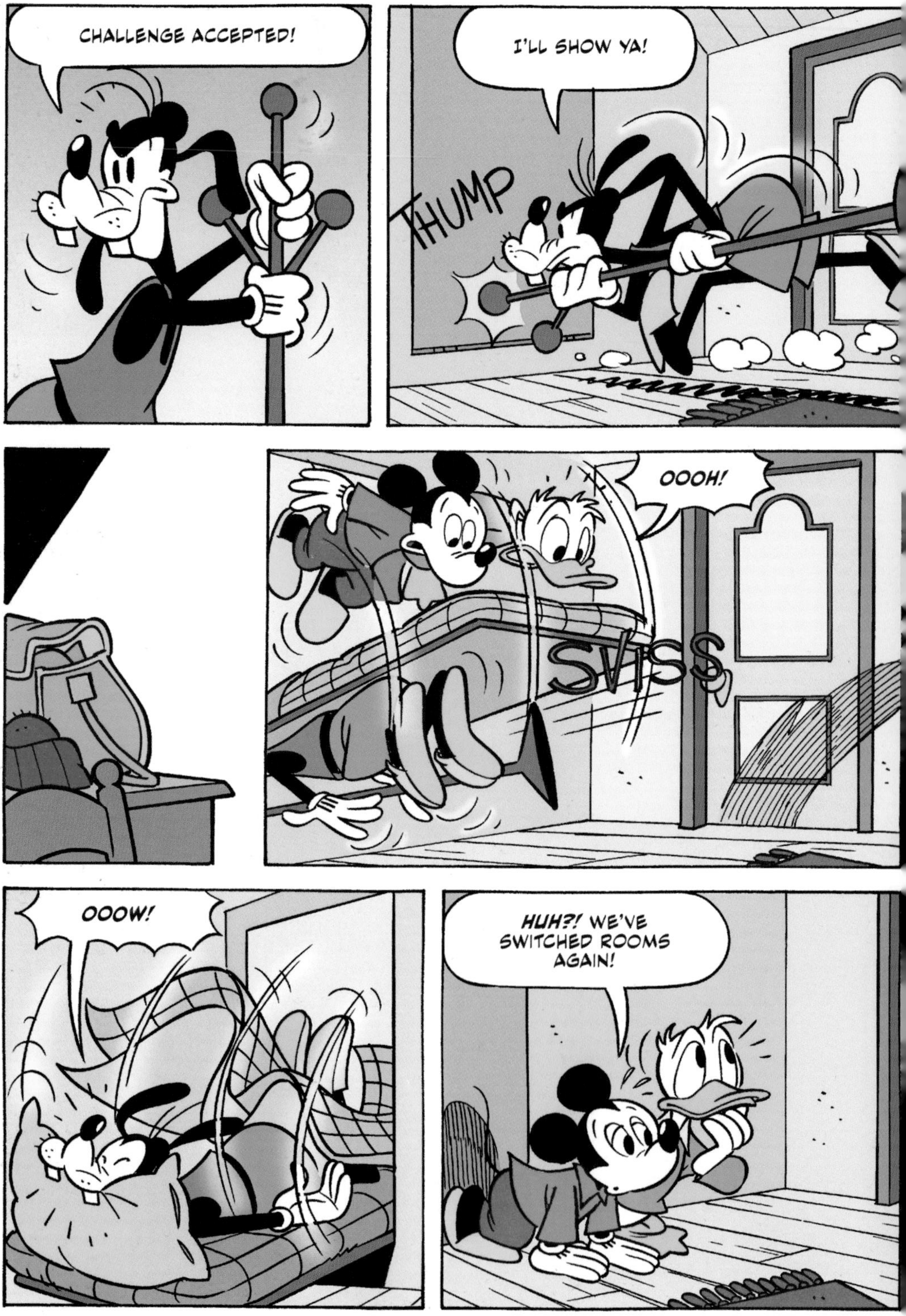
CHALLENGE ACCEPTED!
I'LL SHOW YA!
THUMP
OOOH!
SVISS
OOOW!
HUH?! WE'VE SWITCHED ROOMS AGAIN!

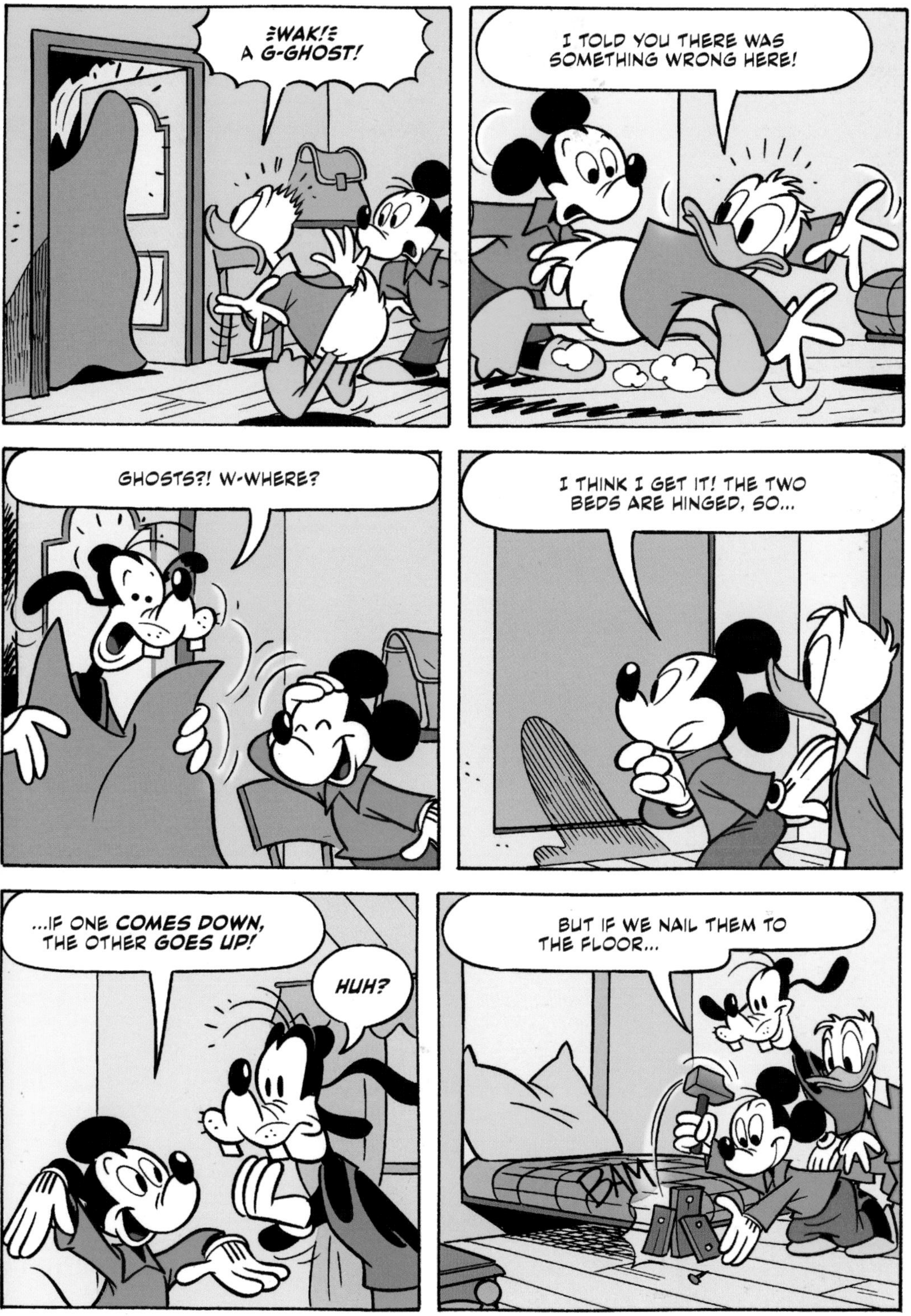

=WAK!= A G-GHOST!
I TOLD YOU THERE WAS SOMETHING WRONG HERE!
GHOSTS?! W-WHERE?
I THINK I GET IT! THE TWO BEDS ARE HINGED, SO...
...IF ONE COMES DOWN, THE OTHER GOES UP!
HUH?
BUT IF WE NAIL THEM TO THE FLOOR...
BAM

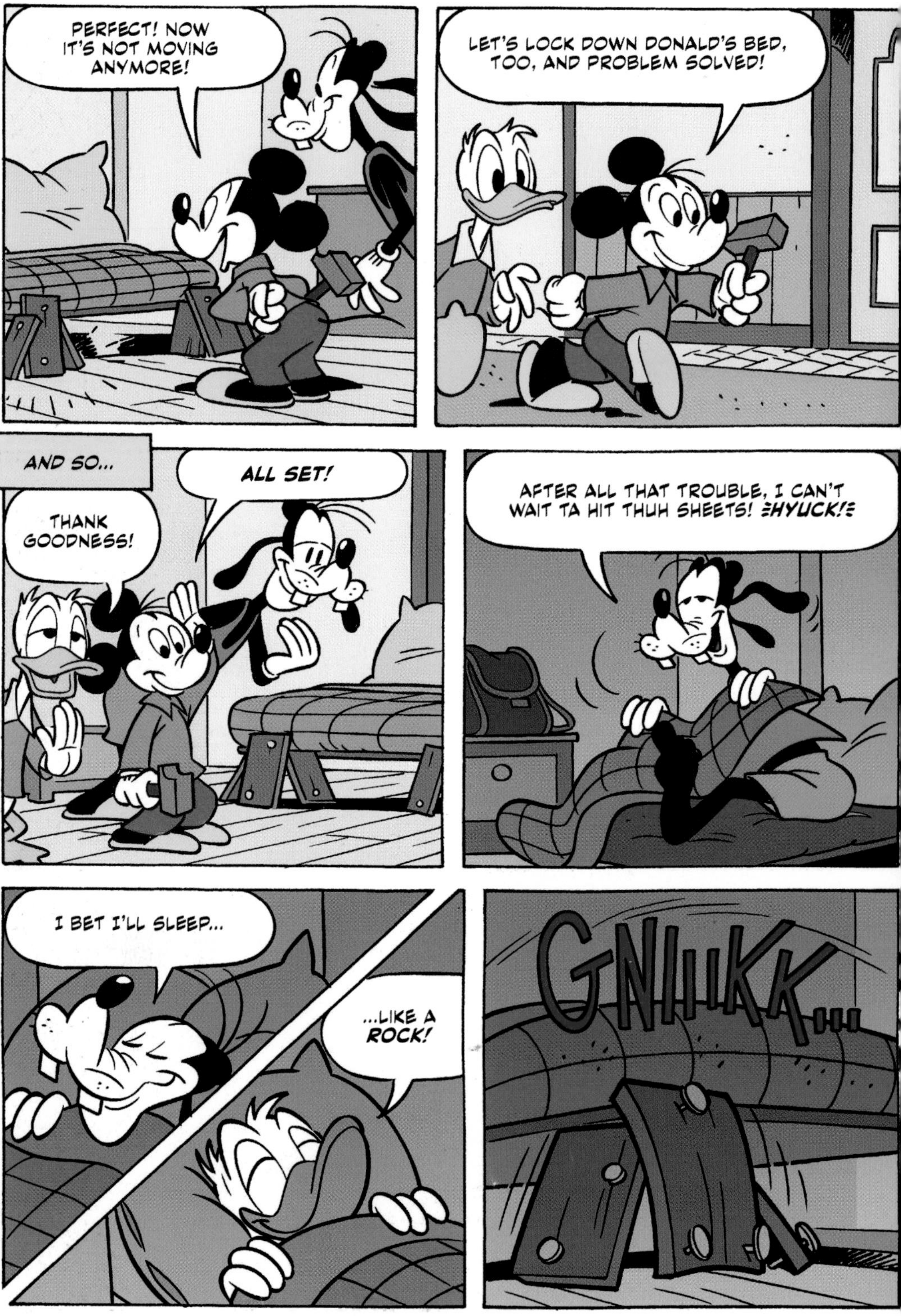
PERFECT! NOW IT'S NOT MOVING ANYMORE!
LET'S LOCK DOWN DONALD'S BED, TOO, AND PROBLEM SOLVED!
AND SO...
ALL SET!
THANK GOODNESS!
AFTER ALL THAT TROUBLE, I CAN'T WAIT TA HIT THUH SHEETS! HYUCK!
I BET I'LL SLEEP...
...LIKE A ROCK!
GNIIIKK...

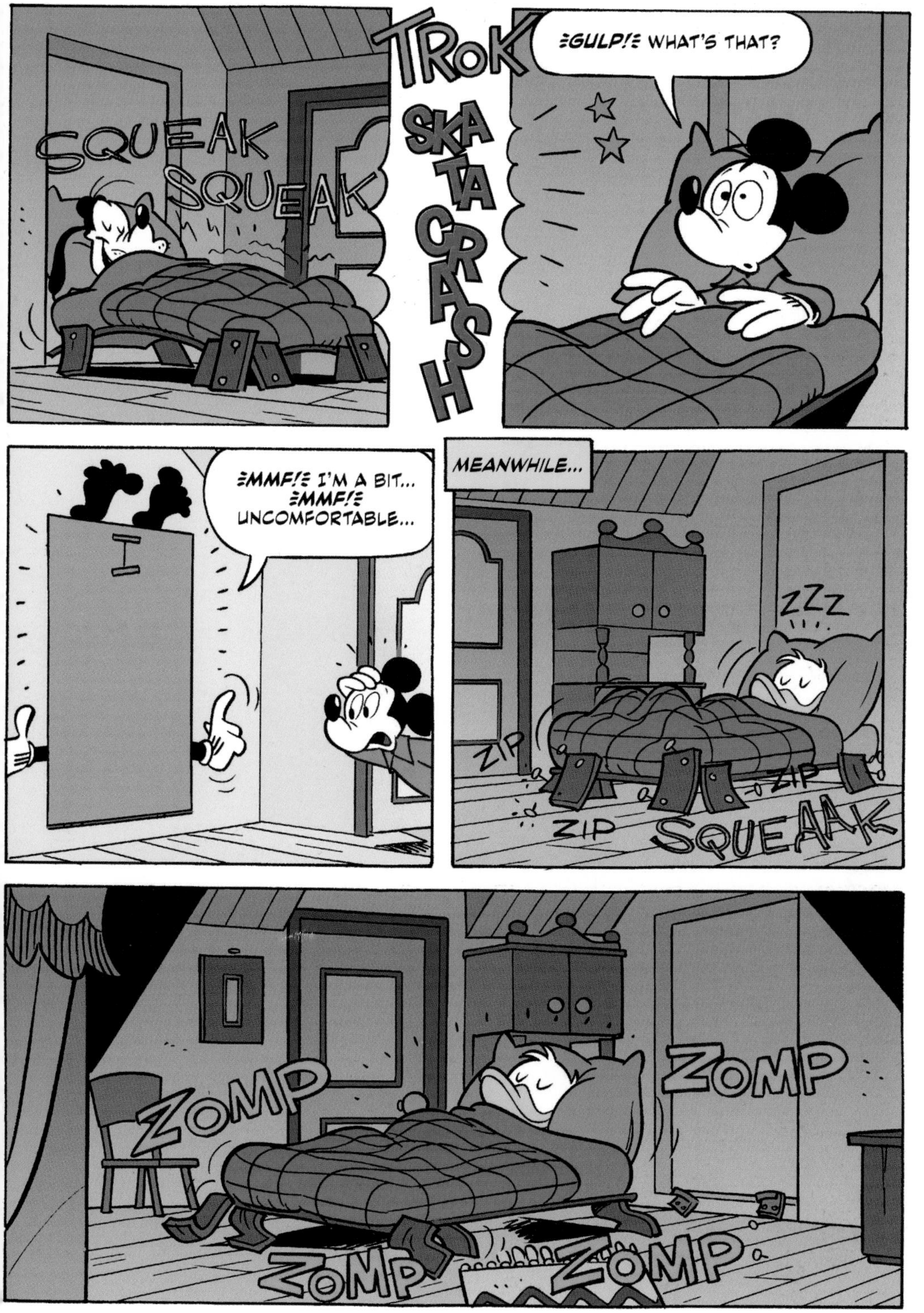
SQUEAK
SQUEAK
TROK
SKATACRASH
GULP! WHAT'S THAT?
MMF! I'M A BIT... MMF! UNCOMFORTABLE...
MEANWHILE...
ZZZ
ZIP
ZIP
ZIP
SQUEAAK
ZOMP
ZOMP
ZOMP
ZOMP

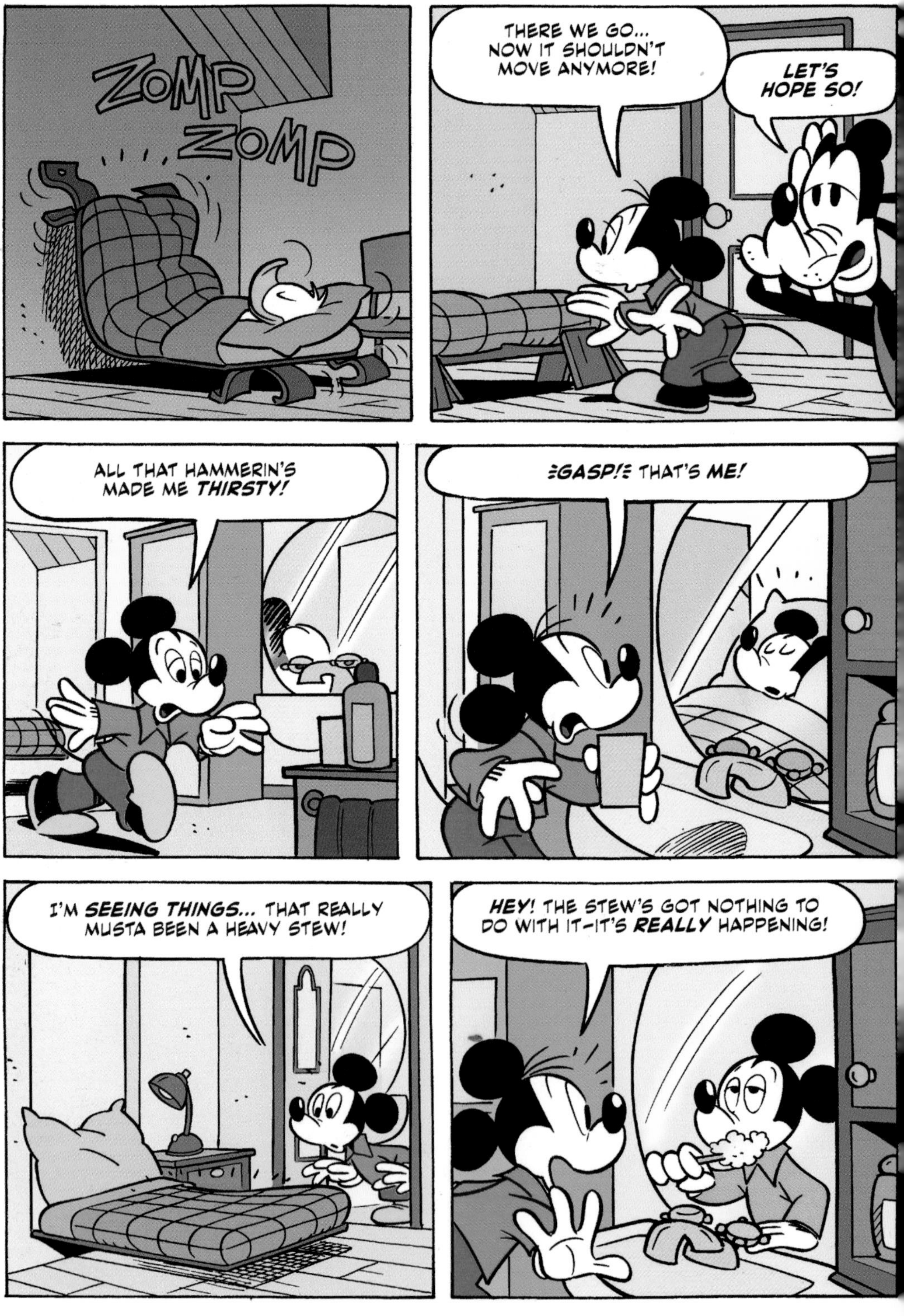
ZOMP
ZOMP
THERE WE GO... NOW IT SHOULDN'T MOVE ANYMORE!
LET'S HOPE SO!
ALL THAT HAMMERIN'S MADE ME THIRSTY!
GASP! THAT'S ME!
I'M SEEING THINGS... THAT REALLY MUSTA BEEN A HEAVY STEW!
HEY! THE STEW'S GOT NOTHING TO DO WITH IT—IT'S REALLY HAPPENING!

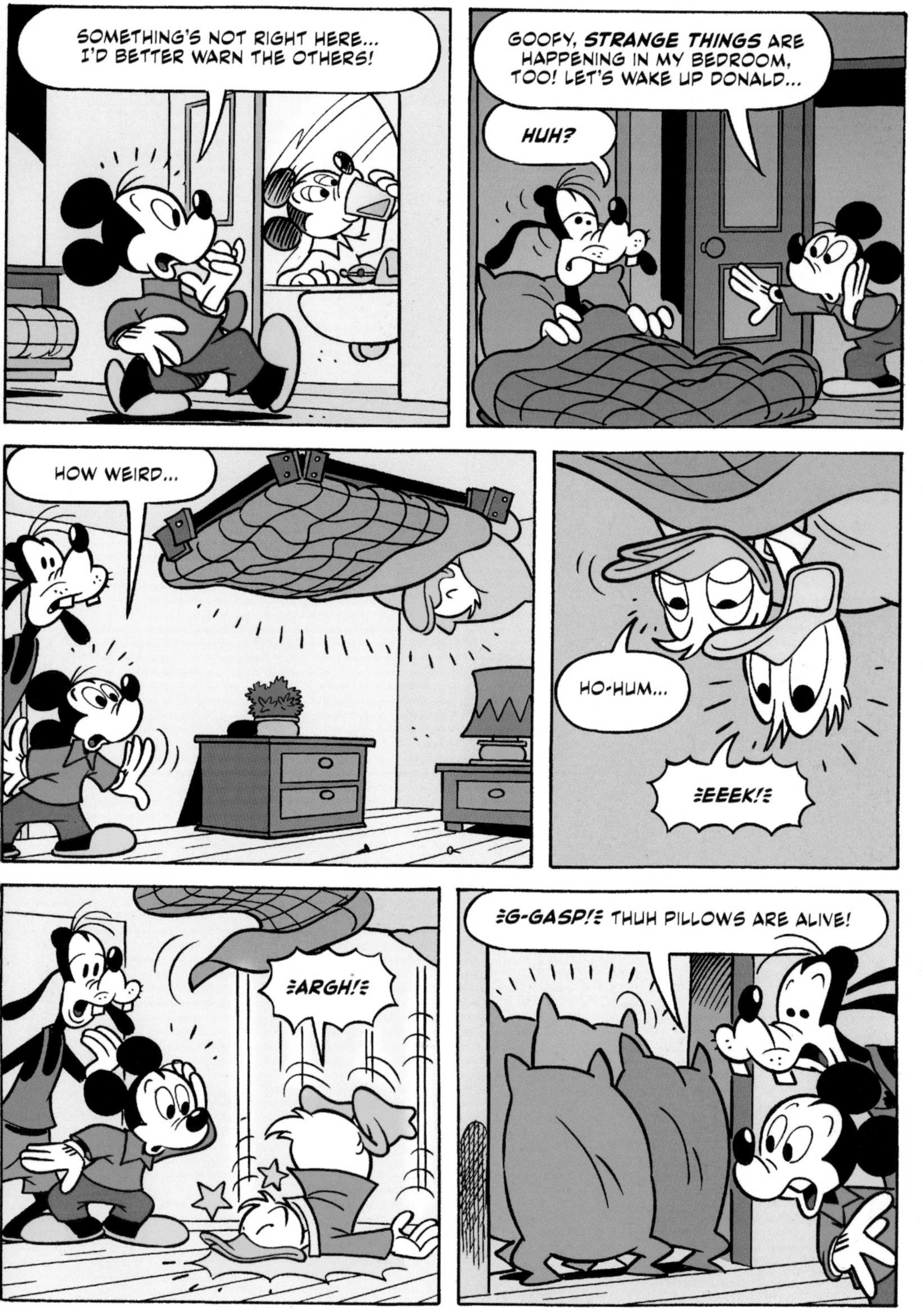
SOMETHING'S NOT RIGHT HERE... I'D BETTER WARN THE OTHERS!
GOOFY, STRANGE THINGS ARE HAPPENING IN MY BEDROOM, TOO! LET'S WAKE UP DONALD...
HUH?
HOW WEIRD...
HO-HUM...
EEEK!
ARGH!
G-GASP! THUH PILLOWS ARE ALIVE!

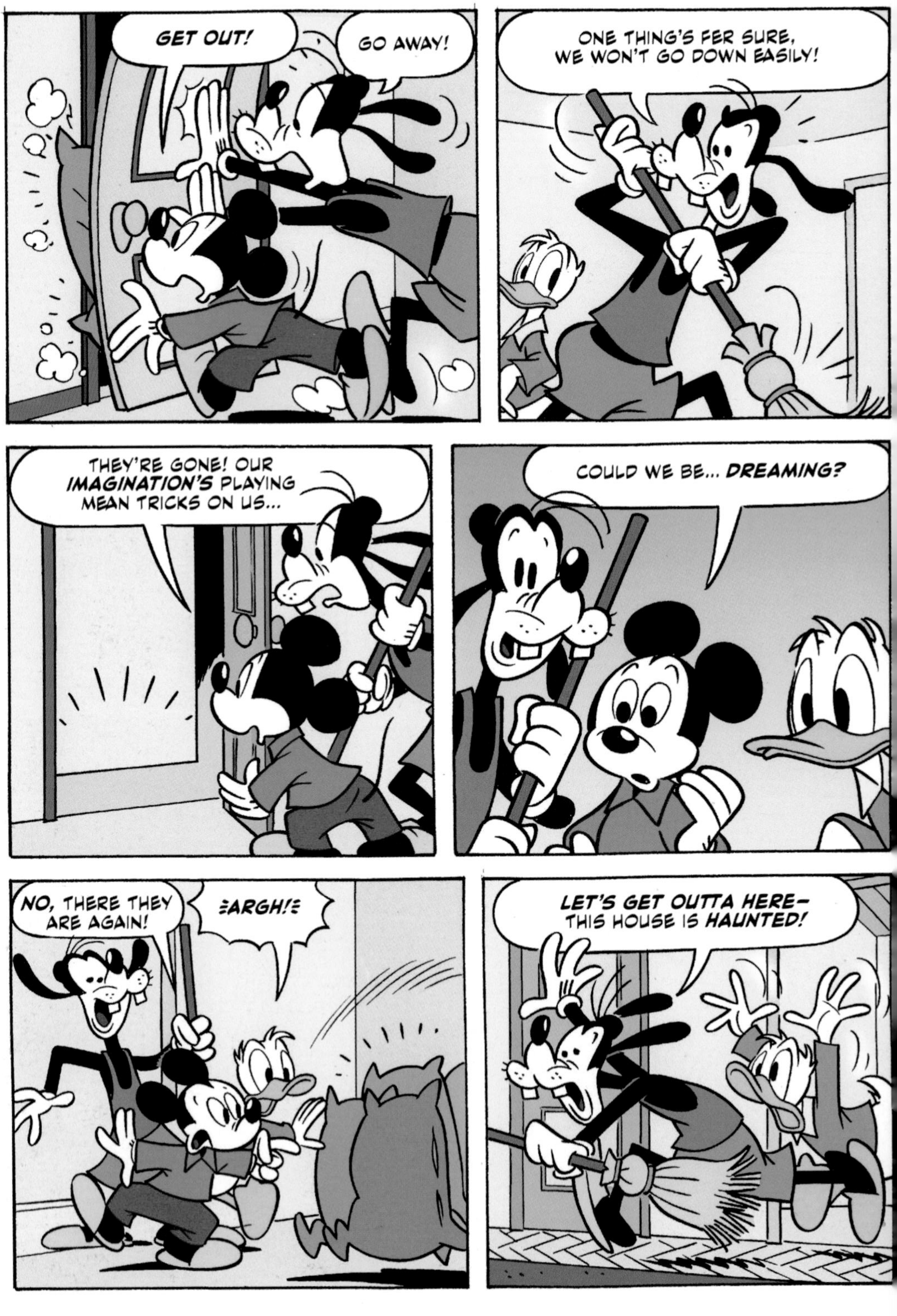
GET OUT!
GO AWAY!
ONE THING'S FER SURE, WE WON'T GO DOWN EASILY!
THEY'RE GONE! OUR IMAGINATION'S PLAYING MEAN TRICKS ON US...
COULD WE BE... DREAMING?
NO, THERE THEY ARE AGAIN!
ARGH!
LET'S GET OUTTA HERE— THIS HOUSE IS HAUNTED!

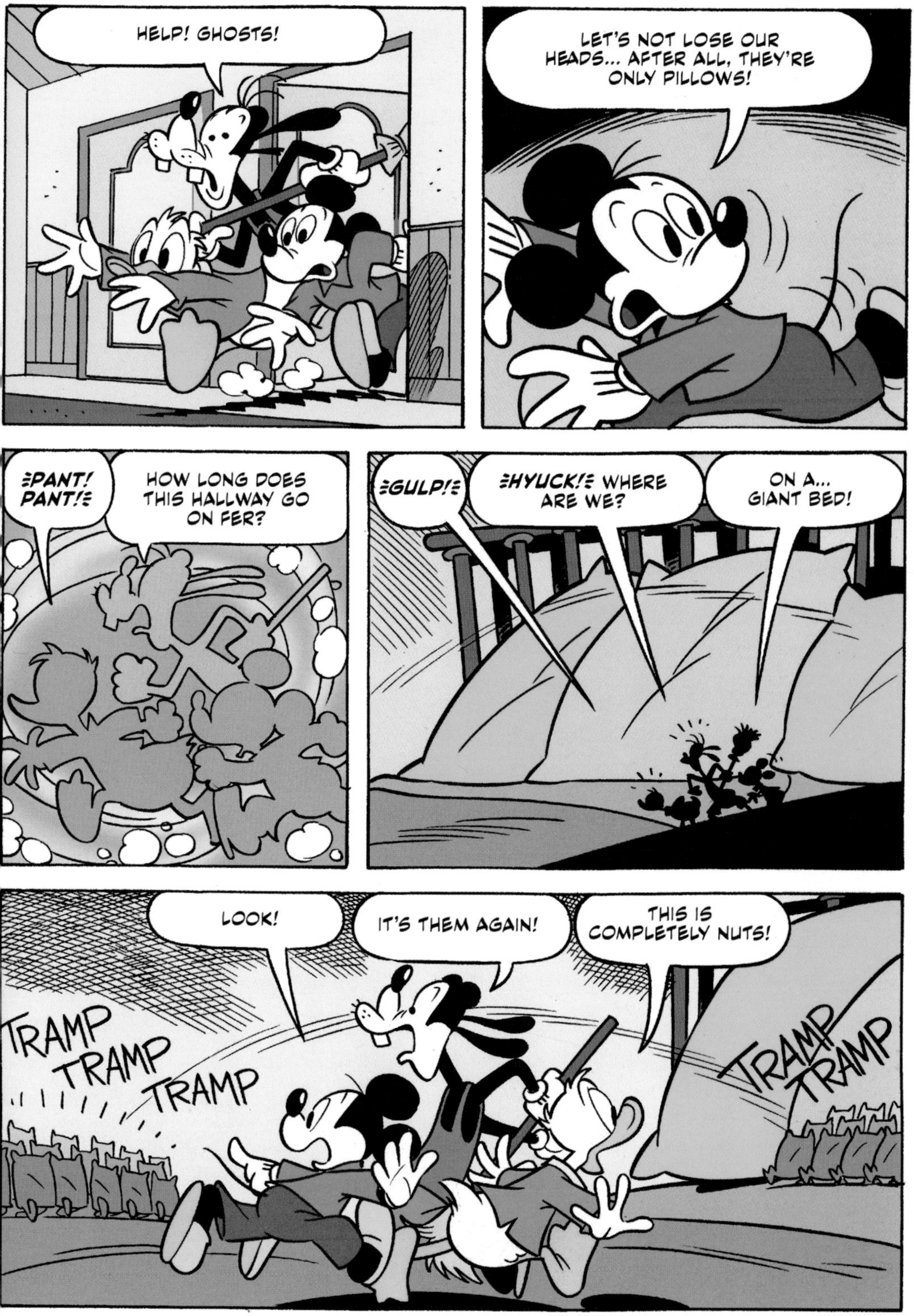
HELP! GHOSTS!
LET'S NOT LOSE OUR HEADS... AFTER ALL, THEY'RE ONLY PILLOWS!
PANT! PANT!
HOW LONG DOES THIS HALLWAY GO ON FER?
GULP!
HYUCK! WHERE ARE WE?
ON A... GIANT BED!
LOOK!
IT'S THEM AGAIN!
THIS IS COMPLETELY NUTS!
TRAMP TRAMP TRAMP
TRAMP TRAMP

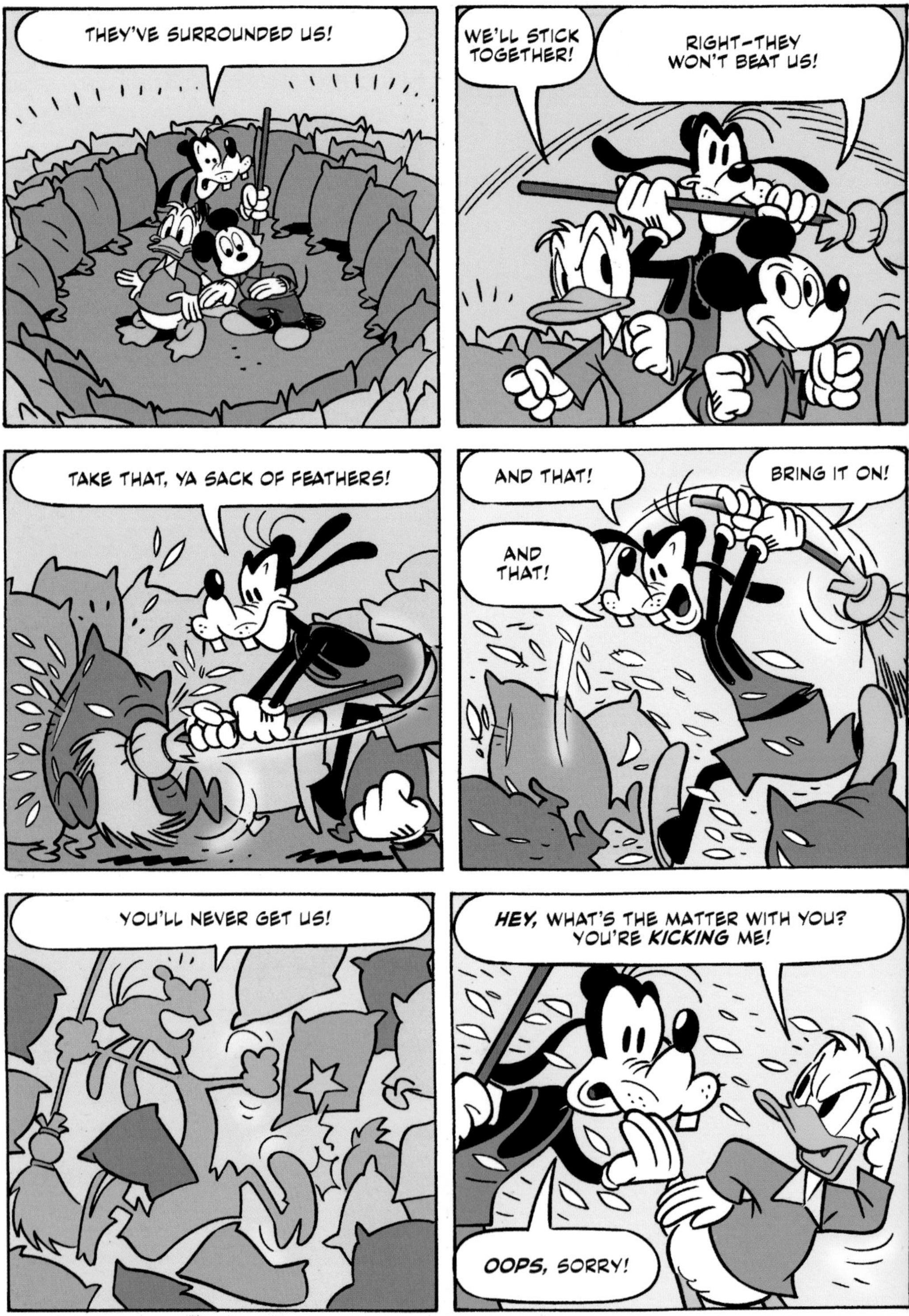
THEY'VE SURROUNDED US!
WE'LL STICK TOGETHER!
RIGHT—THEY WON'T BEAT US!
TAKE THAT, YA SACK OF FEATHERS!
AND THAT!
BRING IT ON!
AND THAT!
YOU'LL NEVER GET US!
HEY, WHAT'S THE MATTER WITH YOU? YOU'RE KICKING ME!
OOPS, SORRY!

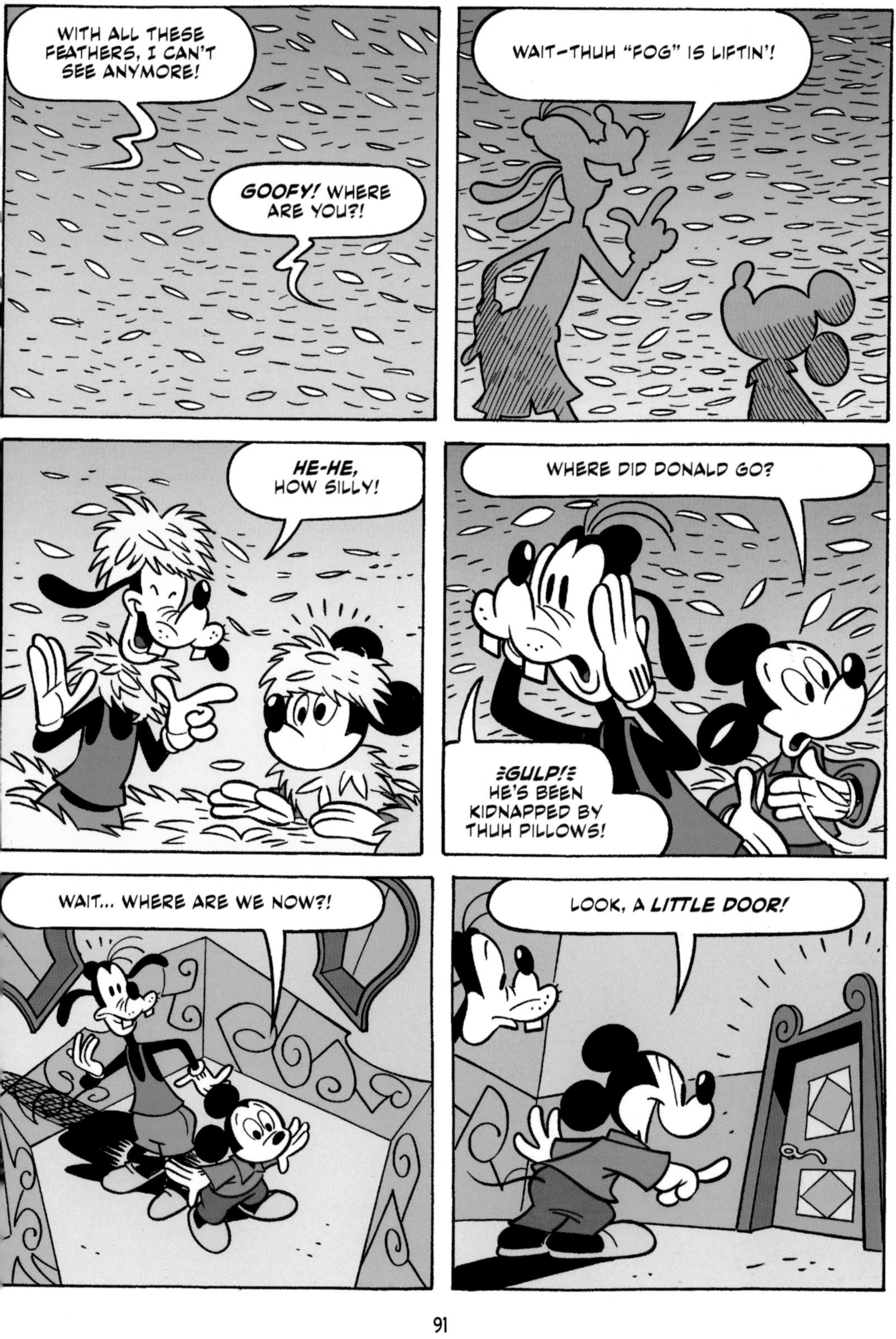
WITH ALL THESE FEATHERS, I CAN'T SEE ANYMORE!
GOOFY! WHERE ARE YOU?!
WAIT–THUH "FOG" IS LIFTIN'!
HE-HE, HOW SILLY!
WHERE DID DONALD GO?
GULP! HE'S BEEN KIDNAPPED BY THUH PILLOWS!
WAIT... WHERE ARE WE NOW?!
LOOK, A LITTLE DOOR!

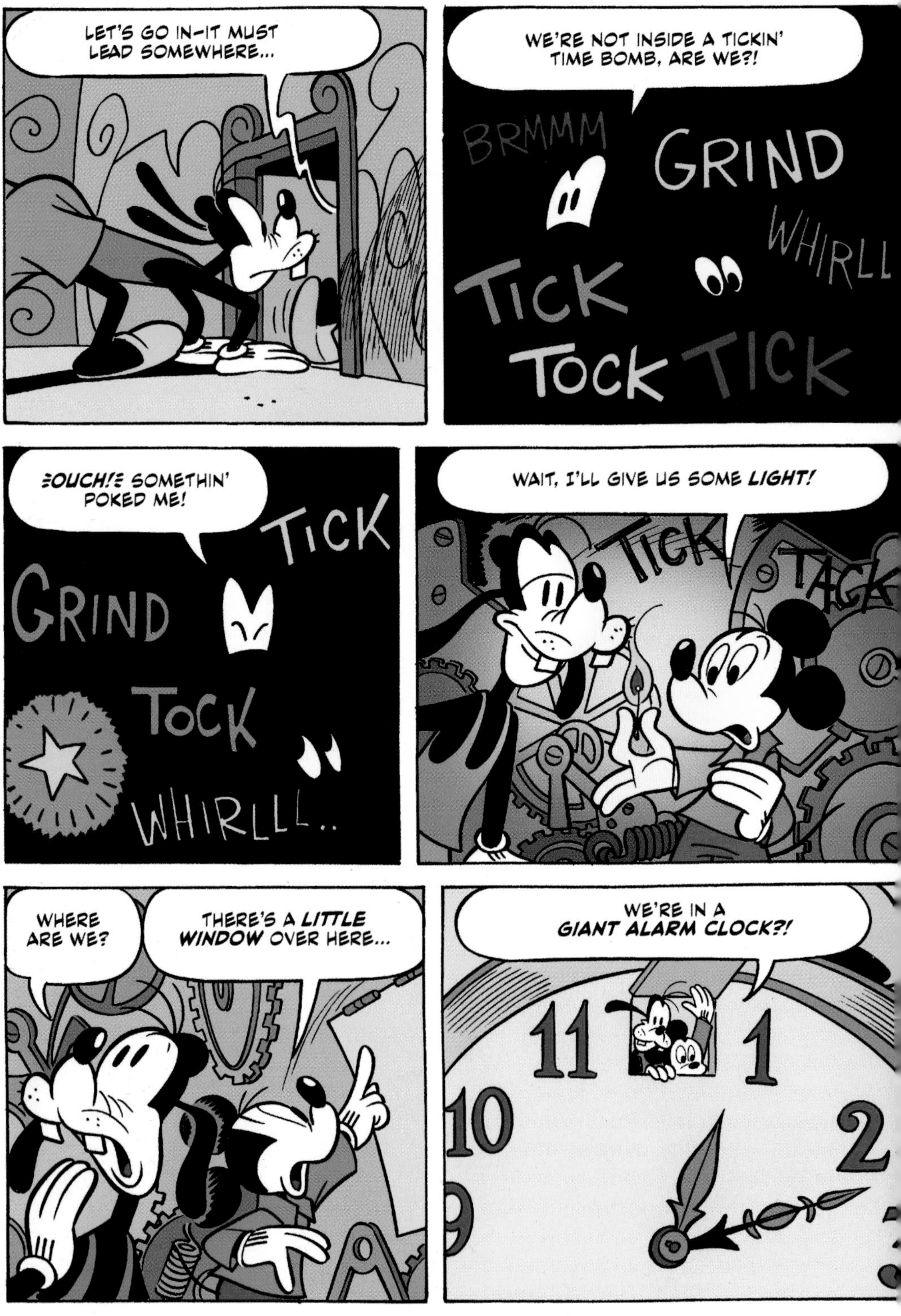
LET'S GO IN—IT MUST LEAD SOMEWHERE...
WE'RE NOT INSIDE A TICKIN' TIME BOMB, ARE WE?!
BRMMM
GRIND
WHIRLL
TICK
TOCK
TICK
OUCH! SOMETHIN' POKED ME!
TICK
GRIND
TOCK
WHIRLLL..
WAIT, I'LL GIVE US SOME LIGHT!
TICK
TACK
WHERE ARE WE?
THERE'S A LITTLE WINDOW OVER HERE...
WE'RE IN A GIANT ALARM CLOCK?!

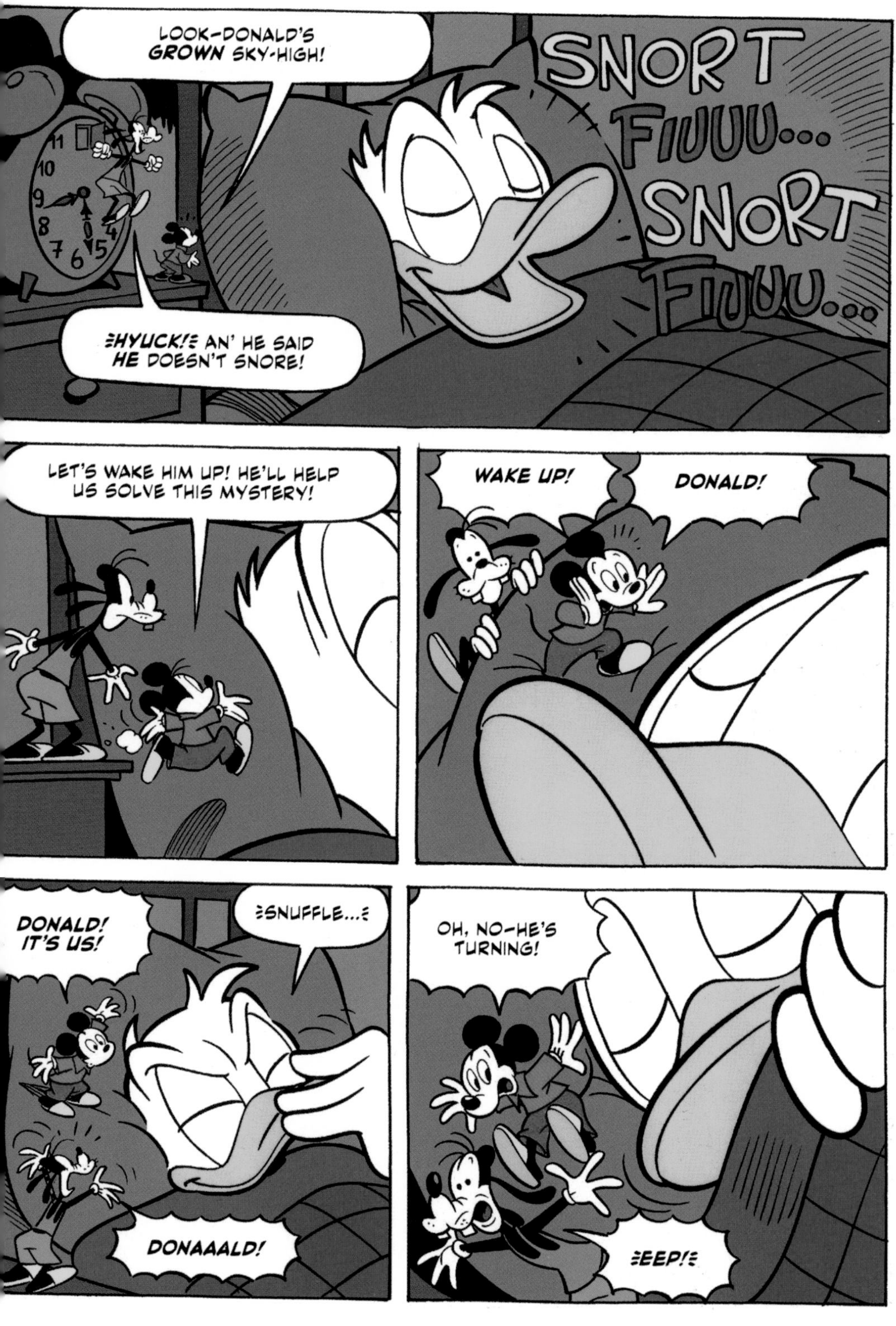

LOOK-DONALD'S GROWN SKY-HIGH!
SNORT
FIUUU...
SNORT
FIUUU...
HYUCK! AN' HE SAID HE DOESN'T SNORE!
LET'S WAKE HIM UP! HE'LL HELP US SOLVE THIS MYSTERY!
WAKE UP!
DONALD!
DONALD! IT'S US!
SNUFFLE...
DONAAALD!
OH, NO-HE'S TURNING!
EEP!

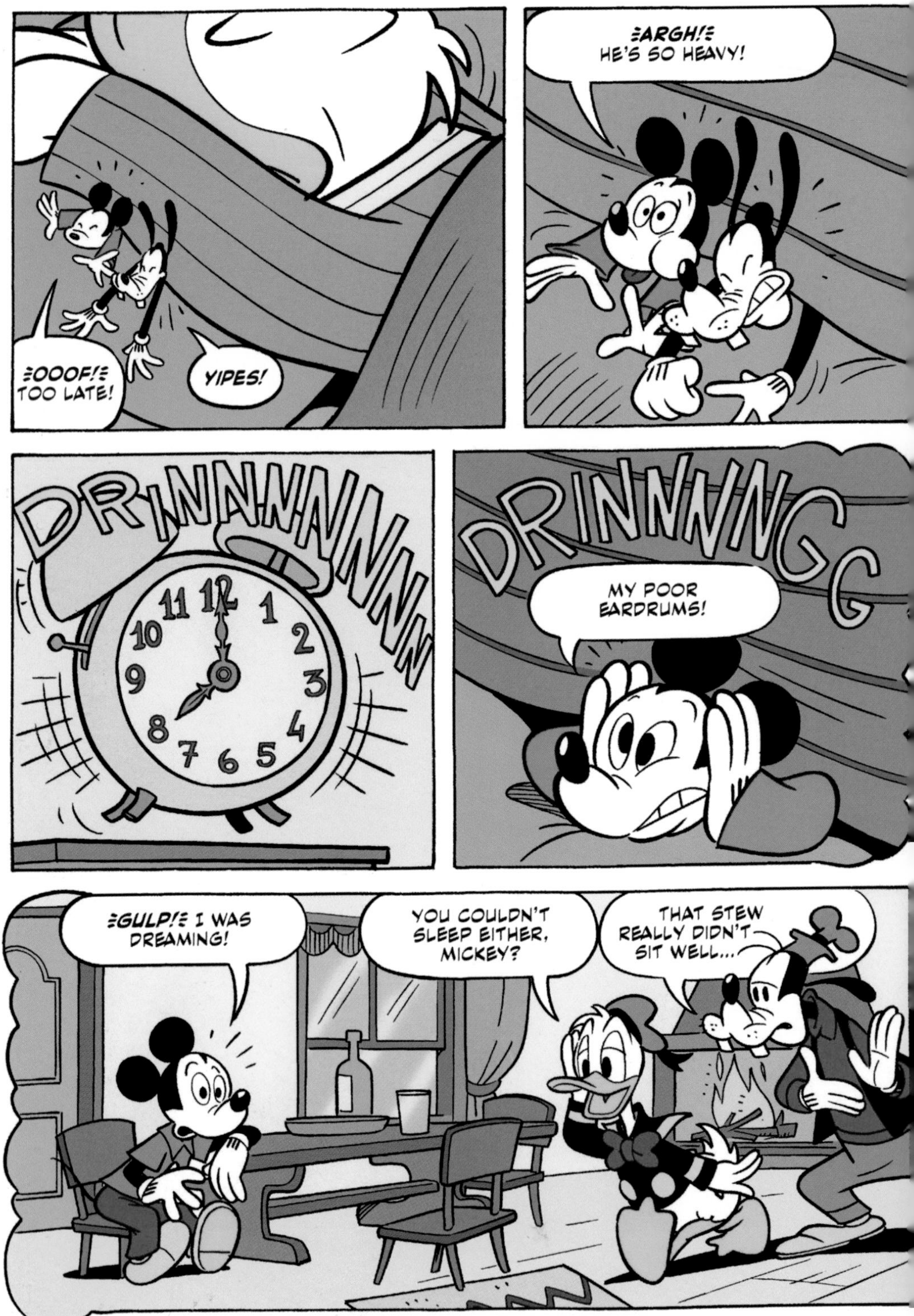

OOOF! TOO LATE!
YIPES!
ARGH! HE'S SO HEAVY!
DRINNNNNNNNNN
DRINNNNNGG
MY POOR EARDRUMS!
GULP! I WAS DREAMING!
YOU COULDN'T SLEEP EITHER, MICKEY?
THAT STEW REALLY DIDN'T SIT WELL...

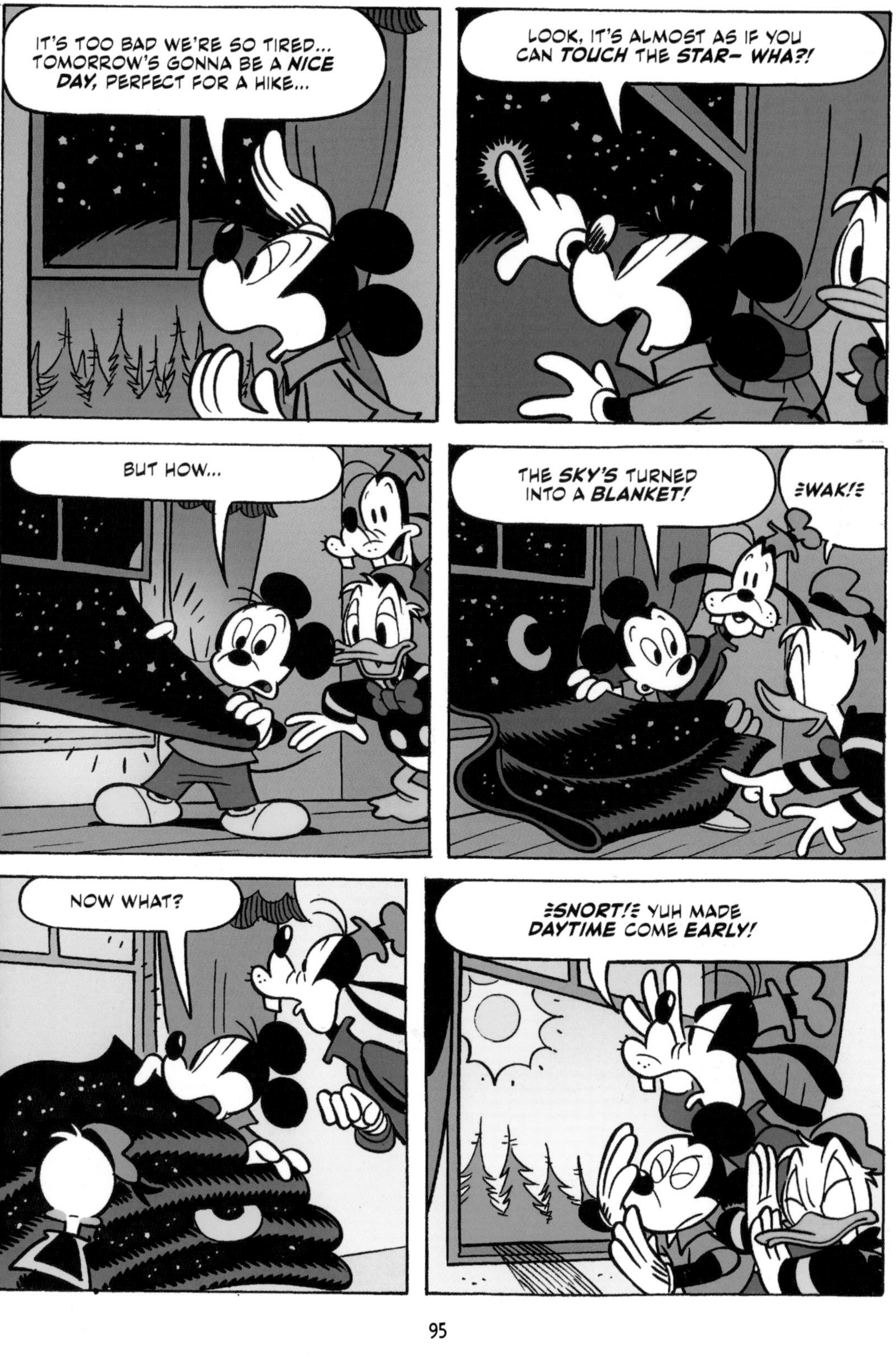
IT'S TOO BAD WE'RE SO TIRED... TOMORROW'S GONNA BE A NICE DAY, PERFECT FOR A HIKE...
LOOK, IT'S ALMOST AS IF YOU CAN TOUCH THE STAR– WHA?!
BUT HOW...
THE SKY'S TURNED INTO A BLANKET!
WAK!
NOW WHAT?
SNORT! YUH MADE DAYTIME COME EARLY!

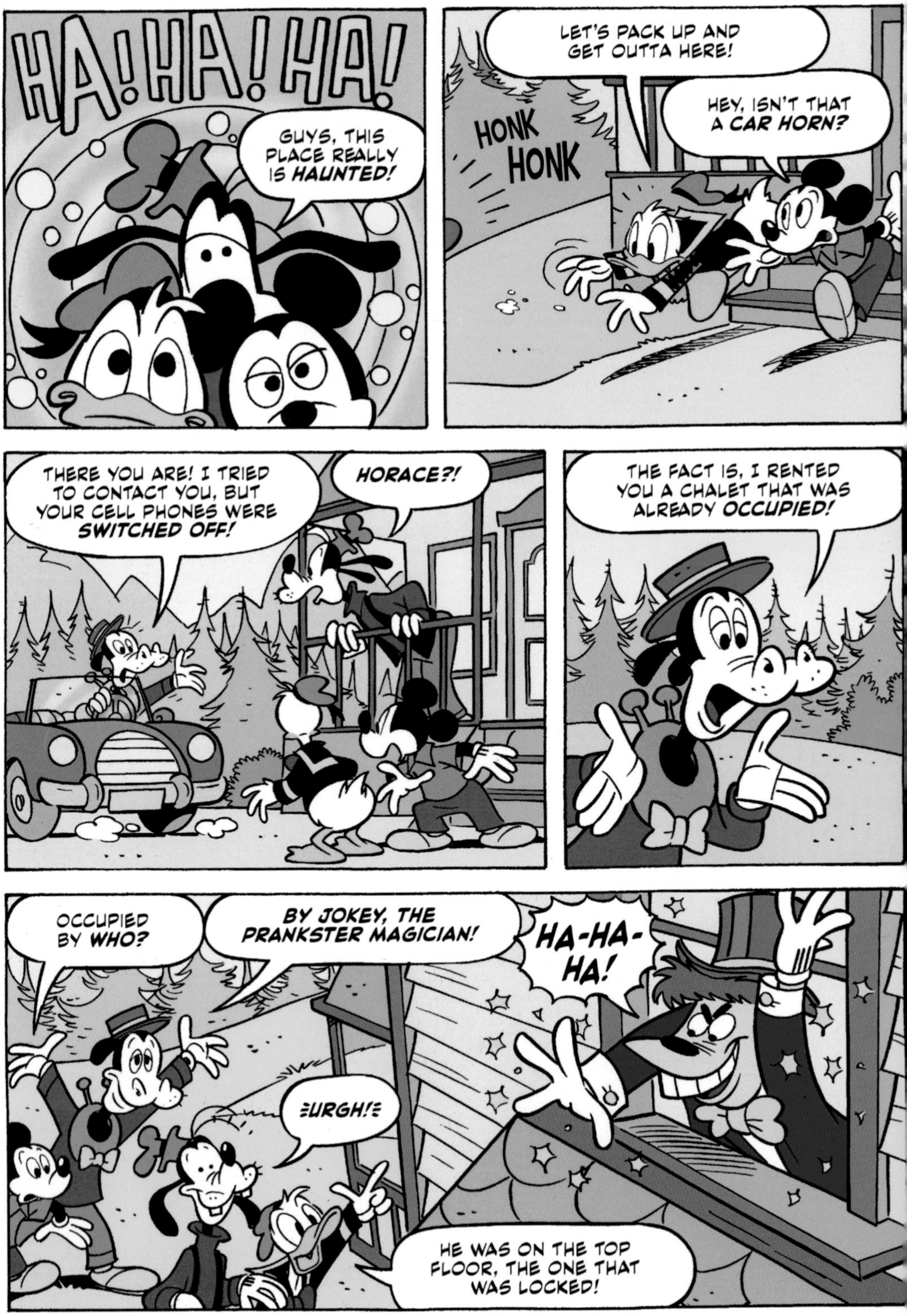
HA! HA! HA!
GUYS, THIS PLACE REALLY IS HAUNTED!
LET'S PACK UP AND GET OUTTA HERE!
HONK HONK
HEY, ISN'T THAT A CAR HORN?
THERE YOU ARE! I TRIED TO CONTACT YOU, BUT YOUR CELL PHONES WERE SWITCHED OFF!
HORACE?!
THE FACT IS, I RENTED YOU A CHALET THAT WAS ALREADY OCCUPIED!
OCCUPIED BY WHO?
BY JOKEY, THE PRANKSTER MAGICIAN!
HA-HA-HA!
URGH!
HE WAS ON THE TOP FLOOR, THE ONE THAT WAS LOCKED!

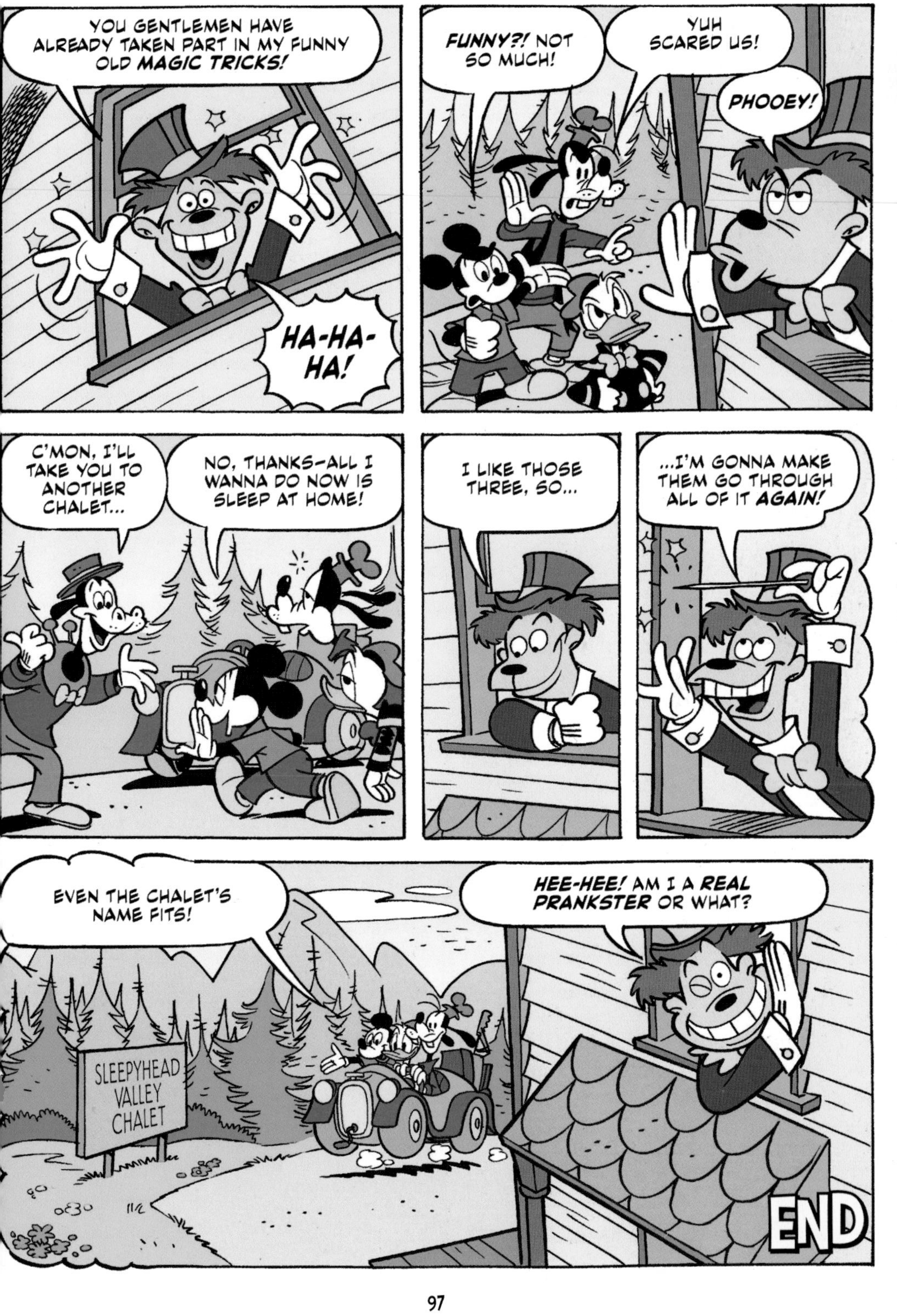
YOU GENTLEMEN HAVE ALREADY TAKEN PART IN MY FUNNY OLD MAGIC TRICKS!
HA-HA-HA!
FUNNY?! NOT SO MUCH!
YUH SCARED US!
PHOOEY!
C'MON, I'LL TAKE YOU TO ANOTHER CHALET...
NO, THANKS—ALL I WANNA DO NOW IS SLEEP AT HOME!
I LIKE THOSE THREE, SO...
...I'M GONNA MAKE THEM GO THROUGH ALL OF IT AGAIN!
EVEN THE CHALET'S NAME FITS!
HEE-HEE! AM I A REAL PRANKSTER OR WHAT?
SLEEPYHEAD VALLEY CHALET
END

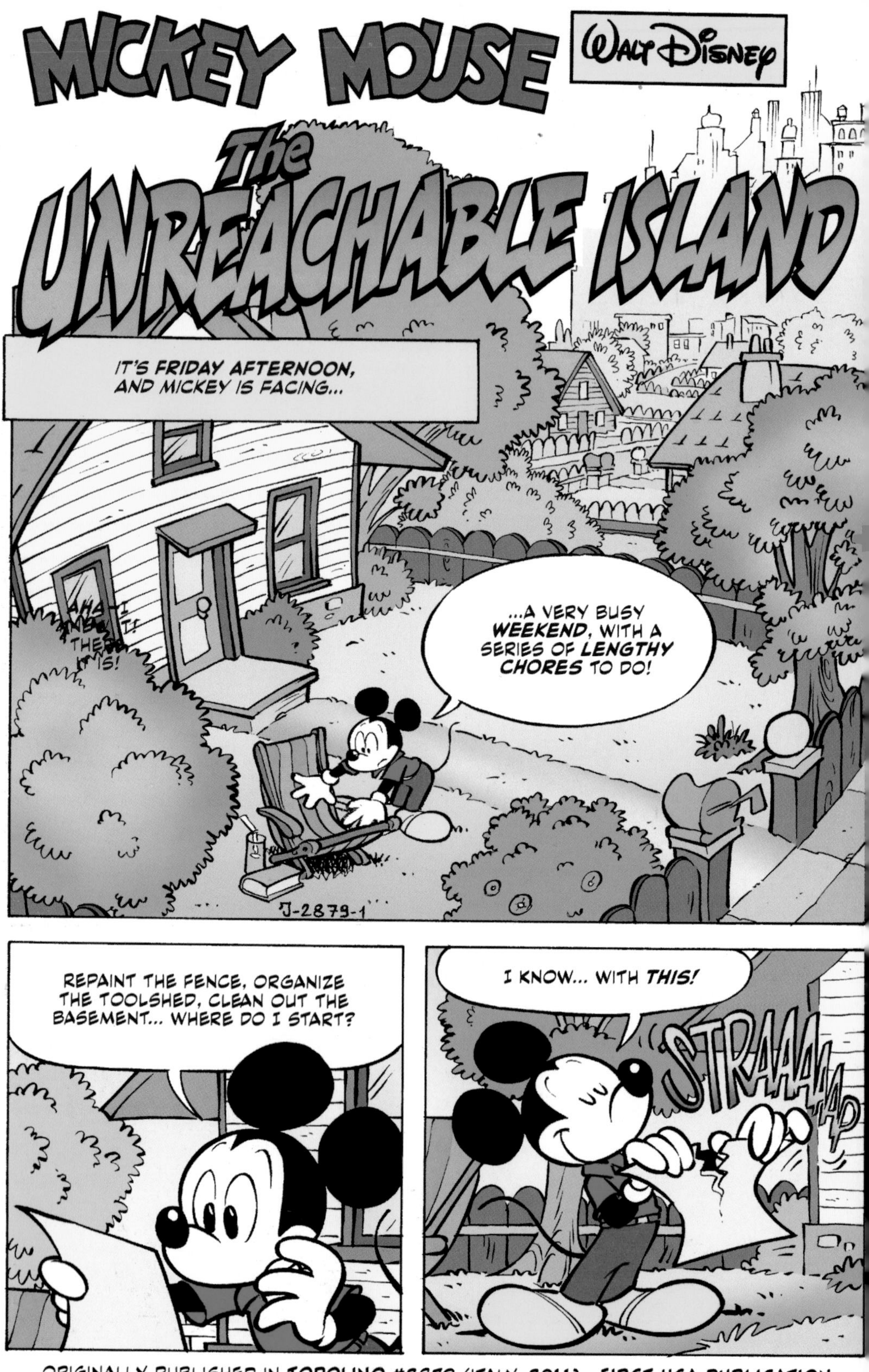
MICKEY MOUSE
WALT DISNEY
The UNREACHABLE ISLAND
IT'S FRIDAY AFTERNOON, AND MICKEY IS FACING...
...A VERY BUSY WEEKEND, WITH A SERIES OF LENGTHY CHORES TO DO!
J-2879-1
REPAINT THE FENCE, ORGANIZE THE TOOLSHED, CLEAN OUT THE BASEMENT... WHERE DO I START?
I KNOW... WITH THIS!
STRAAAAAP

ORIGINALLY PUBLISHED IN **TOPOLINO #2879** (ITALY, 2011) • **FIRST USA PUBLICATION**

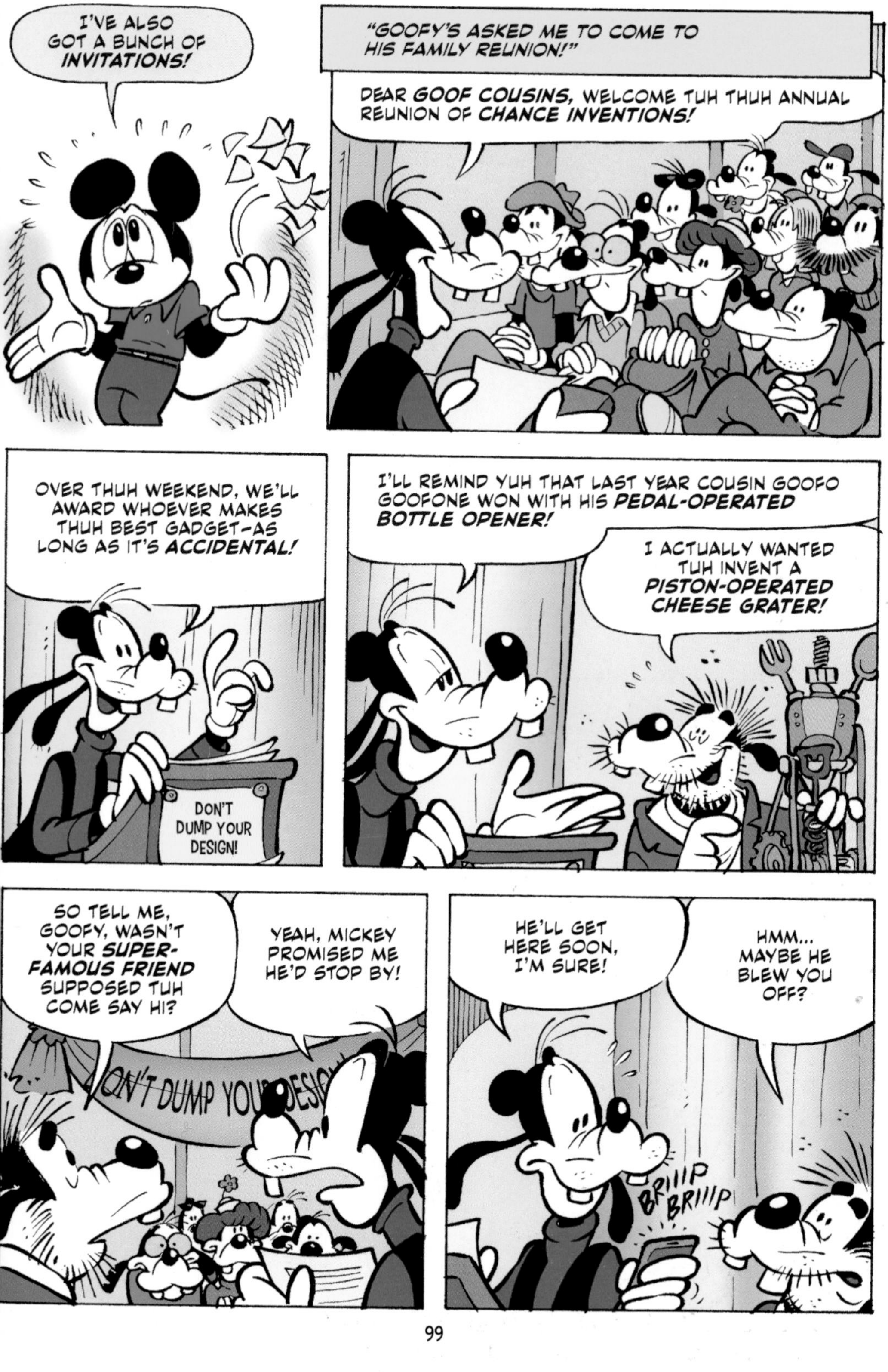

I'VE ALSO GOT A BUNCH OF INVITATIONS!
"GOOFY'S ASKED ME TO COME TO HIS FAMILY REUNION!"
DEAR GOOF COUSINS, WELCOME TUH THUH ANNUAL REUNION OF CHANCE INVENTIONS!
OVER THUH WEEKEND, WE'LL AWARD WHOEVER MAKES THUH BEST GADGET—AS LONG AS IT'S ACCIDENTAL!
DON'T DUMP YOUR DESIGN!
I'LL REMIND YUH THAT LAST YEAR COUSIN GOOFO GOOFONE WON WITH HIS PEDAL-OPERATED BOTTLE OPENER!
I ACTUALLY WANTED TUH INVENT A PISTON-OPERATED CHEESE GRATER!
SO TELL ME, GOOFY, WASN'T YOUR SUPER-FAMOUS FRIEND SUPPOSED TUH COME SAY HI?
YEAH, MICKEY PROMISED ME HE'D STOP BY!
HE'LL GET HERE SOON, I'M SURE!
HMM... MAYBE HE BLEW YOU OFF?
BRIIIP BRIIIP

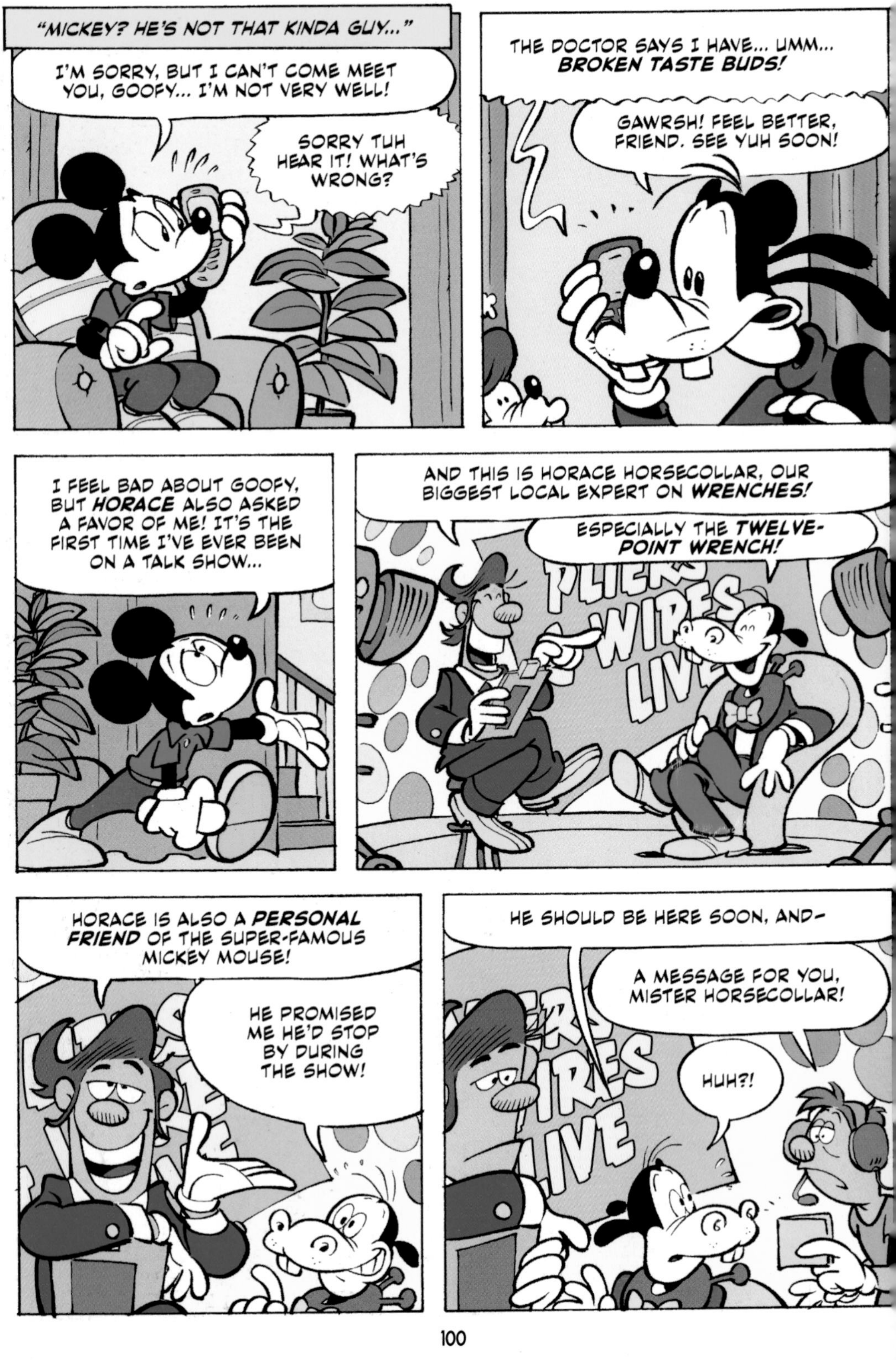
"MICKEY? HE'S NOT THAT KINDA GUY..."
I'M SORRY, BUT I CAN'T COME MEET YOU, GOOFY... I'M NOT VERY WELL!
SORRY TUH HEAR IT! WHAT'S WRONG?
THE DOCTOR SAYS I HAVE... UMM... **BROKEN TASTE BUDS!**
GAWRSH! FEEL BETTER, FRIEND. SEE YUH SOON!
I FEEL BAD ABOUT GOOFY, BUT **HORACE** ALSO ASKED A FAVOR OF ME! IT'S THE FIRST TIME I'VE EVER BEEN ON A TALK SHOW...
AND THIS IS HORACE HORSECOLLAR, OUR BIGGEST LOCAL EXPERT ON **WRENCHES!**
ESPECIALLY THE **TWELVE-POINT WRENCH!**
PLIERS WIRES LIVE
HORACE IS ALSO A **PERSONAL FRIEND** OF THE SUPER-FAMOUS MICKEY MOUSE!
HE PROMISED ME HE'D STOP BY DURING THE SHOW!
HE SHOULD BE HERE SOON, AND–
A MESSAGE FOR YOU, MISTER HORSECOLLAR!
HUH?!

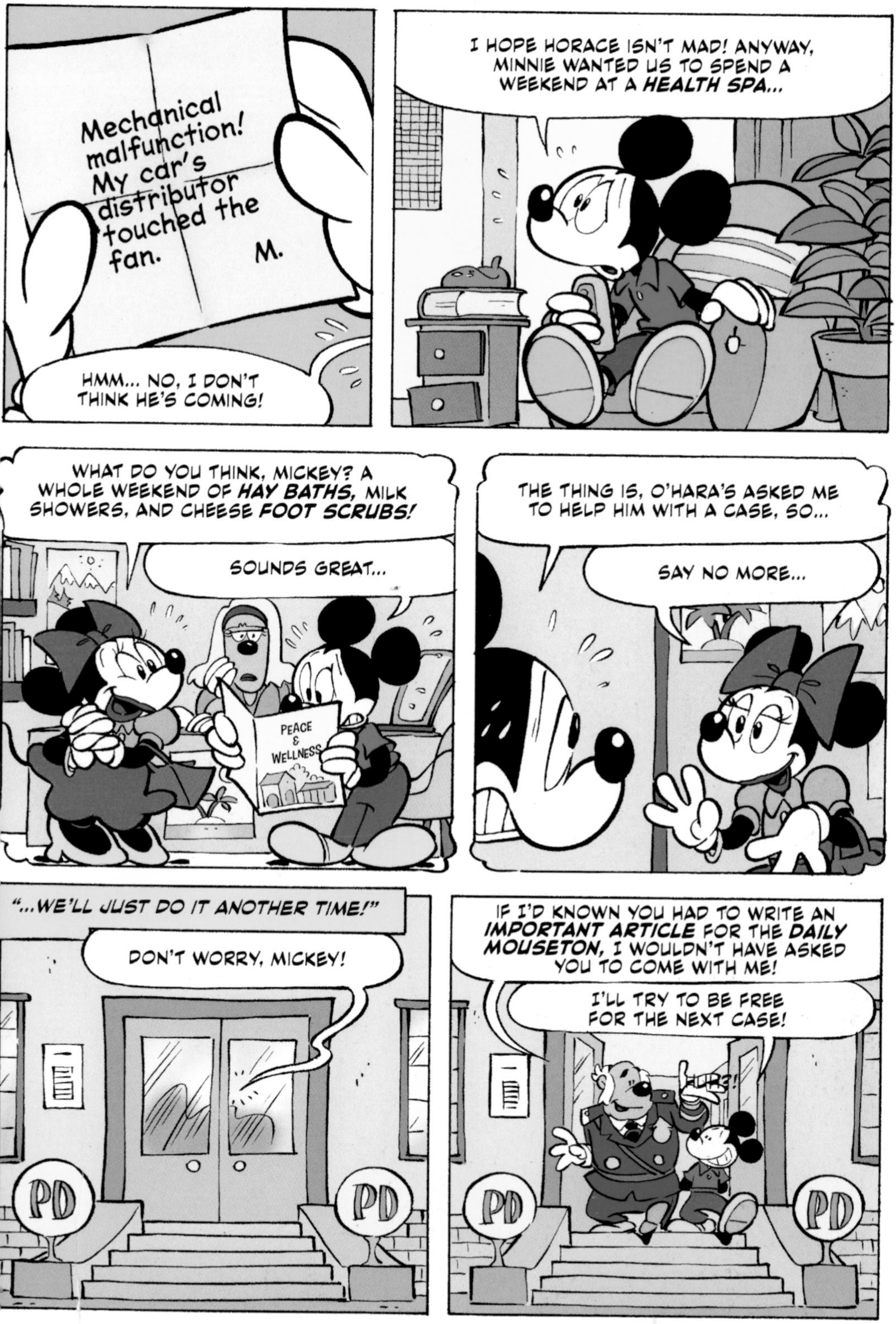
Mechanical malfunction! My car's distributor touched the fan. M.
HMM... NO, I DON'T THINK HE'S COMING!
I HOPE HORACE ISN'T MAD! ANYWAY, MINNIE WANTED US TO SPEND A WEEKEND AT A HEALTH SPA...
WHAT DO YOU THINK, MICKEY? A WHOLE WEEKEND OF HAY BATHS, MILK SHOWERS, AND CHEESE FOOT SCRUBS!
SOUNDS GREAT...
PEACE & WELLNESS
THE THING IS, O'HARA'S ASKED ME TO HELP HIM WITH A CASE, SO...
SAY NO MORE...
"...WE'LL JUST DO IT ANOTHER TIME!"
DON'T WORRY, MICKEY!
PD
PD
IF I'D KNOWN YOU HAD TO WRITE AN IMPORTANT ARTICLE FOR THE DAILY MOUSETON, I WOULDN'T HAVE ASKED YOU TO COME WITH ME!
I'LL TRY TO BE FREE FOR THE NEXT CASE!
PD
PD

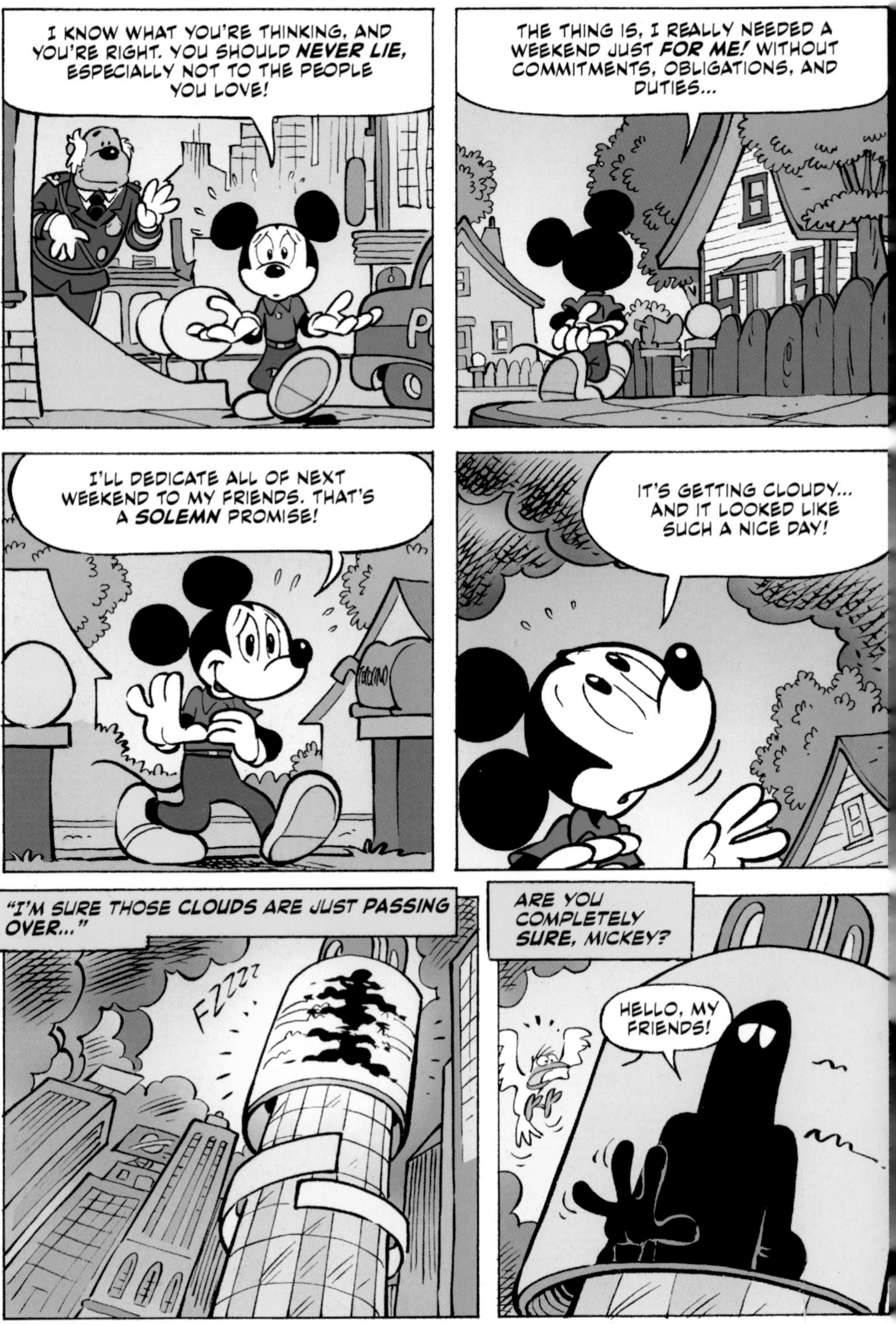
I KNOW WHAT YOU'RE THINKING, AND YOU'RE RIGHT. YOU SHOULD NEVER LIE, ESPECIALLY NOT TO THE PEOPLE YOU LOVE!
THE THING IS, I REALLY NEEDED A WEEKEND JUST FOR ME! WITHOUT COMMITMENTS, OBLIGATIONS, AND DUTIES...
I'LL DEDICATE ALL OF NEXT WEEKEND TO MY FRIENDS. THAT'S A SOLEMN PROMISE!
IT'S GETTING CLOUDY... AND IT LOOKED LIKE SUCH A NICE DAY!
"I'M SURE THOSE CLOUDS ARE JUST PASSING OVER..."
FZZZZ
ARE YOU COMPLETELY SURE, MICKEY?
HELLO, MY FRIENDS!

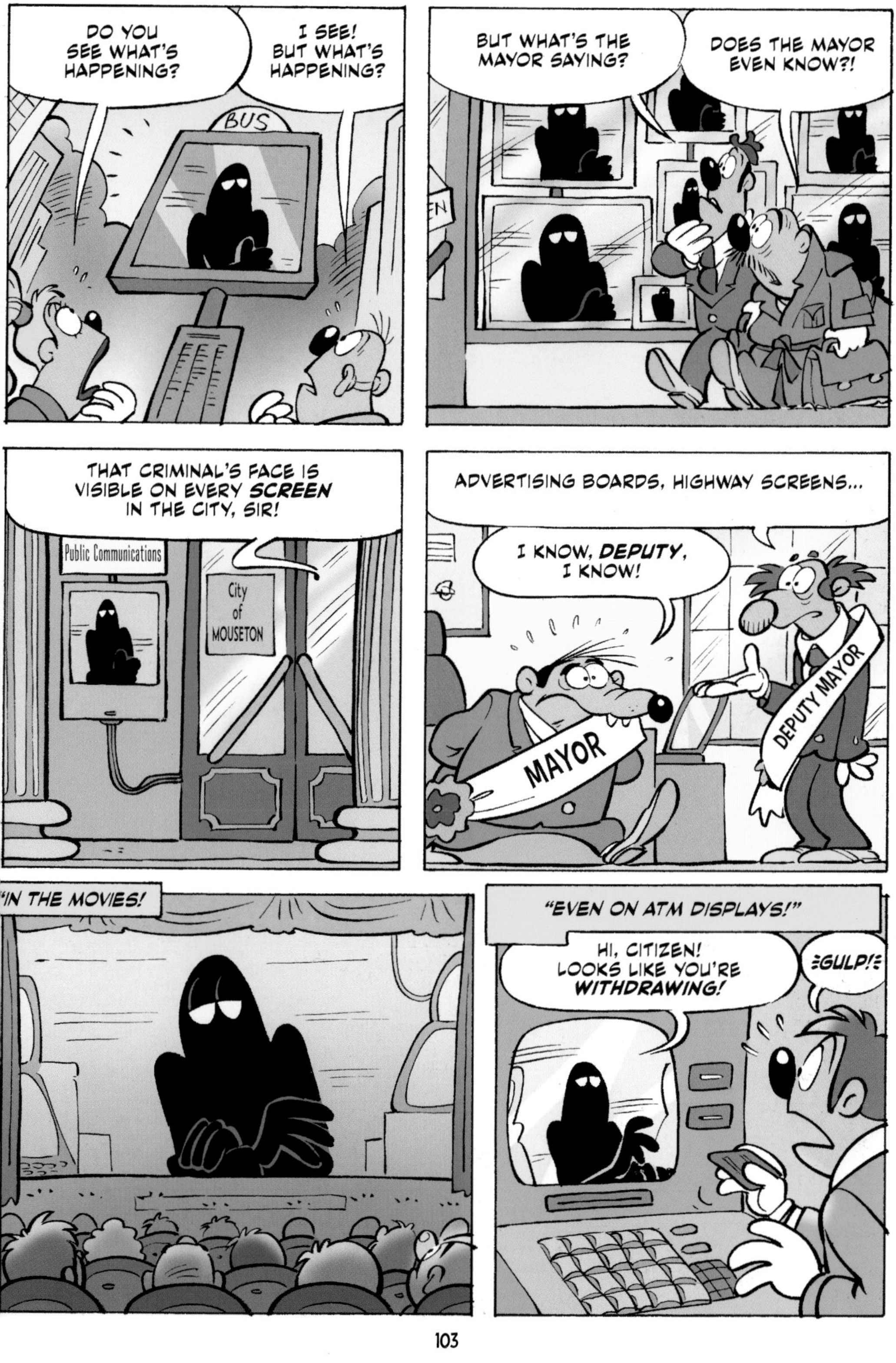
DO YOU SEE WHAT'S HAPPENING?
I SEE! BUT WHAT'S HAPPENING?
BUS
BUT WHAT'S THE MAYOR SAYING?
DOES THE MAYOR EVEN KNOW?!
THAT CRIMINAL'S FACE IS VISIBLE ON EVERY SCREEN IN THE CITY, SIR!
Public Communications
City of MOUSETON
ADVERTISING BOARDS, HIGHWAY SCREENS...
I KNOW, DEPUTY, I KNOW!
MAYOR
DEPUTY MAYOR
"IN THE MOVIES!
"EVEN ON ATM DISPLAYS!"
HI, CITIZEN! LOOKS LIKE YOU'RE WITHDRAWING!
GULP!

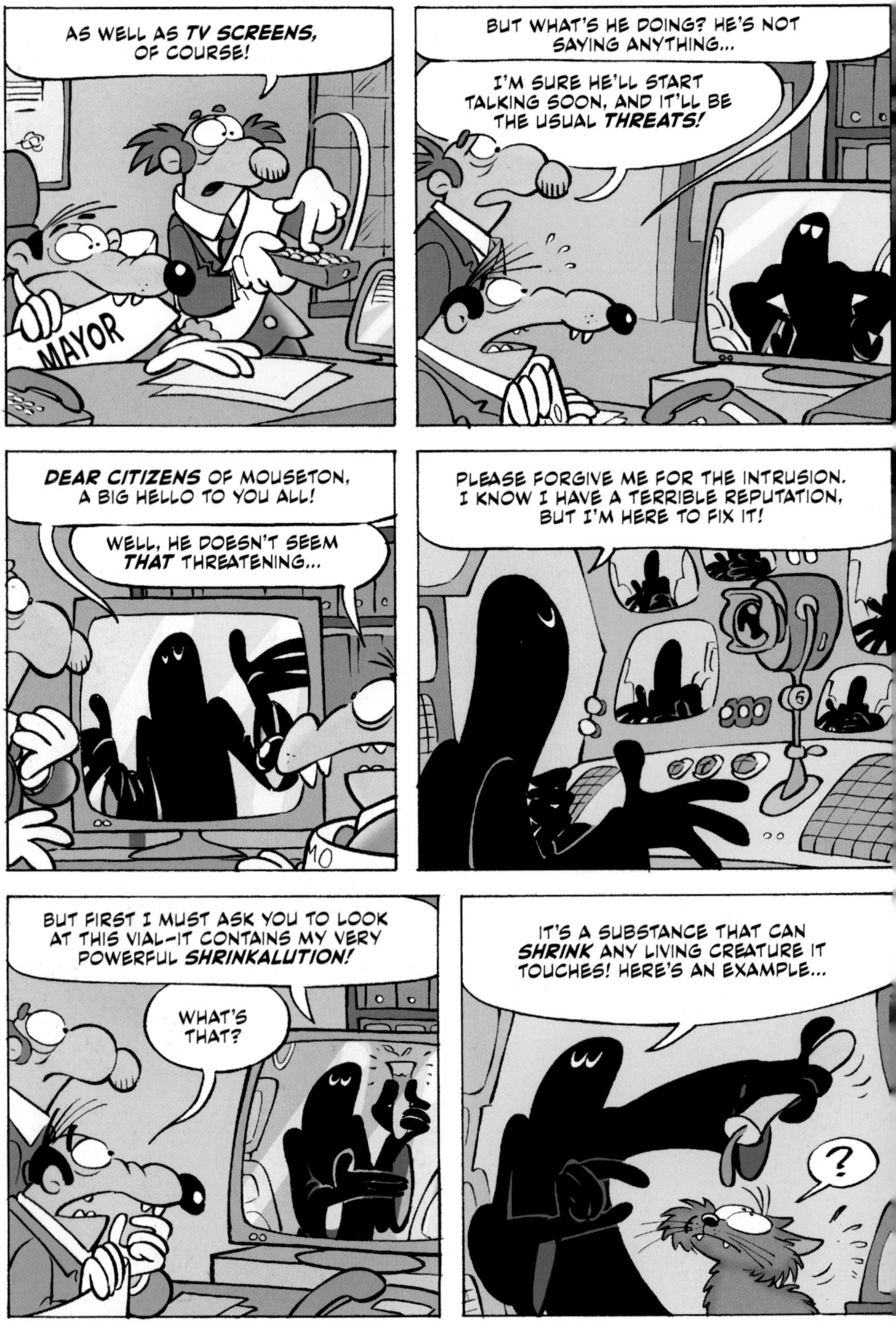
AS WELL AS TV SCREENS, OF COURSE!
MAYOR
BUT WHAT'S HE DOING? HE'S NOT SAYING ANYTHING...
I'M SURE HE'LL START TALKING SOON, AND IT'LL BE THE USUAL THREATS!
DEAR CITIZENS OF MOUSETON, A BIG HELLO TO YOU ALL!
WELL, HE DOESN'T SEEM THAT THREATENING...
PLEASE FORGIVE ME FOR THE INTRUSION. I KNOW I HAVE A TERRIBLE REPUTATION, BUT I'M HERE TO FIX IT!
BUT FIRST I MUST ASK YOU TO LOOK AT THIS VIAL—IT CONTAINS MY VERY POWERFUL SHRINKALUTION!
WHAT'S THAT?
IT'S A SUBSTANCE THAT CAN SHRINK ANY LIVING CREATURE IT TOUCHES! HERE'S AN EXAMPLE...
?

≡MEOOOW!≡

WOOOO OOOOSH

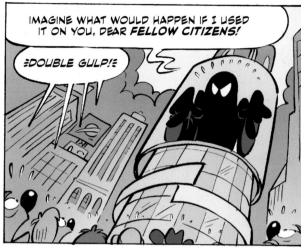

IMAGINE WHAT WOULD HAPPEN IF I USED IT ON YOU, DEAR *FELLOW CITIZENS!*

≡DOUBLE GULP!≡

THERE WAS A TIME WHEN I WOULD HAVE BLACKMAILED YOU, BUT I WANT TO COME BACK AND BE PART OF THE COMMUNITY!

FROM NOW ON, MOUSETON WON'T HAVE TO WORRY ABOUT ME ANYMORE!

I'LL DELIVER THIS LITTLE VIAL TO THE MAYOR, AND I WON'T ASK FOR ANYTHING IN EXCHANGE...

...EXCEPT FOR A *TINY LITTLE FAVOR!*

WHAT'S THAT?

GET THIS *LITTLE RAT* OUT OF MY HAIR ONCE AND FOR ALL! AND I KNOW JUST HOW...

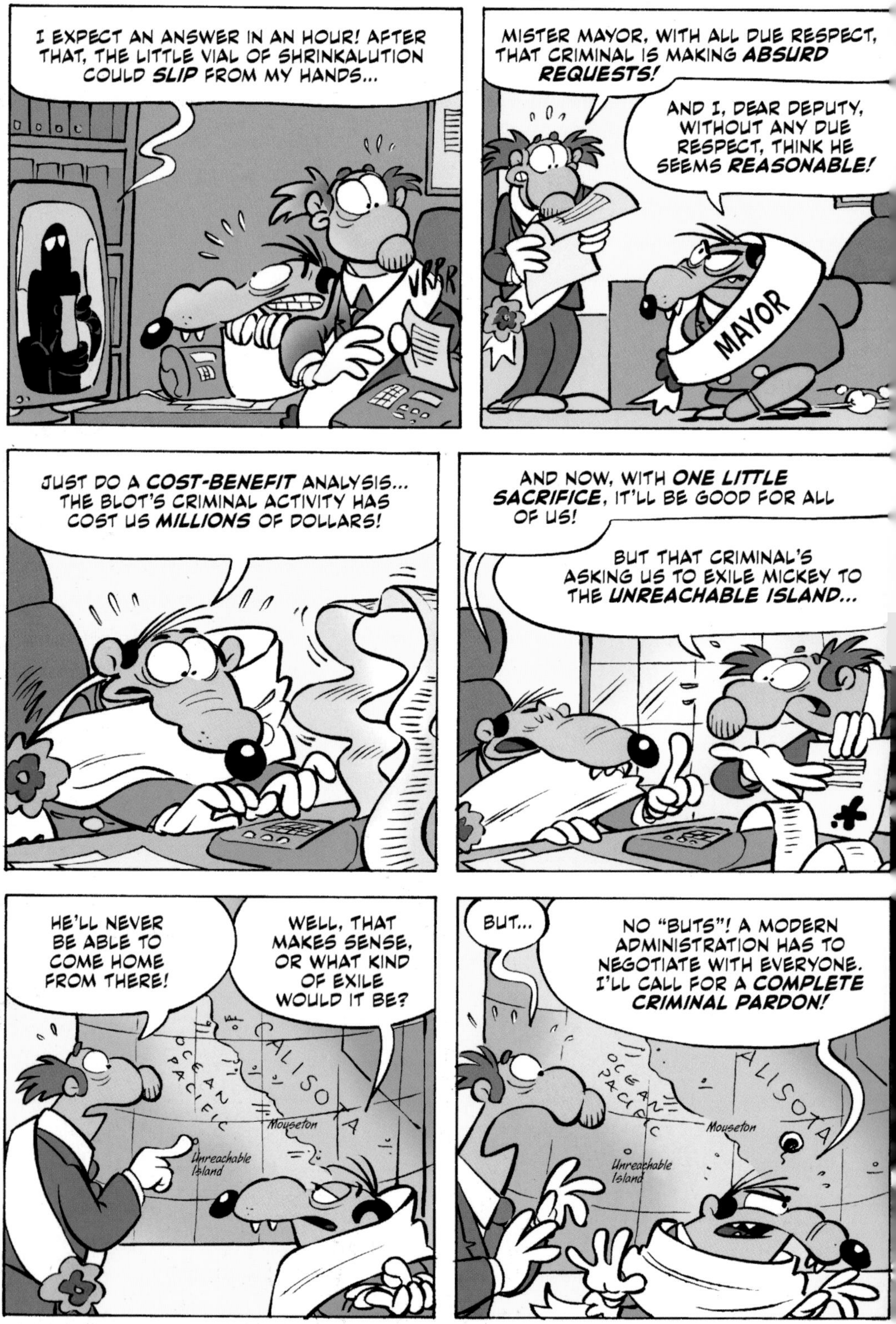
I EXPECT AN ANSWER IN AN HOUR! AFTER THAT, THE LITTLE VIAL OF SHRINKALUTION COULD SLIP FROM MY HANDS...
VRRR
MISTER MAYOR, WITH ALL DUE RESPECT, THAT CRIMINAL IS MAKING ABSURD REQUESTS!
AND I, DEAR DEPUTY, WITHOUT ANY DUE RESPECT, THINK HE SEEMS REASONABLE!
MAYOR
JUST DO A COST-BENEFIT ANALYSIS... THE BLOT'S CRIMINAL ACTIVITY HAS COST US MILLIONS OF DOLLARS!
AND NOW, WITH ONE LITTLE SACRIFICE, IT'LL BE GOOD FOR ALL OF US!
BUT THAT CRIMINAL'S ASKING US TO EXILE MICKEY TO THE UNREACHABLE ISLAND...
HE'LL NEVER BE ABLE TO COME HOME FROM THERE!
WELL, THAT MAKES SENSE, OR WHAT KIND OF EXILE WOULD IT BE?
CALISOTA
OCEAN PACIFIC
Mouseton
Unreachable Island
BUT...
NO "BUTS"! A MODERN ADMINISTRATION HAS TO NEGOTIATE WITH EVERYONE. I'LL CALL FOR A COMPLETE CRIMINAL PARDON!

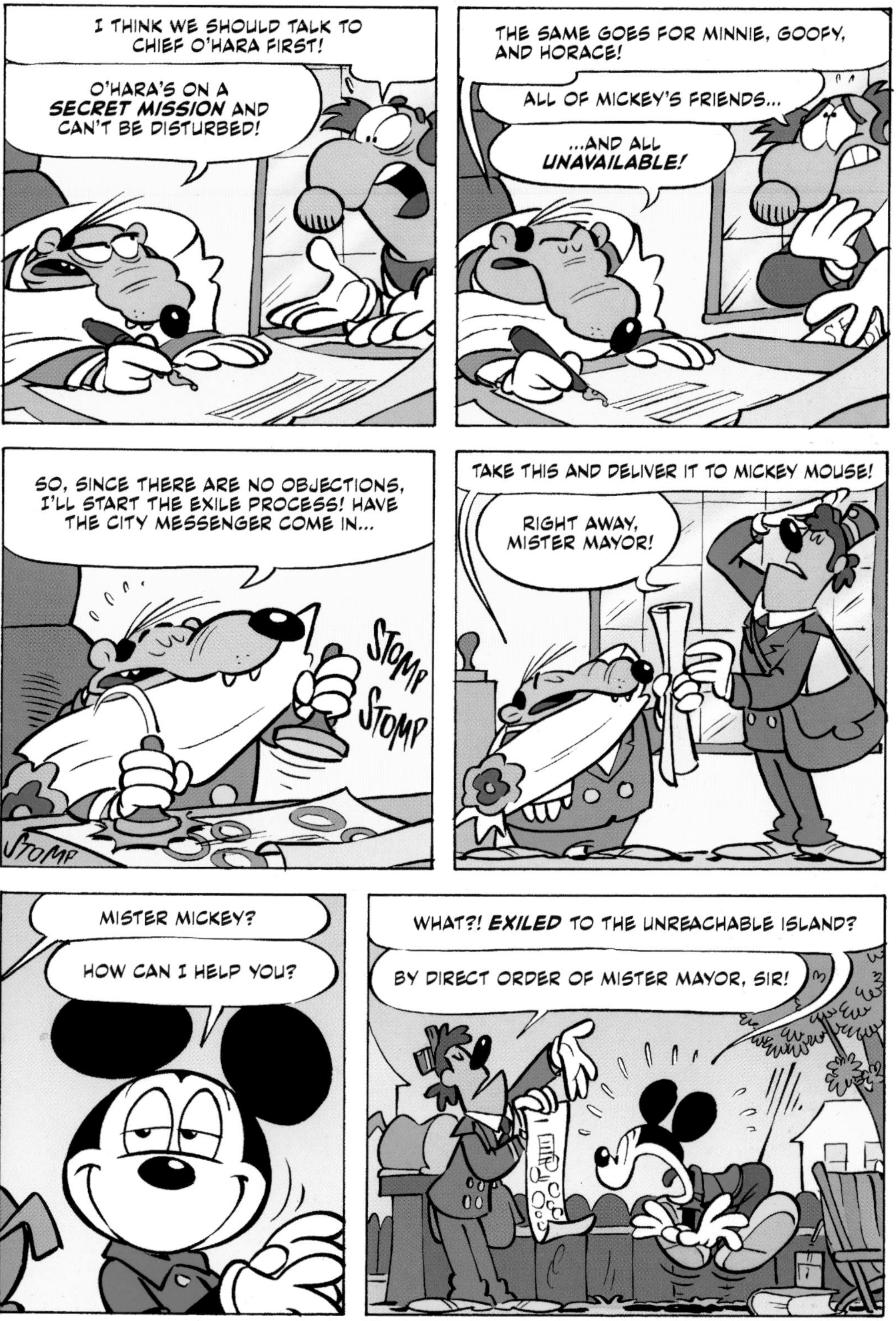
I THINK WE SHOULD TALK TO CHIEF O'HARA FIRST!
O'HARA'S ON A **SECRET MISSION** AND CAN'T BE DISTURBED!
THE SAME GOES FOR MINNIE, GOOFY, AND HORACE!
ALL OF MICKEY'S FRIENDS...
...AND ALL **UNAVAILABLE!**
SO, SINCE THERE ARE NO OBJECTIONS, I'LL START THE EXILE PROCESS! HAVE THE CITY MESSENGER COME IN...
STOMP
STOMP
STOMP
TAKE THIS AND DELIVER IT TO MICKEY MOUSE!
RIGHT AWAY, MISTER MAYOR!
MISTER MICKEY?
HOW CAN I HELP YOU?
WHAT?! **EXILED** TO THE UNREACHABLE ISLAND?
BY DIRECT ORDER OF MISTER MAYOR, SIR!

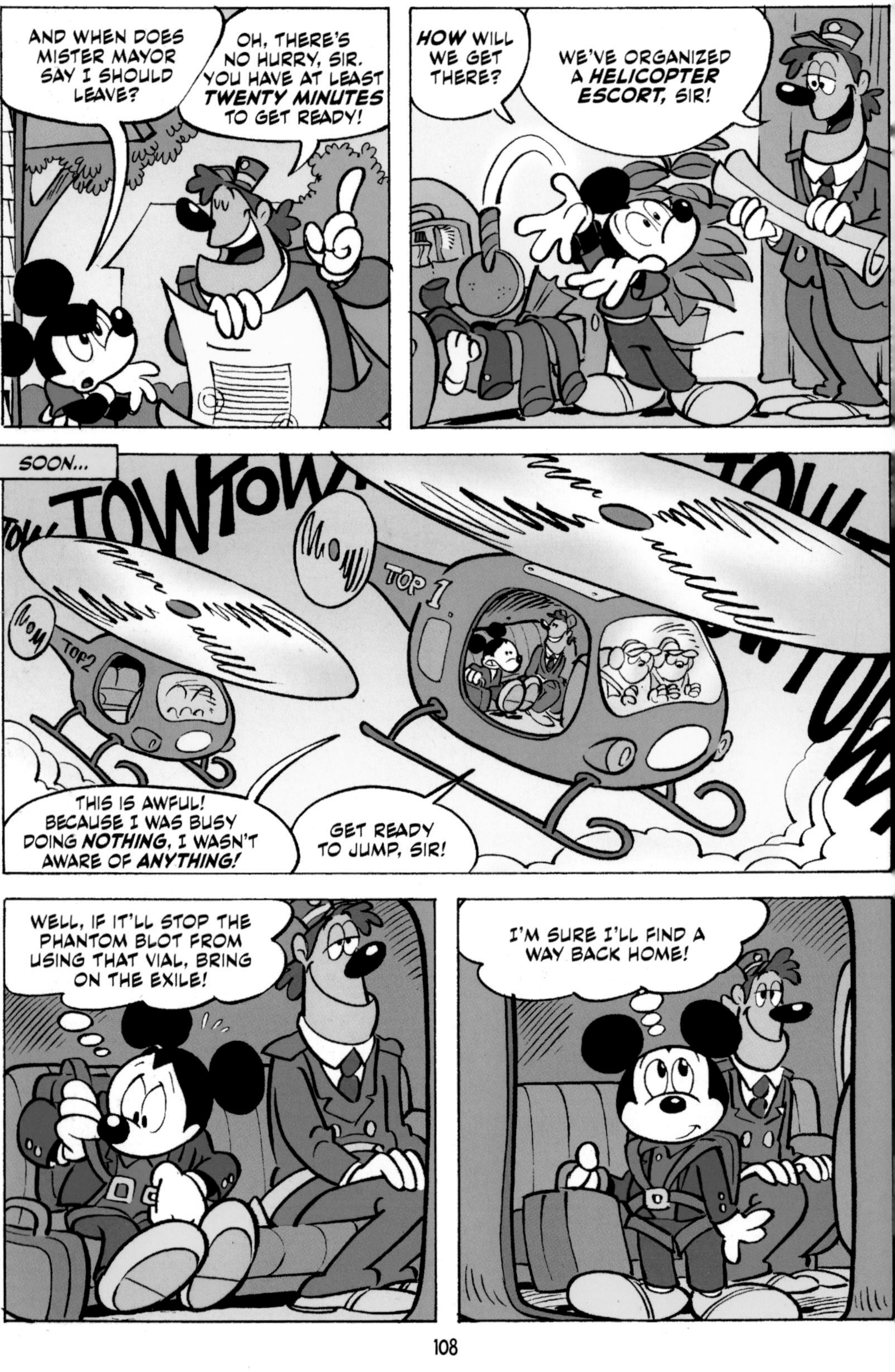
AND WHEN DOES MISTER MAYOR SAY I SHOULD LEAVE?
OH, THERE'S NO HURRY, SIR. YOU HAVE AT LEAST **TWENTY MINUTES** TO GET READY!
HOW WILL WE GET THERE?
WE'VE ORGANIZED A **HELICOPTER ESCORT,** SIR!
SOON...
TOWTOW
TOP 1
TOP2
THIS IS AWFUL! BECAUSE I WAS BUSY DOING **NOTHING**, I WASN'T AWARE OF **ANYTHING!**
GET READY TO JUMP, SIR!
WELL, IF IT'LL STOP THE PHANTOM BLOT FROM USING THAT VIAL, BRING ON THE EXILE!
I'M SURE I'LL FIND A WAY BACK HOME!

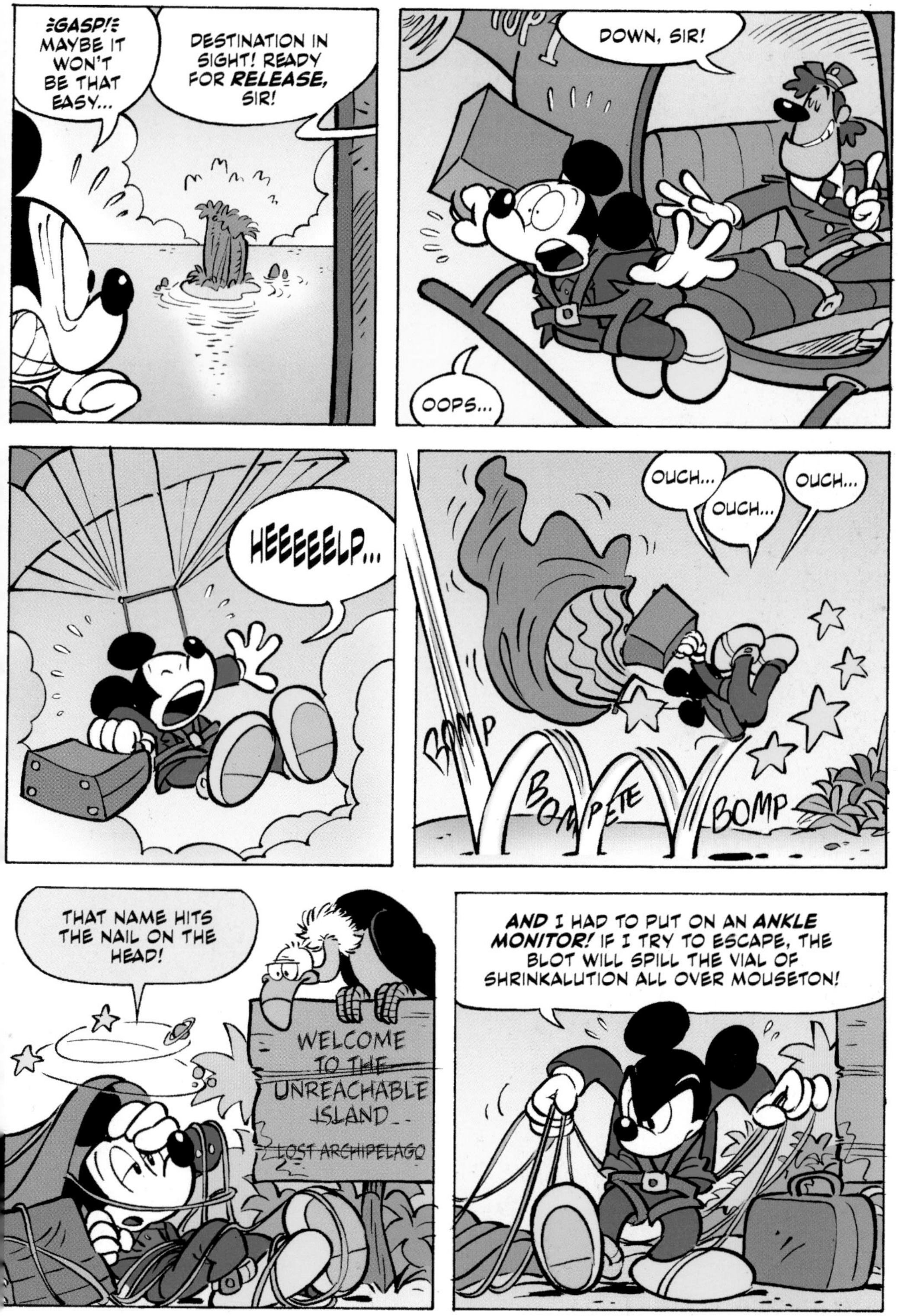
GASP! MAYBE IT WON'T BE THAT EASY...
DESTINATION IN SIGHT! READY FOR RELEASE, SIR!
DOWN, SIR!
OOPS...
HEEEEELP...
OUCH...
OUCH...
OUCH...
BOMP
BOMPETE
BOMP
THAT NAME HITS THE NAIL ON THE HEAD!
WELCOME TO THE UNREACHABLE ISLAND
LOST ARCHIPELAGO
AND I HAD TO PUT ON AN ANKLE MONITOR! IF I TRY TO ESCAPE, THE BLOT WILL SPILL THE VIAL OF SHRINKALUTION ALL OVER MOUSETON!

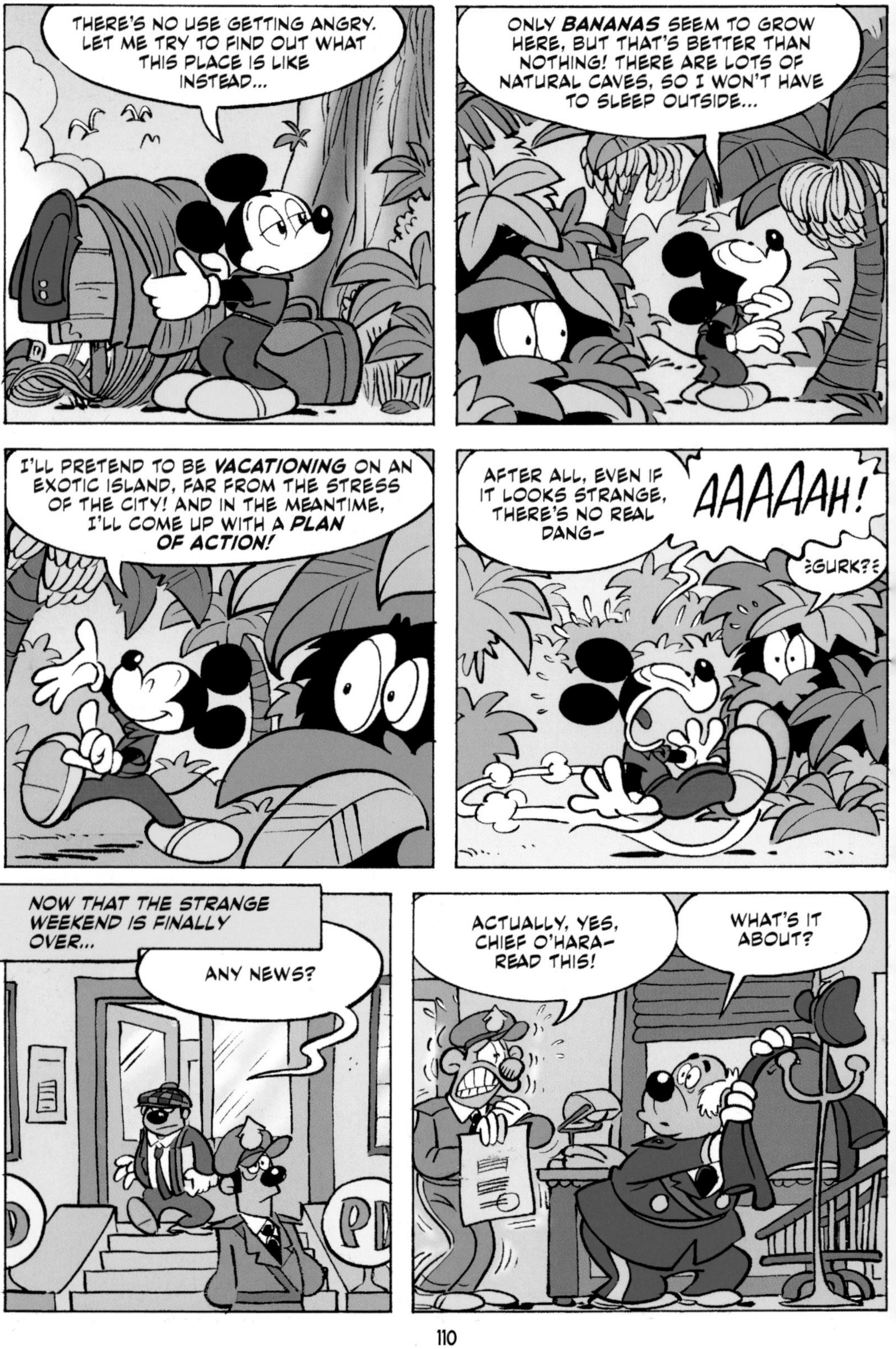
THERE'S NO USE GETTING ANGRY. LET ME TRY TO FIND OUT WHAT THIS PLACE IS LIKE INSTEAD...
ONLY BANANAS SEEM TO GROW HERE, BUT THAT'S BETTER THAN NOTHING! THERE ARE LOTS OF NATURAL CAVES, SO I WON'T HAVE TO SLEEP OUTSIDE...
I'LL PRETEND TO BE VACATIONING ON AN EXOTIC ISLAND, FAR FROM THE STRESS OF THE CITY! AND IN THE MEANTIME, I'LL COME UP WITH A PLAN OF ACTION!
AFTER ALL, EVEN IF IT LOOKS STRANGE, THERE'S NO REAL DANG–
AAAAAH!
GURK?
NOW THAT THE STRANGE WEEKEND IS FINALLY OVER...
ANY NEWS?
ACTUALLY, YES, CHIEF O'HARA– READ THIS!
WHAT'S IT ABOUT?

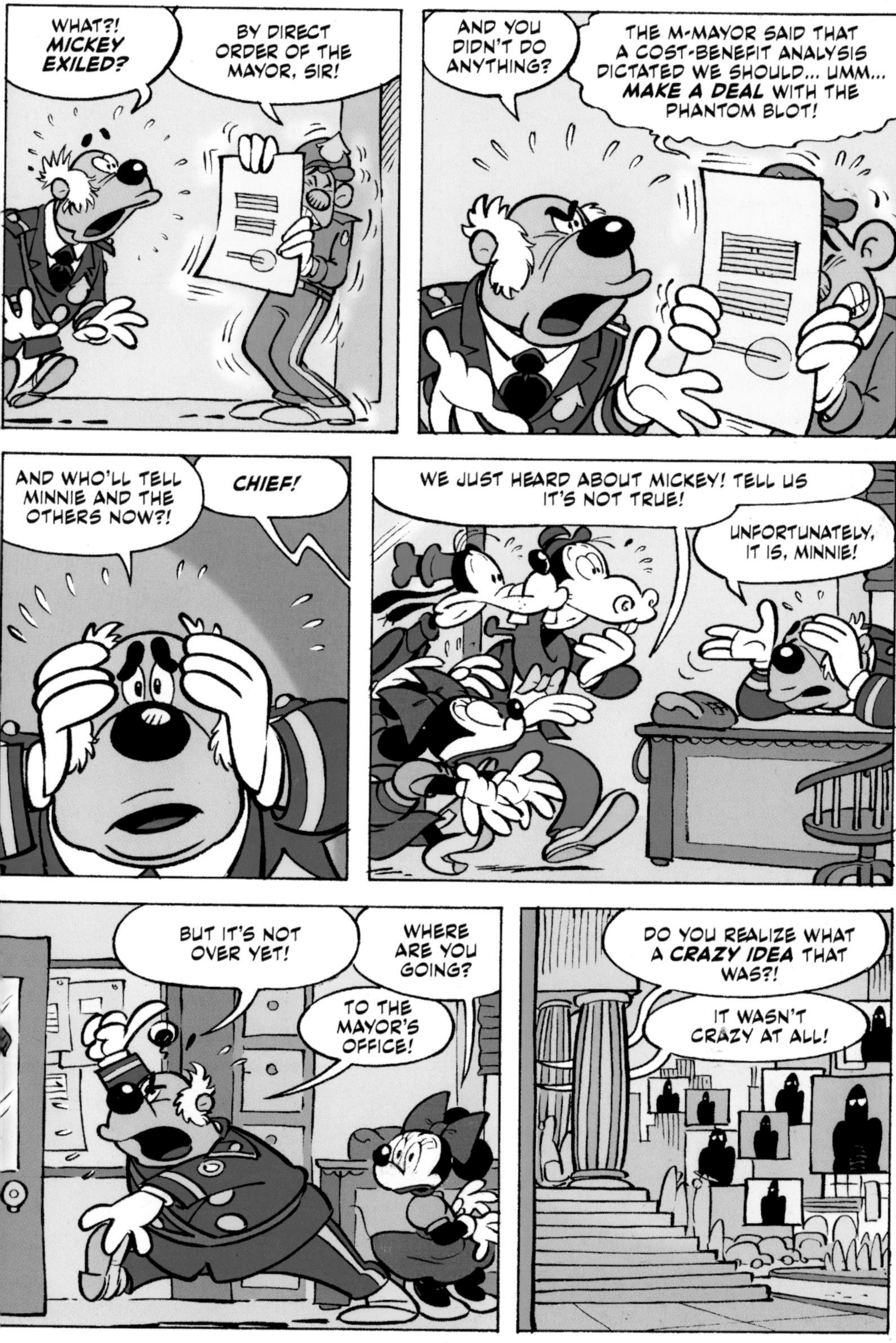
WHAT?! *MICKEY EXILED?*
BY DIRECT ORDER OF THE MAYOR, SIR!
AND YOU DIDN'T DO ANYTHING?
THE M-MAYOR SAID THAT A COST-BENEFIT ANALYSIS DICTATED WE SHOULD... UMM... *MAKE A DEAL* WITH THE PHANTOM BLOT!
AND WHO'LL TELL MINNIE AND THE OTHERS NOW?!
CHIEF!
WE JUST HEARD ABOUT MICKEY! TELL US IT'S NOT TRUE!
UNFORTUNATELY, IT IS, MINNIE!
BUT IT'S NOT OVER YET!
WHERE ARE YOU GOING?
TO THE MAYOR'S OFFICE!
DO YOU REALIZE WHAT A *CRAZY IDEA* THAT WAS?!
IT WASN'T CRAZY AT ALL!

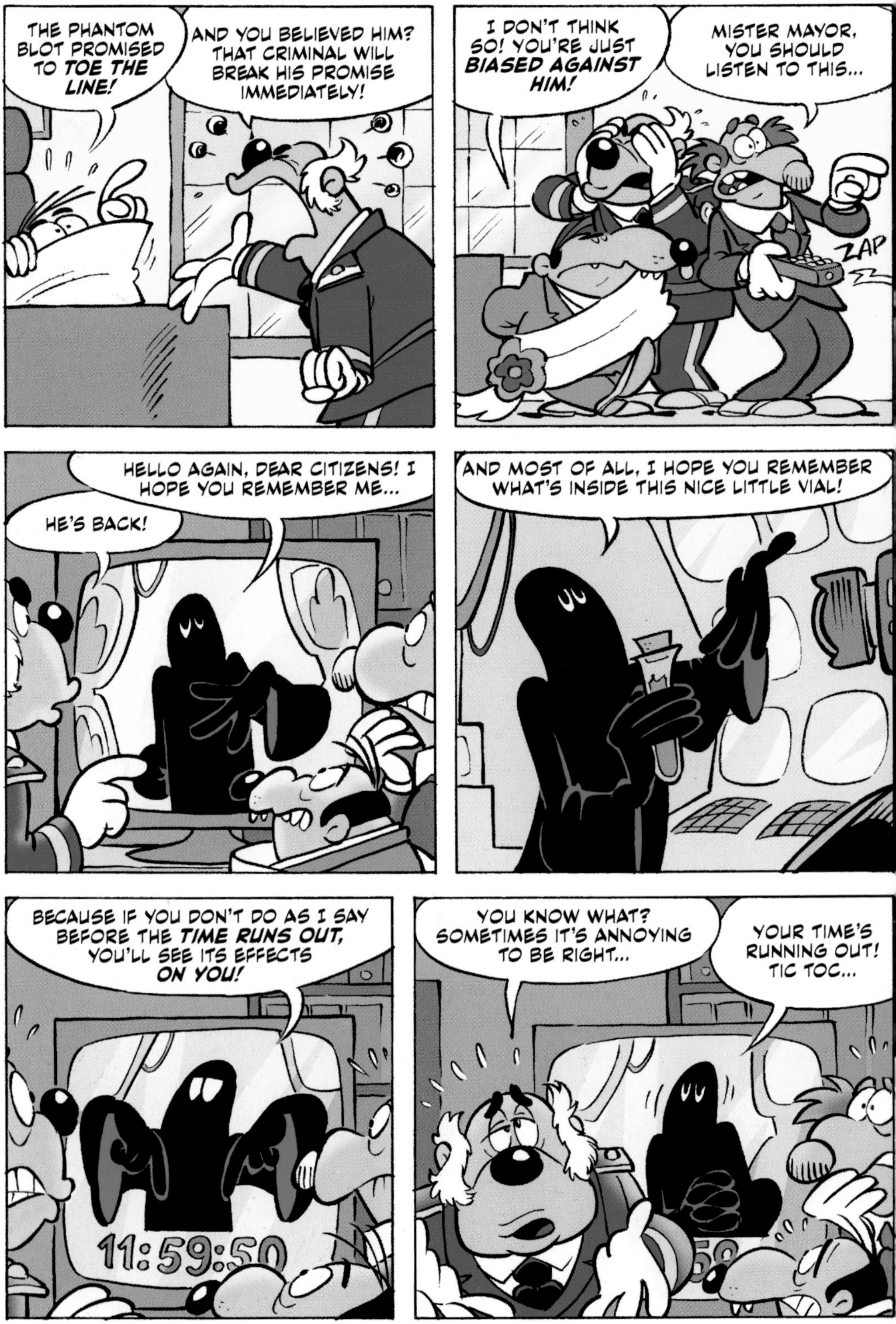
THE PHANTOM BLOT PROMISED TO TOE THE LINE!
AND YOU BELIEVED HIM? THAT CRIMINAL WILL BREAK HIS PROMISE IMMEDIATELY!
I DON'T THINK SO! YOU'RE JUST BIASED AGAINST HIM!
MISTER MAYOR, YOU SHOULD LISTEN TO THIS...
ZAP
HELLO AGAIN, DEAR CITIZENS! I HOPE YOU REMEMBER ME...
HE'S BACK!
AND MOST OF ALL, I HOPE YOU REMEMBER WHAT'S INSIDE THIS NICE LITTLE VIAL!
BECAUSE IF YOU DON'T DO AS I SAY BEFORE THE TIME RUNS OUT, YOU'LL SEE ITS EFFECTS ON YOU!
11:59:50
YOU KNOW WHAT? SOMETIMES IT'S ANNOYING TO BE RIGHT...
YOUR TIME'S RUNNING OUT! TIC TOC...

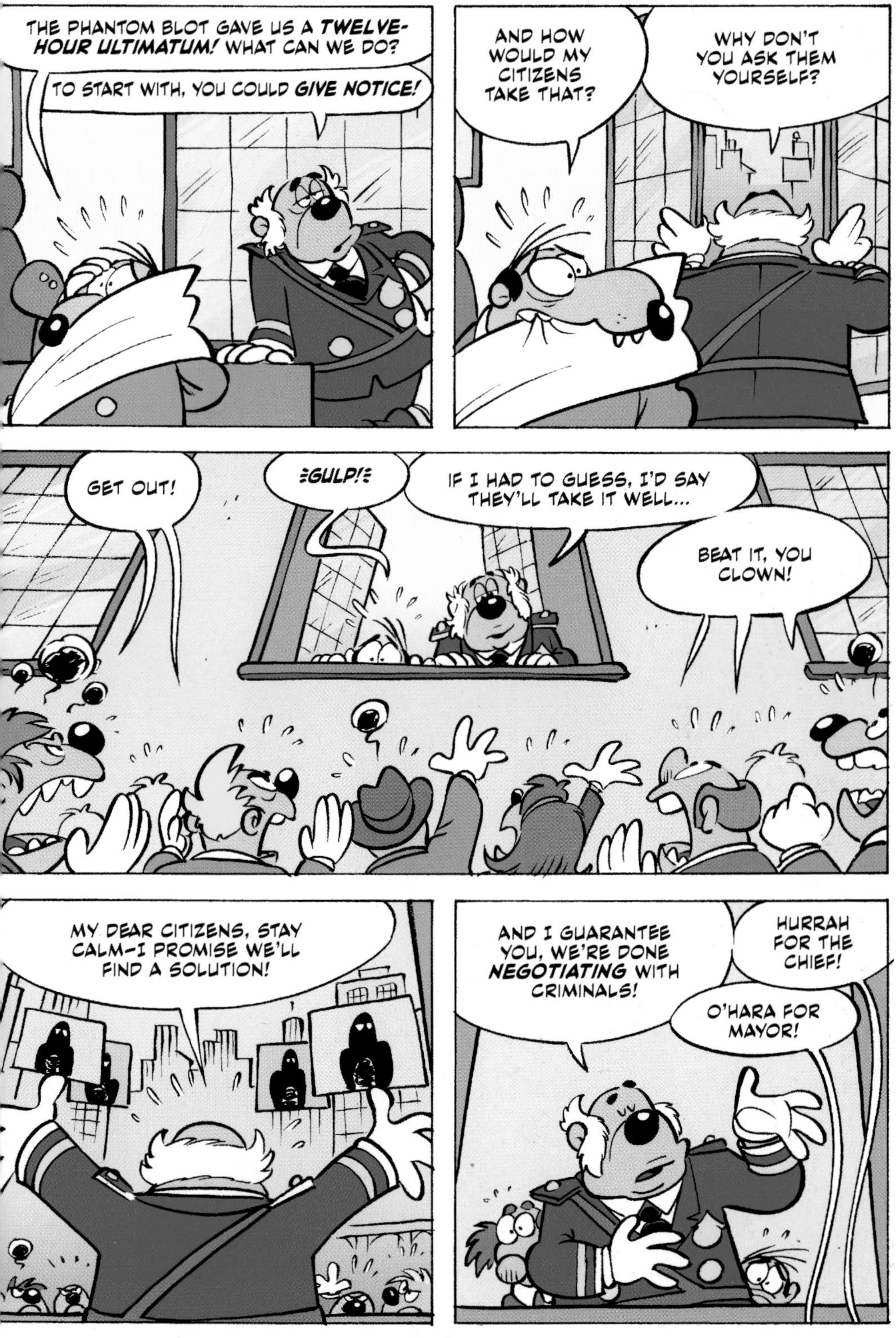
THE PHANTOM BLOT GAVE US A TWELVE-HOUR ULTIMATUM! WHAT CAN WE DO?
TO START WITH, YOU COULD GIVE NOTICE!
AND HOW WOULD MY CITIZENS TAKE THAT?
WHY DON'T YOU ASK THEM YOURSELF?
GET OUT!
GULP!
IF I HAD TO GUESS, I'D SAY THEY'LL TAKE IT WELL...
BEAT IT, YOU CLOWN!
MY DEAR CITIZENS, STAY CALM–I PROMISE WE'LL FIND A SOLUTION!
AND I GUARANTEE YOU, WE'RE DONE NEGOTIATING WITH CRIMINALS!
HURRAH FOR THE CHIEF!
O'HARA FOR MAYOR!

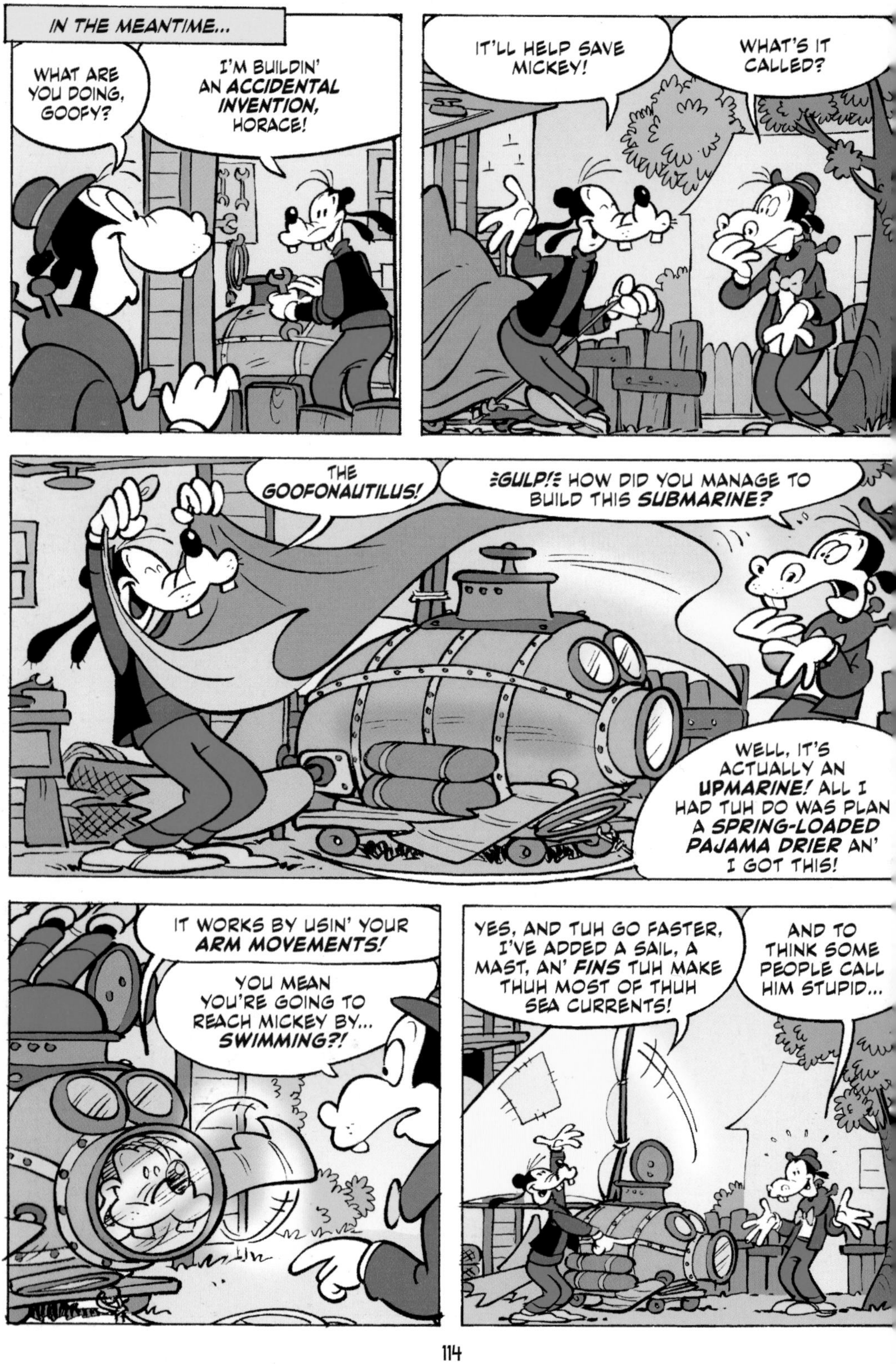
IN THE MEANTIME...
WHAT ARE YOU DOING, GOOFY?
I'M BUILDIN' AN ACCIDENTAL INVENTION, HORACE!
IT'LL HELP SAVE MICKEY!
WHAT'S IT CALLED?
THE GOOFONAUTILUS!
GULP! HOW DID YOU MANAGE TO BUILD THIS SUBMARINE?
WELL, IT'S ACTUALLY AN UPMARINE! ALL I HAD TUH DO WAS PLAN A SPRING-LOADED PAJAMA DRIER AN' I GOT THIS!
IT WORKS BY USIN' YOUR ARM MOVEMENTS!
YOU MEAN YOU'RE GOING TO REACH MICKEY BY... SWIMMING?!
YES, AND TUH GO FASTER, I'VE ADDED A SAIL, A MAST, AN' FINS TUH MAKE THUH MOST OF THUH SEA CURRENTS!
AND TO THINK SOME PEOPLE CALL HIM STUPID...

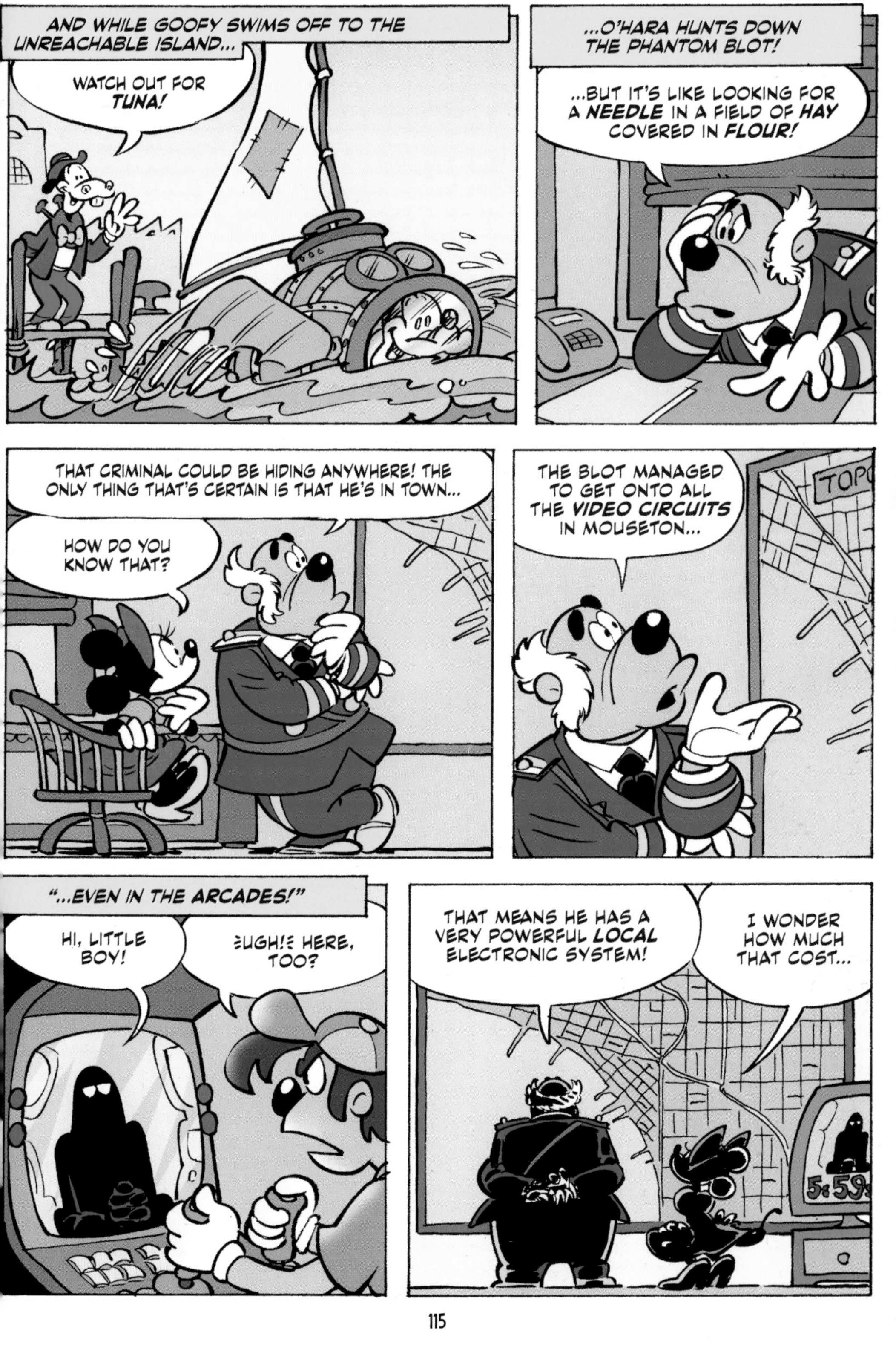
AND WHILE GOOFY SWIMS OFF TO THE UNREACHABLE ISLAND...
WATCH OUT FOR TUNA!
...O'HARA HUNTS DOWN THE PHANTOM BLOT!
...BUT IT'S LIKE LOOKING FOR A NEEDLE IN A FIELD OF HAY COVERED IN FLOUR!
THAT CRIMINAL COULD BE HIDING ANYWHERE! THE ONLY THING THAT'S CERTAIN IS THAT HE'S IN TOWN...
HOW DO YOU KNOW THAT?
THE BLOT MANAGED TO GET ONTO ALL THE VIDEO CIRCUITS IN MOUSETON...
TOPO
"...EVEN IN THE ARCADES!"
HI, LITTLE BOY!
UGH! HERE, TOO?
THAT MEANS HE HAS A VERY POWERFUL LOCAL ELECTRONIC SYSTEM!
I WONDER HOW MUCH THAT COST...

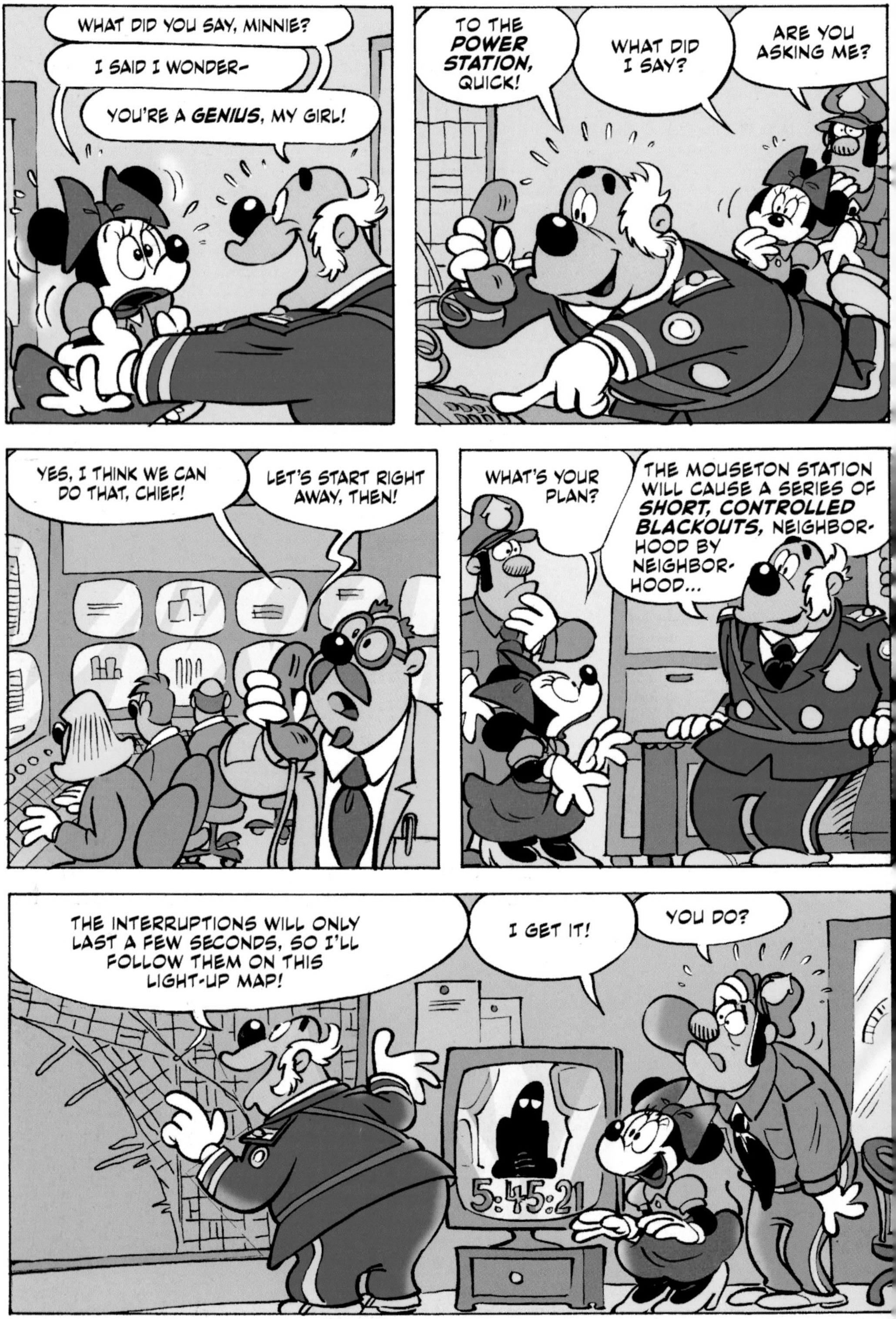
WHAT DID YOU SAY, MINNIE?
I SAID I WONDER-
YOU'RE A GENIUS, MY GIRL!
TO THE POWER STATION, QUICK!
WHAT DID I SAY?
ARE YOU ASKING ME?
YES, I THINK WE CAN DO THAT, CHIEF!
LET'S START RIGHT AWAY, THEN!
WHAT'S YOUR PLAN?
THE MOUSETON STATION WILL CAUSE A SERIES OF SHORT, CONTROLLED BLACKOUTS, NEIGHBORHOOD BY NEIGHBORHOOD...
THE INTERRUPTIONS WILL ONLY LAST A FEW SECONDS, SO I'LL FOLLOW THEM ON THIS LIGHT-UP MAP!
I GET IT!
YOU DO?
5:45:21

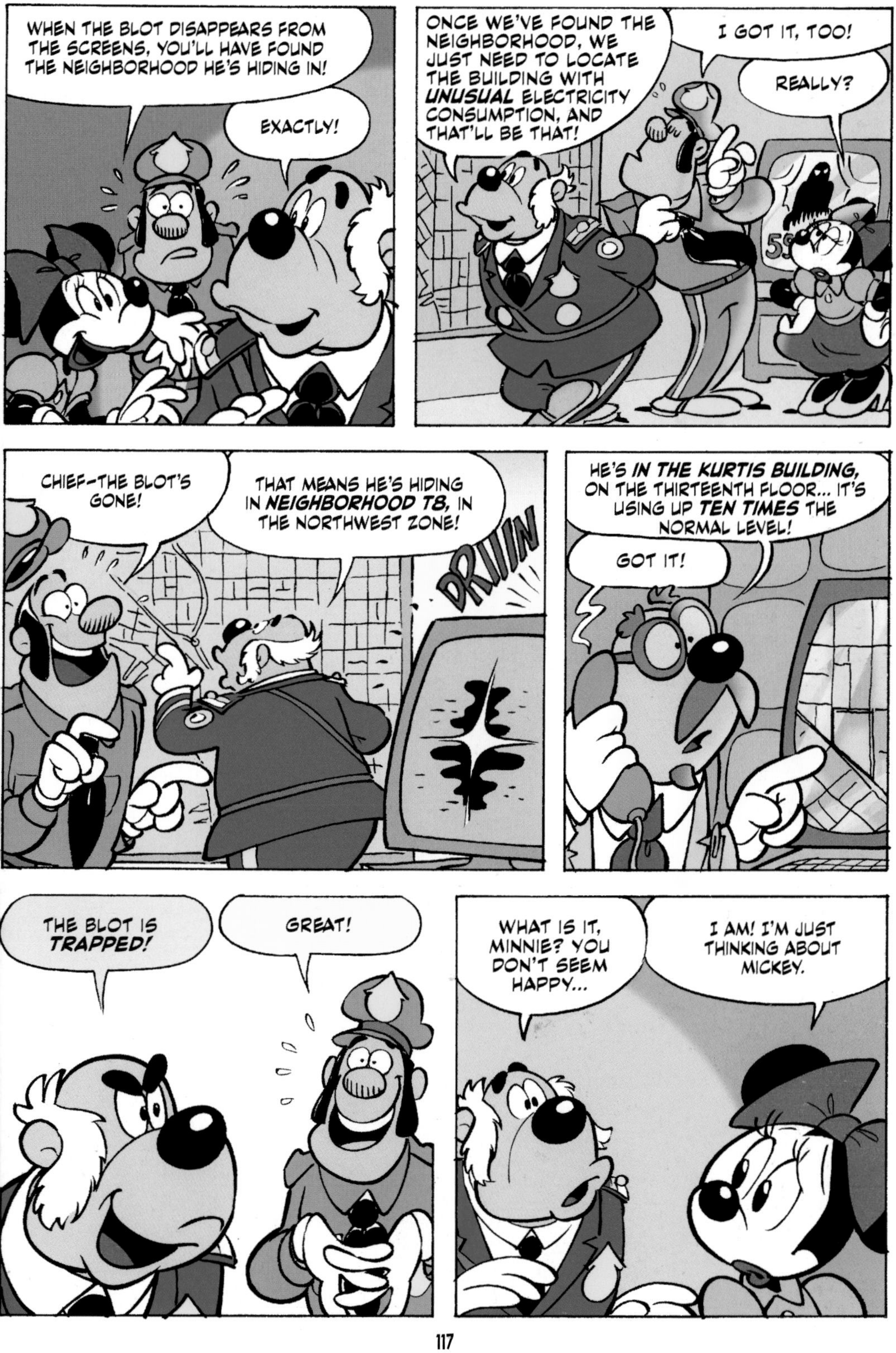

WHEN THE BLOT DISAPPEARS FROM THE SCREENS, YOU'LL HAVE FOUND THE NEIGHBORHOOD HE'S HIDING IN!
EXACTLY!
ONCE WE'VE FOUND THE NEIGHBORHOOD, WE JUST NEED TO LOCATE THE BUILDING WITH ***UNUSUAL*** ELECTRICITY CONSUMPTION, AND THAT'LL BE THAT!
I GOT IT, TOO!
REALLY?
CHIEF—THE BLOT'S GONE!
THAT MEANS HE'S HIDING IN ***NEIGHBORHOOD T8,*** IN THE NORTHWEST ZONE!
BRIIIN
HE'S ***IN THE KURTIS BUILDING,*** ON THE THIRTEENTH FLOOR... IT'S USING UP ***TEN TIMES*** THE NORMAL LEVEL!
GOT IT!
THE BLOT IS ***TRAPPED!***
GREAT!
WHAT IS IT, MINNIE? YOU DON'T SEEM HAPPY...
I AM! I'M JUST THINKING ABOUT MICKEY.

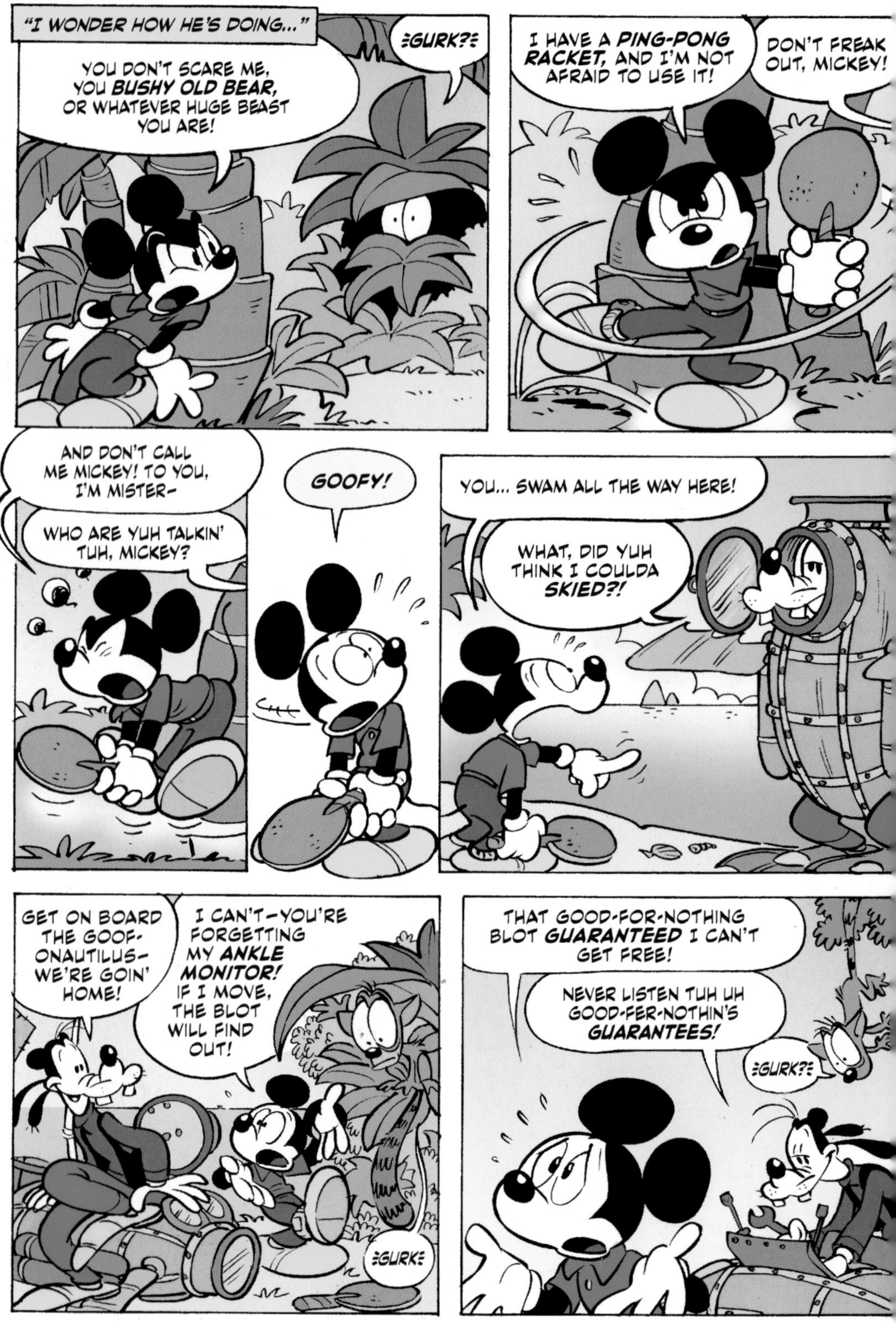
"I WONDER HOW HE'S DOING..."
YOU DON'T SCARE ME, YOU BUSHY OLD BEAR, OR WHATEVER HUGE BEAST YOU ARE!
GURK?
I HAVE A PING-PONG RACKET, AND I'M NOT AFRAID TO USE IT!
DON'T FREAK OUT, MICKEY!
AND DON'T CALL ME MICKEY! TO YOU, I'M MISTER-
WHO ARE YUH TALKIN' TUH, MICKEY?
GOOFY!
YOU... SWAM ALL THE WAY HERE!
WHAT, DID YUH THINK I COULDA SKIED?!
GET ON BOARD THE GOOF-ONAUTILUS-WE'RE GOIN' HOME!
I CAN'T-YOU'RE FORGETTING MY ANKLE MONITOR! IF I MOVE, THE BLOT WILL FIND OUT!
GURK
THAT GOOD-FOR-NOTHING BLOT GUARANTEED I CAN'T GET FREE!
NEVER LISTEN TUH UH GOOD-FER-NOTHIN'S GUARANTEES!
GURK?

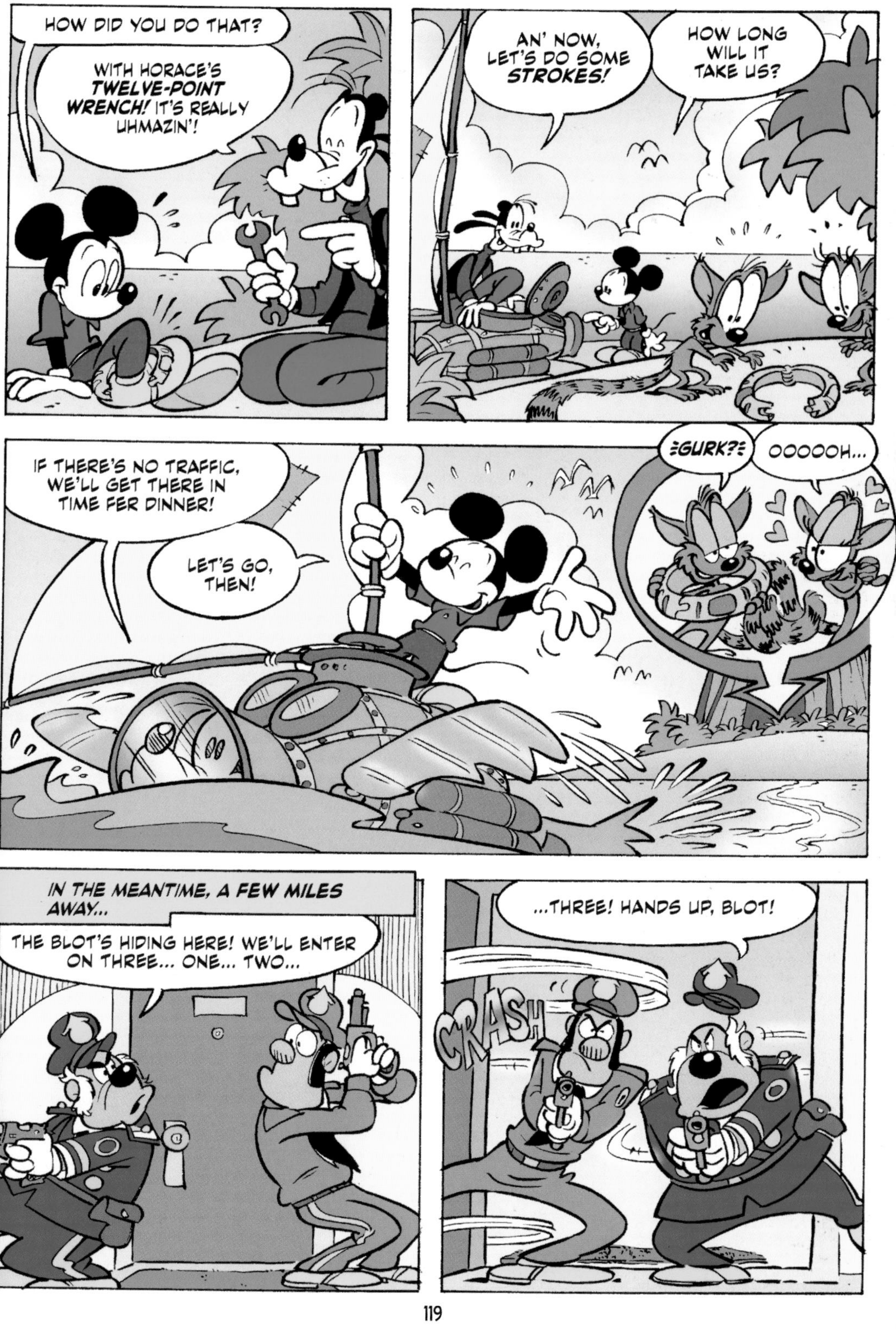
HOW DID YOU DO THAT?
WITH HORACE'S TWELVE-POINT WRENCH! IT'S REALLY UHMAZIN'!
AN' NOW, LET'S DO SOME STROKES!
HOW LONG WILL IT TAKE US?
IF THERE'S NO TRAFFIC, WE'LL GET THERE IN TIME FER DINNER!
LET'S GO, THEN!
GURK?
OOOOOH...
IN THE MEANTIME, A FEW MILES AWAY...
THE BLOT'S HIDING HERE! WE'LL ENTER ON THREE... ONE... TWO...
...THREE! HANDS UP, BLOT!
CRASH

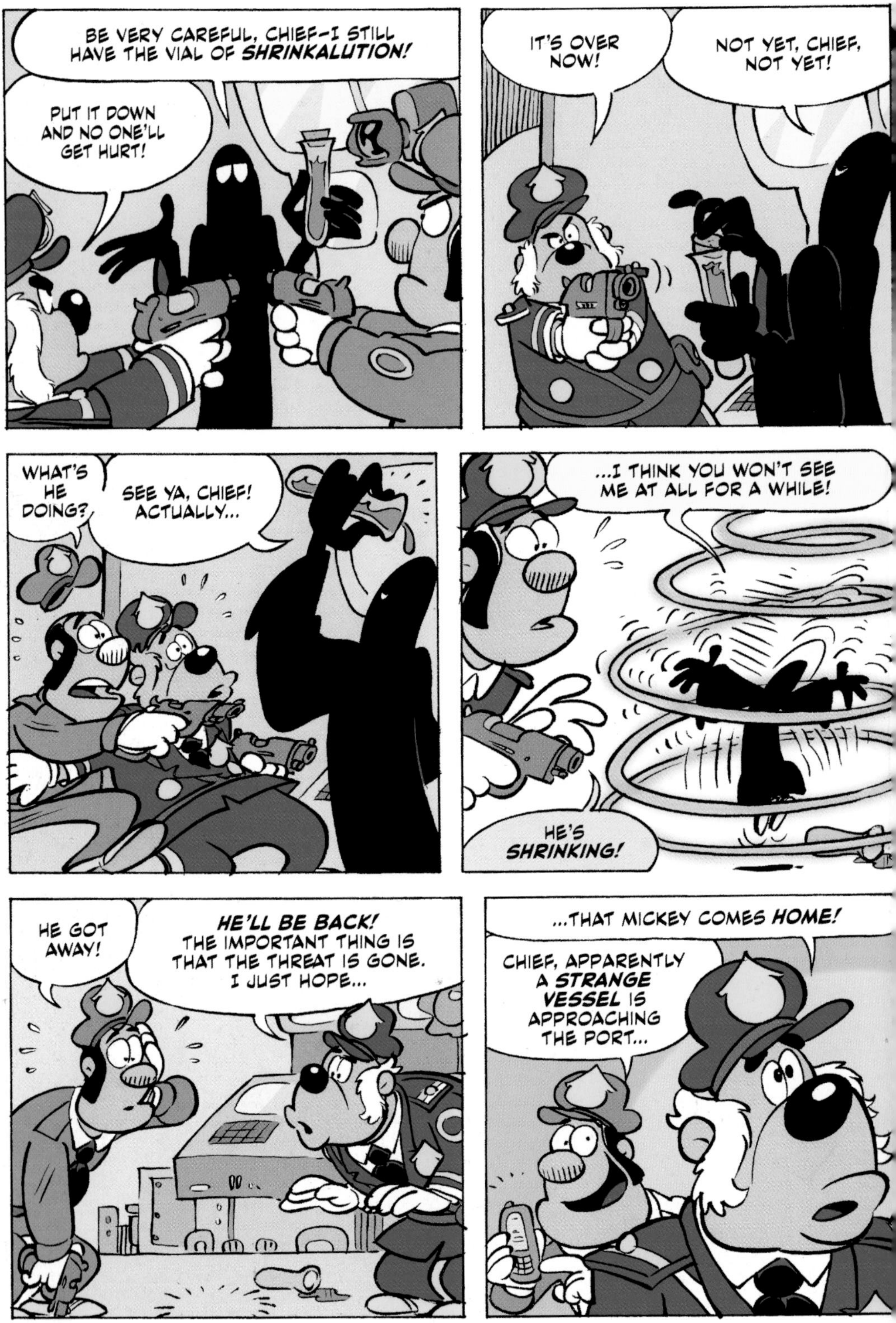
BE VERY CAREFUL, CHIEF–I STILL HAVE THE VIAL OF SHRINKALUTION!
PUT IT DOWN AND NO ONE'LL GET HURT!
IT'S OVER NOW!
NOT YET, CHIEF, NOT YET!
WHAT'S HE DOING?
SEE YA, CHIEF! ACTUALLY...
...I THINK YOU WON'T SEE ME AT ALL FOR A WHILE!
HE'S SHRINKING!
HE GOT AWAY!
HE'LL BE BACK! THE IMPORTANT THING IS THAT THE THREAT IS GONE. I JUST HOPE...
...THAT MICKEY COMES HOME!
CHIEF, APPARENTLY A STRANGE VESSEL IS APPROACHING THE PORT...

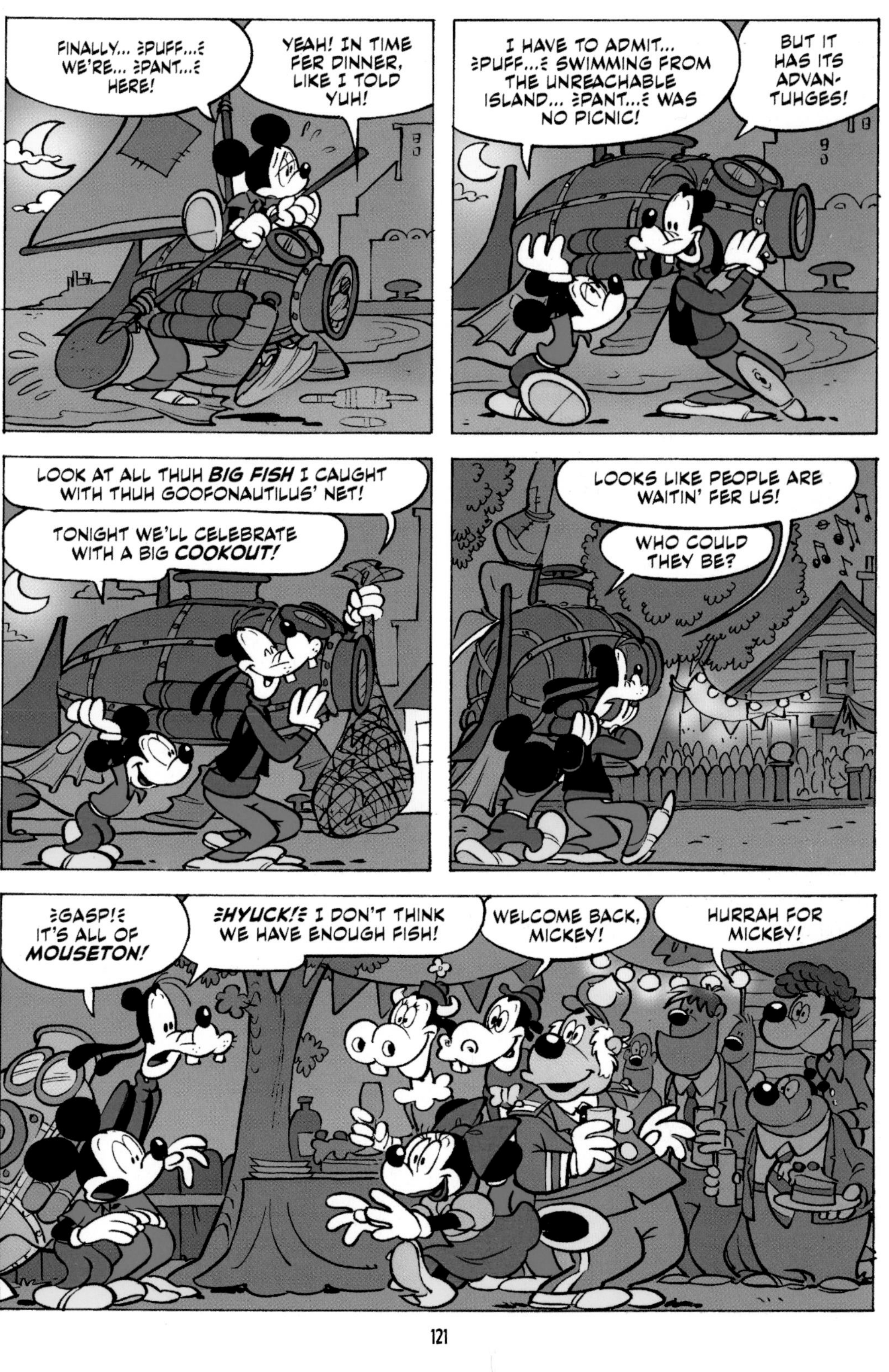
FINALLY... ≷PUFF...≶ WE'RE... ≷PANT...≶ HERE!
YEAH! IN TIME FER DINNER, LIKE I TOLD YUH!
I HAVE TO ADMIT... ≷PUFF...≶ SWIMMING FROM THE UNREACHABLE ISLAND... ≷PANT...≶ WAS NO PICNIC!
BUT IT HAS ITS ADVAN-TUHGES!
LOOK AT ALL THUH **BIG FISH** I CAUGHT WITH THUH GOOFONAUTILUS' NET!
TONIGHT WE'LL CELEBRATE WITH A BIG **COOKOUT!**
LOOKS LIKE PEOPLE ARE WAITIN' FER US!
WHO COULD THEY BE?
≷GASP!≶ IT'S ALL OF **MOUSETON!**
≷HYUCK!≶ I DON'T THINK WE HAVE ENOUGH FISH!
WELCOME BACK, MICKEY!
HURRAH FOR MICKEY!

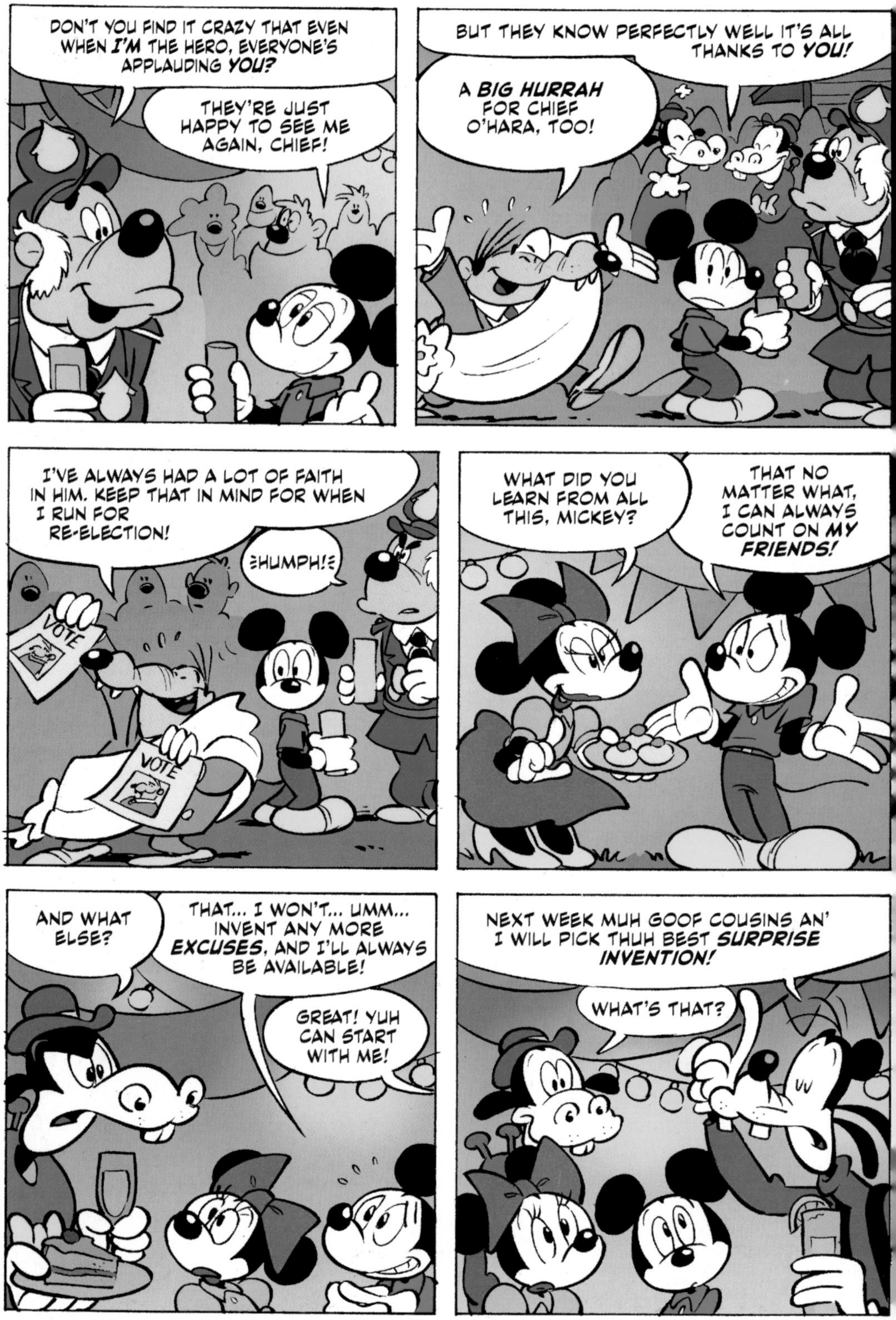
DON'T YOU FIND IT CRAZY THAT EVEN WHEN I'M THE HERO, EVERYONE'S APPLAUDING YOU?
THEY'RE JUST HAPPY TO SEE ME AGAIN, CHIEF!
BUT THEY KNOW PERFECTLY WELL IT'S ALL THANKS TO YOU!
A BIG HURRAH FOR CHIEF O'HARA, TOO!
I'VE ALWAYS HAD A LOT OF FAITH IN HIM. KEEP THAT IN MIND FOR WHEN I RUN FOR RE-ELECTION!
HUMPH!
VOTE
VOTE
WHAT DID YOU LEARN FROM ALL THIS, MICKEY?
THAT NO MATTER WHAT, I CAN ALWAYS COUNT ON MY FRIENDS!
AND WHAT ELSE?
THAT... I WON'T... UMM... INVENT ANY MORE EXCUSES, AND I'LL ALWAYS BE AVAILABLE!
GREAT! YUH CAN START WITH ME!
NEXT WEEK MUH GOOF COUSINS AN' I WILL PICK THUH BEST SURPRISE INVENTION!
WHAT'S THAT?

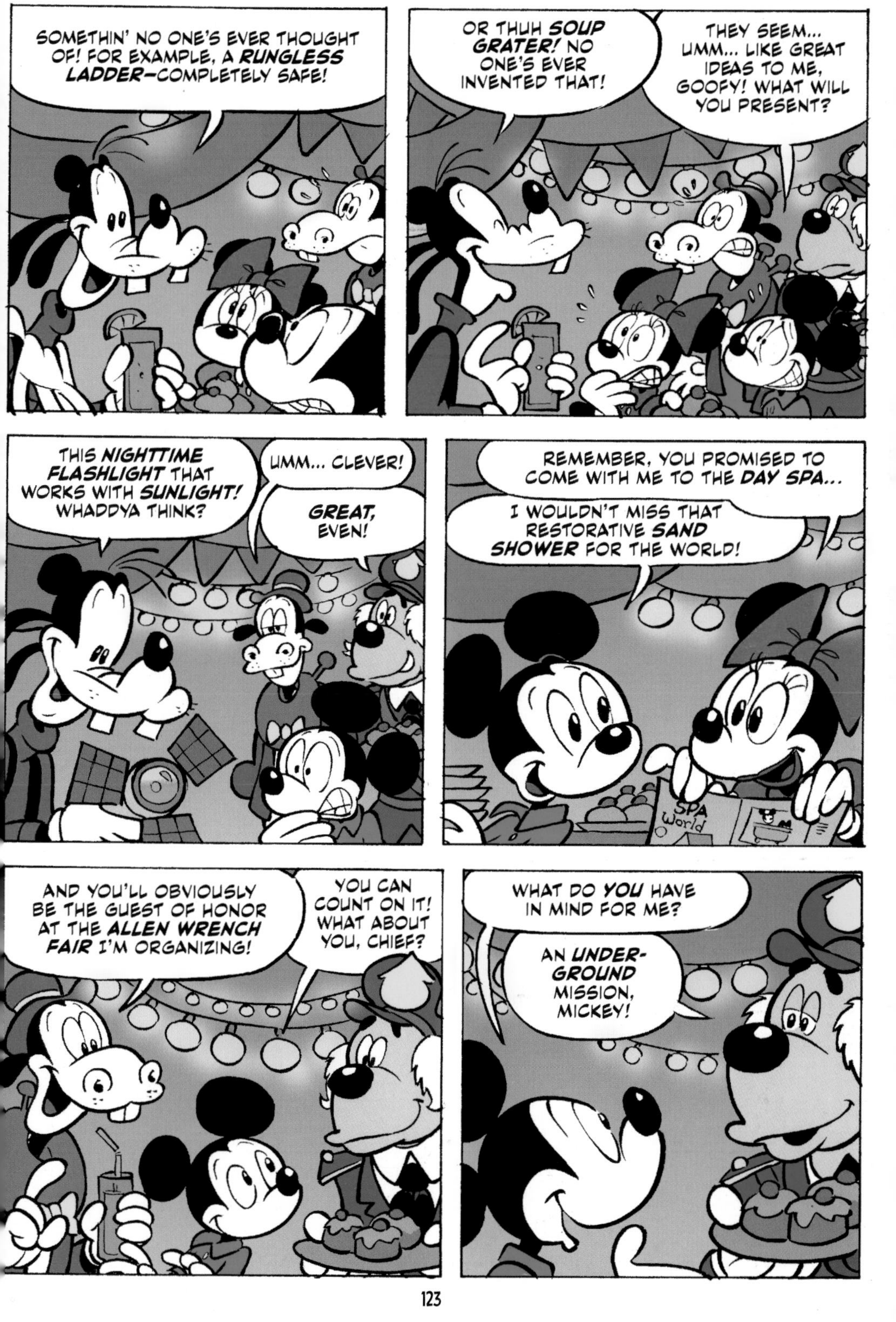
SOMETHIN' NO ONE'S EVER THOUGHT OF! FOR EXAMPLE, A RUNGLESS LADDER—COMPLETELY SAFE!
OR THUH SOUP GRATER! NO ONE'S EVER INVENTED THAT!
THEY SEEM... UMM... LIKE GREAT IDEAS TO ME, GOOFY! WHAT WILL YOU PRESENT?
THIS NIGHTTIME FLASHLIGHT THAT WORKS WITH SUNLIGHT! WHADDYA THINK?
UMM... CLEVER!
GREAT, EVEN!
REMEMBER, YOU PROMISED TO COME WITH ME TO THE DAY SPA...
I WOULDN'T MISS THAT RESTORATIVE SAND SHOWER FOR THE WORLD!
SPA World
AND YOU'LL OBVIOUSLY BE THE GUEST OF HONOR AT THE ALLEN WRENCH FAIR I'M ORGANIZING!
YOU CAN COUNT ON IT! WHAT ABOUT YOU, CHIEF?
WHAT DO YOU HAVE IN MIND FOR ME?
AN UNDER-GROUND MISSION, MICKEY!

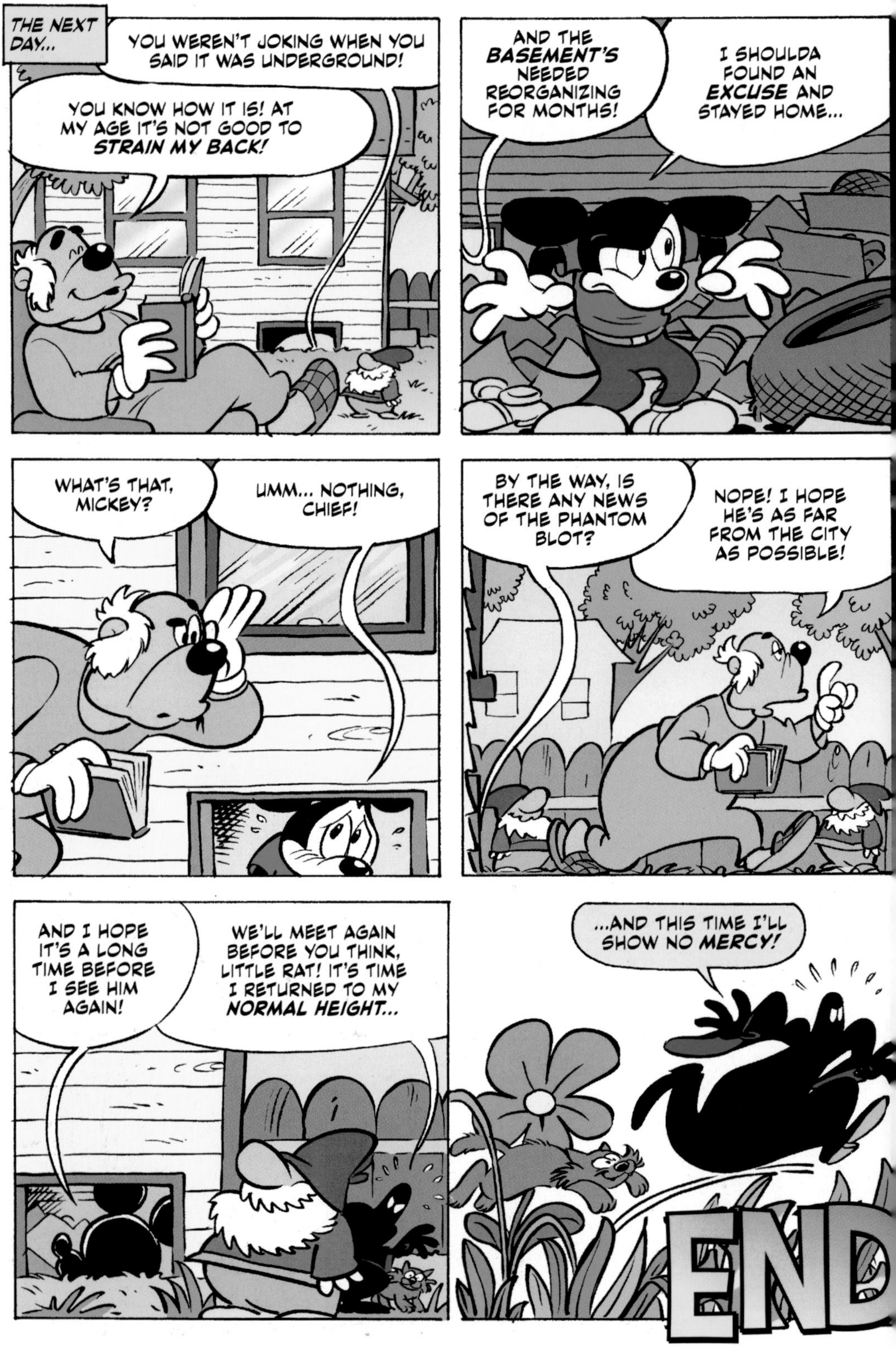
THE NEXT DAY...
YOU WEREN'T JOKING WHEN YOU SAID IT WAS UNDERGROUND!
YOU KNOW HOW IT IS! AT MY AGE IT'S NOT GOOD TO STRAIN MY BACK!
AND THE BASEMENT'S NEEDED REORGANIZING FOR MONTHS!
I SHOULDA FOUND AN EXCUSE AND STAYED HOME...
WHAT'S THAT, MICKEY?
UMM... NOTHING, CHIEF!
BY THE WAY, IS THERE ANY NEWS OF THE PHANTOM BLOT?
NOPE! I HOPE HE'S AS FAR FROM THE CITY AS POSSIBLE!
AND I HOPE IT'S A LONG TIME BEFORE I SEE HIM AGAIN!
WE'LL MEET AGAIN BEFORE YOU THINK, LITTLE RAT! IT'S TIME I RETURNED TO MY NORMAL HEIGHT...
...AND THIS TIME I'LL SHOW NO MERCY!
END

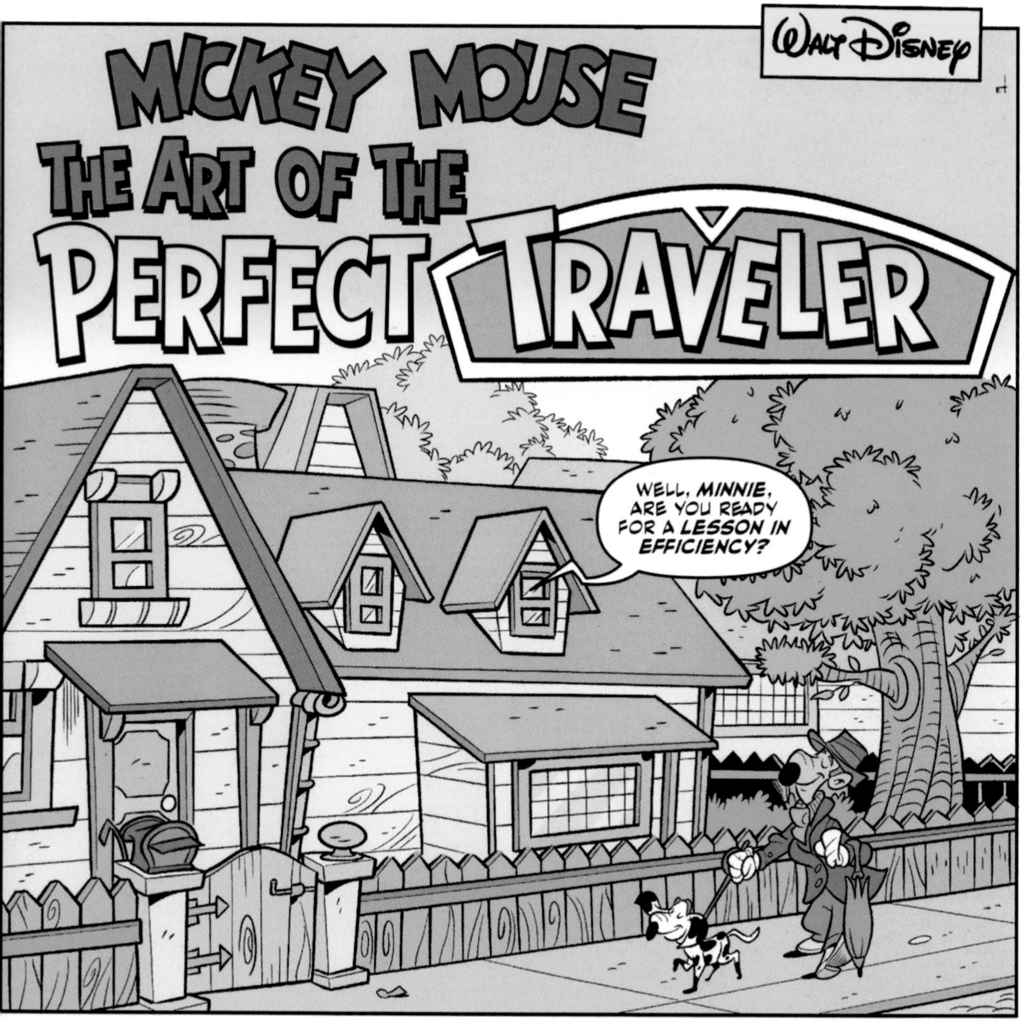
WALT DISNEY
MICKEY MOUSE
THE ART OF THE PERFECT TRAVELER
WELL, *MINNIE*, ARE YOU READY FOR A *LESSON IN EFFICIENCY?*

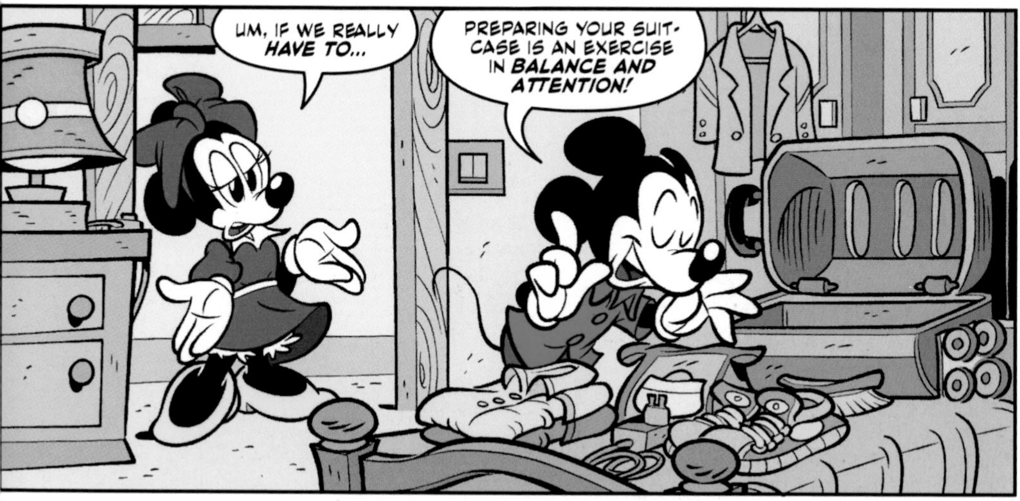
UM, IF WE REALLY *HAVE TO...*
PREPARING YOUR SUIT-CASE IS AN EXERCISE IN *BALANCE AND ATTENTION!*

ORIGINALLY PUBLISHED IN **TOPOLINO #3185** (ITALY, 2016) • **FIRST USA PUBLICATION**

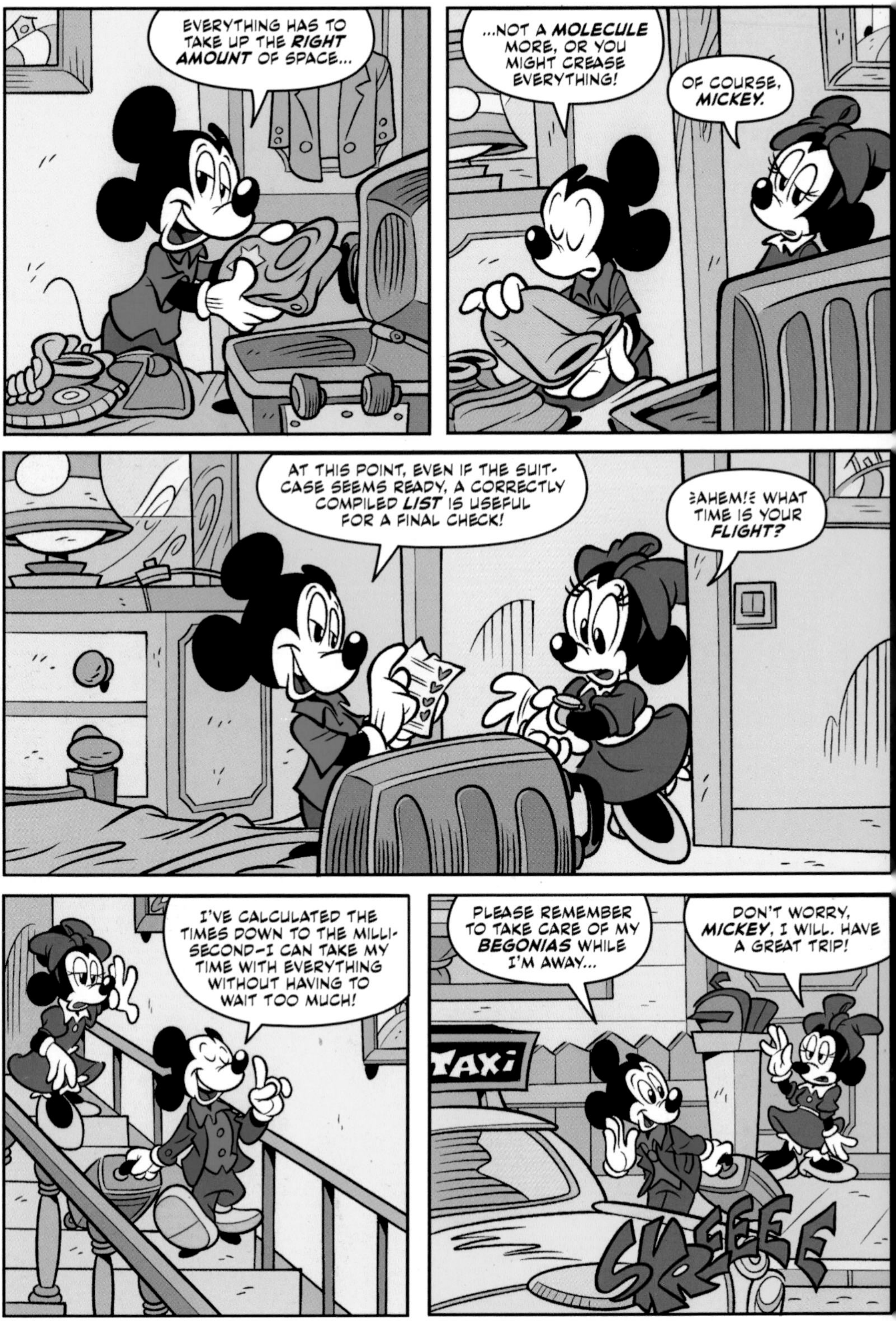
EVERYTHING HAS TO TAKE UP THE RIGHT AMOUNT OF SPACE...
...NOT A MOLECULE MORE, OR YOU MIGHT CREASE EVERYTHING!
OF COURSE, MICKEY.
AT THIS POINT, EVEN IF THE SUIT-CASE SEEMS READY, A CORRECTLY COMPILED LIST IS USEFUL FOR A FINAL CHECK!
AHEM! WHAT TIME IS YOUR FLIGHT?
I'VE CALCULATED THE TIMES DOWN TO THE MILLI-SECOND—I CAN TAKE MY TIME WITH EVERYTHING WITHOUT HAVING TO WAIT TOO MUCH!
PLEASE REMEMBER TO TAKE CARE OF MY BEGONIAS WHILE I'M AWAY...
DON'T WORRY, MICKEY, I WILL. HAVE A GREAT TRIP!
TAXI
SKREEEE

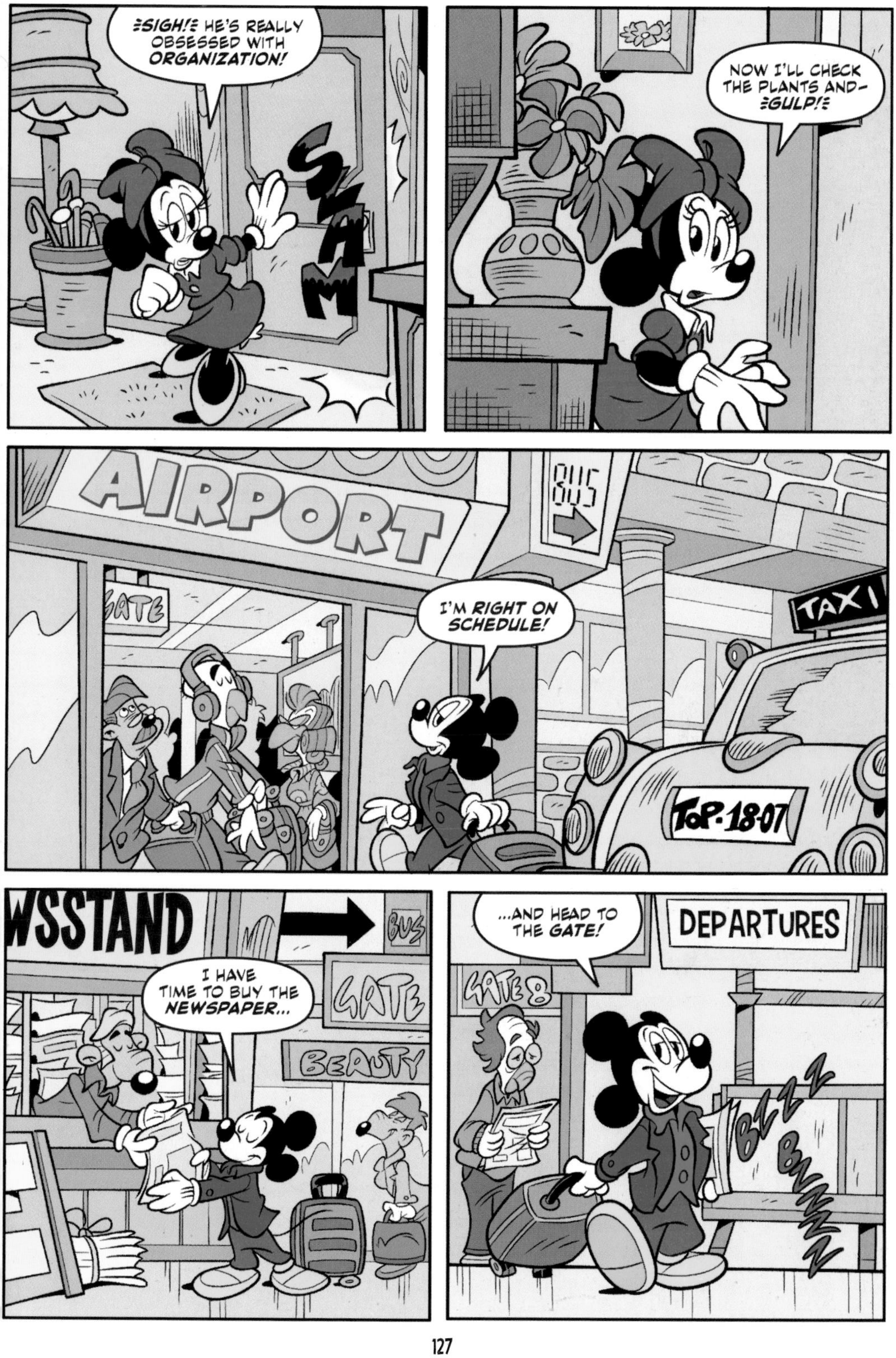
SIGH! HE'S REALLY OBSESSED WITH ORGANIZATION!
SLAM
NOW I'LL CHECK THE PLANTS AND– GULP!
AIRPORT
BUS
GATE
I'M RIGHT ON SCHEDULE!
TAXI
TOP-18-07
WSSTAND
BUS
I HAVE TIME TO BUY THE NEWSPAPER...
GATE
BEAUTY
...AND HEAD TO THE GATE!
DEPARTURES
GATE 8

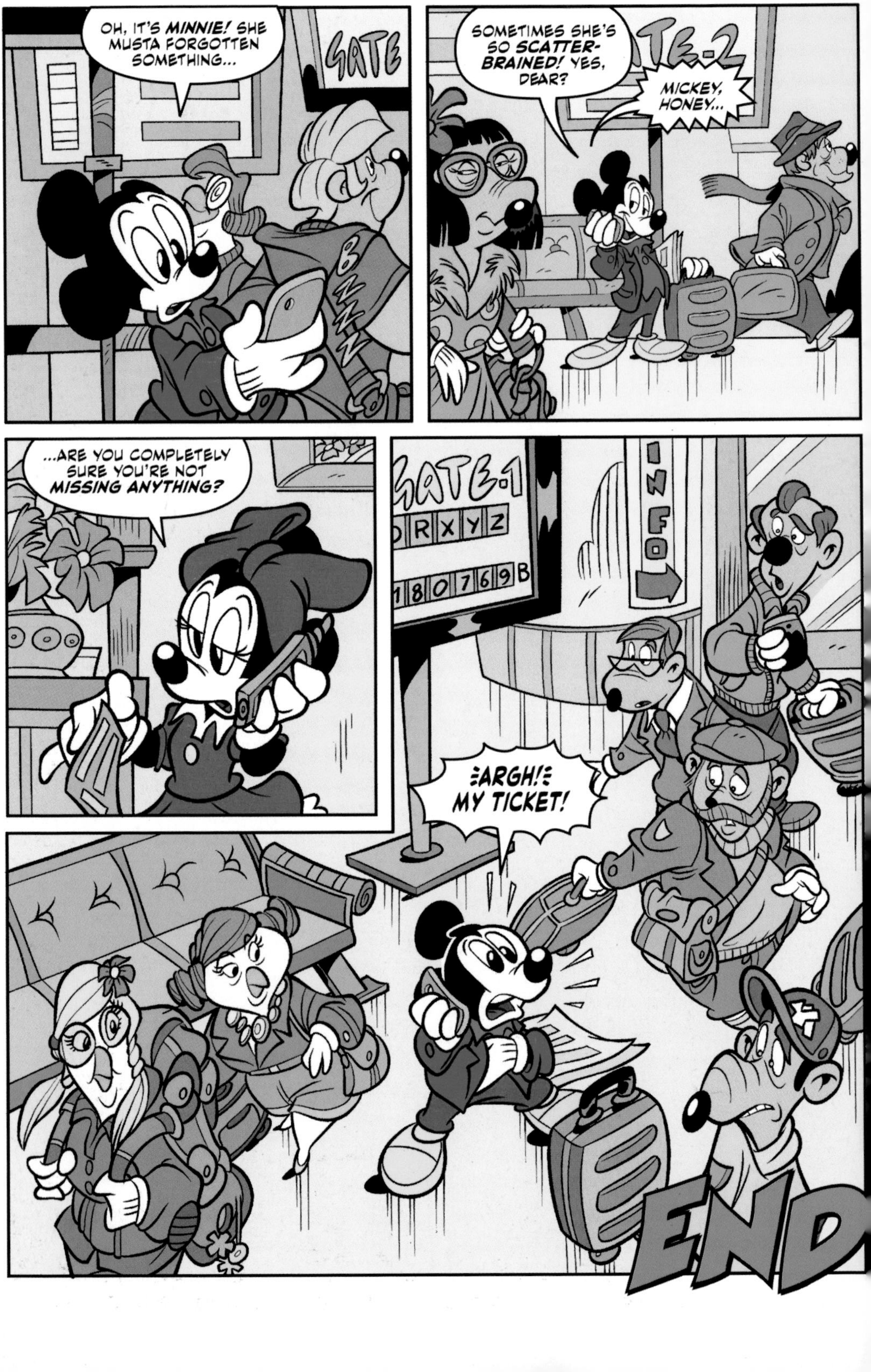

OH, IT'S MINNIE! SHE MUSTA FORGOTTEN SOMETHING...
GATE
SOMETIMES SHE'S SO SCATTER-BRAINED! YES, DEAR?
MICKEY, HONEY...
...ARE YOU COMPLETELY SURE YOU'RE NOT MISSING ANYTHING?
GATE 1
INFO
ARGH! MY TICKET!
END

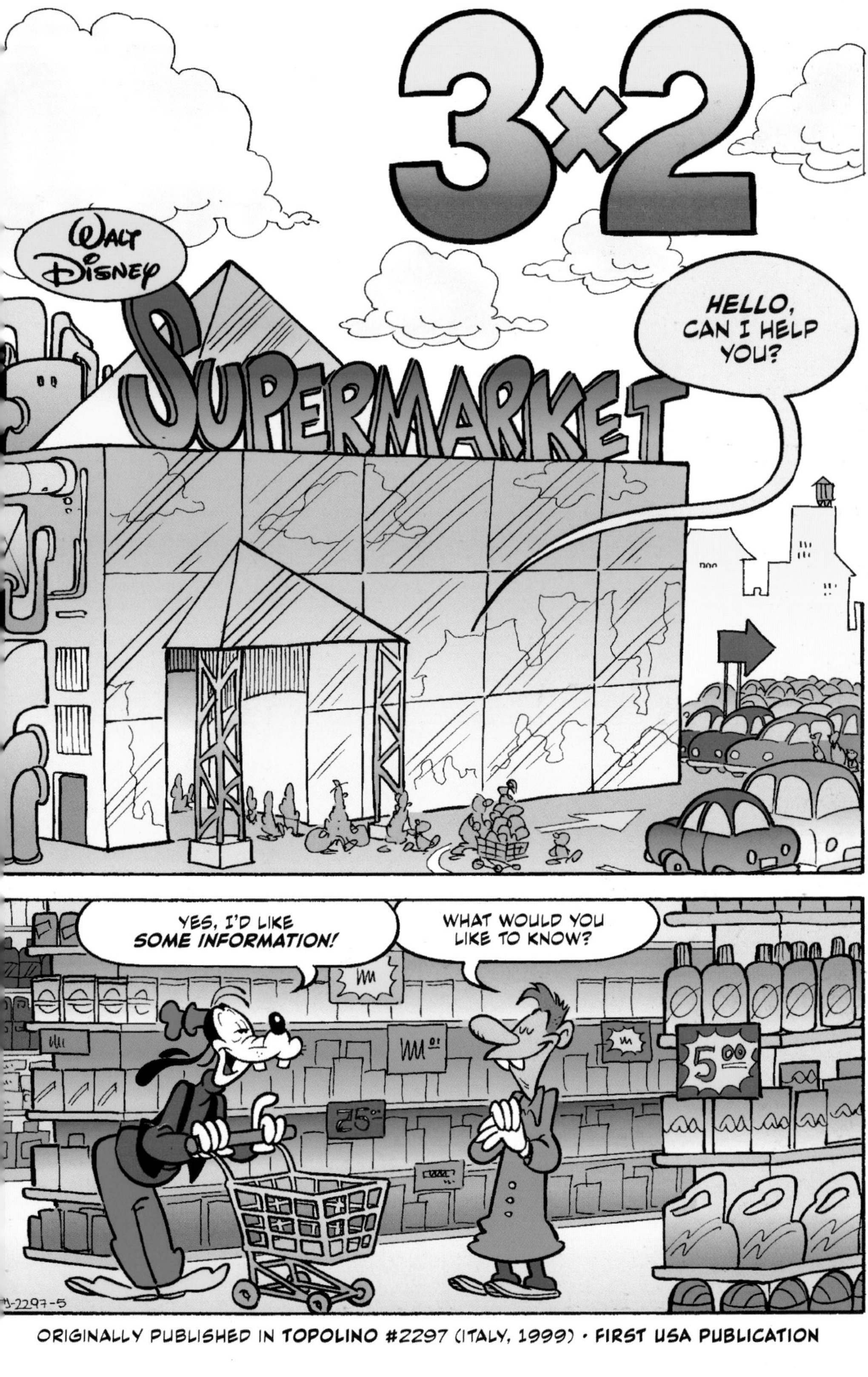
3×2
WALT DISNEY
SUPERMARKET
HELLO, CAN I HELP YOU?
YES, I'D LIKE SOME INFORMATION!
WHAT WOULD YOU LIKE TO KNOW?
5.00

ORIGINALLY PUBLISHED IN **TOPOLINO #2297** (ITALY, 1999) • **FIRST USA PUBLICATION**

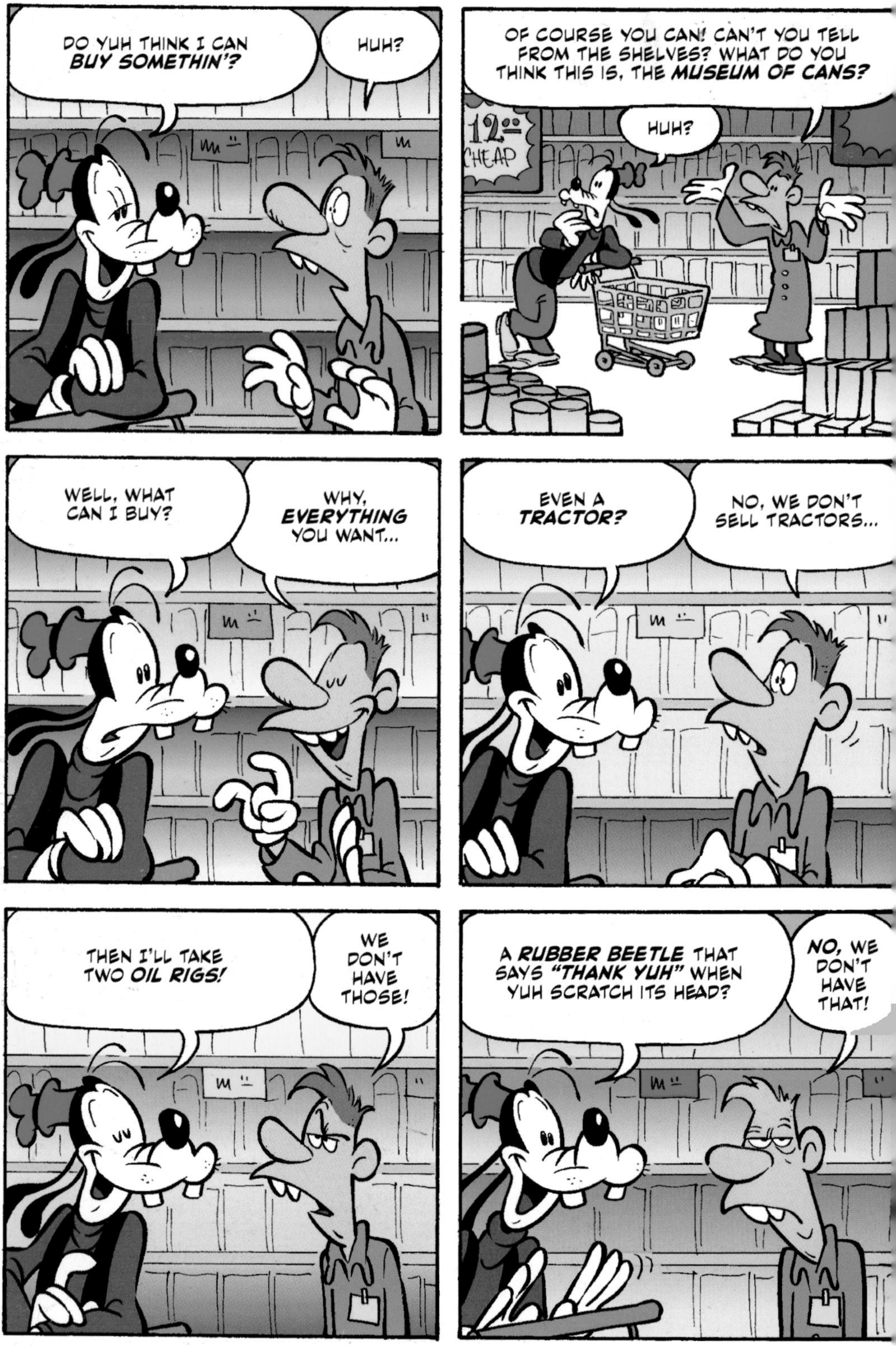
DO YUH THINK I CAN BUY SOMETHIN'?
HUH?
OF COURSE YOU CAN! CAN'T YOU TELL FROM THE SHELVES? WHAT DO YOU THINK THIS IS, THE MUSEUM OF CANS?
HUH?
12¢ CHEAP
WELL, WHAT CAN I BUY?
WHY, EVERYTHING YOU WANT...
EVEN A TRACTOR?
NO, WE DON'T SELL TRACTORS...
THEN I'LL TAKE TWO OIL RIGS!
WE DON'T HAVE THOSE!
A RUBBER BEETLE THAT SAYS "THANK YUH" WHEN YUH SCRATCH ITS HEAD?
NO, WE DON'T HAVE THAT!

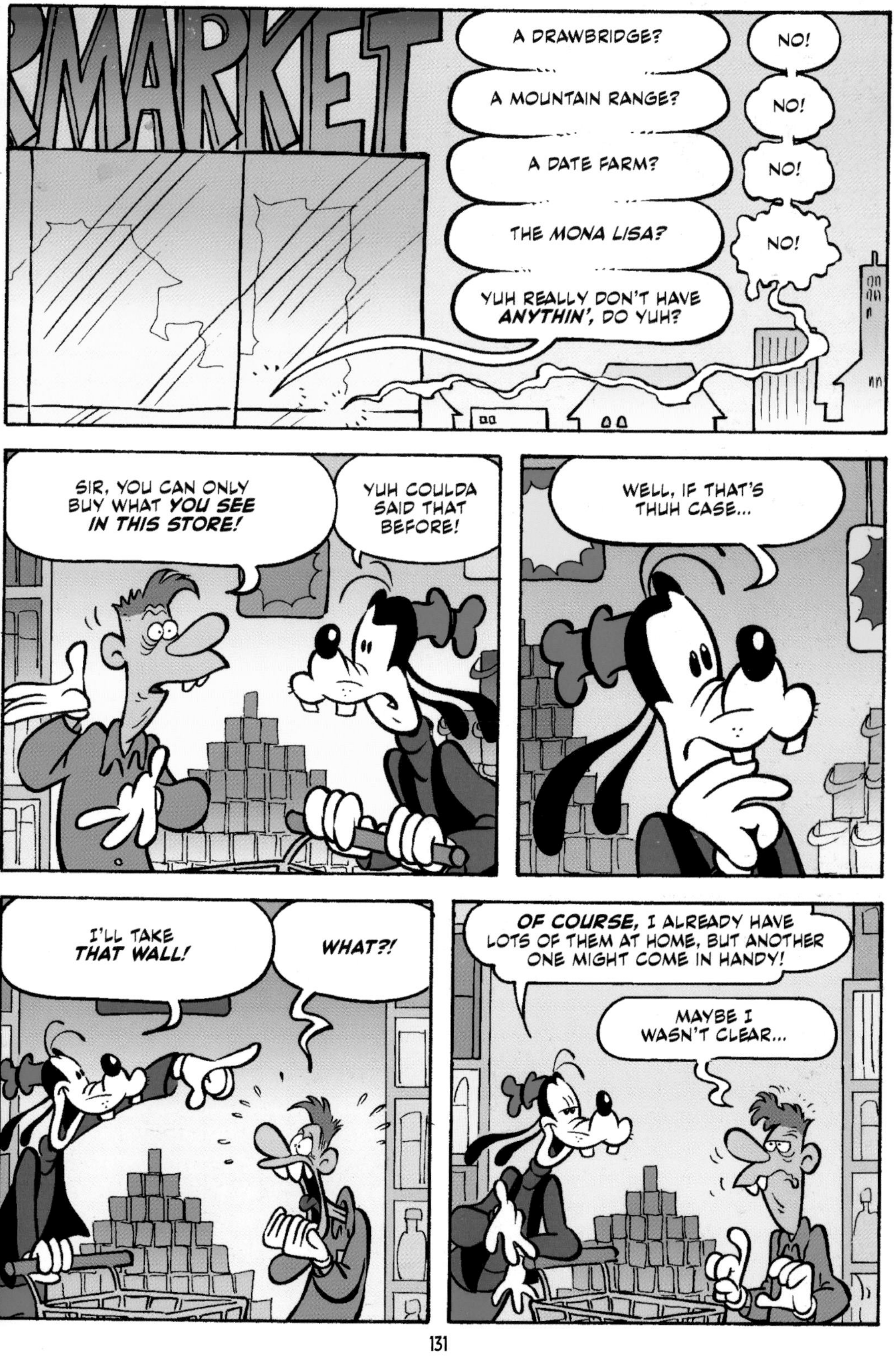
A DRAWBRIDGE?
NO!
A MOUNTAIN RANGE?
NO!
A DATE FARM?
NO!
THE MONA LISA?
NO!
YUH REALLY DON'T HAVE ANYTHIN', DO YUH?
SIR, YOU CAN ONLY BUY WHAT YOU SEE IN THIS STORE!
YUH COULDA SAID THAT BEFORE!
WELL, IF THAT'S THUH CASE...
I'LL TAKE THAT WALL!
WHAT?!
OF COURSE, I ALREADY HAVE LOTS OF THEM AT HOME, BUT ANOTHER ONE MIGHT COME IN HANDY!
MAYBE I WASN'T CLEAR...

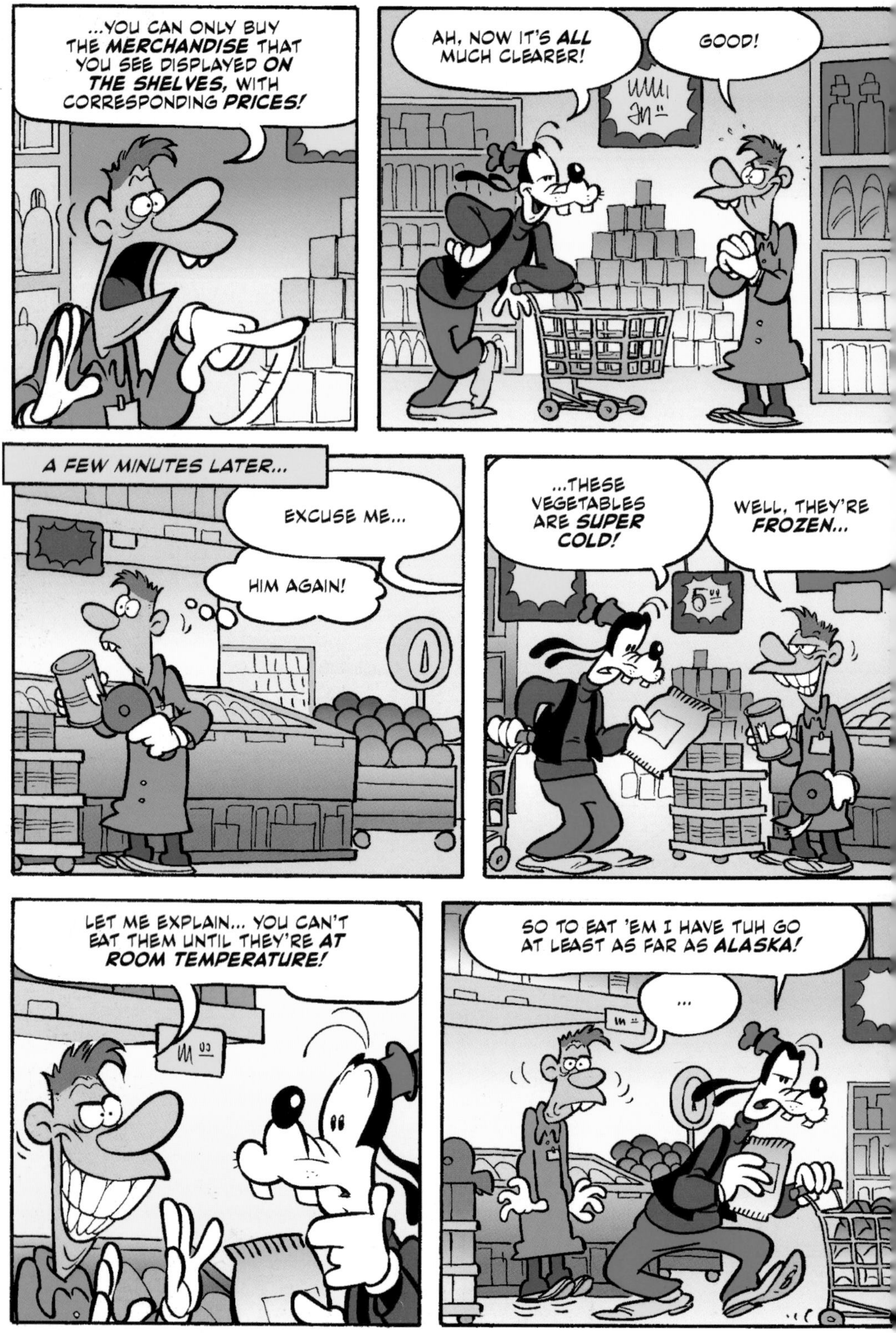
...YOU CAN ONLY BUY THE MERCHANDISE THAT YOU SEE DISPLAYED ON THE SHELVES, WITH CORRESPONDING PRICES!
AH, NOW IT'S ALL MUCH CLEARER!
GOOD!
A FEW MINUTES LATER...
EXCUSE ME...
HIM AGAIN!
...THESE VEGETABLES ARE SUPER COLD!
WELL, THEY'RE FROZEN...
LET ME EXPLAIN... YOU CAN'T EAT THEM UNTIL THEY'RE AT ROOM TEMPERATURE!
SO TO EAT 'EM I HAVE TUH GO AT LEAST AS FAR AS ALASKA!
...

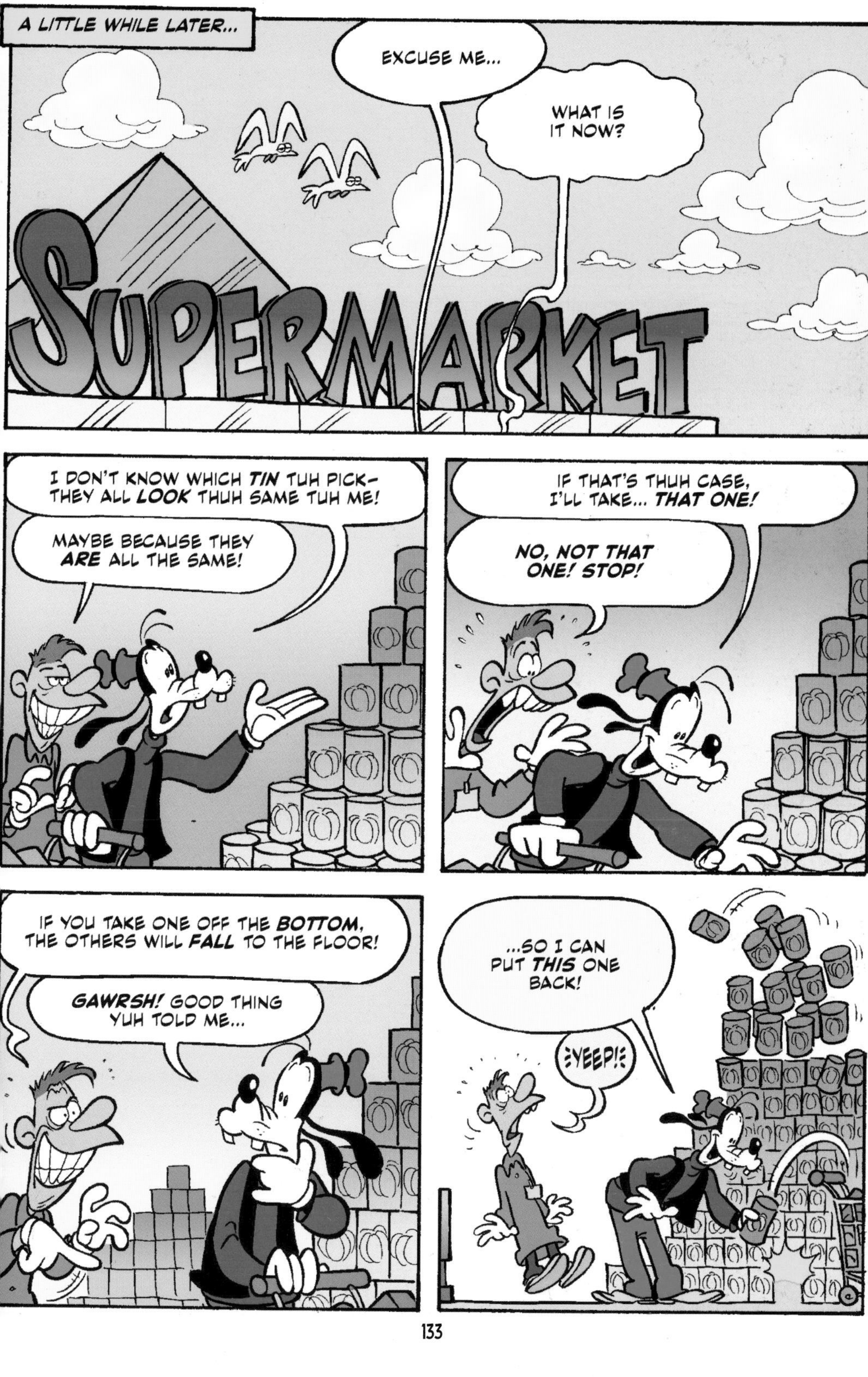
A LITTLE WHILE LATER...
EXCUSE ME...
WHAT IS IT NOW?
SUPERMARKET
I DON'T KNOW WHICH TIN TUH PICK–THEY ALL LOOK THUH SAME TUH ME!
MAYBE BECAUSE THEY ARE ALL THE SAME!
IF THAT'S THUH CASE, I'LL TAKE... THAT ONE!
NO, NOT THAT ONE! STOP!
IF YOU TAKE ONE OFF THE BOTTOM, THE OTHERS WILL FALL TO THE FLOOR!
GAWRSH! GOOD THING YUH TOLD ME...
...SO I CAN PUT THIS ONE BACK!
YEEP!

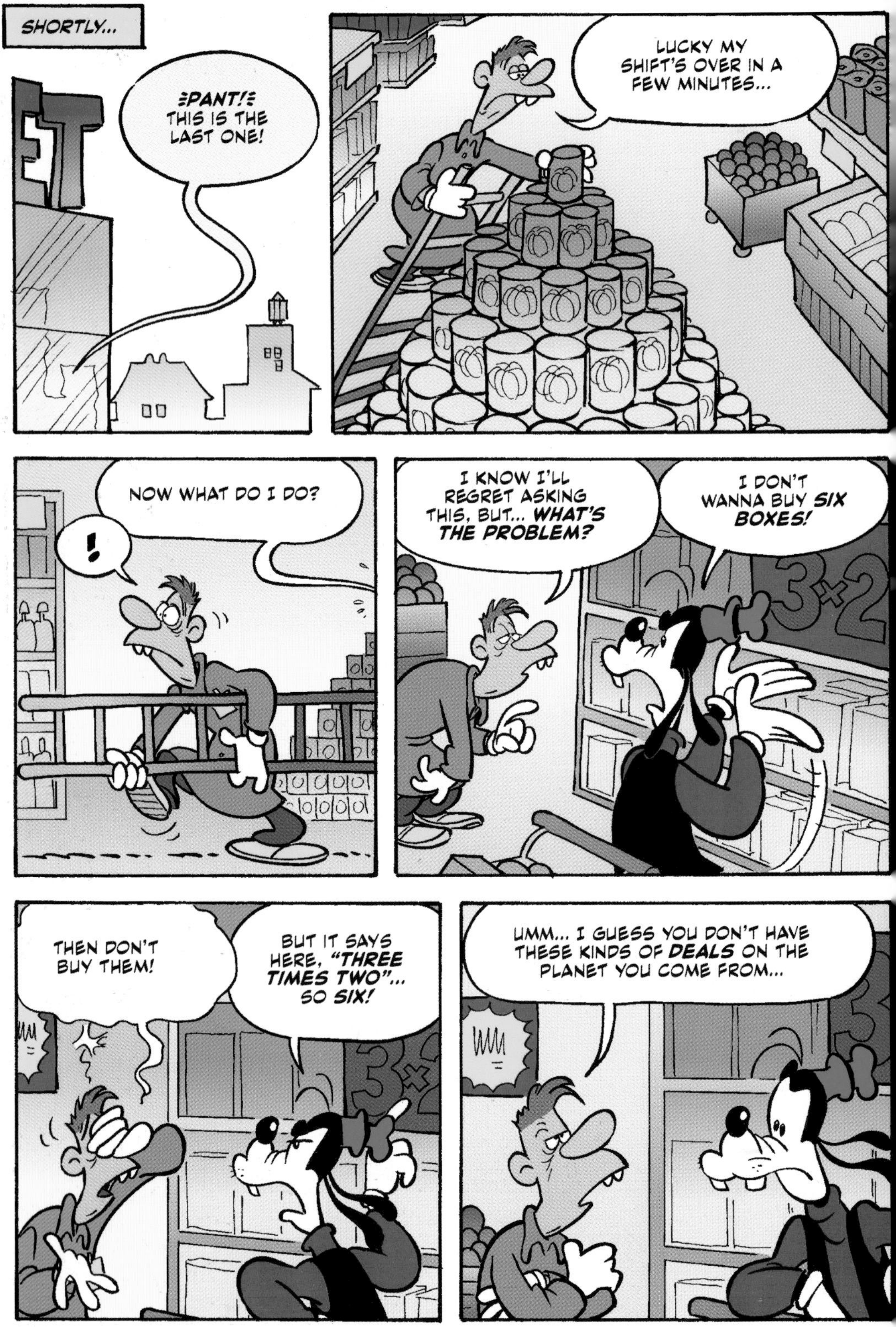
SHORTLY...
PANT! THIS IS THE LAST ONE!
LUCKY MY SHIFT'S OVER IN A FEW MINUTES...
NOW WHAT DO I DO?
!
I KNOW I'LL REGRET ASKING THIS, BUT... WHAT'S THE PROBLEM?
I DON'T WANNA BUY SIX BOXES!
3x2
THEN DON'T BUY THEM!
BUT IT SAYS HERE, "THREE TIMES TWO"... SO SIX!
UMM... I GUESS YOU DON'T HAVE THESE KINDS OF DEALS ON THE PLANET YOU COME FROM...

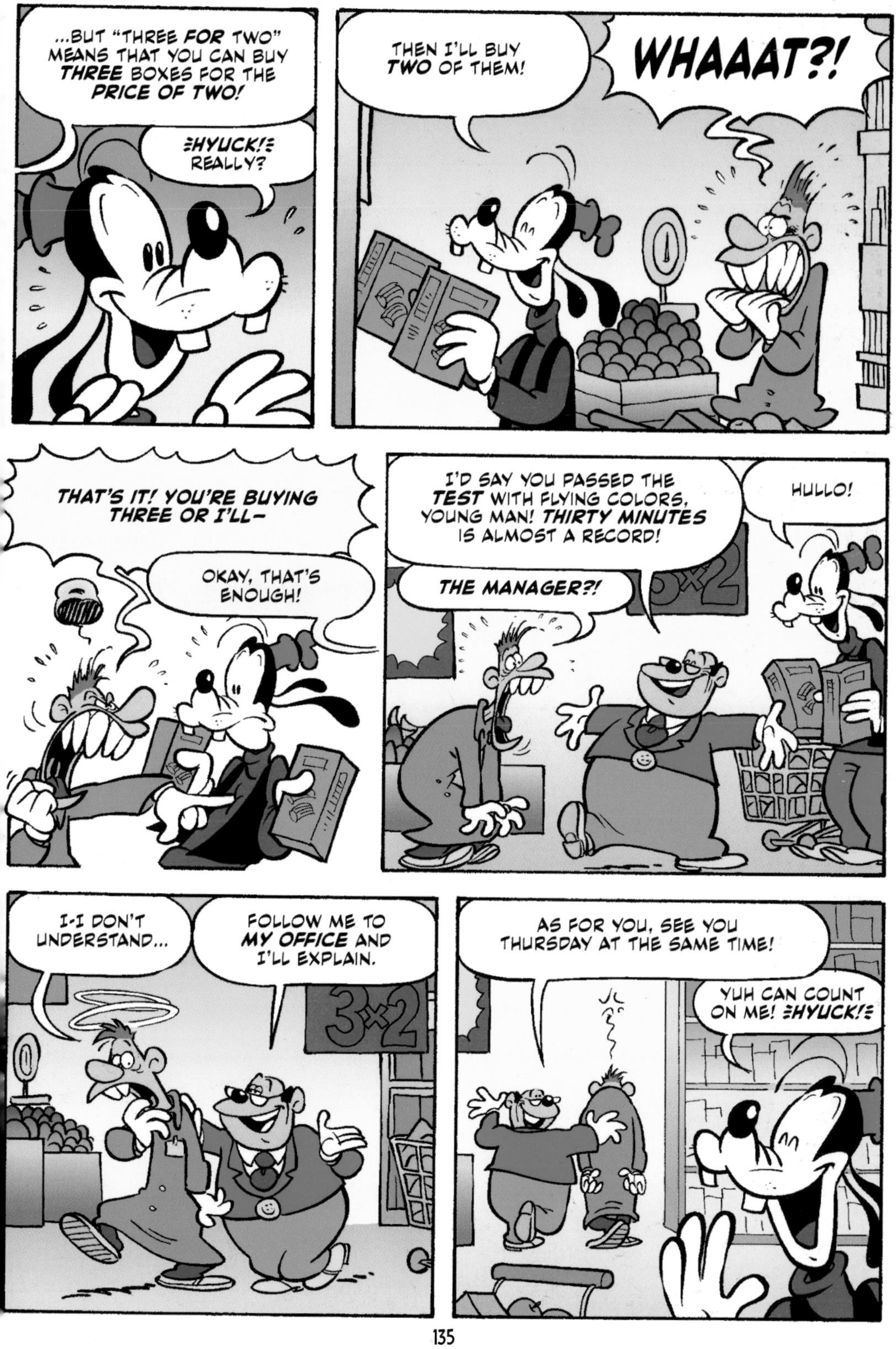
...BUT "THREE FOR TWO" MEANS THAT YOU CAN BUY THREE BOXES FOR THE PRICE OF TWO!
HYUCK! REALLY?
THEN I'LL BUY TWO OF THEM!
WHAAAT?!
THAT'S IT! YOU'RE BUYING THREE OR I'LL–
OKAY, THAT'S ENOUGH!
THE MANAGER?!
I'D SAY YOU PASSED THE TEST WITH FLYING COLORS, YOUNG MAN! THIRTY MINUTES IS ALMOST A RECORD!
HULLO!
3×2
I-I DON'T UNDERSTAND...
FOLLOW ME TO MY OFFICE AND I'LL EXPLAIN.
3×2
AS FOR YOU, SEE YOU THURSDAY AT THE SAME TIME!
YUH CAN COUNT ON ME! HYUCK!

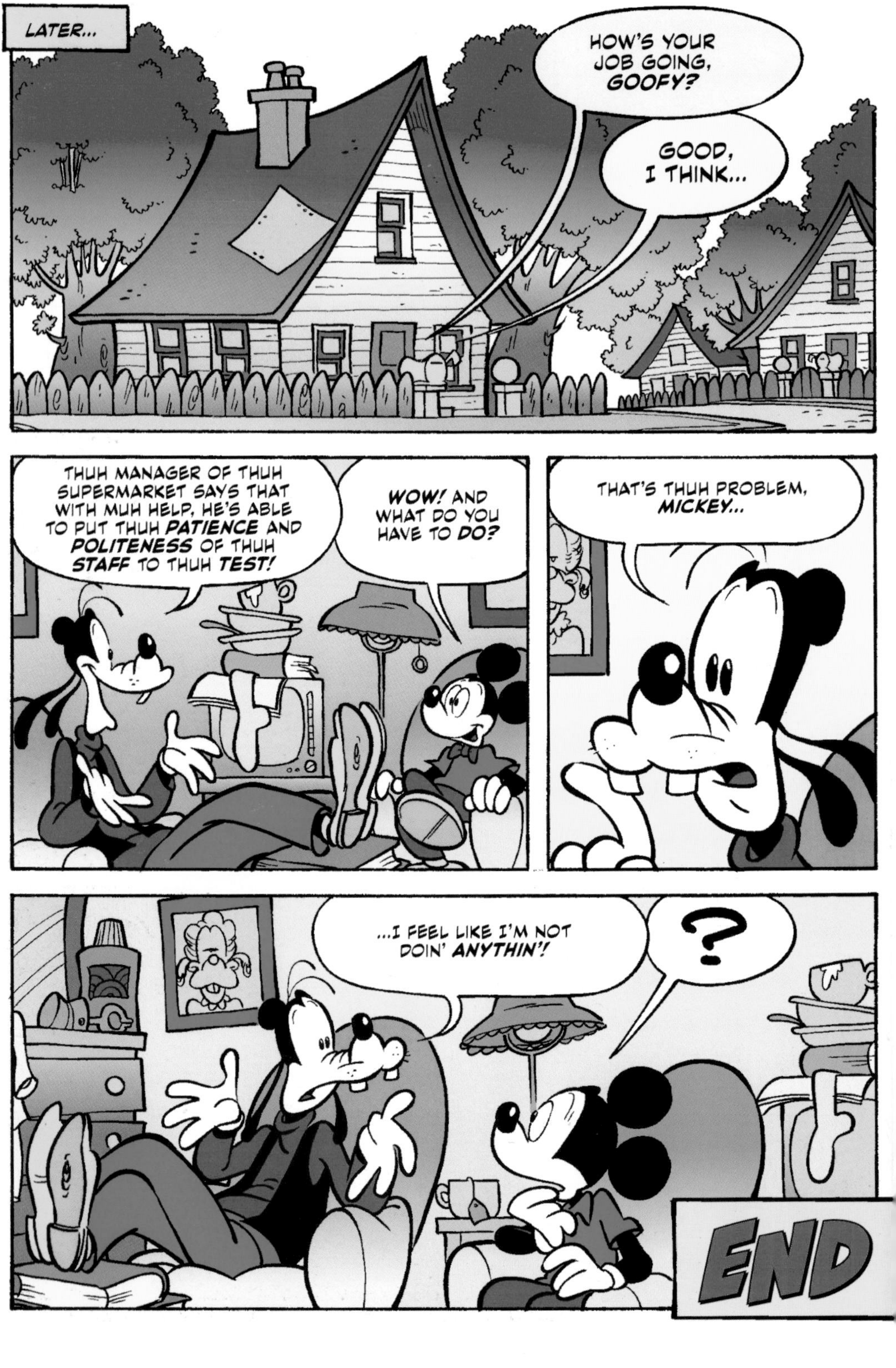
LATER...
HOW'S YOUR JOB GOING, GOOFY?
GOOD, I THINK...
THUH MANAGER OF THUH SUPERMARKET SAYS THAT WITH MUH HELP, HE'S ABLE TO PUT THUH PATIENCE AND POLITENESS OF THUH STAFF TO THUH TEST!
WOW! AND WHAT DO YOU HAVE TO DO?
THAT'S THUH PROBLEM, MICKEY...
...I FEEL LIKE I'M NOT DOIN' ANYTHIN'!
?
END

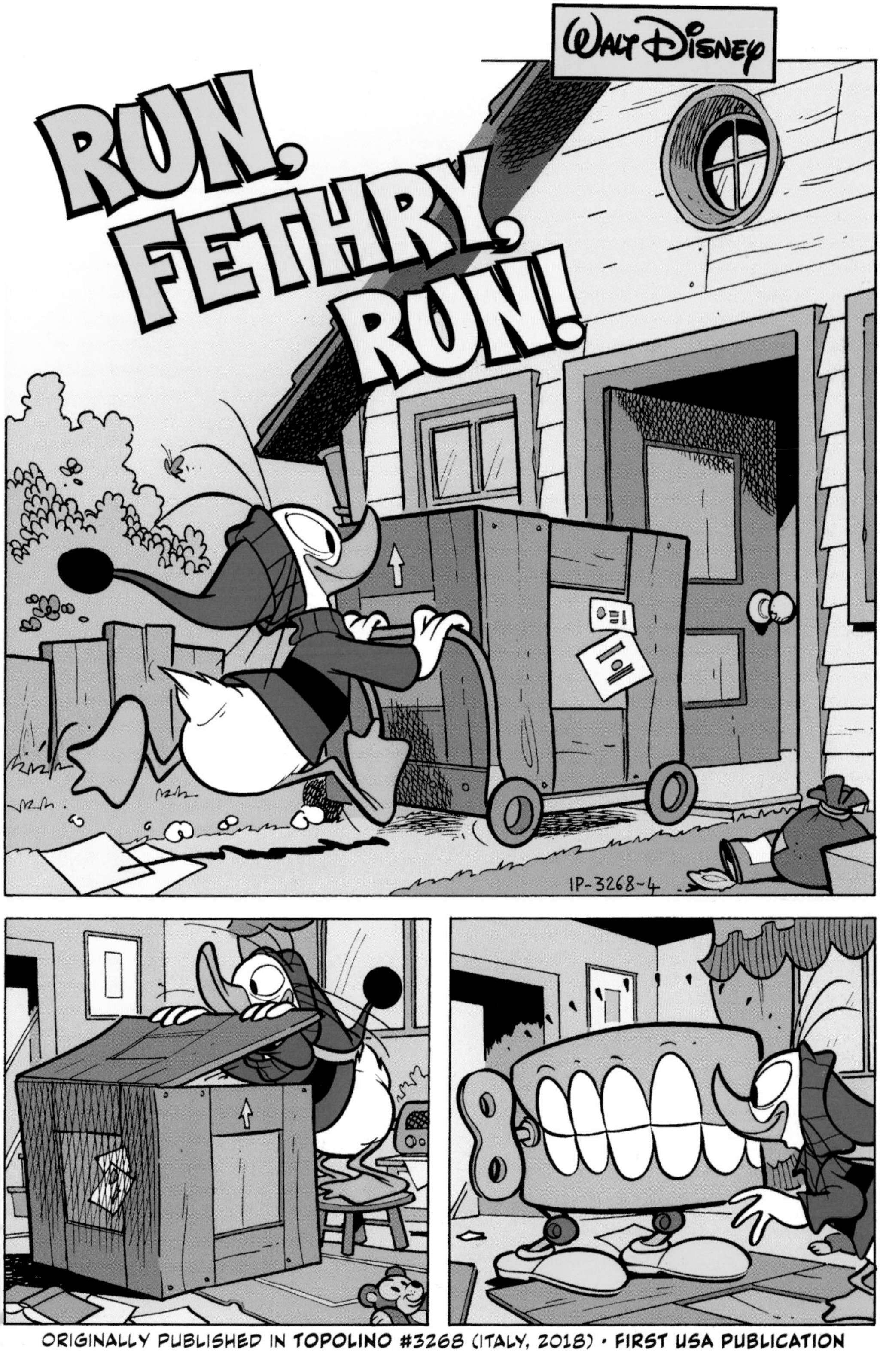
Walt Disney
RUN, FETHRY, RUN!
IP-3268-4

ORIGINALLY PUBLISHED IN TOPOLINO #3268 (ITALY, 2018) • FIRST USA PUBLICATION

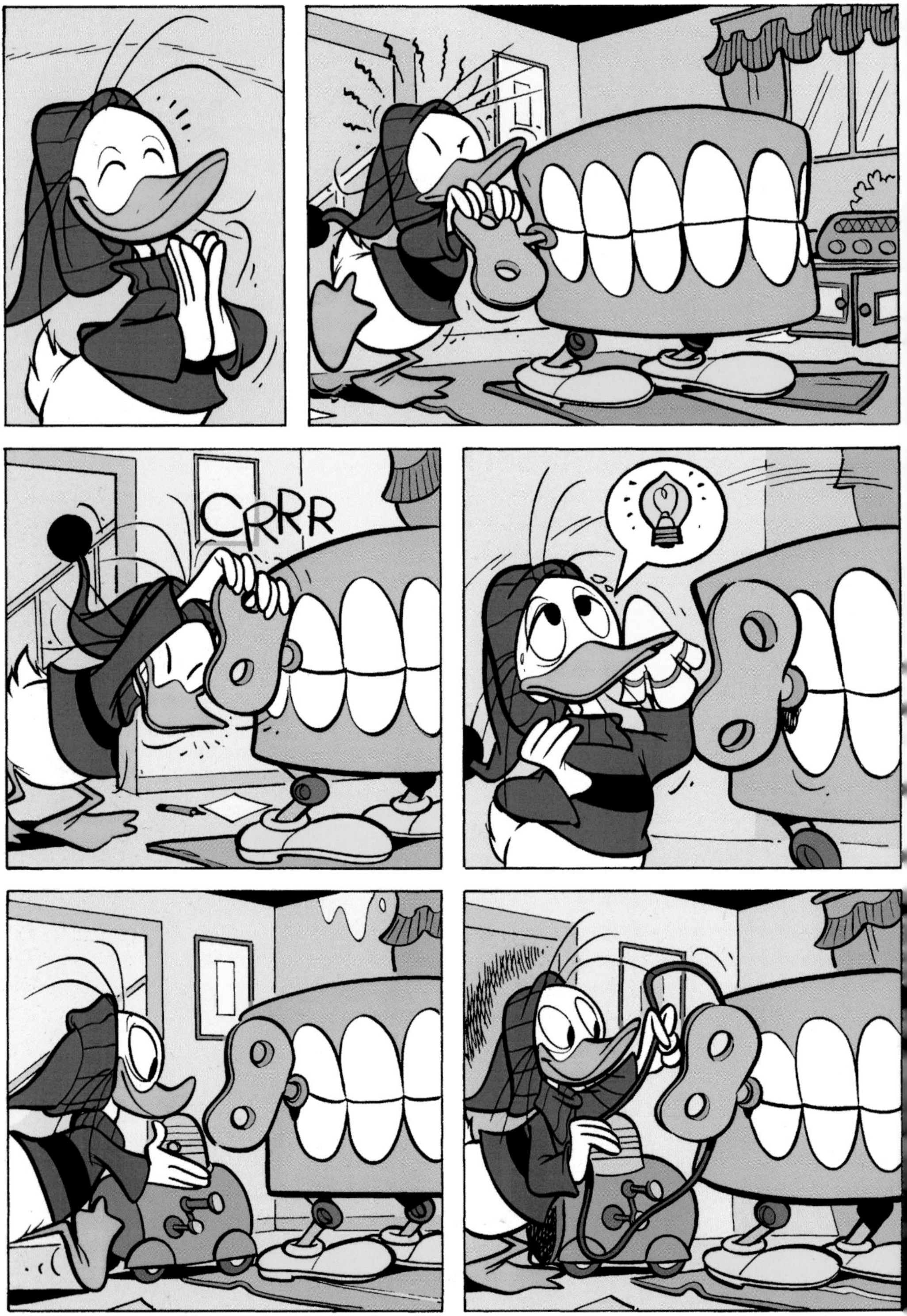
CRRR

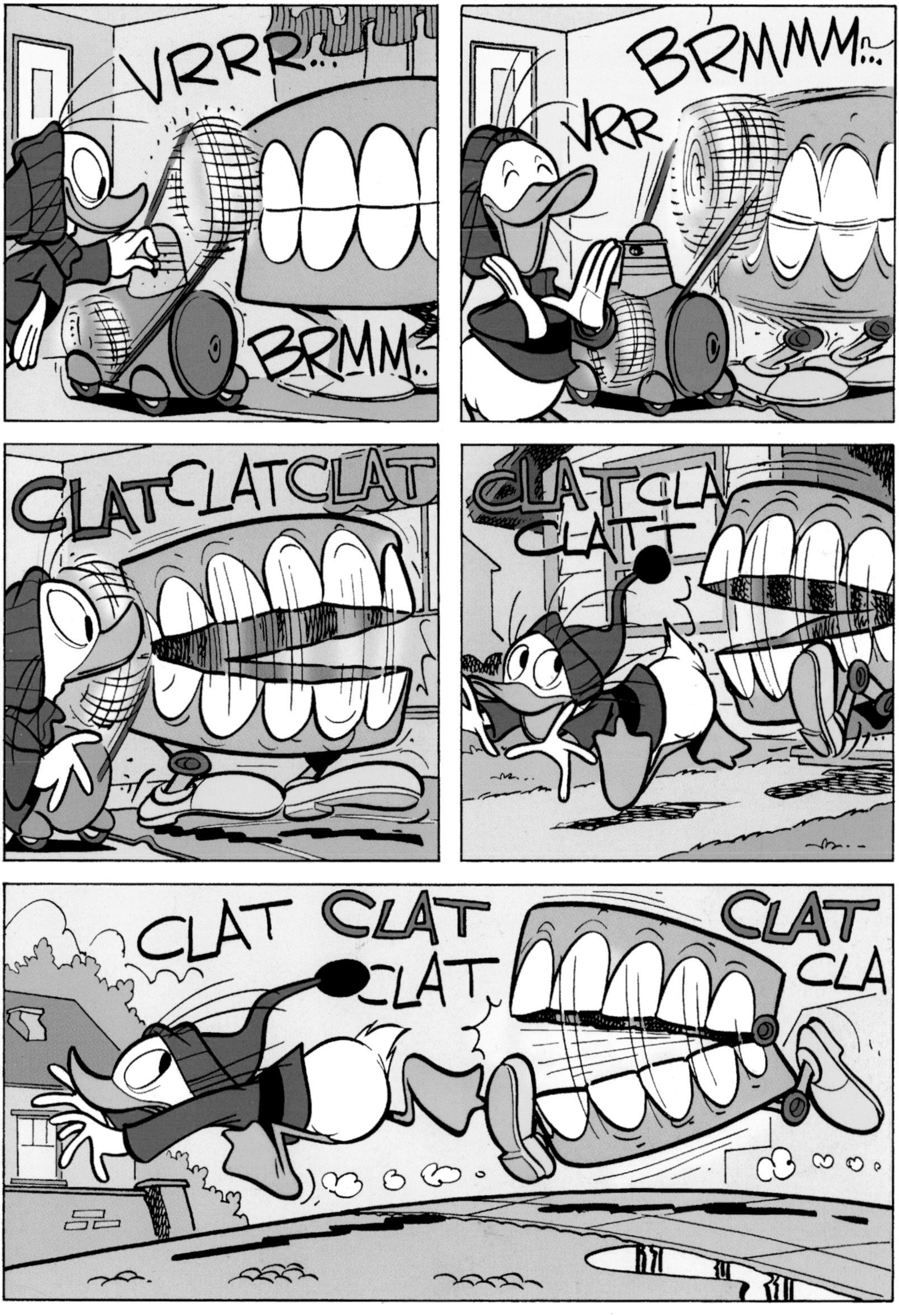
VRRRR...
BRMM..
BRMMM...
VRR
CLATCLATCLAT
CLATCLA
CLATT
CLAT CLAT
CLAT
CLAT
CLA

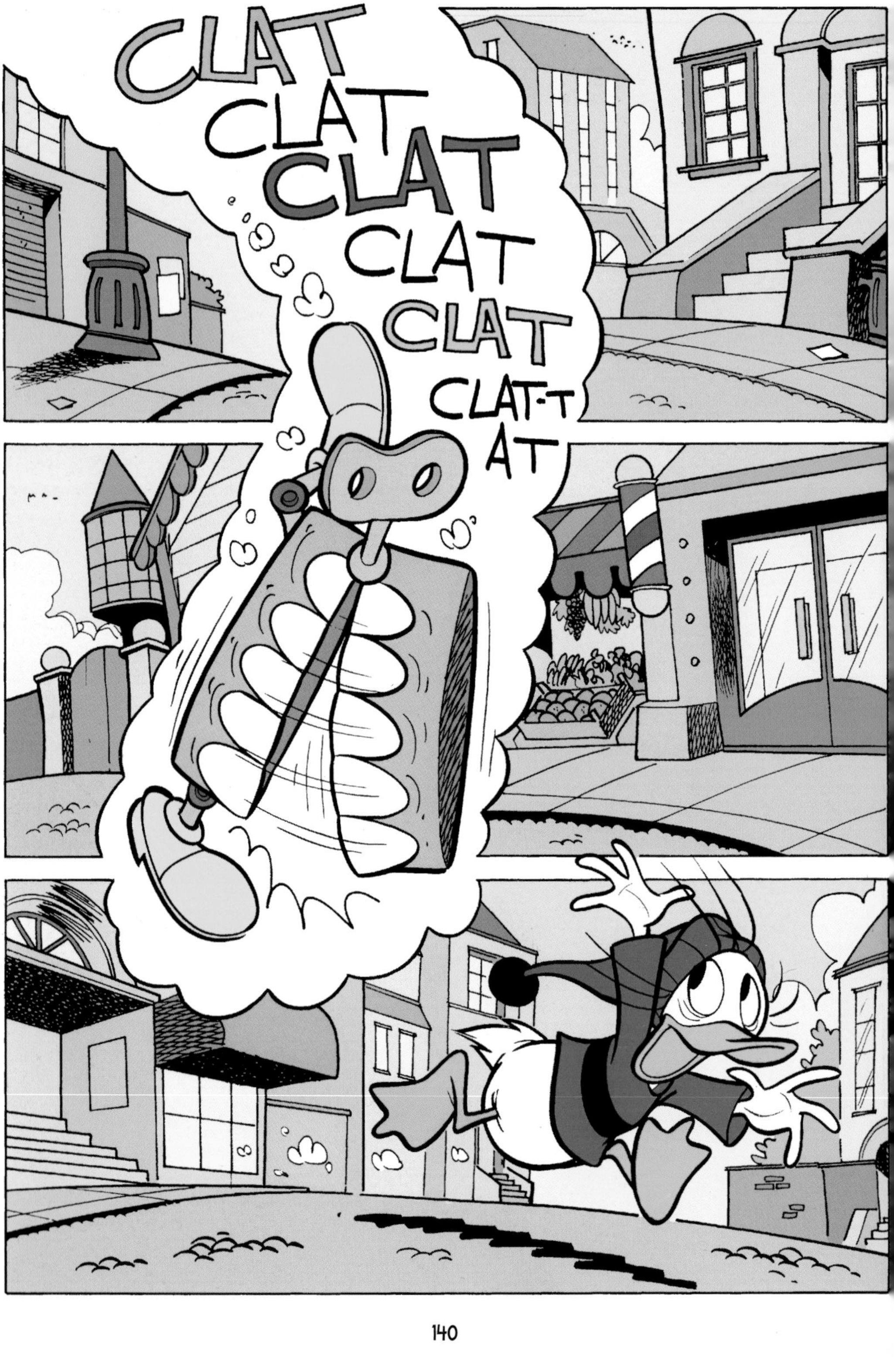
CLAT
CLAT
CLAT
CLAT
CLAT
CLAT-T
AT

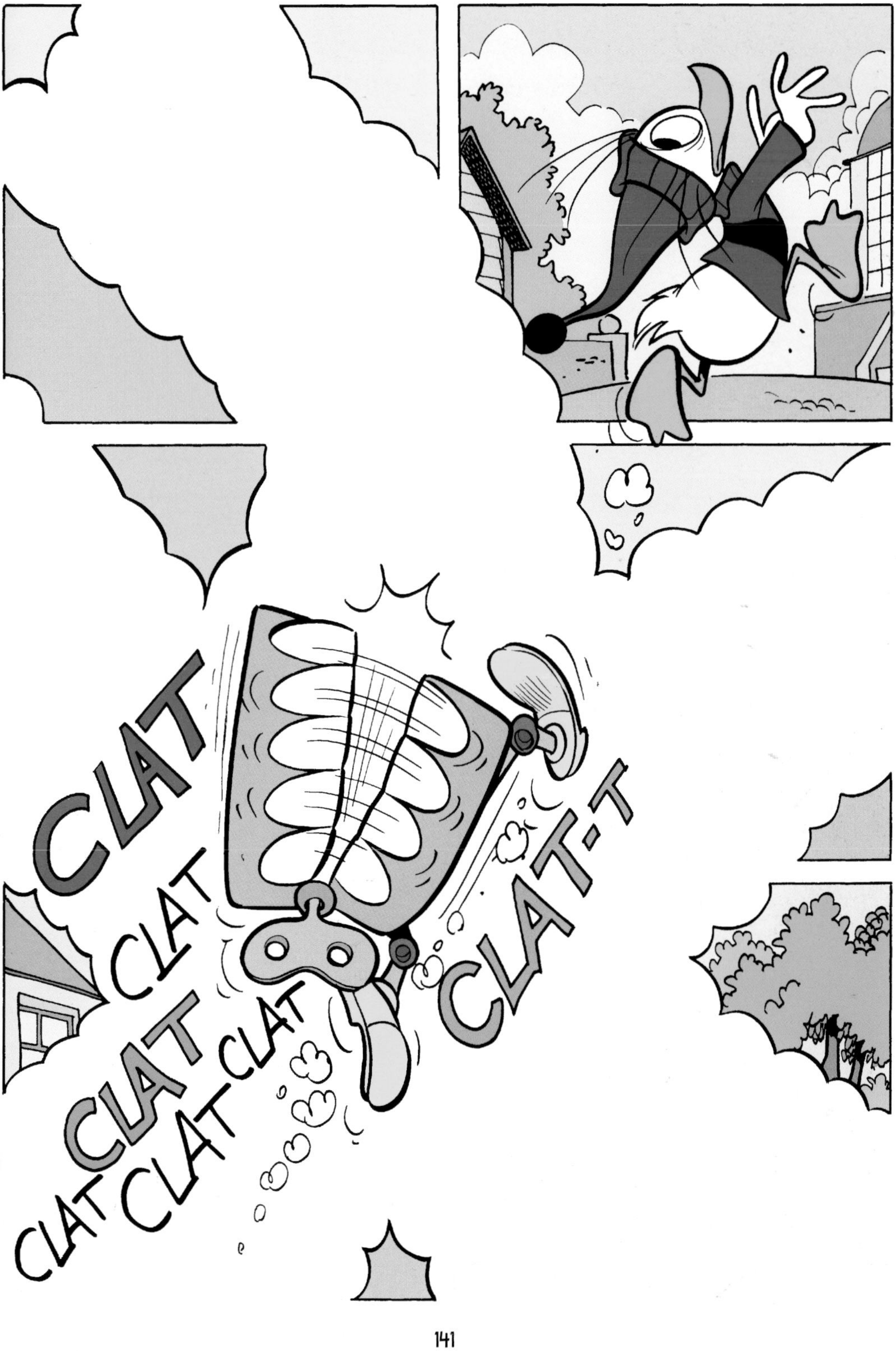
CLAT
CLAT
CLAT
CLAT CLAT CLAT CLAT
CLAT-T

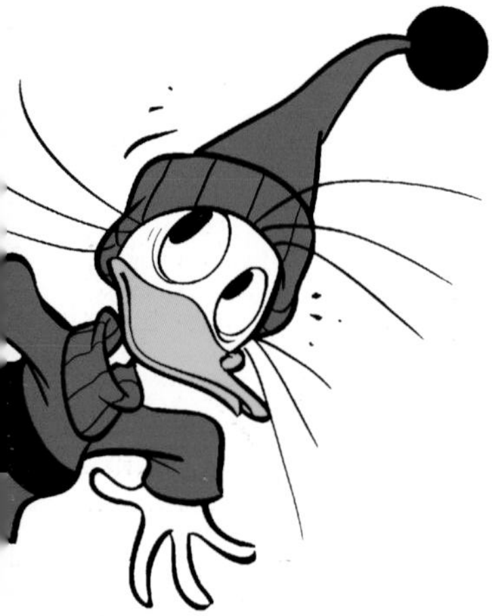

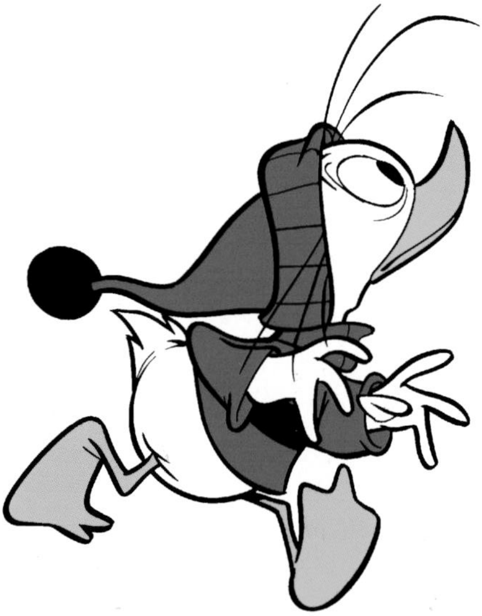

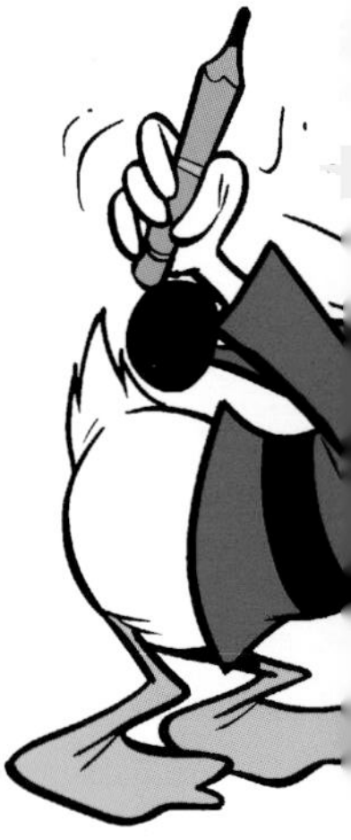

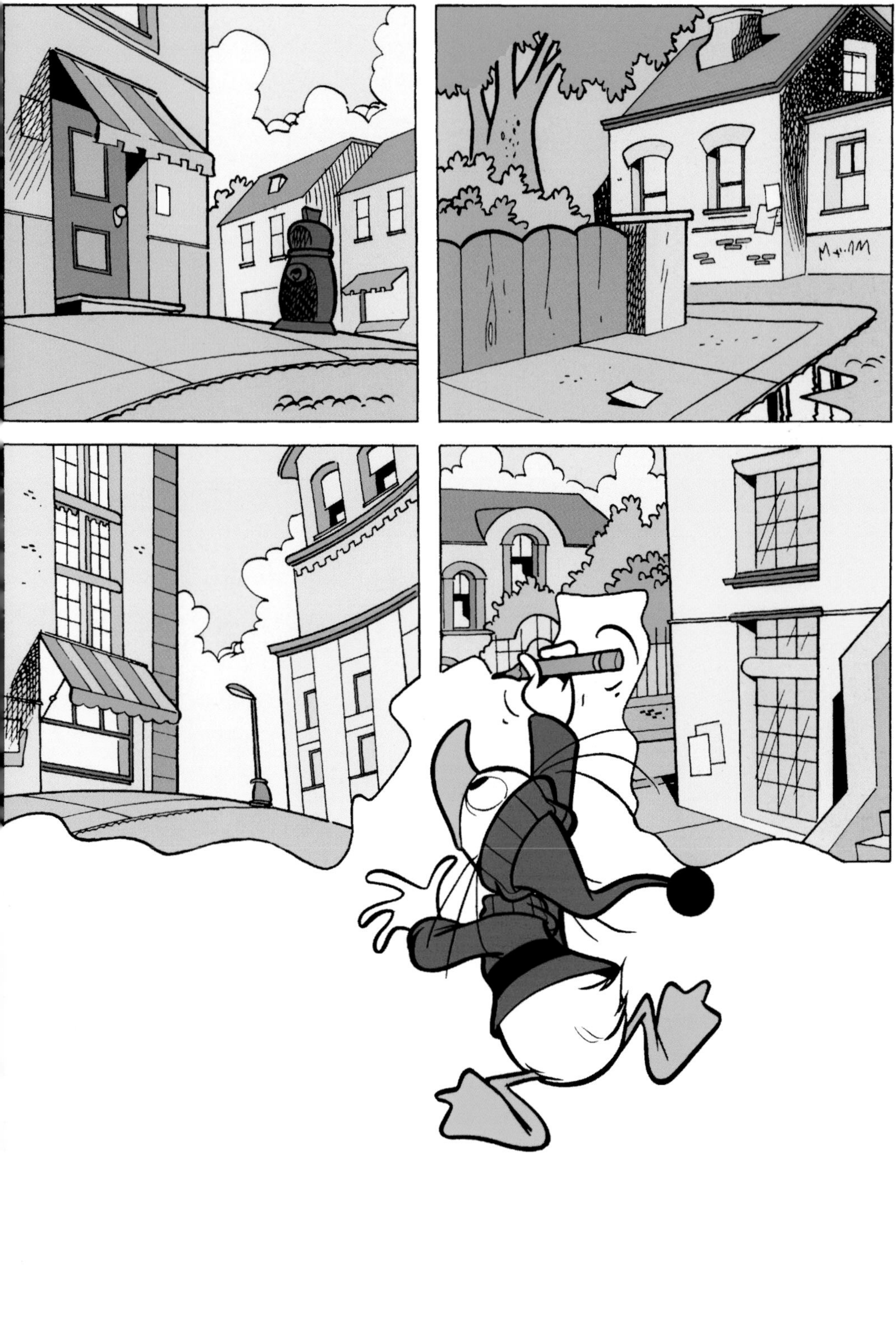

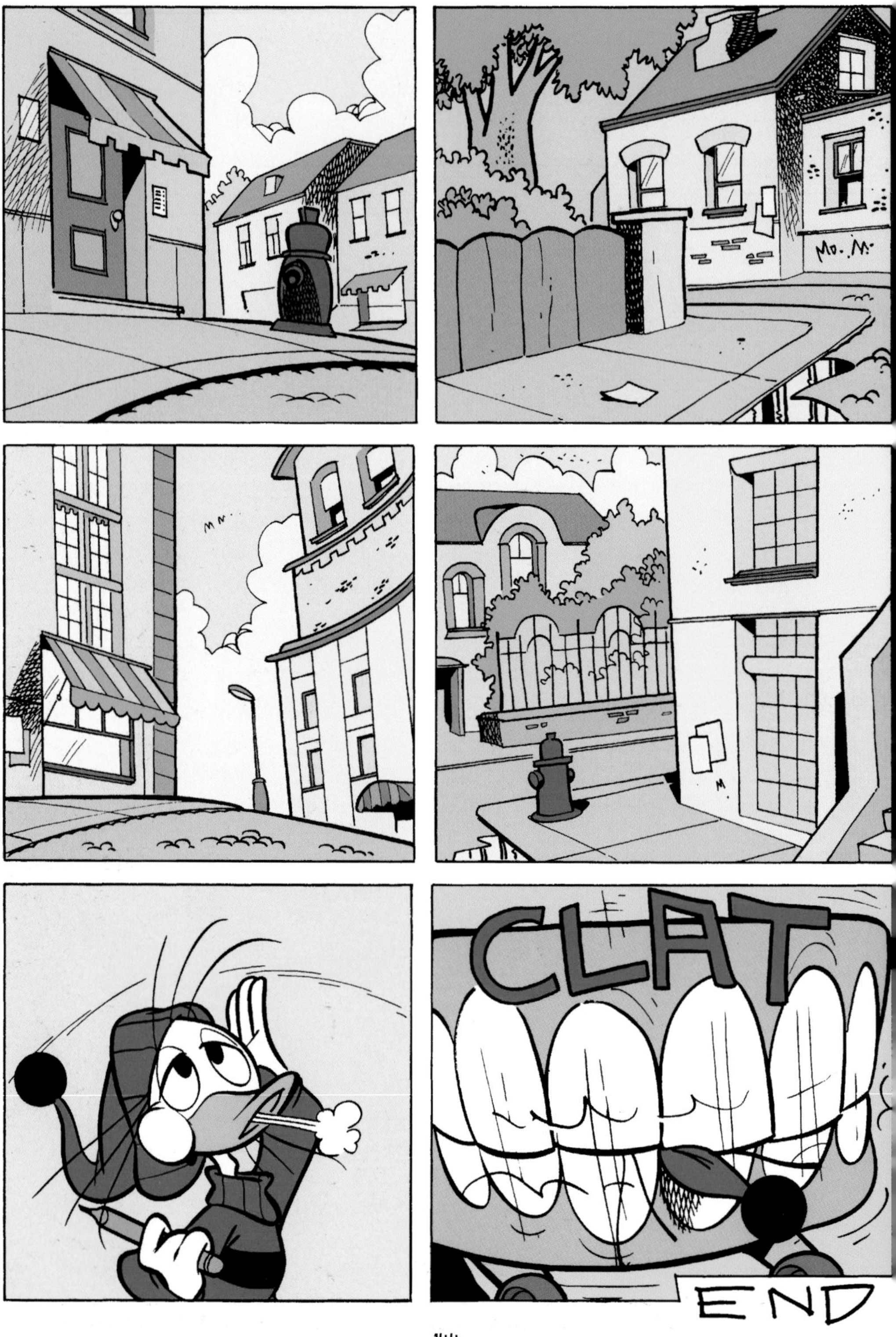
CLAT
END

WALT DISNEY

FETHRY AT WORK

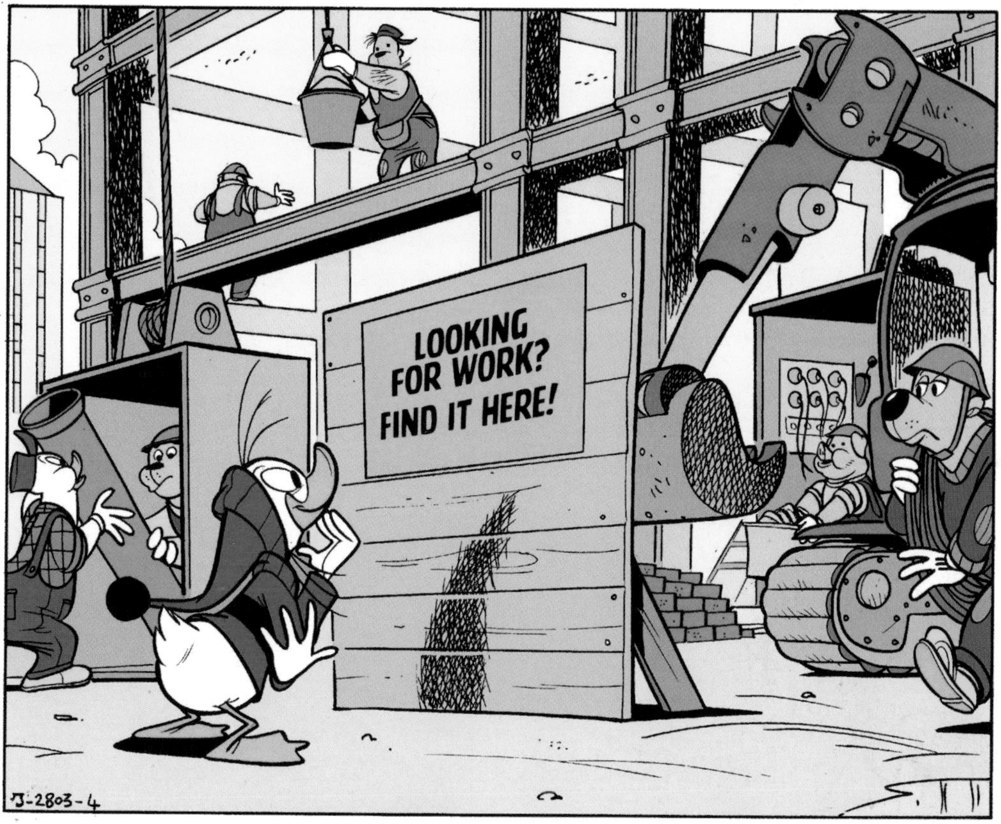
LOOKING FOR WORK? FIND IT HERE!
J-2803-4

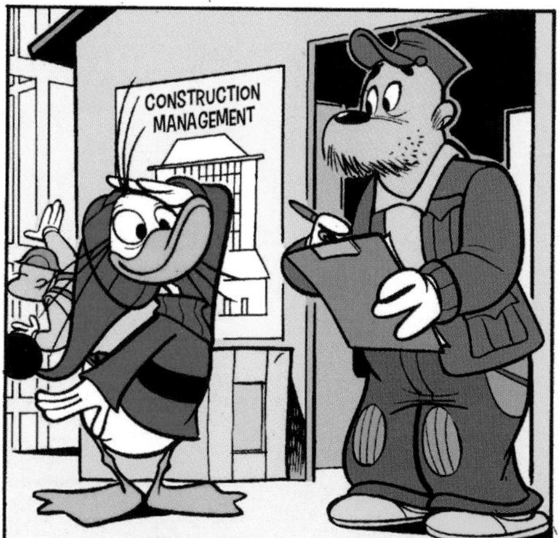
CONSTRUCTION MANAGEMENT

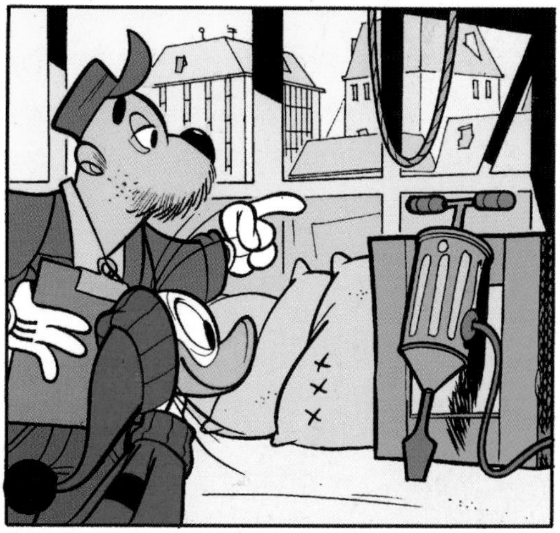

ORIGINALLY PUBLISHED IN TOPOLINO #2803 (ITALY, 2009) • FIRST USA PUBLICATION

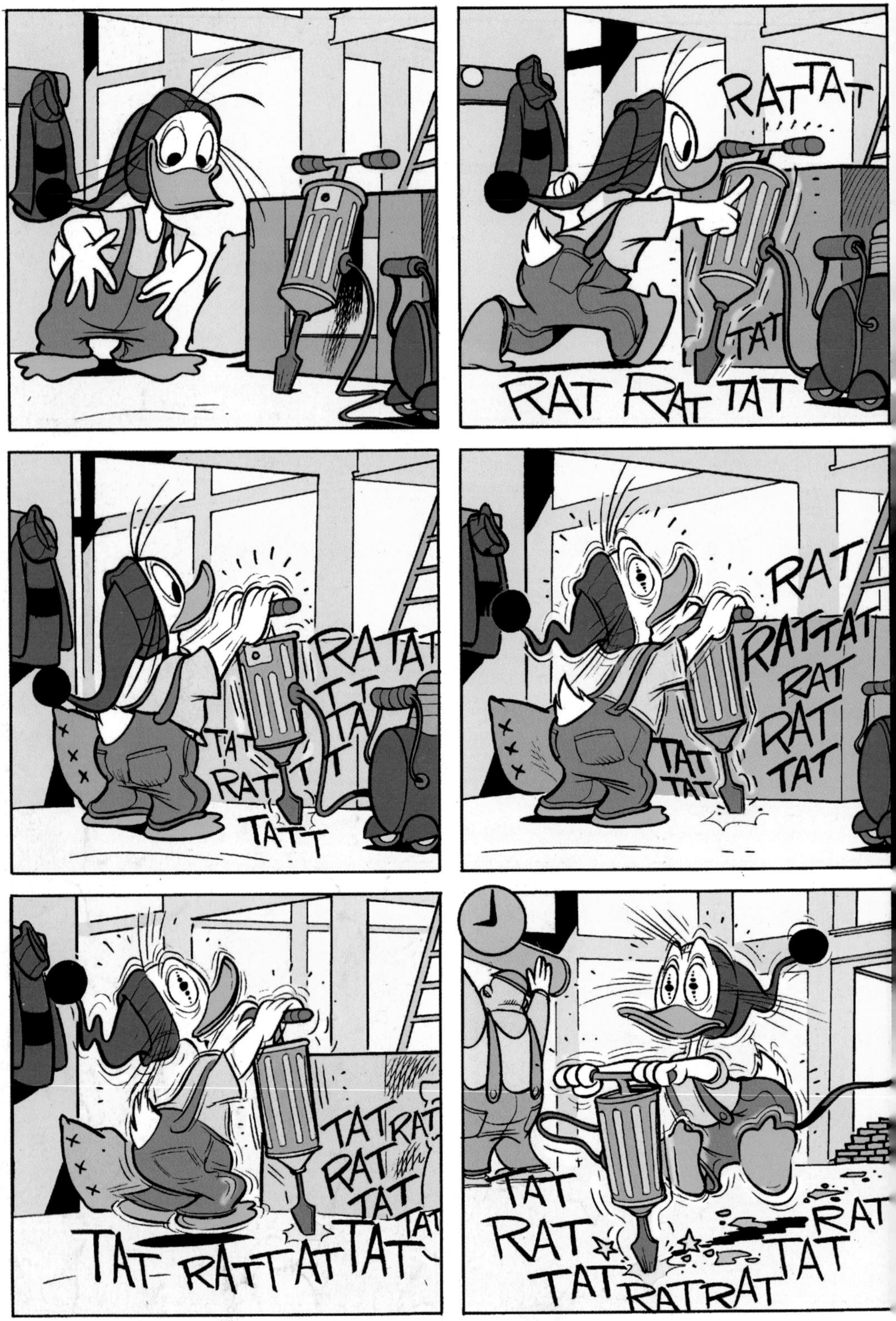
RAT TAT T
TAT
RAT RAT TAT
RATATAT
TAT
RAT
TATT
RAT
RATTAT
RAT
RAT
TAT
TAT
TAT
TATRAT
RAT
TAT
TAT- RATTATTAT
TAT
RAT
TAT
RATRAT
TAT
RAT

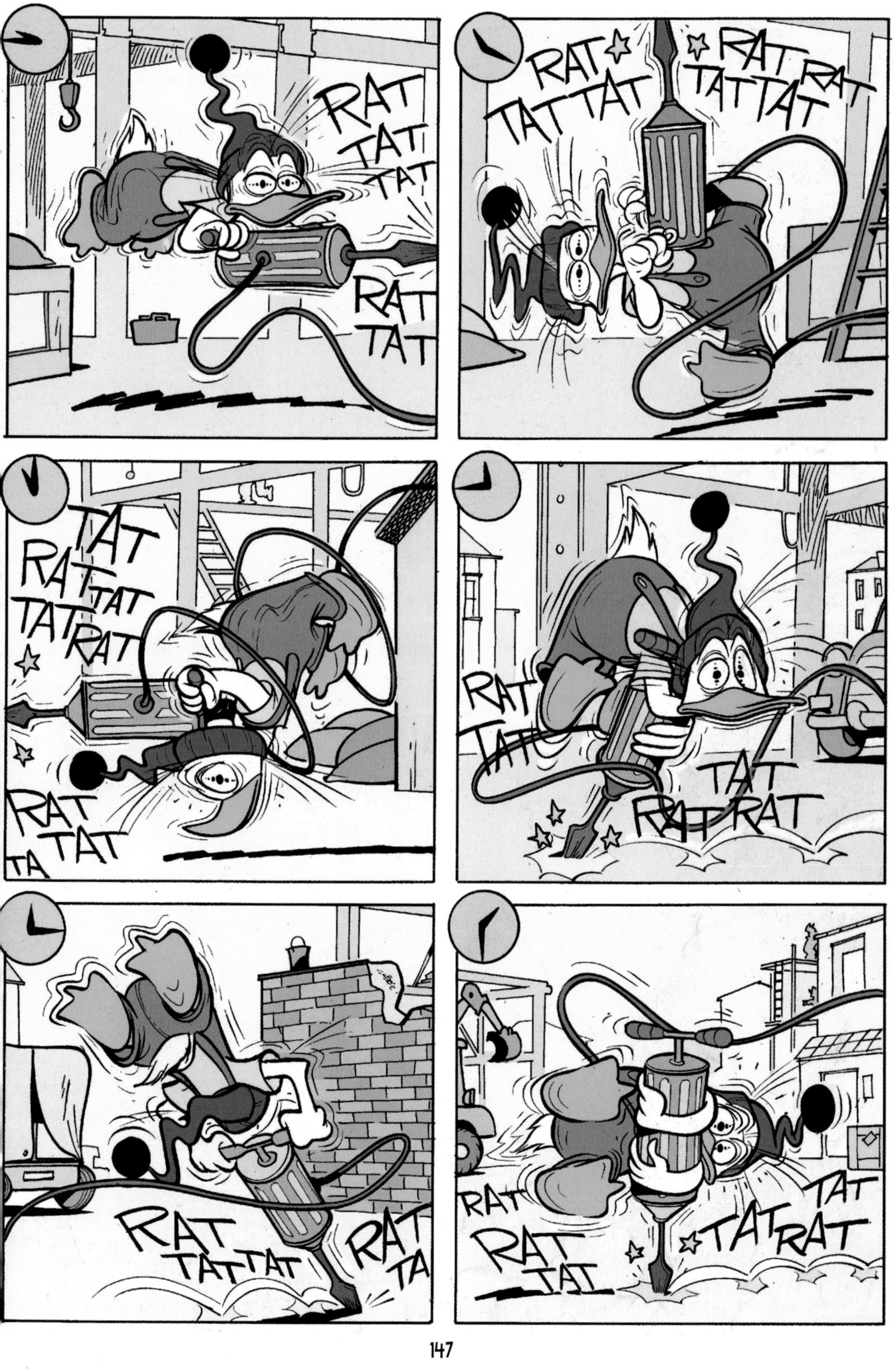
RAT
TAT
TAT
RAT
TAT
RAT
TAT TAT
RAT RAT
TAT TAT TAT
TAT
RAT TAT
TAT RAT
RAT
TAT
TA
RAT
TAT
TAT
RAT RAT
RAT
TAT TAT
RAT
TA
RAT
RAT
TAT
TAT
TAT RAT

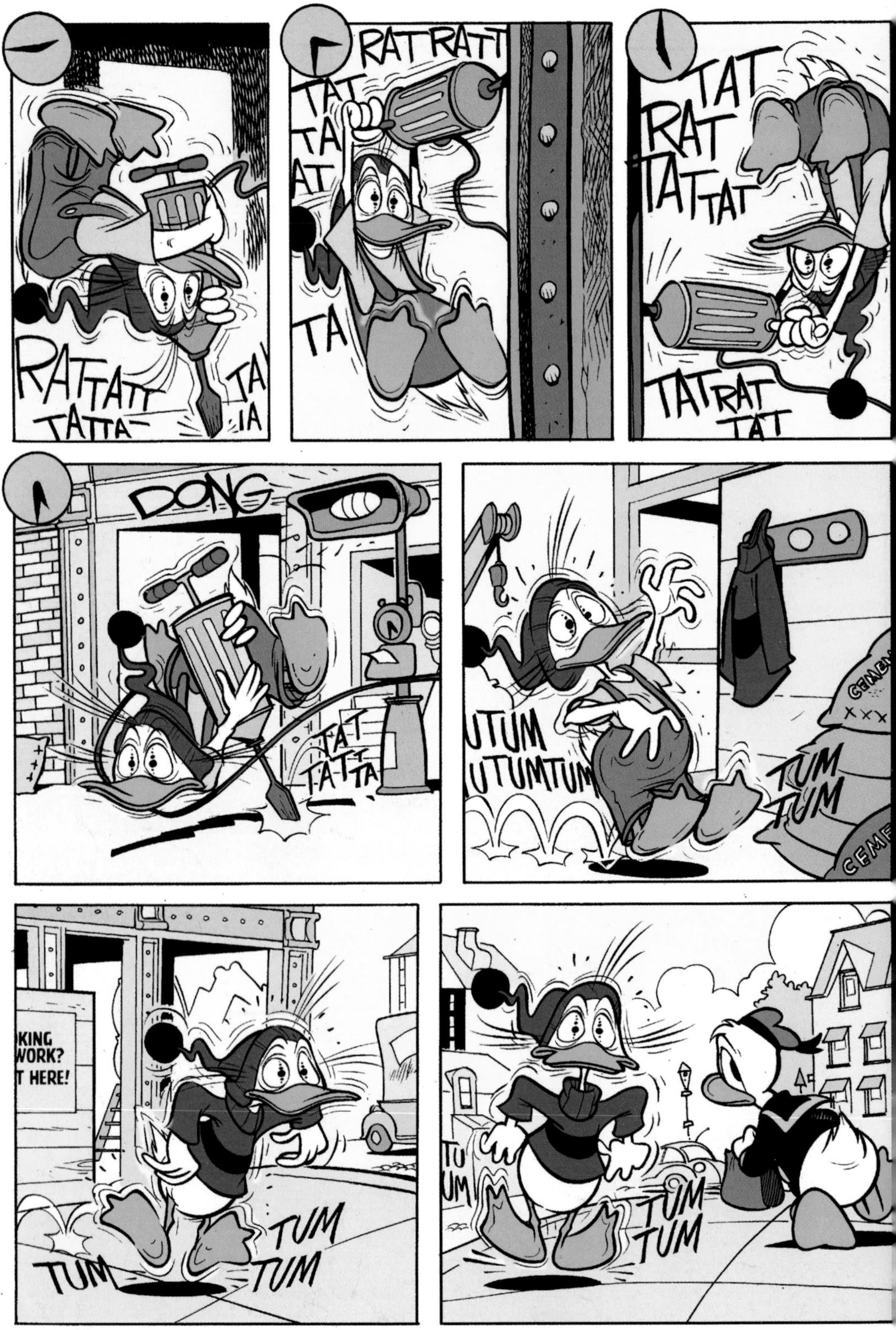
RAT TATT
TATTA
RAT RATT
TAT
TA
TAT
TA
TAT
RAT
TAT TAT
TAT RAT
TAT
DONG
TAT
TATTA
UTUM
UTUMTUM
TUM
TUM
OKING
WORK?
T HERE!
TUM
TUM
TUM
TUM
TUM

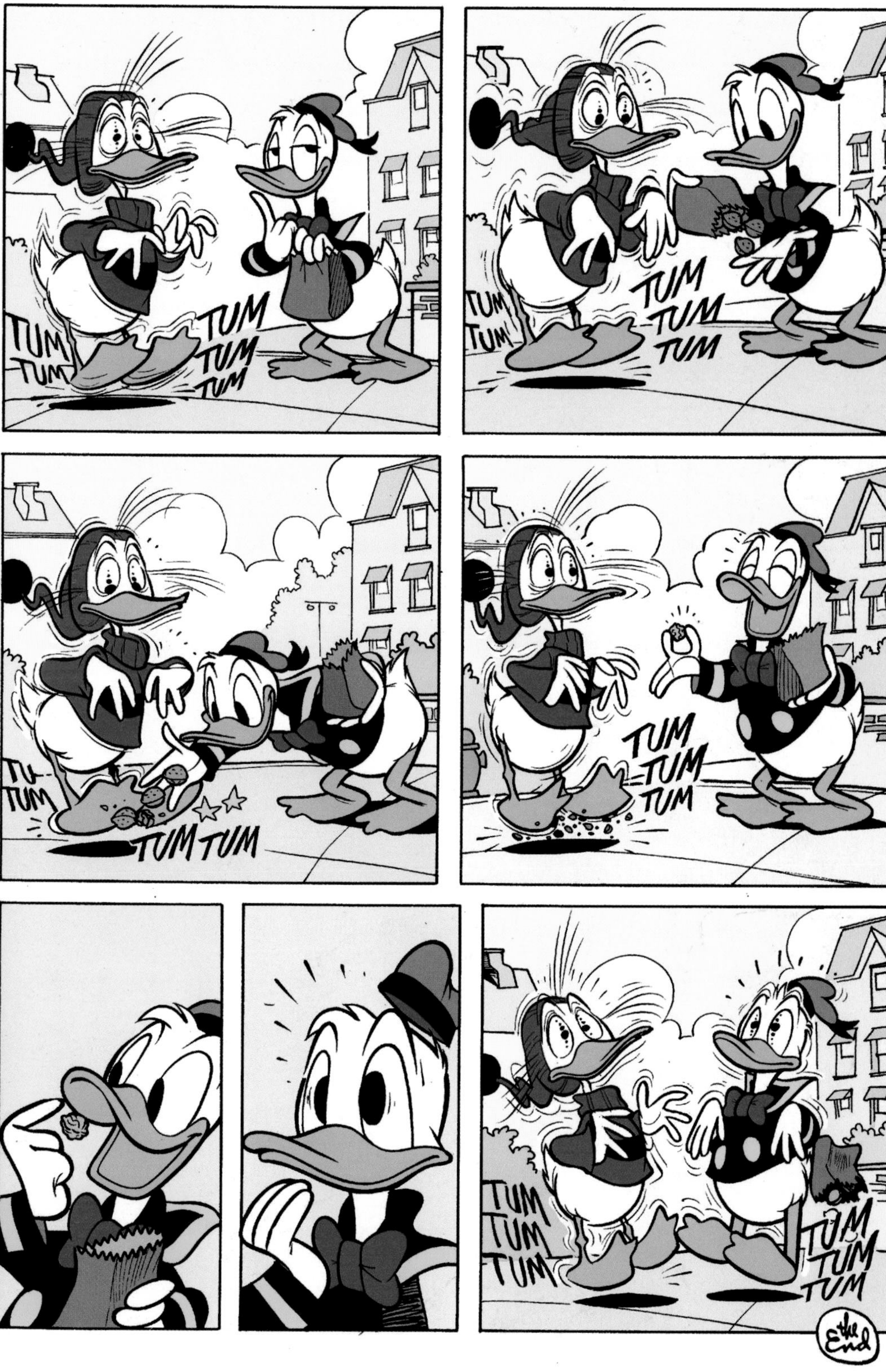
TUM
TUM
TUM
TUM
TUM
TUM
TUM
TUM
TUM
TUM
TU-
TUM
TUM TUM
TUM
TUM
TUM
TUM
TUM
TUM
TUM
TUM
TUM
the End

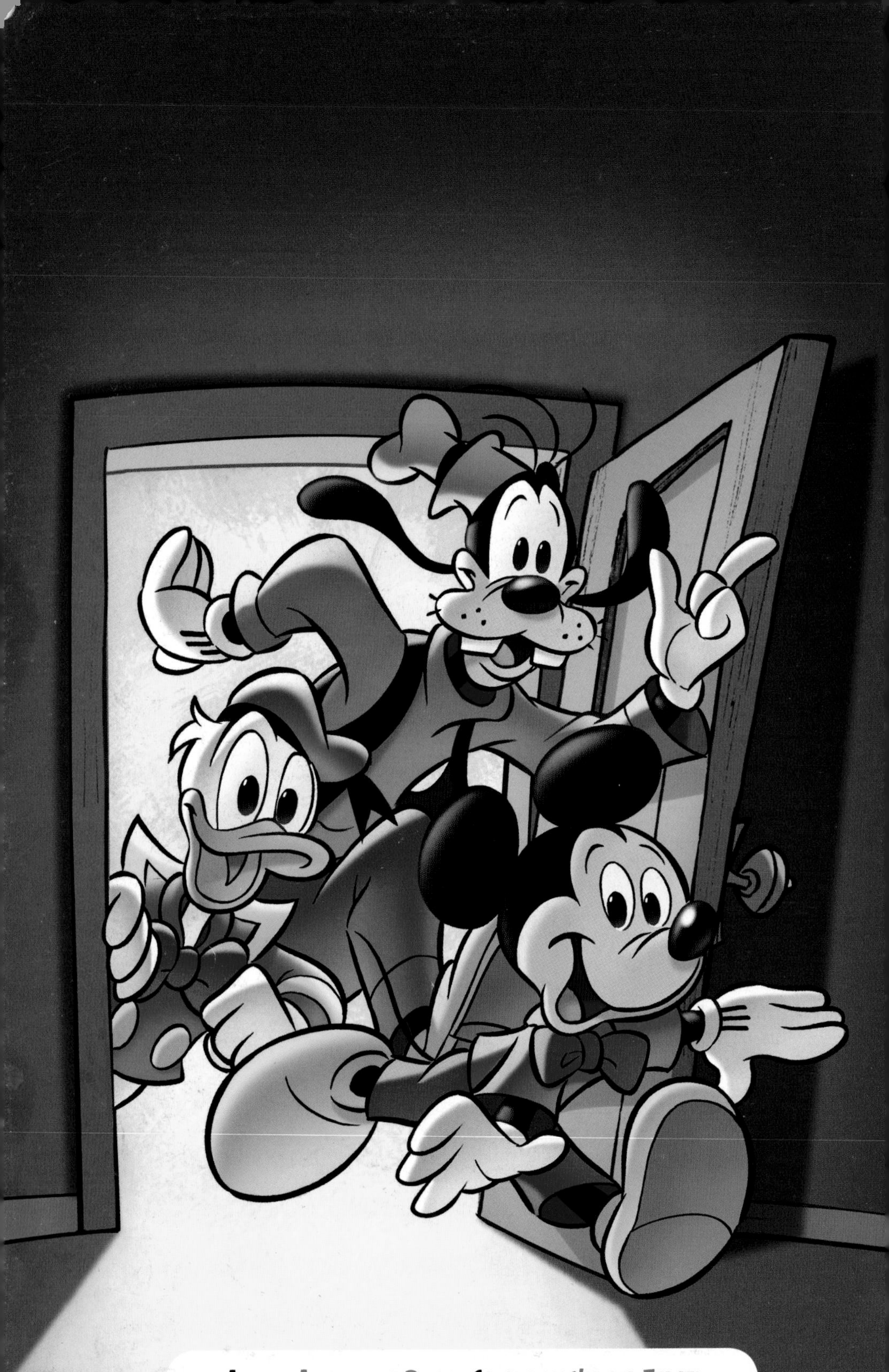

Art by Alessandro Perina Colors by Valeria Turati

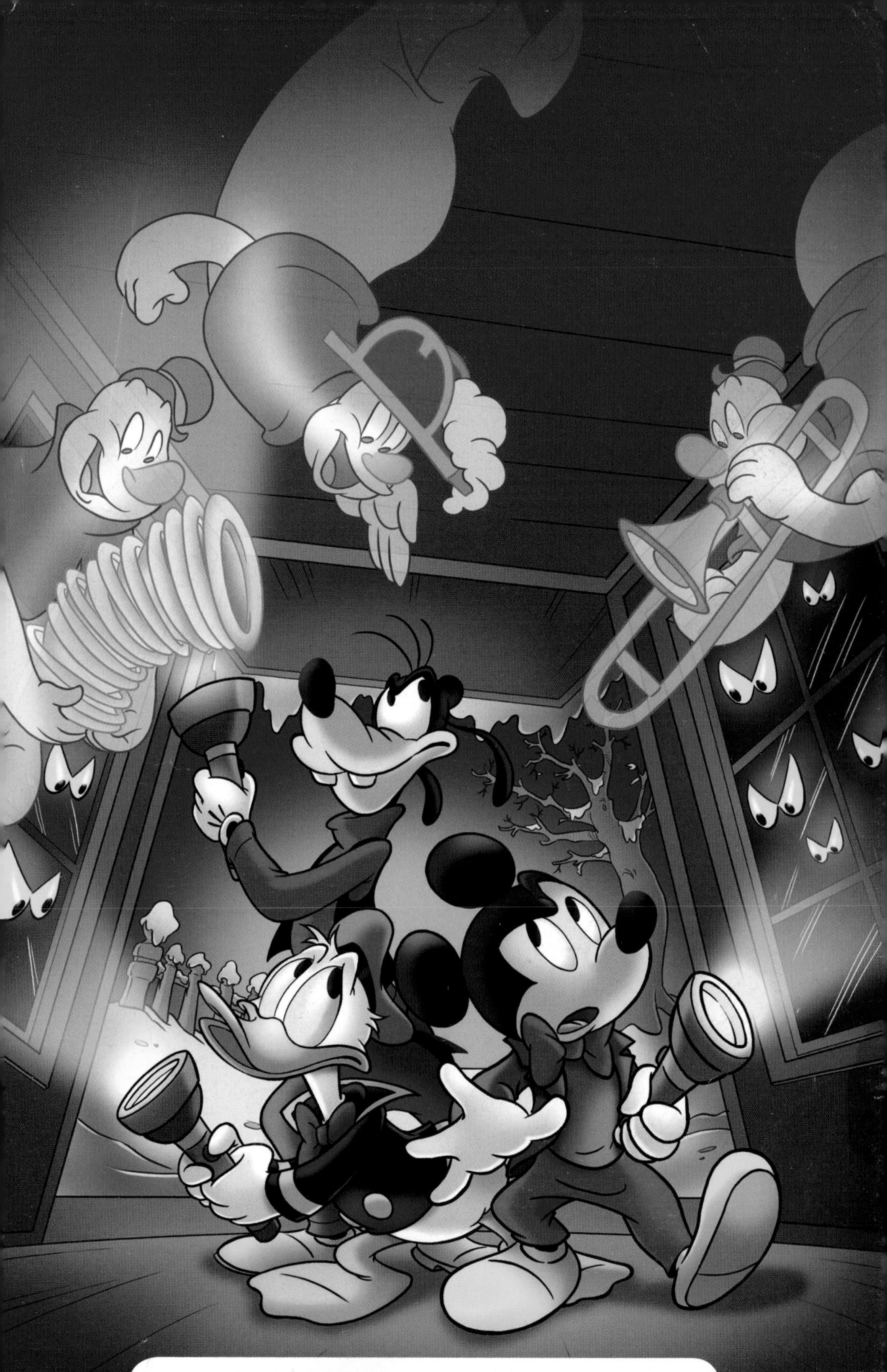

ART BY PAOLO CAMPINOTI COLORS BY MARCO COLLETTI

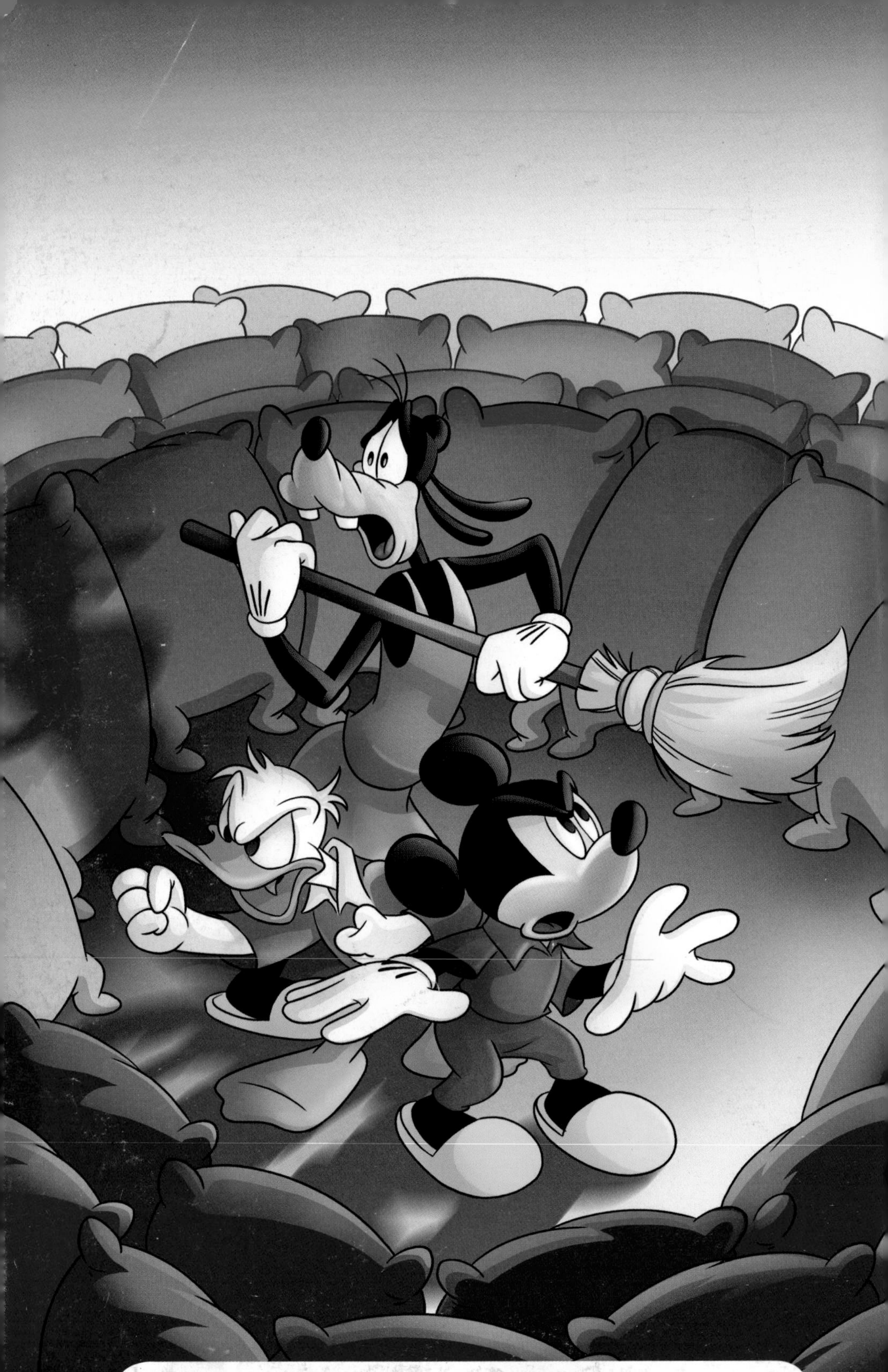

Art by Paolo Campinoti Colors by Fabio Lo Monaco for FEIm Art Studio